ALSO BY

ELENA FERRANTE

The Days of Abandonment
Troubling Love
The Lost Daughter
The Beach at Night
Frantumaglia

MY BRILLIANT FRIEND
(The Neapolitan Quartet)

My Brilliant Friend
The Story of a New Name
Those Who Leave and Those Who Stay
The Story of the Lost Child

MY BRILLIANT
FRIEND

Elena Ferrante

MY BRILLIANT FRIEND

Book One:
Childhood, Adolescence

*Translated from the Italian
by Ann Goldstein*

Europa
editions

Europa Editions
214 West 29th Street
New York, N.Y. 10001
www.europaeditions.com
info@europaeditions.com

Copyright © 2012 by Edizioni E/O
First Publication 2012 by Europa Editions
Twenty-second printing, 2016

Translation by Ann Goldstein
Original title: *L'amica geniale*
Translation copyright © 2012 by Europa Editions

Library of Congress Cataloging in Publication Data is available
ISBN 978-1-60945-078-6

Ferrante, Elena
My Brilliant Friend

Book design by Emanuele Ragnisco
www.mekkanografici.com

Cover photo © Anthony Boccaccio/Getty Images

Prepress by Grafica Punto Print – Rome

Printed in the USA

THE LORD: Therein thou'rt free, according to thy merits;
The like of thee have never moved My hate.
Of all the bold, denying Spirits,
The waggish knave least trouble doth create.
Man's active nature, flagging, seeks too soon the level;
Unqualified repose he learns to crave;
Whence, willingly, the comrade him I gave,
Who works, excites, and must create, as Devil.

J. W. GOETHE, *Faust*,
translation by Bayard Taylor

CONTENTS

MY BRILLIANT FRIEND

INDEX OF CHARACTERS

The Cerullo family (the shoemaker's family):
Fernando Cerullo, shoemaker.
Nunzia Cerullo, wife of Fernando and Lila's mother.
Raffaella Cerullo, called *Lina*, and by Elena *Lila*.
Rino Cerullo, Lila's older brother, also a shoemaker.
Rino, also the name of one of Lila's children.
Other children.

The Greco family (the porter's family):
Elena Greco, called *Lenuccia* or *Lenù*. She is the oldest, and
    after her are *Peppe*, *Gianni*, and *Elisa*.
The *father* is a porter at the city hall.
The *mother* is a housewife.

The Carracci family (Don Achille's family):
Don Achille Carracci, the ogre of fairy tales.
Maria Carracci, wife of Don Achille.
Stefano Carracci, son of Don Achille, grocer in the family store.
Pinuccia and *Alfonso Carracci*, Don Achille's two other chil-
    dren.

The Peluso family (the carpenter's family):
Alfredo Peluso, carpenter.
Giuseppina Peluso, wife of Alfredo.
Pasquale Peluso, older son of Alfredo and Giuseppina, con-
    struction worker.

Carmela Peluso, who is also called *Carmen*, sister of Pasquale, salesclerk in a dry-goods store.
Other children.

The Cappuccio family (the mad widow's family):
Melina, a relative of Lila's mother, a mad widow.
Melina's *husband*, who unloaded crates at the fruit and vegetable market.
Ada Cappuccio, Melina's daughter.
Antonio Cappuccio, her brother, a mechanic.
Other children.

The Sarratore family (the railroad worker poet's family):
Donato Sarratore, conductor.
Lidia Sarratore, wife of Donato.
Nino Sarratore, the oldest of the five children of Donato and Lidia.
Marisa Sarratore, daughter of Donato and Lidia.
Pino, *Clelia*, and *Ciro Sarratore*, younger children of Donato and Lidia.

The Scanno family (the fruit and vegetable seller's family):
Nicola Scanno, fruit and vegetable seller.
Assunta Scanno, wife of Nicola.
Enzo Scanno, son of Nicola and Assunta, also a fruit and vegetable seller.
Other children.

The Solara family (the family of the owner of the Solara bar-pastry shop):
Silvio Solara, owner of the bar-pastry shop.
Manuela Solara, wife of Silvio.
Marcello and *Michele Solara*, sons of Silvio and Manuela.

The Spagnuolo family (the baker's family):
Signor Spagnuolo, pastry maker at the bar-pastry shop Solara.
Rosa Spagnuolo, wife of the pastry maker.
Gigliola Spagnuolo, daughter of the pastry maker.
Other children.

Gino, son of the pharmacist.

The teachers:
Maestro Ferraro, teacher and librarian.
Maestra Oliviero, teacher.
Professor Gerace, high school teacher.
Professor Galiani, high school teacher.

Nella Incardo, Maestra Oliviero's cousin, who lives on Ischia.

PROLOGUE

Eliminating All the Traces

1.

This morning Rino telephoned. I thought he wanted money again and I was ready to say no. But that was not the reason for the phone call: his mother was gone.

"Since when?"

"Since two weeks ago."

"And you're calling me now?"

My tone must have seemed hostile, even though I wasn't angry or offended; there was just a touch of sarcasm. He tried to respond but he did so in an awkward, muddled way, half in dialect, half in Italian. He said he was sure that his mother was wandering around Naples as usual.

"Even at night?"

"You know how she is."

"I do, but does two weeks of absence seem normal?"

"Yes. You haven't seen her for a while, Elena, she's gotten worse: she's never sleepy, she comes in, goes out, does what she likes."

Anyway, in the end he had started to get worried. He had asked everyone, made the rounds of the hospitals: he had even gone to the police. Nothing, his mother wasn't anywhere. What a good son: a large man, forty years old, who hadn't worked in his life, just a small-time crook and spendthrift. I could imagine how carefully he had done his searching. Not at all. He had no brain, and in his heart he had only himself.

"She's not with you?" he asked suddenly.

His mother? Here in Turin? He knew the situation perfectly

well, he was speaking only to speak. Yes, he liked to travel, he had come to my house at least a dozen times, without being invited. His mother, whom I would have welcomed with pleasure, had never left Naples in her life. I answered:

"No, she's not with me."

"You're sure?"

"Rino, please, I told you she's not here."

"Then where has she gone?"

He began to cry and I let him act out his desperation, sobs that began fake and became real. When he stopped I said:

"Please, for once behave as she would like: don't look for her."

"What do you mean?"

"Just what I said. It's pointless. Learn to stand on your own two feet and don't call me again, either."

I hung up.

2.

Rino's mother is named Raffaella Cerullo, but everyone has always called her Lina. Not me, I've never used either her first name or her last. To me, for more than sixty years, she's been Lila. If I were to call her Lina or Raffaella, suddenly, like that, she would think our friendship was over.

It's been at least three decades since she told me that she wanted to disappear without leaving a trace, and I'm the only one who knows what she means. She never had in mind any sort of flight, a change of identity, the dream of making a new life somewhere else. And she never thought of suicide, repulsed by the idea that Rino would have anything to do with her body, and be forced to attend to the details. She meant something different: she wanted to vanish; she wanted every one of her cells to disappear, nothing of her ever to be found. And since

I know her well, or at least I think I know her, I take it for granted that she has found a way to disappear, to leave not so much as a hair anywhere in this world.

3.

Days passed. I looked at my e-mail, at my regular mail, but not with any hope. I often wrote to her, and she almost never responded: this was her habit. She preferred the telephone or long nights of talk when I went to Naples.

I opened my drawers, the metal boxes where I keep all kinds of things. Not much there. I've thrown away a lot of stuff, especially anything that had to do with her, and she knows it. I discovered that I have nothing of hers, not a picture, not a note, not a little gift. I was surprised myself. Is it possible that in all those years she left me nothing of herself, or, worse, that I didn't want to keep anything of her? It is.

This time I telephoned Rino; I did it unwillingly. He didn't answer on the house phone or on his cell phone. He called me in the evening, when it was convenient. He spoke in the tone of voice he uses to arouse pity.

"I saw that you called. Do you have any news?"

"No. Do you?"

"Nothing."

He rambled incoherently. He wanted to go on TV, on the show that looks for missing persons, make an appeal, ask his mamma's forgiveness for everything, beg her to return.

I listened patiently, then asked him: "Did you look in her closet?"

"What for?"

Naturally the most obvious thing would never occur to him. "Go and look."

He went, and he realized that there was nothing there, not

one of his mother's dresses, summer or winter, only old hangers. I sent him to search the whole house. Her shoes were gone. The few books: gone. All the photographs: gone. The movies: gone. Her computer had disappeared, including the old-fashioned diskettes and everything, everything to do with her experience as an electronics wizard who had begun to operate computers in the late sixties, in the days of punch cards. Rino was astonished. I said to him:

"Take as much time as you want, but then call and tell me if you've found even a single hairpin that belongs to her."

He called the next day, greatly agitated.

"There's nothing."

"Nothing at all?"

"No. She cut herself out of all the photographs of the two of us, even those from when I was little."

"You looked carefully?"

"Everywhere."

"Even in the cellar?"

"I told you, everywhere. And the box with her papers is gone: I don't know, old birth certificates, telephone bills, receipts. What does it mean? Did someone steal everything? What are they looking for? What do they want from my mother and me?"

I reassured him, I told him to calm down. It was unlikely that anyone wanted anything, especially from him.

"Can I come and stay with you for a while?"

"No."

"Please, I can't sleep."

"That's your problem, Rino, I don't know what to do about it."

I hung up and when he called back I didn't answer. I sat down at my desk.

Lila is overdoing it as usual, I thought.

She was expanding the concept of trace out of all proportion. She wanted not only to disappear herself, now, at the age of sixty-six, but also to eliminate the entire life that she had left behind.

I was really angry.

We'll see who wins this time, I said to myself. I turned on the computer and began to write—all the details of our story, everything that still remained in my memory.

CHILDHOOD

The Story of Don Achille

1.

My friendship with Lila began the day we decided to go up the dark stairs that led, step after step, flight after flight, to the door of Don Achille's apartment.

I remember the violet light of the courtyard, the smells of a warm spring evening. The mothers were making dinner, it was time to go home, but we delayed, challenging each other, without ever saying a word, testing our courage. For some time, in school and outside of it, that was what we had been doing. Lila would thrust her hand and then her whole arm into the black mouth of a manhole, and I, in turn, immediately did the same, my heart pounding, hoping that the cockroaches wouldn't run over my skin, that the rats wouldn't bite me. Lila climbed up to Signora Spagnuolo's ground-floor window, and, hanging from the iron bar that the clothesline was attached to, swung back and forth, then lowered herself down to the sidewalk, and I immediately did the same, although I was afraid of falling and hurting myself. Lila stuck into her skin the rusted safety pin that she had found on the street somewhere but kept in her pocket like the gift of a fairy godmother; I watched the metal point as it dug a whitish tunnel into her palm, and then, when she pulled it out and handed it to me, I did the same.

At some point she gave me one of her firm looks, eyes narrowed, and headed toward the building where Don Achille lived. I was frozen with fear. Don Achille was the ogre of fairy tales, I was absolutely forbidden to go near him, speak to him, look at him, spy on him, I was to act as if neither he nor his family existed. Regarding him there was, in my house but not only mine, a fear and a hatred whose origin I didn't know. The way my father talked about him, I imagined a huge man, covered with purple boils, violent in spite of the "don," which to me suggested a calm authority. He was a being created out of some unidentifiable material, iron, glass, nettles, but alive, alive, the hot breath streaming from his nose and mouth. I thought that if I merely saw him from a distance he would drive something sharp and burning into my eyes. So if I was mad enough to approach the door of his house he would kill me.

I waited to see if Lila would have second thoughts and turn back. I knew what she wanted to do, I had hoped that she would forget about it, but in vain. The street lamps were not yet lighted, nor were the lights on the stairs. From the apartments came irritable voices. To follow Lila I had to leave the bluish light of the courtyard and enter the black of the doorway. When I finally made up my mind, I saw nothing at first, there was only an odor of old junk and DDT. Then I got used to the darkness and found Lila sitting on the first step of the first flight of stairs. She got up and we began to climb.

We kept to the side where the wall was, she two steps ahead, I two steps behind, torn between shortening the distance or letting it increase. I can still feel my shoulder inching along the flaking wall and the idea that the steps were very high, higher than those in the building where I lived. I was trembling. Every footfall, every voice was Don Achille creeping up behind us or coming down toward us with a long knife, the kind used for slicing open a chicken breast. There was an odor of sautéing garlic. Maria, Don Achille's wife, would put me in the pan of boiling oil, the children would eat me, he would suck my head the way my father did with mullets.

We stopped often, and each time I hoped that Lila would decide to turn back. I was all sweaty, I don't know about her. Every so often she looked up, but I couldn't tell at what, all that was visible was the gray areas of the big windows at every landing. Suddenly the lights came on, but they were faint, dusty, leaving broad zones of shadow, full of dangers. We waited to see if it was Don Achille who had turned the switch, but we heard nothing, neither footsteps nor the opening or closing of a door. Then Lila continued on, and I followed.

She thought that what we were doing was just and necessary; I had forgotten every good reason, and certainly was there only because she was. We climbed slowly toward the greatest of our terrors of that time, we went to expose ourselves to fear and interrogate it.

At the fourth flight Lila did something unexpected. She stopped to wait for me, and when I reached her she gave me her hand. This gesture changed everything between us forever.

2.

It was her fault. Not too long before—ten days, a month, who can say, we knew nothing about time, in those days—she had treacherously taken my doll and thrown her down into a cellar. Now we were climbing toward fear; then we had felt obliged to descend, quickly, into the unknown. Up or down, it seemed to us that we were always going toward something terrible that had existed before us yet had always been waiting for us, just for us. When you haven't been in the world long, it's hard to comprehend what disasters are at the origin of a sense of disaster: maybe you don't even feel the need to. Adults, waiting for tomorrow, move in a present behind which is yesterday or the day before yesterday or at most last week: they don't want to think about the rest. Children don't know the meaning of yesterday, of the day before yesterday, or even of tomorrow, everything is this, now: the street is this, the doorway is this, the stairs are this, this is Mamma, this is Papa, this is the

day, this the night. I was small and really my doll knew more
than I did. I talked to her, she talked to me. She had a plastic
face and plastic hair and plastic eyes. She wore a blue dress that
my mother had made for her in a rare moment of happiness,
and she was beautiful. Lila's doll, on the other hand, had a cloth
body of a yellowish color, filled with sawdust, and she seemed
to me ugly and grimy. The two spied on each other, they sized
each other up, they were ready to flee into our arms if a storm
burst, if there was thunder, if someone bigger and stronger,
with sharp teeth, wanted to snatch them away.

We played in the courtyard but as if we weren't playing
together. Lila sat on the ground, on one side of a small barred
basement window, I on the other. We liked that place, especially because behind the bars was a metal grating and, against
the grating, on the cement ledge between the bars, we could
arrange the things that belonged to Tina, my doll, and those of
Nu, Lila's doll. There we put rocks, bottle tops, little flowers,
nails, splinters of glass. I overheard what Lila said to Nu and
repeated it in a low voice to Tina, slightly modified. If she took
a bottle top and put it on her doll's head, like a hat, I said to
mine, in dialect, Tina, put on your queen's crown or you'll
catch cold. If Nu played hopscotch in Lila's arms, I soon afterward made Tina do the same. Still, it never happened that we
decided on a game and began playing together. Even that place
we chose without explicit agreement. Lila sat down there, and
I strolled around, pretending to go somewhere else. Then, as if
I'd given it no thought, I, too, settled next to the cellar window, but on the opposite side.

The thing that attracted us most was the cold air that came
from the cellar, a breath that refreshed us in spring and summer. And then we liked the bars with their spiderwebs, the
darkness, and the tight mesh of the grating that, reddish with
rust, curled up both on my side and on Lila's, creating two parallel holes through which we could drop rocks into obscurity

and hear the sound when they hit bottom. It was all beautiful and frightening then. Through those openings the darkness might suddenly seize the dolls, who sometimes were safe in our arms, but more often were placed deliberately next to the twisted grating and thus exposed to the cellar's cold breath, to its threatening noises, rustling, squeaking, scraping.

Nu and Tina weren't happy. The terrors that we tasted every day were theirs. We didn't trust the light on the stones, on the buildings, on the scrubland beyond the neighborhood, on the people inside and outside their houses. We imagined the dark corners, the feelings repressed but always close to exploding. And to those shadowy mouths, the caverns that opened beyond them under the buildings, we attributed everything that frightened us in the light of day. Don Achille, for example, was not only in his apartment on the top floor but also down below, a spider among spiders, a rat among rats, a shape that assumed all shapes. I imagined him with his mouth open because of his long animal fangs, his body of glazed stone and poisonous grasses, always ready to pick up in an enormous black bag anything we dropped through the torn corners of the grate. That bag was a fundamental feature of Don Achille, he always had it, even at home, and into it he put material both living and dead.

Lila knew that I had that fear, my doll talked about it out loud. And so, on the day we exchanged our dolls for the first time—with no discussion, only looks and gestures—as soon as she had Tina, she pushed her through the grate and let her fall into the darkness.

3.

Lila appeared in my life in first grade and immediately impressed me because she was very bad. In that class we were all a little bad, but only when the teacher, Maestra Oliviero, couldn't see us. Lila, on the other hand, was always bad. Once she tore up some blotting paper into little pieces, dipped the pieces one by one in the inkwell, and then fished them out with her pen and threw them at us. I was hit twice in the hair and once on my white collar. The teacher yelled, as she knew how to do, in a voice like a needle, long and pointed, which terrorized us, and ordered her to go and stand behind the blackboard in punishment. Lila didn't obey and didn't even seem frightened; she just kept throwing around pieces of inky paper. So Maestra Oliviero, a heavy woman who seemed very old to us, though she couldn't have been much over forty, came down from the desk, threatening her. The teacher stumbled, it wasn't clear on what, lost her balance, and fell, striking her face against the corner of a desk. She lay on the floor as if dead.

What happened right afterward I don't remember, I remember only the dark bundle of the teacher's motionless body, and Lila staring at her with a serious expression.

I have in my mind so many incidents of this type. We lived in a world in which children and adults were often wounded, blood flowed from the wounds, they festered, and sometimes people died. One of the daughters of Signora Assunta, the fruit and vegetable seller, had stepped on a nail and died of tetanus. Signora Spagnuolo's youngest child had died of croup. A cousin of mine, at the age of twenty, had gone one morning to move some rubble and that night was dead, crushed, the blood pouring out of his ears and mouth. My mother's father had been killed when he fell from a scaffolding at a building site. The father of Signor Peluso was missing an arm, the lathe had caught him unawares. The sister of Giuseppina, Signor Peluso's wife, had died of tuberculosis at twenty-two. The oldest son of Don Achille—I had never seen him, and yet I seemed to remember him—had gone to war and died twice: drowned in the Pacific Ocean, then eaten by sharks. The entire

Melchiorre family had died clinging to each other, screaming with fear, in a bombardment. Old Signorina Clorinda had died inhaling gas instead of air. Giannino, who was in fourth grade when we were in first, had died one day because he had come across a bomb and touched it. Luigina, with whom we had played in the courtyard, or maybe not, she was only a name, had died of typhus. Our world was like that, full of words that killed: croup, tetanus, typhus, gas, war, lathe, rubble, work, bombardment, bomb, tuberculosis, infection. With these words and those years I bring back the many fears that accompanied me all my life.

You could also die of things that seemed normal. You could die, for example, if you were sweating and then drank cold water from the tap without first bathing your wrists: you'd break out in red spots, you'd start coughing, and be unable to breathe. You could die if you ate black cherries and didn't spit out the pits. You could die if you chewed American gum and inadvertently swallowed it. You could die if you banged your temple. The temple, in particular, was a fragile place, we were all careful about it. Being hit with a stone could do it, and throwing stones was the norm. When we left school a gang of boys from the countryside, led by a kid called Enzo or Enzuccio, who was one of the children of Assunta the fruit and vegetable seller, began to throw rocks at us. They were angry because we were smarter than them. When the rocks came at us we ran away, except Lila, who kept walking at her regular pace and sometimes even stopped. She was very good at studying the trajectory of the stones and dodging them with an easy move that today I would call elegant. She had an older brother and maybe she had learned from him, I don't know, I also had brothers, but they were younger than me and from them I had learned nothing. Still, when I realized that she had stayed behind, I stopped to wait for her, even though I was scared.

Already then there was something that kept me from abandoning her. I didn't know her well; we had never spoken to each other, although we were constantly competing, in class and outside it. But in a confused way I felt that if I ran away with the others I would leave with her something of mine that she would never give back.

At first I stayed hidden, around a corner, and leaned out to see if Lila was coming. Then, since she wouldn't budge, I forced myself to rejoin her; I handed her stones, and even threw some myself. But I did it without conviction: I did many things in my life without conviction; I always felt slightly detached from my own actions. Lila, on the other hand, had, from a young age—I can't say now precisely if it was so at six or seven, or when we went together up the stairs that led to Don Achille's and were eight, almost nine—the characteristic of absolute determination. Whether she was gripping the tricolor shaft of the pen or a stone or the handrail on the dark stairs, she communicated the idea that whatever came next— thrust the pen with a precise motion into the wood of the desk, dispense inky bullets, strike the boys from the countryside, climb the stairs to Don Achille's door—she would do without hesitation.

The gang came from the railroad embankment, stocking up on rocks from the trackbed. Enzo, the leader, was a dangerous child, with very short blond hair and pale eyes; he was at least three years older than us, and had repeated a year. He threw small, sharp-edged rocks with great accuracy, and Lila waited for his throws to demonstrate how she evaded them, making him still angrier, and responded with throws that were just as dangerous. Once we hit him in the right calf, and I say we because I had handed Lila a flat stone with jagged edges. The stone slid over Enzo's skin like a razor, leaving a red stain that immediately gushed blood. The child looked at his wounded leg. I have him before my eyes: between thumb and index finger he held the rock that he was about to throw, his arm was raised to throw it, and yet he stopped, bewildered. The boys under his command also looked incredulously at the blood. Lila, however, manifested not the least satisfaction in the outcome of the throw and bent over to pick up another stone. I grabbed her by the arm; it was the first contact between us, an abrupt, frightened contact. I felt that the gang would get more ferocious and I wanted to retreat. But there wasn't time. Enzo, in spite of his bleeding calf, came out of his stupor and threw the rock in his hand. I was still holding on to Lila when the rock hit her in the head and knocked her away from me. A second later she was lying on the sidewalk with a gash in her forehead.

4.

Blood. In general it came from wounds only after horrible curses and disgusting obscenities had been exchanged. That was the standard procedure. My father, though he seemed to me a good man, hurled continuous insults and threats if someone didn't deserve, as he said, to be on the face of the earth. He especially had it in for Don Achille. He always had something to accuse him of, and sometimes I put my hands over my ears in order not to be too disturbed by his brutal words. When he spoke of him to my mother he called him "your cousin" but my mother denied that blood tie (there was a very distant relationship) and added to the insults. Their anger frightened me, I was frightened above all by the thought that Don Achille might have ears so sensitive that he could hear insults even from far away. I was afraid that he might come and murder them.

The sworn enemy of Don Achille, however, was not my father but Signor Peluso, a very good carpenter who was always broke, because he gambled away everything he earned in the back room of the Bar Solara. Peluso was the father of our class-mate Carmela, of Pasquale, who was older, and of two others, children poorer than us, with whom Lila and I sometimes played, and who in school and outside always tried to steal our things, a pen, an eraser, the *cotognata*, so that they went home covered with bruises because we'd hit them.

The times we saw him, Signor Peluso seemed to us the image of despair. On the one hand he lost everything gambling and on the other he was criticized in public because he was no longer able to feed his family. For obscure reasons he attrib-uted his ruin to Don Achille. He charged him with having taken by stealth, as if his shadowy body were a magnet, all the tools for his carpentry work, which made the shop useless. He accused him of having taken the shop itself, and transforming it into a grocery store. For years I imagined the pliers, the saw, the tongs, the hammer, the vise, and thousands and thousands of nails sucked up like a swarm of metal into the matter that made up Don Achille. For years I saw his body—a coarse body, heavy with a mixture of materials—emitting in a swarm salami, provolone, mortadella, lard, and prosciutto.

These things had happened in the dark ages. Don Achille had supposedly revealed himself in all his monstrous nature before we were born. *Before*. Lila often used that formula-tion. But she didn't seem to care as much about what had happened before us—events that were in general obscure, and about which the adults either were silent or spoke with great reticence—as about the fact that there really had been a before. It was this which at the time left her puzzled and occasionally even made her nervous. When we became friends she spoke so much of that absurd thing—*before us*—that she ended up passing on her nervousness to me. It was the long, very long, period when we didn't exist, that period when Don Achille had showed himself to everyone for what he was: an evil being of uncertain animal-mineral physiognomy, who—it seemed—sucked blood from others while never losing any himself, maybe it wasn't even possible to scratch him.

We were in second grade, perhaps, and still hadn't spoken to each other, when the rumor spread that right in front of the Church of the Holy Family, right after Mass, Signor Peluso had started screaming furiously at Don Achille. Don Achille had left his older son Stefano, his daughter Pinuccia, Alfonso, who was our age, and his wife, and, appearing for a moment in his most hair-raising form, had hurled himself at Peluso, picked him up, thrown him against a tree in the public gardens, and left him there, barely conscious, with blood coming out of innumerable wounds in his head and everywhere, and the poor man able to say merely: help.

5.

I feel no nostalgia for our childhood: it was full of violence. Every sort of thing happened, at home and outside, every day, but I don't recall having ever thought that the life we had there was particularly bad. Life was like that, that's all, we grew up with the duty to make it difficult for others before they made it difficult for us. Of course, I would have liked the nice manners that the teacher and the priest preached, but I felt that those ways were not suited to our neighborhood, even if you were a girl. The women fought among themselves more than the men, they pulled each other's hair, they hurt each other. To cause pain was a disease. As a child I imagined tiny, almost invisible animals that arrived in the neighborhood at night, they came from the ponds, from the abandoned train cars beyond the embankment, from the stinking grasses called *fetienti*, from the frogs, the salamanders, the flies, the rocks, the dust, and entered the water and the food and the air, making our mothers, our grandmothers as angry as starving dogs. They were more severely infected than the men, because while men were always getting furious, they calmed down in the end; women, who appeared to be silent, acquiescent, when they were angry flew into a rage that had no end.

Lila was deeply affected by what had happened to Melina Cappuccio, a relative of her mother's. And I, too. Melina lived in the same building as my family, we on the second floor, she on the third. She was only a little over thirty and had six children, but to us she seemed an old woman. Her husband was the same age; he unloaded crates at the fruit and vegetable market. I recall him as short and broad, but handsome, with a proud face. One night he came out of the house as usual and died, perhaps murdered, perhaps of weariness. The funeral was very bitter; the whole neighborhood went, including my parents, and Lila's parents. Then time passed and something happened to Melina. On the outside she remained the same, a gaunt woman with a large nose, her hair already gray, a shrill voice that at night called her children from the window, by name, the syllables drawn out by an angry despair: Aaa-daaa, Miii-chè. At first she was much helped by Donato Sarratore, who lived in the apartment right above hers, on the fourth and top floor. Donato was diligent in his attendance at the Church of the Holy Family and as a good Christian he did a lot for her, collecting money, used clothes, and shoes, settling Antonio, the oldest son, in the auto-repair shop of Gorresio, an acquaintance of his. Melina was so grateful that her gratitude became, in her desolate woman's heart, love, passion. It wasn't clear if Sarratore was ever aware of it. He was a friendly man but very serious—home, church, and job. He worked on a train crew for the state railroad, and had a decent salary on which he supported his wife, Lidia, and five children; the oldest was called Nino. When he wasn't traveling on the Naples-Paola route he devoted himself to fixing this or that in the house, he did the shopping, took the youngest child out in the carriage. These things were very unusual in the neighborhood. It occurred to no one that Donato was generous in that way to lighten the burdens of his wife. No: all the neighborhood men, my father in the lead, considered him a womanish man, even more so because he wrote poems and read them willingly to anyone. It didn't occur even to Melina. The widow preferred to think that, because of his gentle spirit, he was put upon by his wife, and so she decided to do battle against Lidia Sarratore to free him and let him join her permanently. The war that followed at first seemed funny; it was discussed in my house and elsewhere with malicious laughter. Lidia would hang out the sheets fresh from the laundry and Melina climbed up on the windowsill and dirtied them with a reed whose tip she had charred in the fire; Lidia passed under her windows and she spit on her head or emptied buckets of dirty water on her; Lidia made noise during the day walking above her, with her unruly children, and she banged the floor mop against the ceiling all night. Sarratore tried by every means to make peace, but he was too sensitive, too polite. As their vindictiveness increased, the two women began to insult each other if they met on the street or the stairs: harsh, fierce sounds. It was then that they began to frighten me. One of the many terrible scenes of my childhood begins with the shouts of Melina and Lidia, with the insults they hurl from the windows and then on the stairs; it continues with my mother rushing to our door, opening it, and looking out, followed by us children; and ends with the image, for me still unbearable, of the two neighbors rolling down the stairs, entwined, and Melina's head hitting the floor of the landing, a few inches from my shoes, like a white melon that has slipped from your hand.

It's hard to say why at the time we children took the part of Lidia Sarratore. Maybe because she had regular features and blond hair. Or because Donato was hers and we had understood that Melina wanted to take him away from her. Or because Melina's children were ragged and dirty, while Lidia's were washed, well groomed, and the oldest, Nino, who was a few years older than us, was handsome, and we liked him. Lila alone favored Melina, but she never explained why. She said only, once, that if Lidia Sarratore ended up murdered she deserved it, and I thought that it was partly because she was mean in her heart and partly because she and Melina were distant relatives.

One day we were coming home from school, four or five girls. With us was Marisa Sarratore, who usually joined us not because we liked her but because we hoped that, through her, we might meet her older brother, that is to say Nino. It was she who first noticed Melina. The woman was walking slowly from one side of the *stradone*, the wide avenue that ran through the neighborhood, to the other, carrying a paper bag in one hand from which, with the other, she was taking something and eating it. Marisa pointed to her, calling her "the whore," without rancor, but because she was repeating the phrase that her mother used at home. Lila, although she was shorter and very thin, immediately slapped her so hard that she knocked her down: ruthless, as she usually was on occasions of violence, no yelling before or after, no word of warning, cold and determined, not even widening her eyes.

First I went to the aid of Marisa, who was crying, and helped her get up, then I turned to see what Lila was doing. She had left the sidewalk and was going toward Melina, crossing the street without paying attention to the passing trucks. I saw in her, in her posture more than in her face, something that disturbed me and is still hard to define, so for now I'll put it like this: she was moving, cutting across the street, a small, dark, nervous figure, she was acting with her usual determination, she was firm. Firm in what her mother's relative was

doing, firm in the pain, firm in silence as a statue is firm. A fol-
lower. One with Melina, who was holding in her palm the dark
soft soap she had just bought in Don Carlo's cellar, and with
her other hand was taking some and eating it.

6.

The day Maestra Oliviero fell from the desk and hit her
cheekbone against it, I, as I said, thought she was dead, dead
on the job like my grandfather or Melina's husband, and it
seemed to me that as a result Lila, too, would die because of
the terrible punishment she would get. Instead, for a period I
can't define—short, long—nothing happened. They simply
disappeared, both of them, teacher and pupil, from our days
and from memory.

But then everything was surprising. Maestra Oliviero
returned to school alive and began to concern herself with Lila,
not to punish her, as would have seemed to us natural, but to
praise her.

This new phase began when Lila's mother, Signora Cerullo,
was called to school. One morning the janitor knocked and
announced her. Right afterward Nunzia Cerullo came in,
unrecognizable. She, who, like the majority of the neighborhood women, lived untidily in slippers and shabby old dresses,
appeared in her formal black dress (wedding, communion,
christening, funeral), with a shiny black purse and low-heeled
shoes that tortured her swollen feet, and handed the teacher
two paper bags, one containing sugar and the other coffee.

The teacher accepted the gifts with pleasure and, looking at
Lila, who was staring at the desk, spoke to her, and to the
whole class, words whose general sense disoriented me. We
were just learning the alphabet and the numbers from one to
ten. I was the smartest in the class, I could recognize all the let-

ters, I knew how to say one two three four and so on, I was constantly praised for my handwriting, I won the tricolor cockades that the teacher sewed. Yet, surprisingly, Maestra Oliviero, although Lila had made her fall and sent her to the hospital, said that she was the best among us. True that she was the worst-behaved. True that she had done that terrible thing of shooting ink-soaked bits of blotting paper at us. True that if that girl had not acted in such a disruptive manner she, our teacher, would not have fallen and cut her cheek. True that she was compelled to punish her constantly with the wooden rod or by sending her to kneel on the hard floor behind the blackboard. But there was a fact that, as a teacher and also as a person, filled her with joy, a marvelous fact that she had discovered a few days earlier, by chance.

Here she stopped, as if words were not enough, or as if she wished to teach Lila's mother and us that deeds almost always count more than words. She took a piece of chalk and wrote on the blackboard (now I don't remember what, I didn't yet know how to read: so I'm inventing the word) "sun." Then she asked Lila:

"Cerullo, what is written there?"

In the classroom a fascinated silence fell. Lila half smiled, almost a grimace, and flung herself sideways, against her deskmate, who was visibly irritated. Then she read in a sullen tone:

"Sun."

Nunzia Cerullo looked at the teacher, and her look was hesitant, almost fearful. The teacher at first seemed not to understand why her own enthusiasm was not reflected in the mother's eyes. But then she must have guessed that Nunzia didn't know how to read, or, anyway, that she wasn't sure the word "sun" really was written on the blackboard, and she frowned. Then, partly to clarify the situation to Signora Cerullo, partly to praise our classmate, she said to Lila:

"Good, 'sun' is what it says there."

Then she ordered her:

"Come, Cerullo, come to the blackboard."

Lila went unwillingly to the blackboard, the teacher handed her the chalk.

"Write," she said to her, " 'chalk.' "

Lila, very concentrated, in shaky handwriting, placing the letters one a little higher, one a little lower, wrote: "chak."

Oliviero added the "l" and Signora Cerullo, seeing the correction, said in despair to her daughter:

"You made a mistake."

But the teacher immediately reassured her:

"No, no, no. Lila has to practice, yes, but she already knows how to read, she already knows how to write. Who taught her?"

Signora Cerullo, eyes lowered, said: "Not me."

"But at your house or in the building is there someone who might have taught her?"

Nunzia shook her head no emphatically.

Then the teacher turned to Lila and with sincere admiration asked her in front of all of us, "Who taught you to read and write, Cerullo?"

Cerullo, that small dark-haired, dark-eyed child, in a dark smock with a red ribbon at the neck, and only six years old, answered, "Me."

7.

According to Rino, Lila's older brother, she had learned to read at the age of around three by looking at the letters and pictures in his primer. She would sit next to him in the kitchen while he was doing his homework, and she learned more than he did.

Rino was almost six years older than Lila; he was a fearless boy who shone in all the courtyard and street games, especially spinning a top. But reading, writing, arithmetic, learning poems by heart were not for him. When he was scarcely ten his father, Fernando, had begun to take him every day to his tiny shoemaker's shop, in a narrow side street that ran off the *stradone*, to teach him the craft of resoling shoes. We girls, when we met him, smelled on him the odor of dirty feet, of old uppers, of glue, and we made fun of him, we called him shoe-soler. Maybe that's why he boasted that he was at the origin of his sister's virtuosity. But in reality he had never had a primer, and hadn't sat for even a minute, ever, to do homework. Impossible therefore that Lila had learned from his scholastic labors. It was more likely that she had precociously learned how the alphabet worked from the sheets of newspaper in which customers wrapped the old shoes and which her father sometimes brought home and read to the family the most interesting local news items.

Anyway, however it had happened, the fact was this: Lila knew how to read and write, and what I remember of that gray morning when the teacher revealed it to us was, above all, the sense of weakness the news left me with. Right away, from the first day, school had seemed to me a much nicer place than home. It was the place in the neighborhood where I felt safest, I went there with excitement. I paid attention to the lessons, I carried out with the greatest diligence everything that I was told to carry out, I learned. But most of all I liked pleasing the teacher, I liked pleasing everyone. At home I was my father's favorite, and my brothers and sister, too, loved me. The problem was my mother; with her things never took the right course. It seemed to me that, though I was barely six, she did her best to make me understand that I was superfluous in her life. I wasn't agreeable to her nor was she to me. Her body repulsed me, something she probably intuited. She was a dark blonde, blue-eyed, voluptuous. But you never knew where her right eye was looking. Nor did her right leg work properly—she called it the damaged leg. She limped, and her step agitated me, especially at night, when she couldn't sleep and walked along the hall to the kitchen, returned, started again. Sometimes I heard her angrily crushing with her heel the cockroaches that came through the front door, and I imagined her with furious eyes, as when she got mad at me.

Certainly she wasn't happy; the household chores wore her down, and there was never enough money. She often got angry with my father, a porter at the city hall, she shouted that he had to come up with something, she couldn't go on like this. They quarreled. But since my father never raised his voice, even when he lost patience, I always took his part against her, even though he sometimes beat her and could be threatening to me. It was he, and not my mother, who said to me, the first day of school: "Lenuccia, do well with the teacher and we'll let you go to school. But if you're not good, if you're not the best, Papa needs help and you'll go to work." Those words had really scared me, and yet, although he said them, I felt it was my mother who had suggested them, imposed them. I had promised them both that I would be good. And things had immediately gone so well that the teacher often said to me:

"Greco, come and sit next to me."

It was a great privilege. Maestra Oliviero always had an empty chair next to her, and the best students were called on to sit there, as a reward. In the early days, I was always sitting beside her. She urged me on with encouraging words, she praised my blond curls, and thus reinforced in me the wish to do well: completely the opposite of my mother, who, at home, so often rebuked me, sometimes abusively, that I wanted to hide in a dark corner and hope that she wouldn't find me. Then it happened that Signora Cerullo came to class and Maestra Oliviero revealed that Lila was far ahead of us. Not only that: she called on her to sit next to her more often than on me. What that demotion caused inside me I don't know, I find it difficult to say, today, faithfully and clearly what I felt. Perhaps nothing at first, some jealousy, like everyone else. But surely it was then that a worry began to take shape. I thought that, although my legs functioned perfectly well, I ran the constant risk of becoming crippled. I woke with that idea in my head and I got out of bed right away to see if my legs still worked. Maybe that's why I became focused on Lila, who had slender, agile legs, and was always moving them, kicking even when she was sitting next to the teacher, so that the teacher became irritated and soon sent her back to her desk. Something convinced me, then, that if I kept up with her, at her pace, my mother's limp, which had entered into my brain and wouldn't come out, would stop threatening me. I decided that I had to model myself on that girl, never let her out of my sight, even if she got annoyed and chased me away.

8.

I suppose that that was my way of reacting to envy, and hatred, and of suffocating them. Or maybe I disguised in that manner the sense of subordination, the fascination I felt. Certainly I trained myself to accept readily Lila's superiority in everything, and even her oppressions.

Besides, the teacher acted very shrewdly. It was true that she often called on Lila to sit next to her, but she seemed to do it more to make her behave than to reward her. She continued, in fact, to praise Marisa Sarratore, Carmela Peluso, and, especially, me. She let me shine with a vivid light, she encouraged me to become more and more disciplined, more diligent, more serious. When Lila stopped misbehaving and effortlessly outdid me, the teacher praised me first, with moderation, and then went on to exalt her prowess. I felt the poison of defeat more acutely when it was Sarratore or Peluso who did better than me. If, however, I came in second after Lila, I wore a meek expression of acquiescence. In those years I think I feared only one thing: not being paired, in the hierarchy established by Maestra Oliviero, with Lila; not to hear the teacher say proudly, Cerullo and Greco are the best. If one day she had said, the best are Cerullo and Sarratore, or Cerullo and Peluso, I would have died on the spot. So I used all my childish energies not to become first in the class—it seemed to me impossible to succeed there—but not to slip into third, fourth, last place. I devoted myself to studying and to many things that were difficult, alien to me, just so I could keep pace with that terrible, dazzling girl.

Dazzling to me. To our classmates Lila was only terrible. From first grade to fifth, she was, because of the principal and partly also because of Maestra Oliviero, the most hated child in the school and the neighborhood.

At least twice a year the principal had the classes compete against one another, in order to distinguish the most brilliant students and consequently the most competent teachers. Oliviero liked this competition. Our teacher, in permanent conflict with her colleagues, with whom she sometimes seemed near coming to blows, used Lila and me as the blazing proof of how good she was, the best teacher in the neighborhood elementary school. So she would often bring us to other classes, apart from the occasions arranged by the principal, to compete with the other children, girls and boys. Usually, I was sent on reconnaissance, to test the enemy's level of skill. In general I won, but without overdoing it, without humiliating either teachers or students. I was a pretty little girl with blond curls, happy to show off but not aggressive, and I gave an impression of delicacy that was touching. If then I was the best at reciting poems, repeating the times tables, doing division and multiplication, at rattling off the Maritime, Cottian, Graia, and Pennine

Alps, the other teachers gave me a pat anyway, while the students felt how hard I had worked to memorize all those facts, and didn't hate me.

In Lila's case it was different. Even by first grade she was beyond any possible competition. In fact, the teacher said that with a little application she would be able to take the test for second grade and, not yet seven, go into third. Later the gap increased. Lila did really complicated calculations in her head, in her dictations there was not a single mistake, she spoke in dialect like the rest of us but, when necessary, came out with a bookish Italian, using words like "accustomed," "luxuriant," "willingly." So that, when the teacher sent her into the field to give the moods or tenses of verbs or solve math problems, hearts grew bitter. Lila was too much for anyone.

Besides, she offered no openings to kindness. To recognize her virtuosity was for us children to admit that we would never win and so there was no point in competing, and for the teachers to confess to themselves that they had been mediocre children. Her quickness of mind was like a hiss, a dart, a lethal bite. And there was nothing in her appearance that acted as a corrective. She was disheveled, dirty, on her knees and elbows she always had scabs from cuts and scrapes that never had time to heal. Her large, bright eyes could become cracks behind which, before every brilliant response, there was a gaze that appeared not very childlike and perhaps not even human. Every one of her movements said that to harm her would be pointless because, whatever happened, she would find a way of doing worse to you.

The hatred was therefore tangible; I was aware of it. Both girls and boys were irritated by her, but the boys more openly. For a hidden motive of her own, in fact, Maestra Oliviero especially enjoyed taking us to the classes where the girl students and women teachers could not be humiliated so much as the males. And the principal, too, for equally hidden motives, preferred competitions of this type. Later I thought that in the school they were betting money, maybe even a lot, on those meetings of ours. But I was exaggerating: maybe it was just a way of giving vent to old grudges or allowing the principal to keep the less good or less obedient teachers under his control. The fact is that one morning the two of us, who were then in second grade, were taken to a fourth-grade class, Maestro Ferraro's, in which were both Enzo Scanno, the fierce son of the fruit and vegetable seller, and Nino Sarratore, Marisa's brother, whom I loved.

Everyone knew Enzo. He was a repeater and at least a couple of times had been dragged through the classrooms with a card around his neck on which Maestro Ferraro, a tall, very thin man, with very short gray hair, a small, lined face, and worried eyes, had written "Dunce." Nino on the other hand was so good, so meek, so quiet that he was well known and liked, especially by me. Naturally Enzo hardly counted, scholastically speaking, we kept an eye on him only because he was aggressive. Our adversaries, in matters of intelligence, were Nino and—we discovered just then—Alfonso Carracci, the third child of Don Achille, a very neat boy, who was in second grade, like us, but looked younger than his seven years. It was clear that the teacher had brought him there to the fourth-grade class because he had more faith in him than in Nino, who was almost two years older.

There was some tension between Oliviero and Ferraro because of that unexpected summoning of Carracci, then the competition began, in front of the two classes, assembled in one classroom. They asked us verbs, they asked us times tables, they asked us addition, subtraction, multiplication, division (the four operations), first at the blackboard, then in our heads. Of that particular occasion I remember three things. The first is that little Alfonso Carracci defeated me immediately, he was calm and precise, but he had the quality of not gloating. The second is that Nino Sarratore, surprisingly, almost never answered the questions, but appeared dazed, as if he didn't understand what the teachers were asking him. The third is that Lila stood up to the son of Don Achille reluctantly, as if she didn't care if he beat her. The scene grew lively only when they began to do calculations in their heads, addition, subtraction, multiplication, and division. Alfonso, despite Lila's reluctance and, at times, silence, as if she hadn't heard the question, began to slip, making mistakes especially in multiplication and division. On the other hand, if the son of Don Achille failed, Lila wasn't up to it, either, and so they seemed more or less equal. But at a certain point something unexpected happened. At least twice, when Lila didn't answer or Alfonso made a mistake, the voice of Enzo Scanno, filled with contempt, was heard, from a desk at the back, giving the right answer.

This astonished the class, the teachers, the principal, me, and Lila. How was it possible that someone like Enzo, who was lazy, incapable, and delinquent, could do complicated calculations in his head better than me, than Alfonso Carracci, than Nino Sarratore? Suddenly Lila seemed to wake up. Alfonso was quickly out of the running and, with the proud consent of Ferraro, who quickly exchanged champions, a duel began between Lila and Enzo.

The two competed for a long time. The principal, going over Ferraro's head, called the son of the fruit and vegetable seller to the front of the room, next to Lila. Enzo left the back row amid uneasy laughter, his own and his friends', and positioned himself, sullen and uneasy, next to the blackboard, opposite Lila. The duel continued, as they did increasingly difficult calculations in their heads. The boy gave his answers in dialect, as if he were on the street and not in a classroom, and Ferraro corrected his diction, but the figure was always correct. Enzo seemed extremely proud of that moment of glory, amazed himself at how clever he was. Then he began to slip, because Lila had woken up conclusively, and now her eyes had narrowed in determination, and she answered correctly. In the end Enzo lost. He lost but was not resigned. He began to curse, to shout ugly obscenities. Ferraro sent him to kneel behind the blackboard, but he wouldn't go. He was rapped on the knuckles with the rod and then pulled by the ears to the punishment corner. The school day ended like that.

But from then on the gang of boys began to throw rocks at us.

9.

That morning of the duel between Enzo and Lila is important, in our long story. Many modes of behavior started off there that were difficult to decipher. For example it became very clear that Lila could, if she wanted, ration the use of her abilities. That was what she had done with Don Achille's son. She did not want to beat him, but she had also calibrated silences and answers in such a way as not to be beaten. We had not yet become friends and I couldn't ask her why she had behaved like that. But really there was no need to ask questions, I could guess the reason. Like me, she, too, had been forbidden to offend not only Don Achille but also his family.

It was like that. We didn't know the origin of that fear-rancor-hatred-meekness that our parents displayed toward the Carraccis and transmitted to us, but it was there, it was a fact, like the neighborhood, its dirty-white houses, the fetid odor of the landings, the dust of the streets. In all likelihood Nino Sarratore, too, had been silent in order to allow Alfonso to be at his best. Handsome, slender, and nervous, with long lashes, hair neatly combed, he had stammered only a few words and had finally been silent. To continue to love him, I wanted to think that was what it had been. But deep down I had some doubts. Had it been a choice, like Lila's? I wasn't sure. I had stepped aside because Alfonso really was better than me. Lila could have defeated him immediately, yet she had chosen to aim for a tie. And Nino? There was something that confused and perhaps saddened me: not an inability, not even surrender, but, I would say today, a collapse. That stammer, the pallor, the purple that had suddenly swallowed his eyes: how handsome he was, so languid, and yet how much I disliked his languor.

Lila, too, at a certain point had seemed very beautiful to me. In general I was the pretty one, while she was skinny, like a salted anchovy, she gave off an odor of wildness, she had a long face, narrow at the temples, framed by two bands of smooth black hair. But when she decided to vanquish both Alfonso and Enzo, she had lighted up like a holy warrior. Her cheeks flushed, the sign of a flame released by every corner of her body, and for the first time I thought: Lila is prettier than I am. So I was second in everything. I hoped that no one would ever realize it.

But the most important thing that morning was the discovery that a phrase we often used to avoid punishment contained something true, hence uncontrollable, hence dangerous. The formula was: *I didn't do it on purpose*. Enzo, in fact, had not entered the competition deliberately and had not deliberately defeated Alfonso. Lila had deliberately defeated Enzo but had not deliberately defeated Alfonso or deliberately humiliated him; it had been only a necessary step. The conclusion we drew from this convinced us that it was best to do everything on purpose, deliberately, so that you would know what to expect.

Because almost nothing had been done deliberately, many unforeseen things struck us, one after the other. Alfonso went home in tears as a result of his defeat. His brother Stefano, who was fourteen, an apprentice in the grocery store (the former workshop of the carpenter Peluso) owned by his father—who, however, never set foot in it—showed up outside school the next day and said very nasty things to Lila, to the point of threatening her. She yelled an obscenity at him, and he pushed her against a wall and tried to grab her tongue, shouting that he would prick it with a pin. Lila went home and told her brother Rino everything, and the more she talked, the redder he got, his eyes bright. In the meantime Enzo, going home one night without his country gang, was stopped by Stefano and punched and kicked. Rino, in the morning, went to look for Stefano and they had a fight, giving each other a more or less equal beating. A few days later the wife of Don Achille, Donna Maria, knocked on the Cerullos' door and made a scene with Nunzia, shouting and insulting her. A little time passed and one Sunday, after Mass, Fernando Cerullo the shoemaker, the father of Lila and Rino, a small, thin man, timidly accosted Don Achille and apologized, without ever saying what he was apologizing for. I didn't see it, or at least I don't remember it, but it was said that the apologies were made aloud, and in such a way that everyone could hear, even though Don Achille had walked by as if the shoemaker were not speaking to him. Sometime later Lila and I wounded Enzo in the calf with a stone and Enzo threw a stone that hit Lila in the head. While I was shrieking in fear and Lila got up with the blood dripping from under her hair, Enzo, who was also bleeding, climbed down the embankment, and, seeing Lila in that state, he, utterly unpredictably and to our eyes incomprehensibly, began to cry. Then Rino, Lila's adored brother, came to school and, outside, beat up Enzo, who barely defended himself. Rino was older, bigger, and more motivated. Not only that: Enzo didn't mention that beating to his gang or his mother or his father or his brothers or his cousins, who all worked in the countryside and sold fruit and vegetables from a cart. At that point, thanks to him, the feuds ended.

10.

Lila went around proudly for a while, with her head bandaged. Then she took off the bandage and showed anyone who asked the black scar, red at the edges, that stuck out on her forehead under the hairline. Finally people forgot what had happened and if someone stared at the whitish mark left on her skin, she made an aggressive gesture that meant: what are you looking at, mind your own business. To me she never said anything, not even a word of thanks for the rocks I had handed her, for how I had dried the blood with the edge of my smock. But from that moment she began to subject me to proofs of courage that had nothing to do with school.

We saw each other in the courtyard more and more frequently. We showed off our dolls to each other but without appearing to, one in the other's vicinity, as if each of us were alone. At some point we let the dolls meet, as a test, to see if they got along. And so came the day when we sat next to the cellar window with the curled grating and exchanged our dolls, she holding mine and I hers, and Lila abruptly pushed Tina through the opening in the grating and dropped her.

I felt an unbearable sorrow. I was attached to my plastic doll; it was the most precious possession I had. I knew that Lila was mean, but I had never expected her to do something so spiteful to me. For me the doll was alive, to know that she was on the floor of the cellar, amid the thousand beasts that lived there, threw me into despair. But that day I learned a skill at which I later excelled. I held back my despair, I held it back on the edge of my wet eyes, so that Lila said to me in dialect:

"You don't care about her?"

I didn't answer. I felt a violent pain, but I sensed that the pain of quarreling with her would be even stronger. I was as if strangled by two agonies, one already happening, the loss of the doll, and one possible, the loss of Lila. I said nothing, I only acted, without spite, as if it were natural, even if it wasn't natural and I knew I was taking a great risk. I merely threw into the cellar her Nu, the doll she had just given me.

Lila looked at me in disbelief.

"What you do, I do," I recited immediately, aloud, very frightened.

"Now go and get it for me."

"If you go and get mine."

We went together. At the entrance to the building, on the left, was the door that led to the cellars, we knew it well. Because it was broken—one of the panels was hanging on just one hinge—the entrance was blocked by a chain that crudely held the two panels together. Every child was tempted and at the same time terrified by the possibility of forcing the door that little bit that would make it possible to go through to the other side. We did it. We made a space wide enough for our slender, supple bodies to slip through into the cellar.

Once inside, we descended, Lila in the lead, five stone steps into a damp space, dimly lit by the narrow openings at street level. I was afraid, and tried to stay close behind Lila, but she seemed angry, and intent on finding her doll. I groped my way forward. I felt under the soles of my sandals objects that squeaked, glass, gravel, insects. All around were things not identifiable, dark masses, sharp or square or rounded. The faint light that pierced the darkness sometimes fell on something recognizable: the skeleton of a chair, the pole of a lamp, fruit boxes, the bottoms and sides of wardrobes, iron hinges. I got scared by what seemed to me a soft face, with large glass eyes, that lengthened into a chin shaped like a box. I saw it hanging, with its desolate expression, on a rickety wooden stand, and I cried out to Lila, pointing to it. She turned and slowly approached it, with her back to me, carefully extended one hand, and detached it from the stand. Then she turned around. She had put the face with the glass eyes over hers and now her face was enormous, with round, empty eye sockets and no mouth, only that protruding black chin swinging over her chest.

Those are moments which are stamped into memory. I'm not sure, but I must have let out a cry of real terror, because she hurried to say, in an echoing voice, that it was just a mask, an anti-gas mask: that's what her father called it, he had one like it in the storeroom at home. I continued to tremble and moan with fear, which evidently persuaded her to tear the thing off her face and throw it in a corner, causing a loud noise and a lot of dust that thickened amid the tongues of light from the windows.

I calmed down. Lila looked around, identified the opening from which we had dropped Tina and Nu. We went along the rough bumpy wall, we looked into the shadows. The dolls weren't there. Lila repeated in dialect, they're not there, they're not there, they're not there, and searched along the floor with her hands, something I didn't have the courage to do.

Long minutes passed. Once only I seemed to see Tina and with a tug at my heart I bent over to grab her, but it was only a crumpled page of old newspaper. They aren't here, Lila repeated, and headed toward the door. Then I felt lost, unable to stay there by myself and keep searching, unable to leave if I hadn't found my doll.

At the top of the steps she said:

"Don Achille took them, he put them in his black bag."

And at that very moment I heard him, Don Achille: he slithered, he shuffled among the indistinct shapes of things. Then I abandoned Tina to her fate, and ran away, in order not to lose Lila, who was already twisting nimbly between the panels of the broken door.

11.

I believed everything she told me. The shapeless mass of Don Achille running through the underground tunnels, arms dangling, large fingers grasping Nu's head in one hand, in the other Tina's. I suffered terribly. I got sick, had fevers, got better, got sick again. I was overcome by a kind of tactile dysfunction; sometimes I had the impression that, while every animated being around me was speeding up the rhythms of its life, solid surfaces turned soft under my fingers or swelled up, leaving empty spaces between their internal mass and the surface skin. It seemed to me that my own body, if you touched it, was distended, and this saddened me. I was sure that I had cheeks like balloons, hands stuffed with sawdust, earlobes like ripe berries, feet in the shape of loaves of bread. When I returned to the streets and to school, I felt that the space, too, had changed. It seemed to be chained between two dark poles: on one side was the underground air bubble that pressed on the roots of the houses, the threatening cavern the dolls had fallen into; on the other the upper sphere, on the fourth floor of the building where Don Achille, who had stolen them, lived. The two balls were as if screwed to the ends of an iron bar, which in my imagination obliquely crossed the apartments, the streets, the countryside, the tunnel, the railroad tracks, and compressed them. I felt squeezed in that vise along with the mass of everyday things and people, and I had a bad taste in my mouth, a permanent sense of nausea that exhausted me, as if everything, thus compacted, and always tighter, were grinding me up, reducing me to a repulsive cream.

It was an enduring malaise, lasting perhaps years, beyond early adolescence. But unexpectedly, just when it began, I received my first declaration of love.

It was before Lila and I had attempted to climb the stairs to Don Achille's, and my grief at the loss of Tina was still unbearable. I had gone reluctantly to buy bread. My mother had sent me and I was going home, the change clutched in my fist and the loaf still warm against my chest, when I realized that Nino Sarratore was trudging behind me, holding his little brother by the hand. On summer days his mother, Lidia, always sent him out with Pino, who at the time was no more than five, with the injunction never to leave him. Near a corner, a little past the Carraccis' grocery, Nino was about to pass me, but instead of passing he cut off my path, pushed me against the wall, placed his free hand against the wall as a bar, to keep me from running away, and with the other pulled up beside him his brother, a silent witness of his undertaking. Breathlessly he said something I couldn't understand. He was pale, and he smiled, then he became serious, then he smiled again. Finally he said, in school Italian:

"When we grow up I want to marry you."

Then he asked if in the meantime I would be engaged to him. He was a little taller than me, very thin, with a long neck, his ears sticking out a little from his head. He had rebellious hair, and intense eyes with long lashes. The effort he was making to restrain his timidity was touching. Although I also wanted to marry him, I felt like answering:

"No, I can't."

He was stunned, Pino gave him a tug. I ran away.

From that moment I began to sneak into a side street whenever I saw him. And yet he seemed to me so handsome. How many times had I hung around his sister Marisa just to be near him and walk part of the way home with them. But he had made the declaration at the wrong moment. He couldn't know how undone I felt, how much anguish Tina's disappearance had caused me, how exhausting the effort of keeping up with Lila was, how the compressed space of the courtyard, the buildings, the neighborhood cut off my breath. After giving me many long, frightened glances from a distance, he began to avoid me, too. For a while he must have been afraid that I would tell the other girls, and in particular his sister, about the proposal he had made. Everyone knew that Gigliola Spagnuolo, the daughter of the baker, had done that when Enzo had asked her to be his girlfriend. And Enzo had found out and got angry, he had shouted outside school that she was a liar, he had even threatened to kill her with a knife. I, too, was tempted to tell everything, but then I let it go, I didn't tell anyone, not even Lila when we became friends. Slowly I forgot about it myself.

It came to mind again when, some time later, the entire Sarratore family moved. One morning the cart and horse that belonged to Assunta's husband, Nicola, appeared in the courtyard: with that same cart and that same old horse he sold fruit and vegetables with his wife, going up and down the streets of the neighborhood. Nicola had a broad handsome face and the same blue eyes, the same blond hair as his son Enzo. Besides selling fruit and vegetables, he was the mover. And in fact he, Donato Sarratore, Nino himself, and Lidia, too, began to carry things downstairs, all sorts of odds and ends, mattresses, furniture, and piled it on the cart.

As soon as the women heard the sound of wheels in the courtyard, they looked out, including my mother, including me. There was a great curiosity. It seemed that Donato had got a new house directly from the state railroad, in the neighborhood of a square called Piazza Nazionale. Or—said my mother—his wife had obliged him to move to escape the persecutions of Melina, who wanted to take away her husband. Likely. My mother always saw evil where, to my great annoyance, it was sooner or later discovered that evil really was, and her crossed eye seemed made purposely to identify the secret motives of the neighborhood. How would Melina react? Was it true, as I had heard whispered, that she had had a child with Sarratore and then killed it? And was it possible that she would start shouting terrible things, including that? All the females, big and small, were at the windows, perhaps to wave goodbye to the family that was leaving, perhaps to witness the spectacle of rage of that ugly, lean, and widowed woman. I saw that Lila and her mother, Nunzia, were also watching.

I sought Nino's gaze, but he seemed to have other things to do. I was then seized, as usual for no precise reason, by a weariness that made everything around me faint. I thought that perhaps he had made that declaration because he already knew that he would be leaving and wanted to tell me first what he felt for me. I looked at him as he struggled to carry boxes filled to overflowing, and I felt the guilt, the sorrow of having said no. Now he was fleeing like a bird.

Finally the procession of furniture and household goods stopped. Nicola and Donato began to tie everything to the cart with ropes. Lidia Sarratore appeared dressed as if to go to a party, she had even put on a summer hat, of blue straw. She pushed the carriage with her youngest boy in it and beside her she had the two girls, Marisa, who was my age, eight or nine, and Clelia, six. Suddenly there was a noise of things breaking on the second floor. Almost at the same moment Melina began screaming. Her cries were so tortured that Lila, I saw, put her hands over her ears. The pained voice of Ada, Melina's second child, echoed as she cried, Mamma, no, Mamma. After a moment of uncertainty I, too, covered my ears. But meanwhile objects began to fly out the window and curiosity became so strong that I freed my eardrums, as if I needed clear sounds to understand. Melina, however, wasn't uttering words but only aaah, aaah, as if she were wounded. She couldn't be seen, not even an arm or a hand that was throwing things could be seen. Copper pots, glasses, bottles, plates appeared to fly out the window of their own volition, and in the street Lidia Sarratore walked with her head down, leaning over the baby carriage, her daughters behind, while Donato climbed up on the cart amid his property, and Don Nicola guided the horse by the

bridle and meanwhile objects hit the asphalt, bounced, shattered, sending splinters between the nervous hooves of the
beast.

I looked at Lila. Now I saw another face, a face of bewilderment. She must have realized that I was looking at her, and
she immediately disappeared from the window. Meanwhile the
cart started off. Keeping to the wall, without a goodbye to anyone, Lidia and the four youngest children slunk toward the
gate, while Nino seemed unwilling to leave, as if hypnotized by
the waste of fragile objects against the asphalt.

Last I saw flying out the window a sort of black spot. It was
an iron, pure steel. When I still had Tina and played in the
house, I used my mother's, which was identical, prow-shaped,
pretending it was a ship in a storm. The object plummeted
down and with a sharp thud made a hole in the ground, a few
inches from Nino. It nearly—very nearly—killed him.

12.

No boy ever declared to Lila that he loved her, and she
never told me if it grieved her. Gigliola Spagnuolo received
proposals to be someone's girlfriend continuously and I, too,
was much in demand. Lila, on the other hand, wasn't popular,
mostly because she was skinny, dirty, and always had a cut or
bruise of some sort, but also because she had a sharp tongue.
She invented humiliating nicknames and although in front of
the teacher she showed off Italian words that no one knew,
with us she spoke a scathing dialect, full of swear words, which
cut off at its origin any feeling of love. Only Enzo did a thing
that, if it wasn't exactly a request to be her boyfriend, was nevertheless a sign of admiration and respect. Some time after he
had cut her head with the rock and before, it seems to me, he
was rejected by Gigliola Spagnuolo, he ran into us on the

stradone and, before my incredulous eyes, held out to Lila a garland of sorb apples.

"What do I do with it?"

"You eat them."

"Bitter?"

"Let them ripen."

"I don't want them."

"Throw them away."

That was it. Enzo turned his back and hurried off to work. Lila and I started laughing. We didn't talk much, but we had a laugh at everything that happened to us. I said only, in a tone of amusement:

"I like sorb apples."

I was lying, it was a fruit I didn't like. I was attracted by their reddish-yellow color when they were unripe, their compactness that gleamed on sunny days. But when they ripened on the balconies and became brown and soft like small wrinkled pears, and the skin came off easily, displaying a grainy pulp not with a bad taste but spongy in a way that reminded me of the corpses of rats along the *stradone*, then I wouldn't even touch them. I made that statement almost as a test, hoping that Lila would offer them to me: here, take them, you have them. I felt that if she had given me the gift that Enzo had given her I would be happier than if she had given me something of hers. But she didn't, and I still recall the feeling of betrayal when she brought them home. She herself put a nail at the window. I saw her hang the garland on it.

13.

Enzo didn't give her any other gifts. After the fight with Gigliola, who had told everyone about the declaration he had made to her, we saw him less and less. Although he had proved to be extremely good at doing sums in his head, he was lazy, so the teacher didn't suggest that he take the admissions test for the middle school, and he wasn't sorry about it, in fact he was pleased. He enrolled in the trade school, but in fact he was already working with his parents. He got up very early to go with his father to the fruit-and-vegetable market or to drive the cart through the neighborhood, selling produce from the countryside, and so he soon quit school.

We, instead, toward the end of fifth grade, were told that it would be suitable for us to continue in school. The teacher summoned in turn my parents and those of Gigliola and Lila to tell them that we absolutely had to take not only the test for the elementary school diploma but also the one for admission to middle school. I did all I could so that my father would not send my mother, with her limp, her wandering eye, and her stubborn anger, but would go himself, since he was a porter and knew how to be polite. I didn't succeed. She went, she talked to the teacher, and returned home in a sullen mood.

"The teacher wants money. She says she has to give some extra lessons because the test is difficult."

"But what's the point of this test?" my father asked.

"To let her study Latin."

"Why?"

"Because they say she's clever."

"But if she's clever, why does the teacher have to give her lessons that cost money?"

"So she'll be better off and we'll be worse."

They discussed it at length. At first my mother was against it and my father uncertain; then my father became cautiously in favor and my mother resigned herself to being a little less against it; finally they decided to let me take the test, but always provided that if I did not do well they would immediately take me out of school.

Lila's parents on the other hand said no. Nunzia Cerullo made a few somewhat hesitant attempts, but her father wouldn't even talk about it, and in fact hit Rino when he told him that he was wrong. Her parents were inclined not to go and see the teacher, but Maestra Oliviero had the principal summon them, and then Nunzia had to go. Faced with the timid but flat refusal of that frightened woman, Maestra Oliviero, stern but calm, displayed Lila's marvelous compositions, the brilliant solutions to difficult problems, and even the beautifully colored drawings that in class, when she applied herself, enchanted us all, because, pilfering Giotto's pastels, she portrayed in a realistic style princesses with hairdos, jewels, clothes, shoes that had never been seen in any book or even at the parish cinema. When the refusal persisted, the teacher lost her composure and dragged Lila's mother to the principal as if she were a student to be disciplined. But Nunzia couldn't yield, she didn't have permission from her husband. As a result she kept saying no until she, the teacher, and the principal were overcome by exhaustion.

The next day, as we were going to school, Lila said to me in her usual tone: I'm going to take the test anyway. I believed her, to forbid her to do something was pointless, everyone knew it. She seemed the strongest of us girls, stronger than Enzo, than Alfonso, than Stefano, stronger than her brother Rino, stronger than our parents, stronger than all the adults including the teacher and the carabinieri, who could put you in jail. Although she was fragile in appearance, every prohibition lost substance in her presence. She knew how to go beyond the limit without ever truly suffering the consequences. In the end people gave in, and were even, however unwillingly, compelled to praise her.

14.

We were also forbidden to go to Don Achille's, but she decided to go anyway and I followed. In fact, that was when I became convinced that nothing could stop her, and that every disobedient act contained breathtaking opportunities.

We wanted Don Achille to give us back our dolls. So we climbed the stairs: at every step I was on the point of turning around and going back to the courtyard. I still feel Lila's hand grasping mine, and I like to think that she decided to take it not only because she intuited that I wouldn't have the courage to get to the top floor but also because with that gesture she herself sought the force to continue. So, one beside the other, I on the wall side and she on the banister side, sweaty palms clasped, we climbed the last flights. At Don Achille's door my heart was pounding, I could hear it in my ears, but I was consoled by thinking that it was also the sound of Lila's heart. From the apartment came voices, perhaps of Alfonso or Stefano or Pinuccia. After a very long, silent pause before the door, Lila rang the bell. There was silence, then a shuffling. Donna Maria opened the door, wearing a faded green housedress. When she spoke, I saw a brilliant gold tooth in her mouth. She thought we were looking for Alfonso, and was a bit bewildered. Lila said to her in dialect:

"No, we want Don Achille."

"Tell me."

"We have to speak to him."

The woman shouted, "Achì!"

More shuffling. A thickset figure emerged from the shadows. He had a long torso, short legs, arms that hung to his knees, and a cigarette in his mouth; you could see the embers. He asked hoarsely:

"Who is it?"

"The daughter of the shoemaker with Greco's oldest daughter."

Don Achille came into the light, and, for the first time, we saw him clearly. No minerals, no sparkle of glass. His long face was of flesh, and the hair bristled only around his ears; the top of his head was shiny. His eyes were bright, the white veined with small red streams, his mouth wide and thin, his chin heavy, with a crease in the middle. He seemed to me ugly but not the way I imagined.

"Well?"

"The dolls," said Lila.

"What dolls?"

"Ours."

"Your dolls are of no use here."

"You took them down in the cellar."

Don Achille turned and shouted into the apartment:

"Pinù, did you take the doll belonging to the shoemaker's daughter?"

"Me, no."

"Alfò, did you take it?"

Laughter.

Lila said firmly, I don't know where she got all that courage:

"You took them, we saw you."

There was a moment of silence.

" 'You' me?"

"Yes, and you put them in your black bag."

The man, hearing those words, wrinkled his forehead in annoyance.

I couldn't believe that we were there, in front of Don Achille, and Lila was speaking to him like that and he was staring at her in bewilderment, and in the background could be seen Alfonso and Stefano and Pinuccia and Donna Maria, who was setting the table for dinner. I couldn't believe that he was an ordinary person, a little short, a little bald, a little out of proportion, but ordinary. So I waited for him to be abruptly transformed.

Don Achille repeated, as if to understand clearly the meaning of the words:

"I took your dolls and put them in a black bag?"

I felt that he was not angry but unexpectedly pained, as if he were receiving confirmation of something he already knew. He said something in dialect that I didn't understand, Maria cried, "Achì, it's ready."

"I'm coming."

Don Achille stuck a large, broad hand in the back pocket of his pants. We clutched each other's hand tightly, waiting for him to bring out a knife. Instead he took out his wallet, opened it, looked inside, and handed Lila some money, I don't remember how much.

"Go buy yourselves dolls," he said.

Lila grabbed the money and dragged me down the stairs. He muttered, leaning over the banister:

"And remember that they were a gift from me."

I said, in Italian, careful not to trip on the stairs:

"Good evening and enjoy your meal."

15.

Right after Easter, Gigliola Spagnuolo and I started going to the teacher's house to prepare for the admissions test. The teacher lived right next to the parish church of the Holy Family, and her windows looked out on the public gardens; from there you could see, beyond the dense countryside, the pylons of the railroad. Gigliola passed by my window and called me. I was ready, I ran out. I liked those private lessons, two a week, I think. The teacher, at the end of the lesson, offered us little heart-shaped cookies and a soft drink.

Lila didn't come; her parents had not agreed to pay the teacher. But, since we were now good friends, she continued to tell me that she would take the test and would enter the first year of middle school in the same class as me.

"And the books?"

"You'll lend them to me."

Meanwhile, however, with the money from Don Achille, she bought a book: *Little Women*. She decided to buy it because she already knew it and liked it hugely. Maestra Oliviero, in fourth grade, had given the smarter girls books to read. Lila had received *Little Women*, along with the following comment: "This is for older girls, but it will be good for you," and I got the book *Heart*, by Edmondo De Amicis, with not a word of explanation. Lila read both *Little Women* and *Heart*, in a very short time, and said there was no comparison, in her opinion *Little Women* was wonderful. I hadn't managed to read it, I had had a hard time finishing *Heart* before the time set by the teacher for returning it. I was a slow reader, I still am. Lila, when she had to give the book back to Maestra Oliviero, regretted both not being able to reread *Little Women* continuously and not being able to talk about it with me. So one morning she made up her mind. She called me from the street, we went to the ponds, to the place where we had buried the money from Don Achille, in a metal box, took it out, and went to ask Iolanda the stationer, who had had displayed in her window forever a copy of *Little Women*, yellowed by the sun, if it was enough. It was. As soon as we became owners of the book we began to meet in the courtyard to read it, either silently, one next to the other, or aloud. We read it for months, so many times that the book became tattered and sweat-stained, it lost its spine, came unthreaded, sections fell apart. But it was our book, we loved it dearly. I was the guardian, I kept it at home among the schoolbooks, because Lila didn't feel she could keep it in her house. Her father, lately, would get angry if she merely took it out to read.

But Rino protected her. When the subject of the admissions test came up, quarrels exploded continuously between him and his father. Rino was about sixteen at the time, he was a very excitable boy and had started a battle to be paid for the work he did. His reasoning was: I get up at six; I come to the shop and work till eight at night; I want a salary. But those words outraged his father and his mother. Rino had a bed to sleep in, food to eat, why did he want money? His job was to help the family, not impoverish it. But he insisted, he found it unjust to work as hard as his father and not receive a cent. At that point Fernando Cerullo answered him with apparent patience: "I pay you already, Rino, I pay you generously by teaching you the whole trade: soon you'll be able to repair a heel or an edge or put on a new sole; your father is passing on to you everything he knows, and you'll be able to make an entire shoe, with the skill of a professional." But that payment by instruction was not enough for Rino, and so they argued, especially at dinner. They began by talking about money and ended up quarreling about Lila.

"If you pay me I'll take care of sending her to school," Rino said.

"School? Why, did I go to school?"

"No."

"Did you go to school?"

"No."

"Then why should your sister, who is a girl, go to school?"

The matter almost always ended with a slap in the face for Rino, who, one way or another, even if he didn't intend to, had displayed a lack of respect toward his father. The boy, without crying, apologized in a spiteful tone of voice.

Lila was silent during those discussions. She never said so, but I had the impression that while I hated my mother, really hated her, profoundly, she, in spite of everything, wasn't upset with her father. She said that he was full of kindnesses, she said that when there were accounts to do he let her do them, she said that she had heard him say to his friends that his daughter was the most intelligent person in the neighborhood, she said that on her name day he brought her warm chocolate in bed and four biscuits. But what could you do, it didn't enter into his view of the world that she should continue to go to school. Nor did it fall within his economic possibilities: the family was large, they all had to live off the shoe repair shop, including two unmarried sisters of Fernando and Nunzia's parents. So on the matter of school it was like talking to the wall, and her mother all in all had the same opinion. Only her brother had different ideas, and fought boldly against his father. And Lila, for reasons I didn't understand, seemed certain that Rino would win. He would get his salary and would send her to school with the money.

"If there's a fee to pay, he'll pay it for me," she explained.

She was sure that her brother would also give her money for the school books and even for pens, pen case, pastels, globe, the smock and the ribbon. She adored him. She said that, after she went to school, she wanted to earn a lot of money for the sole purpose of making her brother the wealthiest person in the neighborhood.

In that last year of elementary school, wealth became our obsession. We talked about it the way characters in novels talk about searching for treasure. We said, when we're rich we'll do this, we'll do that. To listen to us, you might think that the wealth was hidden somewhere in the neighborhood, in treasure chests that, when opened, would be gleaming with gold, and were waiting only for us to find them. Then, I don't know why, things changed and we began to link school to wealth. We thought that if we studied hard we would be able to write books and that the books would make us rich. Wealth was still the glitter of gold coins stored in countless chests, but to get there all you had to do was go to school and write a book.

"Let's write one together," Lila said once, and that filled me with joy.

Maybe the idea took root when she discovered that the author of *Little Women* had made so much money that she had given some of it to her family. But I wouldn't promise. We argued about it, I said we could start right after the admission test. She agreed, but then she couldn't wait. While I had a lot to study because of the afternoon lessons with Spagnuolo and the teacher, she was freer, she set to work and wrote a novel without me.

I was hurt when she brought it to me to read, but I didn't say anything, in fact I held in check my disappointment and was full of congratulations. There were ten sheets of graph paper, folded and held together with a dressmaker's pin. It had a cover drawn in pastels, and the title, I remember, was *The Blue Fairy*. How exciting it was, how many difficult words there were. I told her to let the teacher read it. She didn't want to. I begged her, I offered to give it to her. Although she wasn't sure, she agreed.

One day when I was at Maestra Oliviero's house for our lesson, I took advantage of Gigliola being in the bathroom to take out *The Blue Fairy*. I said it was a wonderful novel written by Lila and that Lila wanted her to read it. But the teacher, who for five years had been enthusiastic about everything Lila did, except when she was bad, replied coldly:

"Tell Cerullo that she would do well to study for the diploma, instead of wasting time." And although she kept Lila's novel, she left it on the table without even giving it a glance.

That attitude confused me. What had happened? Was she angry with Lila's mother? Had her rage extended to Lila herself? Was she upset about the money that the parents of my friend wouldn't give her? I didn't understand. A few days later I cautiously asked her if she had read *The Blue Fairy*. She answered in an unusual tone, obscurely, as if only she and I could truly understand.

"Do you know what the plebs are, Greco?"

"Yes, the people, the tribunes of the plebs are the Gracchi."

"The plebs are quite a nasty thing."

"Yes."

"And if one wishes to remain a plebeian, he, his children, the children of his children deserve nothing. Forget Cerullo and think of yourself."

Maestra Oliviero never said anything about *The Blue Fairy*. Lila asked about it a couple of times, then she let it go. She said grimly:

"As soon as I have time I'll write another, that one wasn't good."

"It was wonderful."

"It was terrible."

But she became less lively, especially in class, probably because she realized that the teacher had stopped praising her, and sometimes seemed irritated by her excesses of virtuosity. When it came time for the competition at the end of the year she was still the best, but without her old impudence. At the end of the day, the principal presented to those remaining in competition—Lila, Gigliola, and me—an extremely difficult problem that he had invented himself. Gigliola and I struggled in vain. Lila, narrowing her eyes to cracks, applied herself. She was the last to give up. She said, with a timidity unusual for her, that the problem couldn't be solved, because there was a mistake in the premise, but she didn't know what it was. Maestra Oliviero scolded her harshly. I saw Lila standing at the blackboard, chalk in hand, very small and pale, assaulted by volleys of cruel phrases. I felt her suffering, I couldn't bear the trembling of her lower lip and nearly burst into tears.

"When one cannot solve a problem," the teacher concluded coldly, "one does not say, There is a mistake in the problem, one says, I am not capable of solving it."

The principal was silent. As far as I remember, the day ended there.

16.

Shortly before the final test in elementary school Lila pushed me to do another of the many things that I would never have had the courage to do by myself. We decided to skip school, and cross the boundaries of the neighborhood.

It had never happened before. As far back as I could remember, I had never left the four-story white apartment buildings, the courtyard, the parish church, the public gardens, I had never felt the urge to. Trains passed continuously on the other side of the scrubland, trucks and cars passed up and down along the *stradone*, and yet I can't remember a single occasion when I asked myself, my father, my teacher: where are the cars going, the trucks, the trains, to what city, to what world?

Nor had Lila appeared particularly interested, but this time she organized everything. She told me to tell my mother that after school we were all going to the teacher's house for a party to mark the end of the school year, and although I tried to remind her that the teachers had never invited all us girls to their houses for a party, she said that that was the very reason we should say it. The event would seem so exceptional that none of our parents would be bold enough to go to school and ask if it was true or not. As usual, I trusted her, and things went just as she had said. At my house everyone believed it, not only my father and my sister and brothers but even my mother.

The night before, I couldn't sleep. What was beyond the neighborhood, beyond its well-known perimeter? Behind us rose a thickly wooded hill and a few structures in the shelter of the gleaming railroad tracks. In front of us, beyond the *stradone*, stretched a pitted road that skirted the ponds. To the right was a strip of treeless countryside, under an enormous sky. To the left was a tunnel with three entrances, but if you climbed up to the railroad tracks, on clear days you could see, beyond some low houses and walls of tufa and patches of thick vegetation, a blue mountain with one low peak and one a little higher, which was called Vesuvius and was a volcano.

But nothing that we had before our eyes every day, or that could be seen if we clambered up the hill, impressed us. Trained by our schoolbooks to speak with great skill about what we had never seen, we were excited by the invisible. Lila said that in the direction of Vesuvius was the sea. Rino, who had been there, had told her that the water was blue and sparkling, a marvelous sight. On Sundays, especially in summer, but often, too, in winter, he went with friends to swim, and he had promised to take her there. He wasn't the only one, naturally, who had seen the sea, others we knew had also seen it. Once Nino Sarratore and his sister Marisa had talked about it, in the tone of those who found it normal to go every so often to eat *taralli* and seafood. Gigliola Spagnuolo had also been there. She, Nino, and Marisa had, lucky for them, parents who took their children on outings far away, not just around the corner to the public gardens in front of the parish church. Ours weren't like that, they didn't have time, they didn't have money, they didn't have the desire. It was true that I seemed to have a vague bluish memory of the sea, my mother claimed she had taken me as a small child, when she had to have sand treatments for her injured leg. But I didn't much believe my mother, and to Lila, who didn't know anything about it, I admitted that I didn't know anything, either. So she planned to do as Rino had, to set off on the road and get there by herself. She persuaded me to go with her. Tomorrow.

I got up early, I did everything as if I were going to school— my bread and milk, my schoolbag, my smock. I waited for Lila as usual in front of the gate, only instead of going to the right we crossed the *stradone* and turned left, toward the tunnel.

It was early morning and already hot. There was a strong odor of earth and grass drying in the sun. We climbed among tall shrubs, on indistinct paths that led toward the tracks. When we reached an electrical pylon we took off our smocks and put them in the schoolbags, which we hid in the bushes. Then we raced through the scrubland, which we knew well, and flew excitedly down the slope that led to the tunnel. The entrance on the right was very dark: we had never been inside that obscurity. We held each other by the hand and entered. It was a long passage, and the luminous circle of the exit seemed far away. Once we got accustomed to the shadowy light, we saw lines of silvery water that slid along the walls, large puddles. Apprehensively, dazed by the echo of our steps, we kept going. Then Lila let out a shout and laughed at the violent explosion of sound. Immediately I shouted and laughed in turn. From that moment all we did was shout, together and separately: laughter and cries, cries and laughter, for the pleasure of hearing them amplified. The tension diminished, the journey began.

Ahead of us were many hours when no one in our families would look for us. When I think of the pleasure of being free, I think of the start of that day, of coming out of the tunnel and finding ourselves on a road that went straight as far as the eye could see, the road that, according to what Rino had told Lila, if you got to the end arrived at the sea. I felt joyfully open to the unknown. It was entirely different from going down into the cellar or up to Don Achille's house. There was a hazy sun, a strong smell of burning. We walked for a long time between crumbling walls invaded by weeds, low structures from which came voices in dialect, sometimes a clamor. We saw a horse make its way slowly down an embankment and cross the street, whinnying. We saw a young woman looking out from a balcony, combing her hair with a flea comb. We saw a lot of small snotty children who stopped playing and looked at us threateningly. We also saw a fat man in an undershirt who emerged from a tumbledown house, opened his pants, and showed us his penis. But we weren't scared of anything: Don Nicola, Enzo's father, sometimes let us pat his horse, the children were threatening in our courtyard, too, and there was old Don Mimì who showed us his disgusting thing when we were coming home from school. For at least three hours, the road we were walking on did not seem different from the segment that we looked out on every day. And I felt no responsibility for the right road. We held each other by the hand, we walked side by side, but for me, as usual, it was as if Lila were ten steps ahead and knew precisely what to do, where to go. I was used to feeling second in everything, and so I was sure that to her, who had always been first, everything was clear: the pace, the calculation of the time available for going and coming back, the route that would take us to the sea. I felt as if she had everything in her head ordered in such a way that the world around us would never be able to create disorder. I abandoned myself happily. I remember a soft light that seemed to come not from the sky but from the depths of the earth, even though, on the surface, it was poor, and ugly.

Then we began to get tired, to get thirsty and hungry. We hadn't thought of that. Lila slowed down, I slowed down, too. Two or three times I caught her looking at me, as if she had done something mean to me and was sorry. What was happening? I realized that she kept turning around and I started turning around, too. Her hand began to sweat. The tunnel, which was the boundary of the neighborhood, had been out of sight for a long time. By now the road we had just traveled was unfamiliar to us, like the one that stretched ahead. People appeared completely indifferent to our fate. Around us was a landscape of ruin: dented tanks, burned wood, wrecks of cars, cartwheels with broken spokes, damaged furniture, rusting scrap iron. Why was Lila looking back? Why had she stopped talking? What was wrong?

I looked more carefully. The sky, which at first had been

very high, was as if lowered. Behind us everything was becoming black, large heavy clouds lay over the trees, the light poles. In front of us, the light was still dazzling, but as if pressed on the sides by a purplish grayness that would suffocate it. In the distance thunder could be heard. I was afraid, but what frightened me more was Lila's expression, new to me. Her mouth was open, her eyes wide, she was looking nervously ahead, back, to the side, and she was squeezing my hand hard. Is it possible, I wondered, that she's afraid? What was happening to her?

The first fat drops arrived, leaving small brown stains as they hit the dusty road.

"Let's go back," Lila said.

"And the sea?"

"It's too far."

"And home?"

"Also."

"Then let's go to the sea."

"No."

"Why?"

I had never seen her so agitated. There was something—something she had on the tip of her tongue but couldn't make up her mind to tell me—that suddenly impelled her to drag me home in a hurry. I didn't understand: why didn't we keep going? There was time, the sea couldn't be too far, and whether we went back home or continued to go on, we'd get wet just the same, if it rained. It was a type of reasoning I had learned from her and I was bewildered when she didn't apply it.

A violet light cracked the black sky, the thunder was louder. Lila gave me a tug, I found myself running, unwillingly, back toward our own neighborhood. The wind rose, the drops fell more thickly, in a few seconds they were transformed into a cascade of water. It occurred to neither of us to seek shelter. We ran blinded by the rain, our clothes soaked, our bare feet in worn sandals that had no purchase on the now muddy ground. We ran until we were out of breath.

We couldn't keep it up, we slowed down. Lightning, thunder, a lava of rainwater ran along the sides of the road; noisy trucks sped by, raising waves of mud. We walked quickly, our hearts in a tumult, first in a heavy downpour, then in a fine rain, finally under a gray sky. We were soaked, our hair pasted to our heads, our lips livid, eyes frightened. We went back through the tunnel, we crossed the scrubland. The bushes dripping with rain grazed us, making us shiver. We found our schoolbags, we put over our wet clothes the dry smocks, we set out toward home. Tense, her eyes lowered, Lila had let go of my hand.

We quickly understood that things had not happened as we expected. The sky had turned black over the neighborhood just when school was over. My mother had gone to school with an umbrella to take me to the party at the teacher's. She had discovered that I wasn't there, that there was no party. For hours she had been looking for me. When I saw from a distance her painfully limping figure I immediately left Lila, so that she wouldn't get angry with her, and ran toward my mother. She slapped me and hit me with the umbrella, yelling that she would kill me if I did something like that again.

Lila took off. At her house no one had noticed anything.

At night my mother reported everything to my father and compelled him to beat me. He was irritated; he didn't want to, and they ended up fighting. First he hit her, then, angry at himself, he gave me a beating. All night I tried to understand what had really happened. We were supposed to go to the sea and we hadn't gone, I had been punished for nothing. A mysterious inversion of attitudes had occurred: I, despite the rain, would have continued on the road, I felt far from everything and everyone, and distance—I discovered for the first time—

extinguished in me every tie and every worry; Lila had abruptly repented of her own plan, she had given up the sea, she had wanted to return to the confines of the neighborhood. I couldn't figure it out.

The next day I didn't wait for her at the gate, I went alone to school. We met in the public gardens. She discovered the bruises on my arms and asked what had happened. I shrugged, that was how things had turned out.

"All they did was beat you?"

"What should they have done?"

"They're still sending you to study Latin?"

I looked at her in bewilderment.

Was it possible? She had taken me with her hoping that as a punishment my parents would not send me to middle school? Or had she brought me back in such a hurry so that I would avoid that punishment? Or—I wonder today—did she want at different moments both things?

17.

We took the final test in elementary school together. When she realized that I was also taking the admission test for middle school, she lost energy. Something happened that surprised everyone: I passed both tests with all tens, the highest marks; Lila got her diploma with nines and an eight in arithmetic.

She never said a word to me of anger or discontent. She began instead to go around with Carmela Peluso, the daughter of the carpenter-gambler, as if I were no longer enough. Within a few days we became a trio, in which, however, I, who had been first in school, was almost always the third. They talked and joked continuously with each other, or, rather, Lila talked and joked, Carmela listened and was amused. When we went for a walk between the church and the *stradone*, Lila was always in the middle and the two of us on the sides. If I noticed that she tended to be closer to Carmela I suffered and wanted to go home.

In this phase she seemed dazed, like the victim of sun-stroke. It was very hot and we often bathed our heads in the fountain. I remember her with her hair and face dripping as she talked constantly about going to school the next year. It had become her favorite subject and she tackled it as if it were one of the stories she intended to write in order to become rich. Now when she talked she preferred to address Carmela Peluso, who had got her diploma with all sevens and had not taken the admission test for middle school, either.

Lila was very skillful at telling stories—they all seemed true—about the school where we were going, and the teachers, and she made me laugh, she made me worry. One morning, though, I interrupted her.

"Lila," I said, "you can't go to middle school, you didn't take the admission test. Not you and not Carmela."

She got angry. She said she would go just the same, test or no test.

"And Carmela?"

"Yes."

"It's impossible."

"You'll see."

But I must have rattled her. She stopped telling stories about our scholastic future and became silent. Then, with a sudden determination, she started tormenting her family, insisting that she wanted to study Latin, like Gigliola Spa-gnuolo and me. She was especially hard on Rino, who had promised to help her but hadn't. It was pointless to explain to her that there was now nothing to do about it; she became even more unreasonable and mean.

At the start of the summer I began to have a feeling difficult to put into words. I saw that she was agitated, aggressive as she had always been, and I was pleased, I recognized her. But I also felt, behind her old habits, a pain that bothered me. She was suffering, and I didn't like her sorrow. I preferred her when she was different from me, distant from my anxieties. And the uneasiness that the discovery of her fragility brought me was transformed by secret pathways into a need of my own to be superior. As soon as I could, cautiously, especially when Carmela Peluso wasn't there, I found a way to remind her that I had gotten a better report card. As soon as I could, cautiously, I pointed out to her that I would go to middle school and she would not. To not be second, to outdo her, for the first time seemed to me a success. She must have realized it and she became even harsher, but toward her family, not me.

Often, as I waited for her to come down to the courtyard, I heard her shouting from the windows. She hurled insults in the worst street dialect, so vulgar that listening to them made me think of order and respect; it didn't seem right to treat adults like that, or even her brother. Of course, her father, Fernando the shoemaker, when he lost his head turned ugly. But all fathers had fits of anger. And hers, when she didn't provoke him, was a kind, sympathetic man, a hard worker. He looked like an actor named Randolph Scott, but unrefined. He was rough, without pale colors, a black beard covered his cheeks, and he had broad, stubby hands streaked with dirt in every crease and under the nails. He joked easily. When I went to Lila's house he took my nose between index and middle fingers and pretended to pull it off. He wanted to make me believe that he had stolen it and that now, as his prisoner, the nose was struggling to escape and return to my face. I found this funny. But if Rino or Lila or the other children made him angry, even I, hearing him from the street, was afraid.

I don't know what happened, one afternoon. In the hot weather we stayed outside until dinnertime. That day Lila didn't show up, and I went to call her at the windows, which were on the ground floor. I cried, "Lì, Lì, Lì," and my voice joined Fernando's extremely loud voice, his wife's loud voice, my friend's insistent voice. I could hear that something was going on and it terrified me. From the windows came a vulgar Neapolitan and the crash of broken objects. In appearance it was no different from what happened at my house when my mother got angry because there wasn't enough money and my father got angry because she had already spent the part of his wages he had given her. In reality the difference was substantial. My father was restrained even when he was angry, he became violent quietly, keeping his voice from exploding even if the veins on his neck swelled and his eyes were inflamed. Fernando instead yelled, threw things; his rage fed on itself, and he couldn't stop. In fact his wife's attempts to stop him increased his fury, and even if he wasn't mad at her he ended up beating her. I insisted, then, in calling Lila, just to get her out of that tempest of cries, obscenities, sounds of destruction. I cried, "Lì, Lì, Lì," but she—I heard her—kept on insulting her father.

We were ten, soon we would be eleven. I was filling out, Lila remained small and thin, she was light and delicate. Suddenly the shouting stopped and a few seconds later my friend flew out the window, passed over my head, and landed on the asphalt behind me.

I was stunned. Fernando looked out, still screaming horrible threats at his daughter. He had thrown her like a thing.

I looked at her terrified while she tried to get up and said, with an almost amused grimace, "I haven't hurt myself."

But she was bleeding; she had broken her arm.

18.

Fathers could do that and other things to impudent girls. Afterward, Fernando became sullen, and worked more than usual. That summer, Carmela and Lila and I often passed the workshop, but while Rino always gave us a friendly nod of greeting, the shoemaker wouldn't even look at his daughter as long as her arm was in the cast. It was clear that he was sorry. His violent moments as a father were a small thing compared with the widespread violence of the neighborhood. At the Bar Solara, in the heat, between gambling losses and troublesome drunkenness, people often reached the point of *disperazione*— a word that in dialect meant having lost all hope but also being broke—and hence of fights. Silvio Solara, the owner, a large man, with an imposing belly, blue eyes, and a high forehead, had a dark stick behind the bar with which he didn't hesitate to strike anyone who didn't pay for his drinks, who had asked for a loan and didn't repay it within the time limit, who made any sort of agreement and didn't keep it, and often he was helped by his sons, Marcello and Michele, boys the age of Lila's brother, who hit harder than their father. Blows were given and received. Men returned home embittered by their losses, by alcohol, by debts, by deadlines, by beatings, and at the first inopportune word they beat their families, a chain of wrongs that generated wrongs.

Right in the middle of that long season an event took place that upset everyone, but on Lila had a very particular effect. Don Achille, the terrible Don Achille, was murdered in his house in the early afternoon of a surprisingly rainy August day.

He was in the kitchen, and had just opened the window to let in the rain-freshened air. He had got up from bed to do so, interrupting his nap. He had on worn blue pajamas, and on his feet only socks of a yellowish color, blackened at the heels. As soon as he opened the window a gust of rain struck his face and someone plunged a knife into the right side of his neck, halfway between the jaw and the clavicle.

The blood spurted from his neck and hit a copper pot hanging on the wall. The copper was so shiny that the blood looked like an ink stain from which—Lila told us—dripped a wavering black line. The murderer—though she inclined to a murderess—had entered without breaking in, at a time when the children were outside and the adults, if they weren't at work, were lying down. Surely he had entered with a skeleton key. Surely he had intended to strike him in the heart while he was sleeping, but had found him awake and thrust that knife into his throat. Don Achille had turned, with the blade stuck in his neck, eyes staring and the blood pouring out and dripping all over his pajamas. He had fallen to his knees and then, facedown, to the floor.

The murder had made such an impression on Lila that almost every day, with great seriousness, always adding some new details, she compelled us to hear the story as if she had been present. Both Carmela Peluso and I, listening to her, were frightened; Carmela couldn't sleep at night. At the worst moments, when the black line of blood dripped along the copper pot, Lila's eyes became two fierce cracks. Surely she imagined that the murderer was female only because it was easier for her to identify with her.

In that period we often went to the Pelusos' house to play checkers and three-of-a-kind, for which Lila had developed a passion. Carmela's mother let us sit in the dining room, where all the furniture had been made by her husband before Don Achille took away his carpenter's tools and his shop. We sat at the table, which was placed between two sideboards with mirrors, and played. I found Carmela increasingly disagreeable, but I pretended to be her friend at least as much as I was Lila's, in fact sometimes I even let her think that I liked her better. On the other hand I really did like Signora Peluso. She had worked at the tobacco factory, but had recently lost her job and was always at home. Anyway, she was, for better or for worse, a cheerful, fat woman, with a large bosom and bright red cheeks, and although money was scarce she always had something good to offer us. Also her husband seemed more tranquil. Now he was a waiter in a pizzeria, and he tried not to go to the Bar Solara to lose at cards the little he earned.

One morning we were in the dining room playing checkers, Carmela and I against Lila. We were sitting at the table, us two on one side, she on the other. Behind Lila and behind Carmela and me were the identical, dark wood sideboards with the mirrors in spiral frames. I looked at the three of us reflected to infinity and I couldn't concentrate, both because of those images, which disturbed me, and because of the shouts of Alfredo Peluso, who that day was upset and was quarreling with his wife, Giuseppina.

There was a knock at the door and Signora Peluso went to open it. Exclamations, cries. We looked out into the hall and saw the carabinieri, figures we feared greatly. The carabinieri seized Alfredo and dragged him away. He struggled, shouted, called his children by name, Pasquale, Carmela, Ciro, Immacolata, he grabbed the furniture made with his own hands, the chairs, Giuseppina, he swore that he hadn't murdered Don Achille, that he was innocent. Carmela wept desperately, they all wept, I, too, began to weep. But not Lila, Lila had that look she had had years earlier for Melina, but with some difference: now, although she remained still, she appeared to be moving with Alfredo Peluso, whose cries were hoarse, and frightening: *Aaaah*.

It was the most terrible thing we witnessed in the course of our childhood, and made a deep impression on me. Lila attended to Carmela, and consoled her. She said to her that, if it really was her father, he had done well to kill Don Achille, but that in her opinion it wasn't him: surely he was innocent and would soon get out of prison. They whispered together continuously and if I approached they moved a little farther off so that I wouldn't hear.

ADOLESCENCE

The Story of the Shoes

1.

On December 31st of 1958 Lila had her first episode of dissolving margins. The term isn't mine, she always used it. She said that on those occasions the outlines of people and things suddenly dissolved, disappeared. That night, on the terrace where we were celebrating the arrival of 1959, when she was abruptly struck by that sensation, she was frightened and kept it to herself, still unable to name it. It was only years later, one night in November 1980—we were thirty-six, were married, had children—that she recounted in detail what had happened to her then, what still sometimes happened to her, and she used that term for the first time.

We were outside, on the roof terrace of one of the apartment buildings in the neighborhood. Although it was very cold we were wearing light, low-cut dresses, so that we would appear attractive. We looked at the boys, who were cheerful, aggressive, dark figures carried away by the party, the food, the sparkling wine. They were setting off fireworks to celebrate the new year, a ritual in which, as I will explain later, Lila had had a large role, so that now she felt content, watching the streaks of fire in the sky. But suddenly—she told me—in spite of the cold she had begun to sweat. It seemed to her that everyone was shouting too loudly and moving too quickly. This sensation was accompanied by nausea, and she had had the impression that something absolutely material, which had been present around her and around everyone and everything forever, but imperceptible, was breaking down the outlines of persons and things and revealing itself.

Her heart had started beating uncontrollably. She had begun to feel horror at the cries emerging from the throats of all those who were moving about on the terrace amid the smoke, amid the explosions, as if the sound obeyed new, unknown laws. Her nausea increased, the dialect had become unfamiliar, the way our wet throats bathed the words in the liquid of saliva was intolerable. A sense of repulsion had invested all the bodies in movement, their bone structure, the frenzy that shook them. How poorly made we are, she had thought, how insufficient. The broad shoulders, the arms, the legs, the ears, noses, eyes seemed to her attributes of monstrous beings who had fallen from some corner of the black sky. And the disgust, who knows why, was concentrated in particular on her brother Rino, the person who was closest to her, the person she loved most.

She seemed to see him for the first time as he really was: a squat animal form, thickset, the loudest, the fiercest, the greediest, the meanest. The tumult of her heart had overwhelmed her, she felt as if she were suffocating. Too smoky, too foul-smelling, too much flashing fire in the cold. Lila had tried to calm herself, she had said to herself: I have to seize the stream that's passing through me, I have to throw it out from me. But at that point she had heard, among the shouts of joy, a kind of final detonation and something like the breath of a wing beat had passed by her. Someone was shooting not rockets and firecrackers but a gun. Her brother Rino was shouting unbearable obscenities in the direction of the yellow flashes.

On the occasion when she told me that story, Lila also said that the sensation she called dissolving margins, although it had come on her distinctly only that once, wasn't completely new to her. For example, she had often had the sensation of moving for a few fractions of a second into a person or a thing or a number or a syllable, violating its edges. And the day her father threw her out the window she had felt absolutely certain, as she was flying toward the asphalt, that small, very friendly reddish animals were dissolving the composition of the street, transforming it into a smooth, soft material. But that New Year's Eve she had perceived for the first time unknown entities that broke down the outline of the world and demonstrated its terrifying nature. This had deeply shaken her.

2.

When Lila's cast was removed and her arm reappeared, pale but perfectly functioning, her father, Fernando, came to an agreement with himself and, without saying so directly, but through Rino and his wife, Nunzia, allowed her to go to a school to learn I don't know exactly what, stenography, bookkeeping, home economics, or all three.

She went unwillingly. Nunzia was summoned by the teachers because her daughter was often absent without an excuse, disrupted the class, if questioned refused to answer, if she had to do exercises did them in five minutes and then harassed her classmates. At some point she got a nasty flu, she who never got sick, and seemed to welcome it with a sort of abandon, so that the virus quickly sapped her energy. Days passed and she didn't get better. As soon as she tried to go out again, paler than usual, the fever returned. One day I saw her on the street and she looked like a spirit, the spirit of a child who had eaten poisonous berries, such as I had seen illustrated in a book belonging to Maestra Oliviero. Later a rumor spread that she would soon die, which caused me an unbearable anxiety. She recovered, almost in spite of herself. But, with the excuse that her health was poor, she went to school less and less often, and at the end of the year she failed.

Nor did I do well in my first year of middle school. At first I had great expectations, and even if I didn't say so clearly to myself I was glad to be there with Gigliola Spagnuolo rather than with Lila. In some very secret part of myself I looked forward to a school where she would never enter, where, in her absence, I would be the best student, and which I would sometimes tell her about, boasting. But immediately I began to falter, many of the others proved to be better than me. I ended up with Gigliola in a kind of swamp, we were little animals frightened of our own mediocrity, and we struggled all year not to end up at the bottom of the class. I was extremely disappointed. The idea began to quietly form that without Lila I would never feel the pleasure of belonging to that exclusive group of the best.

Every so often, at the entrance to school, I ran into Alfonso, the young son of Don Achille, but we pretended not to know each other. I didn't know what to say to him, I thought that Alfredo Peluso had done a good thing in murdering his father, and words of consolation did not come to me. I couldn't even feel moved by the fact that he had been orphaned, it was as if he bore some responsibility for the fear that for years Don Achille had inspired in me. He had a black band sewn on his jacket, he never laughed, he was always on his own. He was in a different class from mine, and the rumor was that he was really smart. At the end of the year we found out that he had been promoted with an average of eight, which depressed me hugely. Gigliola had to repeat Latin and mathematics, I managed to pass with sixes.

When the grades came out, the teacher summoned my mother, told her in my presence that I had passed Latin only thanks to her generosity, and that without private lessons the next year I certainly wouldn't make it. I felt a double humiliation: I was ashamed because I hadn't done as well as I had in elementary school, and I was ashamed of the difference between the harmonious, modestly dressed figure of the teacher, between her Italian that slightly resembled that of the Iliad, and the misshapen figure of my mother, her old shoes, her dull hair, the dialect bent into an ungrammatical Italian.

My mother, too, must have felt the weight of that humiliation. She went home in a surly mood, she told my father that the teachers weren't happy with me, she needed help in the house and I ought to leave school. They discussed it at length, they quarreled, and in the end my father decided that, since I at least had been promoted, while Gigliola had been held back in two subjects, I deserved to continue.

I spent the summer lethargically, in the courtyard, at the ponds, generally with Gigliola, who often talked about the young university student who came to her house to give her private lessons and who, according to her, was in love with her. I listened but I was bored. Every so often I saw Lila with Carmela Peluso; she, too, had gone to a school for something or other, and she, too, had failed. I felt that Lila no longer wanted to be my friend, and that idea brought on a weary exhaustion. Sometimes, hoping that my mother wouldn't see me, I lay down on the bed and dozed.

One afternoon I really fell asleep and when I woke I felt wet. I went to the bathroom to see what was wrong and discovered that my underpants were stained with blood. Terrified by I don't know what, maybe a scolding from my mother for having hurt myself between my legs, I washed the underpants carefully, wrung them out, and put them on again wet. Then I went out into the heat of the courtyard. My heart was pounding.

I met Lila and Carmela, and walked with them to the parish church. I felt that I was getting wet again, but I tried to calm down by telling myself it was the wet underpants. When the fear became unbearable I whispered to Lila, "I have to tell you something."

"What?"

"I want to tell just you."

I took her by the arm, trying to drag her away from Carmela, but Carmela followed us. I was so worried that in the end I confessed to them both, but addressing only Lila.

"What can it be?" I asked.

Carmela knew all about it. She had had that bleeding for a year already, every month.

"It's normal," she said. "Girls have it naturally: you bleed for a few days, your stomach and your back hurt, but then it goes away."

"Really?"

"Really."

Lila's silence pushed me toward Carmela. The naturalness with which she had said what she knew reassured me and made me like her. I spent all afternoon talking to her, until dinner time. You wouldn't die from that wound, I learned. Rather, "it means that you're grown-up and you can make babies, if a man sticks his thingy in your stomach."

Lila listened without saying anything, or almost anything. We asked if she had blood like us and saw her hesitate, then reluctantly answer no. Suddenly she seemed small, smaller than I had ever seen her. She was three or four inches shorter, all skin and bones, very pale in spite of the days spent outside. And she had failed. And she didn't know what the blood was. And no boy had ever made a declaration to her.

"You'll get it," we both said, in a falsely comforting tone.

"What do I care," she said. "I don't have it because I don't want to, it makes me sick. And anyone who has it makes me sick."

She started to leave but then stopped and asked me, "How's Latin?"

"Wonderful."

"Are you good at it?"

"Very."

She thought about it and muttered, "I failed on purpose. I don't want to go to any school anymore."

"What will you do?"

"Whatever I want."

She left us there in the middle of the courtyard.

For the rest of the summer she didn't appear. I became very friendly with Carmela Peluso, who, although she laughed too much and then complained too much, had absorbed Lila's influence so potently that she became at times a kind of surrogate. In speech Carmela imitated her tone of voice, used some of her recurring expressions, gesticulated in a similar way, and when she walked tried to move like her, even though physically she was more like me: pretty and plump, bursting with health. That sort of misappropriation partly repulsed and partly attracted me. I wavered between irritation at a remake that seemed a caricature and fascination because, even diluted, Lila's habits still enchanted me. It was with those that Carmela finally bound me to her. She told me how terrible the new school had been: everyone teased her and the teachers couldn't stand her. She told of going to the prison of Poggioreale with her mother and siblings to see her father, and how they all wept. She told me that her father was innocent, that it was a black creature who killed Don Achille, part male but mostly female, who lived with the rats and came out of the sewer grates, even in daytime, and did whatever terrible thing had to be done before escaping underground. She told me unexpectedly, with a fatuous little smile, that she was in love with Alfonso Carracci. Right afterward her smile turned to tears: it was a love that tortured her, and sapped her strength, the daughter of the murderer was in love with the son of the victim. It was enough for her to see him crossing the courtyard or passing by on the *stradone* to feel faint.

This was a confidence that made a great impression on me and consolidated our friendship. Carmela swore that she had never talked about it to anyone, not even Lila: if she had decided to open up to me it was because she couldn't bear to keep it inside anymore. I liked her dramatic tone. We examined all the possible consequences of that passion until school started again and I no longer had time to listen to her.

What a story! Not even Lila, perhaps, would have been able to make up such a tale.

3.

A period of unhappiness began. I got fat, and under the skin of my chest two hard shoots sprouted, hair flourished in my armpits and my pubis, I became sad and at the same time anxious. In school I worked harder than I ever had, yet the mathematics problems almost never gave the result expected by the textbook, the Latin sentences seemed to make no sense. As soon as I could I locked myself in the bathroom and looked at myself in the mirror, naked. I no longer knew who I was. I began to suspect that I would keep changing, until from me my mother would emerge, lame, with a crossed eye, and no one would love me anymore. I cried often, without warning. My chest, meanwhile, became large and soft. I felt at the mercy of obscure forces acting inside my body, I was always agitated.

One day as I came out of school, Gino, the pharmacist's son, followed me along the street and said that his classmates claimed that my breasts weren't real, I stuffed them with cotton batting. He laughed as he spoke. He said that he thought they were real, he had bet twenty lire on it. Finally he said that, if he won, he would keep ten lire for himself and would give me ten, but I had to prove that I didn't use padding.

That request frightened me. Since I didn't know how to act, I deliberately resorted to Lila's bold tone:

"Give me the ten lire."

"Why, am I right?"

"Yes."

He ran away, and I was disappointed. But soon he returned with a boy from his class, a skinny boy whose name I don't remember, with a dark down above his lip. Gino said to me, "He has to be there, otherwise the others won't believe I've won."

Again I resorted to Lila's tone.

"First the money."

"And if you have padding?"

"I don't."

He gave me ten lire and we all went, silently, to the top floor of a building near the public gardens. There, next to the iron door that led to the terrace, where I was clearly outlined by slender segments of light, I lifted up my shirt and showed them my breasts. The two stood staring as if they couldn't believe their eyes. Then they turned and ran down the stairs.

I heaved a sigh of relief and went to the Bar Solara to buy myself an ice cream.

That episode remained stamped in my memory: I felt for the first time the magnetic force that my body exercised over men, but above all I realized that Lila acted not only on Carmela but also on me like a demanding ghost. If I had had to make a decision in the pure disorder of emotions in a situation like that, what would I have done? I would have run away. And if I had been with Lila? I would have pulled her by the arm, I would have whispered, Let's go, and then, as usual, I would have stayed, because she, as usual, would have decided to stay. Instead, in her absence, after a slight hesitation I put myself in her place. Or, rather, I had made a place for her in me. If I thought again of the moment when Gino made his request, I felt precisely how I had driven myself away, how I had mimicked Lila's look and tone and behavior in situations of brazen conflict, and I was pleased. But sometimes I wondered, somewhat anxiously: Am I being like Carmela? I didn't think so, it seemed to me that I was different, but I couldn't explain in what sense and my pleasure was spoiled. When I passed Fernando's shop with my ice cream and saw Lila intently arranging shoes on a long table, I was tempted to stop and tell her everything, hear what she thought. But she didn't see me and I kept going.

4.

She was always busy. That year Rino compelled her to enroll in school again, but again she almost never went and again she failed. Her mother asked her to help in the house, her father asked her to be in the shop, and she, all of a sudden, instead of resisting, seemed in fact content to labor for both. The rare times we saw each other—on Sunday after Mass or walking between the public gardens and the *stradone*—she displayed no curiosity about my school, and immediately started talking intensely and with admiration about the work that her father and brother did.

She knew that her father as a boy had wanted to be free, had fled the shop of her grandfather, who was also a shoemaker, and had gone to work in a shoe factory in Casoria, where he had made shoes for everyone, even soldiers going to war. She had discovered that Fernando knew how to make a shoe from beginning to end by hand, but he was also completely at home with the machines and knew how to use them, the post machine, the trimmer, the sander. She talked to me about leather, uppers, leather-goods dealers, leather production, high heels and flat heels, about preparing the thread, about soles and how the sole was applied, colored, and buffed. She used all those words of the trade as if they were magic and her father had learned them in an enchanted world—Casoria, the factory—from which he had returned like a satisfied explorer, so satisfied that now he preferred the family shop, the quiet bench, the hammer, the iron foot, the good smell of glue mixed with that of old shoes. And she drew me inside that vocabulary with such an energetic enthusiasm that her father and Rino, thanks to their ability to enclose people's feet in solid, comfortable shoes, seemed to me the best people in the neighborhood. Above all, I came home with the impression that, not spending my days in a shoemaker's shop, having for a father a banal porter instead, I was excluded from a rare privilege.

I began to feel that my presence in class was pointless. For months and months it seemed to me that every promise had fled from the textbooks, all energy. Coming out of school, dazed by unhappiness, I passed Fernando's shop only to see Lila at her workplace, sitting at a little table in the back, her thin chest with no hint of a bosom, her scrawny neck, her small face. I don't know what she did, exactly, but she was there, active, beyond the glass door, set between the bent head of her father and the bent head of her brother, no books, no lessons, no homework. Sometimes I stopped to look at the boxes of polish in the window, the old shoes newly resoled, new ones put on a form that expanded the leather and widened them, making them more comfortable, as if I were a customer and had an interest in the merchandise. I went away only, and reluctantly, when she saw me and waved to me, and I answered her wave, and she returned to concentrate on her work. But often it was Rino who noticed me first and made funny faces to make me laugh. Embarrassed, I ran away without waiting for Lila to see me.

One Sunday I was surprised to find myself talking passionately about shoes with Carmela Peluso. She would buy the magazine *Sogno* and devour the photo novels. At first it seemed to me a waste of time, then I began to look, too, and we started to read them together, and comment on the stories and what the characters said, which was written in white letters on a black background. Carmela tended to pass without a break from comments on the fictional love stories to comments on the true story of her love for Alfonso. In order not to seem inferior, I once told her about the pharmacist's son, Gino, claiming that he loved me. She didn't believe it. The pharmacist's son was in her eyes a kind of unattainable prince, future heir of the pharmacy, a gentleman who would never marry the daughter of a porter, and I was on the point of telling her about the time he had asked to see my breasts and I had let him and earned ten lire. But we were holding *Sogno* spread out on our knees and my gaze fell on the beautiful high-heeled shoes of one of the actresses. This seemed to me a momentous subject, more than the story of my breasts, and I couldn't resist, I began to praise them and whoever had made such beautiful shoes, and to fantasize that if we wore shoes like that neither Gino nor Alfonso would be able to resist us. The more I talked, though, the more I realized, to my embarrassment, that I was trying to make Lila's new passion my own. Carmela listened to me distractedly, then said she had to go. In shoes and shoemakers she had little or no interest. Although she imitated Lila's habits, she, unlike me, held on to the only things that really absorbed her: the photo novels, love stories.

5.

This entire period had a similar character. I soon had to admit that what I did by myself couldn't excite me, only what Lila touched became important. If she withdrew, if her voice withdrew from things, the things got dirty, dusty. Middle school, Latin, the teachers, the books, the language of books seemed less evocative than the finish of a pair of shoes, and that depressed me.

But one Sunday everything changed again. We had gone, Carmela, Lila, and I, to catechism, we were preparing for our first communion. On the way out Lila said she had something to do and she left us. But I saw that she wasn't heading toward home: to my great surprise she went into the elementary school building.

I walked with Carmela, but when I got bored I said goodbye, walked around the building, and went back. The school was closed on Sunday, how could Lila go into the building? After much hesitation I ventured beyond the entranceway, into the hall. I had never gone into my old school and I felt a strong emotion, I recognized the smell, which brought with it a sensation of comfort, a sense of myself that I no longer had. I went into the only door open on the ground floor. There was a large neon-lit room, whose walls were lined with shelves of old books. I counted a dozen adults, a lot of children. They would take down volumes, page through them, put them back, and choose one. Then they got in line in front of a desk behind which sat an old enemy of Maestra Oliviero's, lean Maestro Ferraro, with his crew-cut gray hair. Ferraro examined the chosen text, marked something in the record book, and the person went out with one or more books.

I looked around: Lila wasn't there, maybe she had already left. What was she doing, she didn't go to school anymore, she loved shoes and old shoes, and yet, without saying anything to me, she came to this place to get books? Did she like this space? Why didn't she ask me to come with her? Why had she left me with Carmela? Why did she talk to me about how soles were ground and not about what she read?

I was angry, and ran away.

For a while school seemed to me more meaningless than ever. Then I was sucked back in by the press of homework and end-of-the-year tests, I was afraid of getting bad grades, I studied a lot but aimlessly. And other preoccupations weighed on me. My mother said that I was indecent with those big breasts I had developed, and she took me to buy a bra. She was more abrupt than usual. She seemed ashamed that I had a bosom, that I got my period. The crude instructions she gave me were rapid and insufficient, barely muttered. I didn't have time to ask her any questions before she turned her back and walked away with her lopsided gait.

The bra made my chest even more noticeable. In the last months of school I was besieged by boys and I quickly realized why. Gino and his friend had spread the rumor that I would show how I was made easily, and every so often someone would ask me to repeat the spectacle. I sneaked away, I compressed my bosom by holding my arms crossed over it, I felt mysteriously guilty and alone with my guilt. The boys persisted, even on the street, even in the courtyard. They laughed, they made fun of me. I tried to keep them off once or twice by acting like Lila, but it didn't work for me, and then I couldn't stand it and burst into tears. Out of fear that they would bother me I stayed in the house. I studied hard, I went out now only to go, very reluctantly, to school.

One morning in May Gino ran after me and asked me, not arrogantly but, rather, with some emotion, if I would be his girlfriend. I said no, out of resentment, revenge, embarrassment, yet proud that the son of the pharmacist wanted me. The next day he asked me again and he didn't stop asking until June, when, with some delay due to the complicated lives of our parents, we made our first communion, the girls in white dresses, like brides.

In those dresses, we lingered in the church square and immediately sinned by talking about love. Carmela couldn't believe that I had refused the son of the pharmacist, and she told Lila. She, surprisingly, instead of slipping away with the air of someone saying Who cares, was interested. We all talked about it.

"Why do you say no?" Lila asked me in dialect.

I answered unexpectedly in proper Italian, to make an impression, to let her understand that, even if I spent my time talking about boyfriends, I wasn't to be treated like Carmela.

"Because I'm not sure of my feelings."

It was a phrase I had learned from reading *Sogno* and Lila seemed struck by it. As if it were one of those contests in elementary school, we began to speak in the language of comics and books, which reduced Carmela to pure and simple listener. Those moments lighted my heart and my head: she and I and all those well-crafted words. In middle school nothing like that ever happened, not with classmates or with teachers; it was wonderful. Step by step Lila convinced me that one achieves security in love only by subjecting the wooer to hard tests. And so, returning suddenly to dialect, she advised me to become Gino's girlfriend but on the condition that all summer he agree to buy ice cream for me, her, and Carmela.

"If he doesn't agree it means it's not true love."

I did as she told me and Gino vanished. It wasn't true love, then, and so I didn't suffer from it. The exchange with Lila had given me a pleasure so intense that I planned to devote myself to her totally, especially in summer, when I would have more free time. Meanwhile I wanted that conversation to become the model for all our next encounters. I felt clever again, as if something had hit me in the head, bringing to the surface images and words.

But the sequel of that episode was not what I expected. Instead of consolidating and making exclusive the relationship between her and me, it attracted a lot of other girls. The conversation, the advice she had given me, its effect had so struck Carmela Peluso that she ended up telling everyone. The result was that the daughter of the shoemaker, who had no bosom and didn't get her period and didn't even have a boyfriend, became in a few days the most reliable dispenser of advice on affairs of the heart. And she, again surprising me, accepted that role. If she wasn't busy in the house or the shop, I saw her talking now with this girl, now with that. I passed by, I greeted her, but she was so absorbed that she didn't hear me. I always caught phrases that seemed to me beautiful, and they made me suffer.

6.

These were desolate days, at the height of which came a humiliation that I should have predicted and which instead I had pretended not to care about: Alfonso Carracci was promoted with an average of eight, Gigliola Spagnuolo was promoted with an average of seven, and I had all sixes and four in Latin. I would have to take the exam again in September in that one subject.

This time it was my father who said it was pointless for me to continue. The schoolbooks had already cost a lot. The Latin dictionary, the Campanini and Carboni, even though it was bought used, had been a big expense. There was no money to send me to private lessons during the summer. But above all it was now clear that I wasn't clever: the young son of Don Achille had passed and I hadn't, the daughter of Spagnuolo the pastry maker had passed and I hadn't: one had to be resigned.

I wept night and day, I made myself ugly on purpose to punish myself. I was the oldest, after me there were two boys and another girl, Elisa: Peppe and Gianni, the two boys, came in turn to console me, now bringing me some fruit, now asking me to play with them. But I felt alone just the same, with a cruel fate, and I couldn't calm down. Then one afternoon I heard my mother come up behind me. She said in dialect, in her usual harsh tone:

"We can't pay for the lessons, but you can try to study by yourself and see if you pass the exam." I looked at her uncertainly. She was the same: lusterless hair, wandering eye, large nose, heavy body. She added, "Nowhere is it written that you can't do it."

That was all she said, or at least it's what I remember. Starting the next day, I began to study, forcing myself never to go to the courtyard or the public gardens.

But one morning I heard someone calling me from the street. It was Lila, who since we finished elementary school had completely gotten out of the habit.

"Lenù," she called.

I looked out.

"I have to tell you something."

"What?"

"Come down."

I went down reluctantly, it irritated me to admit to her that I had to take the exam again. We wandered a bit in the court-yard, in the sun. I asked unwillingly what was new on the sub-ject of boyfriends. I remember that I asked her explicitly if there had been developments between Carmela and Alfonso.

"What sort of developments?"

"She loves him."

She narrowed her eyes. When she did that, turning serious, without a smile, as if leaving the pupils only a crack allowed her to see in a more concentrated way, she reminded me of birds of prey I had seen in films at the parish cinema. But that day it seemed to me she had perceived something that made her angry and at the same time frightened her.

"She didn't tell you anything about her father?" she asked.

"That he's innocent."

"And who is the murderer?"

"A creature half male and half female who hides in the sew-ers and comes out of the grates like the rats."

"So it's true," she said, as if suddenly in pain, and she added that Carmela believed everything she said, that all the girls did.

"I don't want to talk anymore, I don't want to talk to anyone," she muttered, scowling, and I felt that she wasn't speaking with contempt, that the influence she had on us didn't please her, so that for a moment I didn't understand: in her place I would have been extremely proud. In her, though, there was no pride but a kind of impatience mixed with the fear of responsibility.

"But it's good to talk to other people," I murmured.

"Yes, but only if when you talk there's someone who answers."

I felt a burst of joy in my heart. What request was there in that fine sentence? Was she saying that she wanted to talk only to me because I didn't accept everything that came out of her mouth but responded to it? Was she saying that only I knew how to follow the things that went through her mind?

Yes. And she was saying it in a tone that I didn't recognize, that was feeble, although brusque as usual. She had suggested to Carmela, she told me, that in a novel or a film the daughter of the murderer would fall in love with the son of the victim. It was a possibility: to become a true fact a true love would have to arise. But Carmela hadn't understood and right away, the next day, had gone around telling everyone that she was in love with Alfonso: a lie just to show off, whose consequences were unknown. We discussed it. We were twelve years old, but we walked along the hot streets of the neighborhood, amid the dust and flies that the occasional old trucks stirred up as they passed, like two old ladies taking the measure of lives of disappointment, clinging tightly to each other. No one understood us, only we two—I thought—understood one another. We together, we alone, knew how the pall that had weighed on the neighborhood forever, that is, ever since we could remember, might lift at least a little if Peluso, the former carpenter, had not plunged the knife into Don Achille's neck, if it was an inhabitant of the sewers who had done it, if the daughter of the murderer married the son of the victim. There was something unbearable in the things, in the people, in the buildings, in the streets that, only if you reinvented it all, as in a game, became acceptable. The essential, however, was to know how to play, and she and I, only she and I, knew how to do it.

She asked me at one point, without an obvious connection but as if all our conversation could arrive only at that question:

"Are we still friends?"

"Yes."

"Then will you do me a favor?"

I would have done anything for her, on that morning of reconciliation: run away from home, leave the neighborhood, sleep in farmhouses, feed on roots, descend into the sewers through the grates, never turn back, not even if it was cold, not even if it rained. But what she asked seemed to me nothing and at the moment disappointed me. She wanted simply to meet once a day, in the public gardens, even just for an hour, before dinner, and I was to bring the Latin books.

"I won't bother you," she said.

She knew already that I had to take the exam again and wanted to study with me.

7.

In those middle school years many things changed right before our eyes, but day by day, so that they didn't seem to be real changes.

The Bar Solara expanded, became a well-stocked pastry shop—whose skilled pastry maker was Gigliola Spagnuolo's father—which on Sunday was crowded with men, young and old, buying pastries for their families. The two sons of Silvio Solara, Marcello, who was around twenty, and Michele, just a little younger, bought a blue-and-white Fiat 1100 and on Sundays paraded around the streets of the neighborhood.

Peluso's former carpenter shop, which, once in the hands of Don Achille, had become a grocery, was filled with good things that spilled out onto the sidewalk, too. Passing by you caught a whiff of spices, of olives, of salami, of fresh bread, of pork fat and cracklings that made you hungry. The death of Don Achille had slowly detached his threatening shadow from that place and from the whole family. The widow, Donna Maria, had grown very friendly and now managed the store herself, along with Pinuccia, the fifteen-year-old daughter, and Stefano, who was no longer the wild boy who had tried to pierce Lila's tongue but a self-possessed young man, his gaze charming, his smile gentle. The clientele had increased greatly. My mother sent me there to do the shopping, and my father wasn't opposed, partly because when there was no money Stefano wrote everything in a ledger book and we paid at the end of the month.

Assunta, who sold fruit and vegetables on the streets with her husband, Nicola, had had to retire because of bad back pain, and a few months later pneumonia almost killed her husband. Yet those two misfortunes had turned out to be a blessing. Now, going around the streets of the neighborhood every morning with the horse-drawn cart, summer and winter, rain and shine, was the oldest son, Enzo, who had almost nothing about him of the child who threw rocks at us: he had become a stocky youth, with a strong, healthy look, disheveled blond hair, blue eyes, a thick voice with which he praised his wares. He had excellent products and by his gestures alone conveyed an honest, reassuring willingness to serve his customers. He handled the scale adroitly. I liked the speed with which he pushed the weight along the arm to find the right balance, the sound of iron scraping rapidly against iron, then wrapped the potatoes or the fruit and hurried to put the package in Signora Spagnuolo's basket, or Melina's, or my mother's.

Initiatives flourished in the whole neighborhood. A young

dressmaker became a partner in the dry goods store, where Carmela Peluso had just started working as a clerk, and the store expanded, aspiring to become a ladies' clothing shop. The auto-repair shop where Melina's son, Antonio, worked was trying, thanks to the son of the old owner, Gentile Gorresio, to get into motorcycles. In other words everything was quivering, arching upward as if to change its characteristics, not to be known by the accumulated hatreds, tensions, ugliness but, rather, to show a new face. While Lila and I studied Latin in the public gardens, even the pure and simple space around us, the fountain, the shrubbery, a pothole on one side of the street, changed. There was a constant smell of pitch, the steamroller sputtered, advancing slowly over the steamy asphalt, as bare-chested or T-shirted workers paved the streets and the *stradone*. Even the colors changed. Pasquale, Carmela's older brother, was hired to cut down the brush near the railroad tracks. How much he cut—we heard the sound of annihilation for days: the trees groaned, they gave off a scent of fresh green wood, they cleaved the air, they struck the ground after a long rustling that seemed a sigh, and he and others sawed them, split them, pulled up roots that exhaled an odor of underground. The green brush vanished and in its place appeared an area of flat yellow ground. Pasquale had found that job through a stroke of luck. Sometime earlier a friend had told him that people had come to the Bar Solara looking for young men to do night work cutting down trees in a piazza in the center of Naples. He—even though he didn't like Silvio Solara and his sons, he was in that bar because his father was ruined—had to support the family and had gone. He had returned, exhausted, at dawn, his nostrils filled with the odor of living wood, of mangled leaves, and of the sea. Then one thing led to another, and he had been summoned again for that kind of work. And now he was on the construction site near the railroad and we sometimes saw him climbing up the scaffolding of the new buildings that were rising floor by floor, or in a hat made of newspaper, in the sun, eating bread with sausage and greens during his lunch break.

Lila got mad if I looked at Pasquale and was distracted. It was soon obvious, to my great amazement, that she already knew a lot of Latin. She knew the declensions, for example, and also the verbs. Hesitantly I asked her how, and she, with that spiteful expression of a girl who has no time to waste, admitted that during my first year of middle school she had taken a grammar out of the circulating library, the one managed by Maestro Ferraro, and had studied it out of curiosity. The library was a great resource for her. As we talked, she showed me proudly all the cards she had, four: one her own, one in Rino's name, one for her father, and one for her mother. With each she borrowed a book, so she could get four at once. She devoured them, and the following Sunday she brought them back and took four more.

I never asked her what books she had read and what books she was reading, there wasn't time, we had to study. She drilled me, and was furious if I didn't have the answers. Once she slapped me on the arm, hard, with her long, thin hands, and didn't apologize; rather, she said that if I kept making mistakes she would hit me again, and harder. She was enchanted by the Latin dictionary, so large, pages and pages, so heavy—she had never seen one. She constantly looked up words, not only the ones in the exercises but any that occurred to her.

She assigned homework in the tone she had learned from our teacher Maestra Oliviero. She obliged me to translate thirty sentences a day, twenty from Latin to Italian and ten from Italian to Latin. She translated them, too, much more quickly than I did. At the end of the summer, when the exam was approaching, she said warily, having observed skeptically how I looked up words I didn't know in the dictionary, in the

same order in which I found them in the sentence to be translated, fixed on the principal definitions, and only then made an
effort to understand the meaning:

"Did the teacher tell you to do it like that?"

The teacher never said anything, she simply assigned the
exercises. I came up with that method.

She was silent for a moment, then she said to me:

"Read the whole sentence in Latin first, then see where the
verb is. According to the person of the verb you can tell what
the subject is. Once you have the subject you look for the complements: the object if the verb is transitive, or if not other
complements. Try it like that."

I tried. Suddenly translating seemed easy. In September I
went to the exam, I did the written part without a mistake and
answered all the questions in the oral part.

"Who gave you lessons?" the teacher asked, frowning.

"A friend."

"A university student?"

I didn't know what that meant. I said yes.

Lila was waiting for me outside, in the shade. When I came
out I hugged her, I told her that I had done really well and
asked if we would study together the following year. Since it
was she who had first proposed that we meet just to study,
inviting her to continue seemed to me a good way of expressing my joy and gratitude. She detached herself with a gesture
almost of annoyance. She said she just wanted to understand
what that Latin was that those clever ones studied.

"And then?"

"I've understood, that's enough."

"You don't like it?"

"Yes. I'll get some books from the library."

"In Latin?"

"Yes."

"But there's still a lot to study."

"You study for me, and if I have trouble you'll help me. Now I have something to do with my brother."

"What?"

"I'll show you later."

8.

School began again and right away I did well in all the subjects. I couldn't wait for Lila to ask me to help her in Latin or anything else, and so, I think, I studied not so much for school as for her. I became first in the class; even in elementary school I hadn't done so well.

That year it seemed to me that I expanded like pizza dough. I became fuller in the chest, the thighs, the rear. One Sunday when I was going to the gardens, where I was planning to meet Gigliola Spagnuolo, the Solara brothers approached me in the 1100. Marcello, the older, was at the wheel, Michele, the younger, was sitting next to him. They were both handsome, with glossy black hair, white teeth. But of the two I liked Marcello better; he resembled Hector as he was depicted in the school copy of the Iliad. They followed me the whole way, I on the sidewalk and they next to me, in the 1100.

"Have you ever been in a car?"

"No."

"Get in, we'll take you for a ride."

"My father won't let me."

"And we won't tell him. When do you get the chance to ride in a car like this?"

Never, I thought. But meanwhile I said no and kept saying no all the way to the gardens, where the car accelerated and disappeared in a flash beyond the buildings that were under construction. I said no because if my father found out that I had gone in that car, even though he was a good and loving man, even though he loved me very much, he would have beat me to death, while at the same time my little brothers, Peppe and Gianni, young as they were, would feel obliged, now and in the future, to try to kill the Solara brothers. There were no written rules, everyone knew that was how it was. The Solaras knew it, too, since they had been polite, and had merely invited me to get in.

They were not, some time later, with Ada, the oldest daughter of Melina Cappuccio, that is the crazy widow who had caused the scandal when the Sarratores moved. Ada was fourteen. On Sunday, in secret from her mother, she put on lipstick and, with her long, straight legs, and breasts even larger than mine, she looked grown-up and pretty. The Solara brothers made some vulgar remarks to her, Michele grabbed her by the arm, opened the car door, pulled her inside. They brought her back an hour later to the same place, and Ada was a little angry, but also laughing.

But among those who saw her dragged into the car were some who reported it to Antonio, her older brother, who worked as a mechanic in Gorresio's shop. Antonio was a hard worker, disciplined, very shy, obviously wounded by both the untimely death of his father and the unbalanced behavior of his mother. Without saying a single word to friends and relatives he waited in front of the Bar Solara for Marcello and Michele, and when the brothers showed up he confronted them, punching and kicking without even a word of preamble. For a few minutes he managed pretty well, but then the father Solara and one of the barmen came out. They beat Antonio bloody and none of the passersby, none of the customers, intervened to help him.

We girls were divided on this episode. Gigliola Spagnuolo and Carmela Peluso took the part of the Solaras, but only because they were handsome and had an 1100. I wavered. In the presence of my two friends I favored the Solaras and we competed for who loved them most, since in fact they were very handsome and it was impossible not to imagine the impression we would make sitting next to one of them in the car. But I also felt that they had behaved badly with Ada, and that Antonio, even though he wasn't very good-looking, even though he wasn't muscular like the brothers, who went to the gym every day to lift weights, had been courageous in confronting them. So in the presence of Lila, who expressed without half measures that same position, I, too, expressed some reservations.

Once the discussion became so heated that Lila, maybe because she wasn't developed as we were and didn't know the pleasure-fear of having the Solaras' gaze on her, became paler than usual and said that, if what happened to Ada had happened to her, to avoid trouble for her father and her brother Rino she would take care of the two of them herself.

"Because Marcello and Michele don't even look at you," said Gigliola Spagnuolo, and we thought that Lila would get angry.

Instead she said seriously, "It's better that way."

She was as slender as ever, but tense in every fiber. I looked at her hands and marveled: in a short time they had become like Rino's, like her father's, with the skin at the tips yellowish and thick. Even if no one forced her—that wasn't her job, in the shop—she had started to do small tasks, she prepared the thread, took out stitches, glued, even stitched, and now she handled Fernando's tools almost like her brother. That was why that year she never asked me anything about Latin. Eventually, she told me the plan she had in mind, a thing that had nothing to do with books: she was trying to persuade her father to make new shoes. But Fernando didn't want to hear about it. "Making shoes by hand," he told her, "is an art without a future: today there are cars and cars cost money and the money is either in the bank or with the loan sharks, not in the pockets of the Cerullo family." Then she insisted, she filled him with sincere praise: "No one knows how to make shoes the way you do, Papa." Even if that was true, he responded, everything was made in factories now, and since he had worked in the factories he knew very well what lousy stuff came out of them; but there was little to do about it, when people needed new shoes they no longer went to the neighborhood shoemaker, they went to the stores in the center of town, on the Rettifilo, so even if you wanted to make the handcrafted product properly, you wouldn't sell it, you'd be throwing away money and labor, you'd ruin yourself.

Lila wouldn't be convinced and as usual she had drawn Rino to her side. Her brother had first agreed with his father, irritated by the fact that she interfered in things to do with work, where it wasn't a matter of books and he was the expert. Then gradually he had been captivated and now he quarreled with Fernando nearly every day, repeating what she had put into his head.

"Let's at least try it."

"No."

"Have you seen the car the Solaras have, have you seen how well the Carraccis' grocery is doing?"

"I've seen that the dry goods store that wanted to be a dressmaker's gave it up and I've seen that Gorresio, because of his son's stupidity, has bitten off more than he can chew with his motorcycles."

"But the Solaras keep expanding."

"Mind your own business and forget the Solaras."

"Near the train tracks a new neighborhood is being developed."

"Who gives a damn."

"Papa, people are earning and they want to spend."

"People spend on food because you have to eat every day. As for shoes, first of all you don't eat them, and, second, when they break you fix them and they can last twenty years. Our work, right now, is to repair shoes and that's it."

I liked how that boy, who was always nice to me but capable of a brutality that frightened even his father a little, always, in every circumstance, supported his sister. I envied Lila that brother who was so solid, and sometimes I thought that the real difference between her and me was that I had only little brothers, and so no one with the power to encourage me and support me against my mother, freeing my mind, while Lila could count on Rino, who could defend her against anyone, whatever came into her mind. But really, I thought that Fernando was right, and was on his side. And discussing it with Lila, I discovered that she thought so, too.

Once she showed me the designs for shoes that she wanted to make with her brother, both men's and women's. They were beautiful designs, drawn on graph paper, rich in precisely colored details, as if she had had a chance to examine shoes like that close up in some world parallel to ours and then had fixed them on paper. In reality she had invented them in their entirety and in every part, as she had done in elementary school when she drew princesses, so that, although they were normal shoes, they didn't resemble any that were seen in the neighborhood, or even those of the actresses in the photo novels.

"Do you like them?"

"They're really elegant."

"Rino says they're difficult."

"But he knows how to make them?"

"He swears he can."

"And your father?"

"He certainly could do it."

"Then make them."

"Papa doesn't want to."

"Why?"

"He said that as long as I'm playing, fine, but he and Rino can't waste time with me."

"What does that mean?"

"It means that to actually do things takes time and money."

She was on the point of showing me the figures she had put down, in secret from Rino, to understand how much it really would cost to make them. Then she stopped, folded up the pages she was holding, and told me it was pointless to waste time: her father was right.

"But then?"

"We ought to try anyway."

"Fernando will get mad."

"If you don't try, nothing ever changes."

What had to change, in her view, was always the same thing: poor, we had to become rich; having nothing, we had to reach a point where we had everything. I tried to remind her of the old plan of writing novels like the author of *Little Women*. I was stuck there, it was important to me. I was learning Latin just for that, and deep inside I was convinced that she took so many books from Maestro Ferraro's circulating library only because, even though she wasn't going to school anymore, even though she was now obsessed with shoes, she still wanted to write a novel with me and make a lot of money. Instead, she shrugged in her careless way, she had changed her idea of *Little Women*. "Now," she explained, "to become truly rich you need a business." So she thought of starting with a single pair of shoes, just to demonstrate to her father how beautiful and comfortable they were; then, once Fernando was convinced, production would start: two pairs of shoes today, four tomorrow, thirty in a month, four hundred in a year, so that, within a short time, they, she, her father, Rino, her mother, her other siblings, would set up a shoe factory, with machines and at least fifty workers: the Cerullo shoe factory.

"A shoe factory?"

"Yes."

She spoke with great conviction, as she knew how to do, with sentences, in Italian, that depicted before my eyes the factory sign, Cerullo; the brand name stamped on the uppers, Cerullo; and then the Cerullo shoes, all splendid, all elegant, as in her drawings, shoes that once you put them on, she said, are so beautiful and so comfortable that at night you go to sleep without taking them off.

We laughed, we were having fun.

Then Lila paused. She seemed to realize that we were playing, as we had with our dolls years earlier, with Tina and Nu in front of the cellar grating, and she said, with an urgency for concreteness, which emphasized the impression she gave off, of being part child, part old woman, which was, it seemed to me, becoming her characteristic trait:

"You know why the Solara brothers think they're the masters of the neighborhood?"

"Because they're aggressive."

"No, because they have money."

"You think so?"

"Of course. Have you noticed that they've never bothered Pinuccia Carracci?"

"Yes."

"And you know why they acted the way they did with Ada?"

"No."

"Because Ada doesn't have a father, her brother Antonio counts for nothing, and she helps Melina clean the stairs of the buildings."

As a result, either we, too, had to make money, more than the Solaras, or, to protect ourselves against the brothers, we had to do them serious harm. She showed me a sharp shoemaker's knife that she had taken from her father's workshop.

"They won't touch me, because I'm ugly and I don't have

my period," she said, "but with you they might. If anything happens, tell me."

I looked at her in confusion. We were almost thirteen, we knew nothing about institutions, laws, justice. We repeated, and did so with conviction, what we had heard and seen around us since early childhood. Justice was not served by violence? Hadn't Signor Peluso killed Don Achille? I went home. I realized that with those last words she had admitted that I was important to her, and I was happy.

9.

I passed the exams at the end of middle school with eights, and a nine in Italian and nine in Latin. I was the best in the school: better than Alfonso, who had an average of eight, and much better than Gino. For days and days I enjoyed that absolute superiority. I was much praised by my father, who began to boast to everyone about his oldest daughter who had gotten nine in Italian and nine, no less, in Latin. My mother, to my surprise, while she was in the kitchen washing vegetables, said to me, without turning:

"You can wear my silver bracelet Sunday, but don't lose it."

I had less success in the courtyard. There only love and boyfriends counted. When I said to Carmela Peluso that I was the best in the school she immediately started talking to me about the way Alfonso looked at her when he went by. Gigliola Spagnuolo was bitter because she had to repeat the exams for Latin and mathematics and tried to regain prestige by saying that Gino was after her but she was keeping him at a distance because she was in love with Marcello Solara and maybe Marcello also loved her. Even Lila didn't show particular pleasure. When I listed my grades, subject by subject, she said laughing, in her malicious tone, "You didn't get ten?"

I was disappointed. You only got ten in behavior, the teachers never gave anyone a ten in important subjects. But that sentence was enough to make a latent thought become suddenly open: if she had come to school with me, in the same class, if they had let her, she would have had all tens, and this I had always known, and she also knew, and now she was making a point of it.

I went home with the pain of being first without really being first. Further, my parents began to talk about where they could find a place for me, now that I had a middle-school diploma. My mother wanted to ask the stationer to take me as an assistant: in her view, clever as I was, I was suited to selling pens, pencils, notebooks, and schoolbooks. My father imagined future dealings with his acquaintances at the city hall that would settle me in a prestigious post. I felt a sadness inside that, although it wasn't defined, grew and grew and grew, to the point where I didn't even feel like going out on Sunday.

I was no longer pleased with myself, everything seemed tarnished. I looked in the mirror and didn't see what I would have liked to see. My blond hair had turned brown. I had a broad, squashed nose. My whole body continued to expand but without increasing in height. And my skin, too, was spoiled: on my forehead, my chin, and around my jaws, archipelagos of reddish swellings multiplied, then turned purple, finally developed yellowish tips. I began, by my own choice, to help my mother clean the house, to cook, to keep up with the mess that my brothers made, to take care of Elisa, my little sister. In my spare time I didn't go out, I sat and read novels I got from the library: Grazia Deledda, Pirandello, Chekhov, Gogol, Tolstoy, Dostoyevsky. Sometimes I felt a strong need to go and see Lila at the shop and talk to her about the characters I liked best, sentences I had learned by heart, but then I let it go: she would say something mean; she would start talking about the plans she was making with Rino, shoes, shoe factory, money, and I would slowly feel that the novels I read were pointless and that my life was bleak, along with the future, and what I would become: a fat pimply salesclerk in the stationery store across from the parish church, an old maid employee of the local government, sooner or later cross-eyed and lame.

One Sunday, inspired by an invitation that had arrived in the mail in my name, in which Maestro Ferraro summoned me to the library that morning, I finally decided to react. I tried to make myself pretty, as it seemed to me I had been in childhood, as I wished to believe I still was. I spent some time squeezing the pimples, but my face was only more inflamed; I put on my mother's silver bracelet; I let down my hair. Still I was dissatisfied. Depressed I went out into the heat that lay on the neighborhood like a hand swollen with fever in that season, and made my way to the library.

I immediately realized, from the small crowd of parents and elementary- and middle-school children flowing toward the main entrance, that something wasn't normal. I went in. There were rows of chairs already occupied, colored festoons, the priest, Maestro Ferraro, even the principal of the elementary school and Maestra Oliviero. Ferraro, I discovered, had had the idea of awarding a book to the readers who, according to his records, had been most assiduous. Since the ceremony was about to begin and lending was suspended for the moment, I sat at the back of the room. I looked for Lila, but saw only Gigliola Spagnuolo with Gino and Alfonso. I moved restlessly in my chair, uneasy. After a while Carmela Peluso and her brother Pasquale sat down next to me. Hi, hi. I covered my blotchy cheeks better with my hair.

The small ceremony began. The winners were: first Raffaella Cerullo, second Fernando Cerullo, third Nunzia Cerullo, fourth Rino Cerullo, fifth Elena Greco, that is, me.

I wanted to laugh, and so did Pasquale. We looked at each

other, suffocating our laughter, while Carmela whispered insistently, "Why are you laughing?" We didn't answer: we looked at each other again and laughed with our hands over our mouths. Thus, still feeling that laughter in my eyes, and with an unexpected sense of well-being, after the teacher had asked repeatedly and in vain if anyone from the Cerullo family was in the room, he called me, fifth on the list, to receive my prize. Praising me generously, Ferraro gave me *Three Men in a Boat*, by Jerome K. Jerome. I thanked him and asked, in a whisper, "May I also take the prizes for the Cerullo family, so I can deliver them?"

The teacher gave me the prize books for all the Cerullos. As we went out, while Carmela resentfully joined Gigliola, who was happily chatting with Alfonso and Gino, Pasquale said to me, in dialect, things that made me laugh even more, about Rino losing his eyesight over his books, Fernando the shoemaker who didn't sleep at night because he was reading, Signora Nunzia who read standing up, next to the stove, while she was cooking pasta with potatoes, in one hand a novel and in the other the spoon. He had been in elementary school with Rino, in the same class, at the same desk—he said, tears of amusement in his eyes—and both of them, he and his friend, even though they took turns helping each other, after six or seven years of school, including repeats, managed to read at most: Tobacconist, Grocery, Post Office. Then he asked me what the prize for his former schoolmate was.

"*Bruges-la-Morte.*"

"Are there ghosts?"

"I don't know."

"May I come along when you give it to him? Rather, may I give it to him, with my own hands?"

We burst out laughing again.

"Yes."

"They've given Rinuccio a prize. Crazy. It's Lina who reads everything, good Lord, that girl is clever."

The attentions of Pasquale Peluso consoled me greatly, I liked that he made me laugh. Maybe I'm not so ugly, I thought, maybe I can't see myself.

At that moment I heard someone calling me. It was Maestra Oliviero.

I went over and she looked at me, as always evaluating, and said, as if confirming the legitimacy of a more generous judgment about my looks:

"How pretty you are, how big you've gotten."

"It's not true, Maestra."

"It's true, you're a star, healthy, nice, and plump. And also clever. I heard that you were the top student in the school."

"Yes."

"Now what will you do?"

"I'll go to work."

She darkened.

"Don't even mention it, you have to go on studying."

I looked at her in surprise. What was there left to study? I didn't know anything about the order of schools, I didn't have a clear idea what there was after the middle school diploma. Words like high school, university were for me without substance, like many of the words I came across in novels.

"I can't, my parents won't let me."

"What did the literature teacher give you in Latin?"

"Nine."

"Sure?"

"Yes."

"Then I'll talk to your parents."

I started to leave, a little scared, I have to admit. If Maestra Oliviero really went to my father and mother to tell them to let me continue in school, it would again unleash quarrels that I didn't want to face. I preferred things as they were: help my mother, work in the stationery store, accept the ugliness and the pimples, be healthy, nice, and plump, as Maestra Oliviero said, and toil in poverty. Hadn't Lila been doing it for at least three years already, apart from her crazy dreams as the sister and daughter of shoemakers?

"Thank you, Maestra," I said. "Goodbye."

But Oliviero held me by one arm.

"Don't waste time with him," she said, indicating Pasquale, who was waiting for me. "He's a construction worker, he'll never go farther than that. And then he comes from a bad family, his father is a Communist, and murdered Don Achille. I absolutely don't want to see you with him—he's surely a Communist like his father."

I nodded in assent and went off without saying goodbye to Pasquale, who seemed bewildered. Then, with pleasure, I heard him following me, a dozen steps behind. He wasn't good-looking, but I wasn't pretty anymore, either. He had curly black hair, he was dark-skinned, and sunburned, he had a wide mouth and was the son of a murderer, maybe even a Communist.

I turned the word over and over in my head, *Communist*, a word that was meaningless to me, but which the teacher had immediately branded with negativity. Communist, Communist, Communist. It captivated me. Communist and son of a murderer.

Meanwhile, around the corner, Pasquale caught up with me. We walked together until we were a few steps from my house and, laughing again, made a date for the next day, when we would go to the shoemaker's shop to give the books to Lila and Rino. Before we parted Pasquale also said that the following Sunday he, his sister, and anyone who wanted were going to Gigliola's house to learn to dance. He asked if I wanted to go, maybe with Lila. I was astonished, I already knew that my mother would never let me. But still I said, all right, I'll think about it. Then he held out his hand, and I, who was not used to such gestures, hesitated, just brushed his, which was hard and rough, and withdrew mine.

"Are you always going to be a construction worker?" I asked, even though I already knew that he was.

"Yes."

"And you're a Communist?"

He looked at me perplexed.

"Yes."

"And you go to see your father at Poggioreale?"

He turned serious: "When I can."

"Bye."

"Bye."

10.

Maestra Oliviero, that same afternoon, presented herself at my house without warning, throwing my father into utter despair and embittering my mother. She made them both swear that they would enroll me in the nearest classical high school. She offered to find me the books I would need herself. She reported to my father, but looking at me severely, that she had seen me alone with Pasquale Peluso, company that was completely unsuitable for me, who embodied such high hopes.

My parents didn't dare contradict her. They swore solemnly that they would send me to the first year of high school, and my father said, in a menacing tone, "Lenù, don't you dare ever speak to Pasquale Peluso again." Before she left, the teacher asked me about Lila, still in the presence of my parents. I answered that she was helping her father and her brother, she kept the accounts and the shop in order. She made a grimace of contempt, she asked me: "Does she know you got a nine in Latin?"

I nodded yes.

"Tell her that now you're going to study Greek, too. Tell her."

She took leave of my parents with an air of pride.

"This girl," she exclaimed, "will bring us great satisfaction."

That evening, while my mother, furious, was saying that now there was no choice but to send me to the school for rich people, otherwise Oliviero would wear her out by tormenting her and would even fail little Elisa in reprisal; while my father, as if this were the main problem, threatened to break both my legs if he heard that I had been alone with Pasquale Peluso, we heard a loud cry that silenced us. It was Ada, Melina's daughter, crying for help.

We ran to the window, there was a great commotion in the courtyard. It seemed that Melina, who after the Sarratores moved had generally behaved herself—a little melancholy, yes, a little absentminded, but in essence her eccentricities had become infrequent and harmless, like singing loudly while she washed the stairs of the buildings, or dumping buckets of dirty water into the street without paying attention to passersby—was having a new crisis of madness, a sort of crazy outburst of joy. She was laughing, jumping on the bed, and pulling up her skirt, displaying her fleshless thighs and her underpants to her frightened children. This my mother found out, by questioning from her window the other women looking out of their windows. I saw that Nunzia Cerullo and Lila were hurrying to see what was happening and I tried to slip out the door to join them, but my mother stopped me. She smoothed her hair and, with her limping gait, went herself to see what was going on.

When she returned she was indignant. Someone had delivered a book to Melina. A book, yes, a book. To her, who had at most two years of elementary school and had never read a book in her life. The book bore on the cover the name of Donato Sarratore. Inside, on the first page, it had an inscription in pen to Melina and also marked, with red ink, were the poems he had written for her.

My father, hearing that strange news, insulted the railway-worker poet obscenely. My mother said someone should undertake to bash the disgusting head of that disgusting man. All night we heard Melina singing with happiness, we heard the voices of her children, especially Antonio and Ada, trying to calm her but failing.

I, however, was overcome with amazement. On a single day I had attracted the attention of a young man like Pasquale, a new school had opened up before me, and I had discovered that a person who until some time earlier had lived in the neighborhood, in the building across from ours, had published a book. This last fact proved that Lila had been right to think that such a thing could even happen to us. Of course, she had given it up now, but perhaps I, by going to that difficult school called high school, fortified by the love of Pasquale, could write one myself, as Sarratore had done. Who knows, if everything worked out for the best I would become rich before Lila with her shoe designs and her shoe factory.

11.

The next day I went secretly to meet Pasquale Peluso. He arrived out of breath and sweaty in his work clothes, spotted all over with splotches of white plaster. On the way I told him the story of Donato and Melina. I told him that in these latest events was the proof that Melina wasn't mad, that Donato really had been in love with her and still loved her. But as I spoke, even as Pasquale agreed with me, revealing a sensitivity about things to do with love, I realized that, of these developments, what continued to excite me more than anything else was the fact that Donato Sarratore had published a book. That employee of the state railroad had become the author of a volume that Maestro Ferraro might very well put in the library and lend. Therefore, I said to Pasquale, we had all known not an ordinary man, put upon by the nagging of his wife, Lidia, but a poet. Therefore, right before our eyes a tragic love had been born, inspired by a person we knew very well, that is to say Melina. I was very excited, my heart was pounding. But I realized that here Pasquale couldn't follow me, he said yes only so as not to contradict me. And in fact after a while he became evasive, and began to ask me questions about Lila: how she had been at school, what I thought of her, if we were close friends. I answered willingly: it was the first time anyone had asked me about our friendship and I talked about it enthusiastically the whole way. Also for the first time, I felt how, having to search for words on a subject where I didn't have words ready, I tended to reduce the relationship between Lila and me to extreme declarations that were all exaggeratedly positive.

When we got to the shoemaker's shop we were still talking about it. Fernando had gone home for the afternoon rest, but Lila and Rino stood next to each other scowling, bent over something that they looked at with hostility, and as soon as they saw us outside the glass door they put it away. I handed Maestro Ferraro's gifts to Lila, while Pasquale teased Rino, opening the prize under his nose and saying, "After you've read the story of this Bruges-the-dead tell me if you liked it and maybe I'll read it, too." They laughed a lot, and every so often whispered to each other remarks about Bruges, which were surely obscene. But I noticed that Pasquale, although he was joking with Rino, looked furtively at Lila. Why was he looking at her like that, what was he looking for, what did he see there? They were long, intense looks that she didn't seem to be aware of, while—it seemed to me—Rino was even more aware of them than I was, and he soon drew Pasquale out into the street as if to keep us from hearing what was so funny about Bruges, but in reality irritated by the way his friend was looking at his sister.

I went with Lila to the back of the shop, trying to perceive in her what had attracted Pasquale's attention. She seemed to me the same slender girl, skin and bone, pale, except perhaps for the larger shape of her eyes and a slight curve in her chest. She arranged the books with other books she had, amid the old shoes and some notebooks with battered covers. I mentioned Melina's madness, but above all I tried to communicate my excitement at the fact that we could say we knew someone who had just published a book, Donato Sarratore. I murmured in Italian: "Think, his son Nino was in school with us; think, the whole Sarratore family might become rich." She gave a skeptical half smile.

"With this?" she said. She held out her hand and showed me Sarratore's book.

Antonio, Melina's oldest son, had given it to her to get it out of the sight and hands of his mother. I held it, I examined the slim volume. It was called *Attempts at Serenity*. The cover was red, with a drawing of the sun shining on a mountaintop. It was exciting to read, right above the title: "Donato Sarratore." I opened it, read aloud the dedication in pen: *To Melina who nurtured my poetry. Donato. Naples, 12 June 1958*. I was moved, I felt a shiver at the back of my neck, at the roots of my hair. I said, "Nino will have a better car than the Solaras."

But Lila had one of her intense looks and I saw that she was focused on the book I had in my hand. "If it happens we'll know about it," she muttered. "For now those poems have done only damage."

"Why?"

"Sarratore didn't have the courage to go in person to Melina and in his place he sent her the book."

"Isn't it a fine thing?"

"Who knows. Now Melina expects him, and if Sarratore doesn't come she'll suffer more than she's suffered till now."

What wonderful conversations. I looked at her white,

smooth skin, not a blemish. I looked at her lips, the delicate shape of her ears. Yes, I thought, maybe she's changing, and not only physically but in the way she expresses herself. It seemed to me—articulated in words of today—that not only did she know how to put things well but she was developing a gift that I was already familiar with: more effectively than she had as a child, she took the facts and in a natural way charged them with tension; she intensified reality as she reduced it to words, she injected it with energy. But I also realized, with pleasure, that, as soon as she began to do this, I felt able to do the same, and I tried and it came easily. This—I thought contentedly—distinguishes me from Carmela and all the others: I get excited with her, here, at the very moment when she's speaking to me. What beautiful strong hands she had, what graceful gestures came to her, what looks.

But while Lila talked about love, while I talked about it, the pleasure was spoiled by an ugly thought. I suddenly realized that I had been mistaken: Pasquale the construction worker, the Communist, the son of the murderer, had wanted to go there with me not for me but for her, to have the chance to see her.

12.

The thought took my breath away for a moment. When the two young men returned, interrupting our conversation, Pasquale confessed, laughing, that he had left the work site without saying anything to the boss, so he had to go back right away. I noticed that he looked at Lila again, for a long time, intensely, almost against his will, perhaps to signal to her: I'm running the risk of losing my job just for you. Addressing Rino, he said:

"Sunday we're all going dancing at Gigliola's, even Lenuccia's coming, will you two come?"

"Sunday is a long way off, we'll think about it later," Rino answered.

Pasquale gave a last look at Lila, who paid no attention to him, then he slipped away without asking if I wanted to go with him.

I felt an irritation that made me nervous. I began touching the most inflamed areas of my cheeks with my fingers, then I realized it and forced myself not to. While Rino took out from under the bench the things he had been working on before we arrived, and was studying them in bewilderment, I started talking again to Lila about books, about love affairs. We inflated excessively Sarratore, Melina's love madness, the role of the book. What would happen? What reactions would be unleashed not by the reading of the poems but by the object itself, the fact that its cover, the title, the name and surname had again stirred that woman's heart? We talked so fervently that Rino suddenly lost patience and shouted at us: "Will you stop it? Lila, let's get to work, otherwise Papa will return and we won't be able to do anything."

We stopped. I glanced at what they were doing: a wooden form besieged by a tangle of soles, strips of skin, pieces of thick leather, amid knives and awls and various other tools. Lila told me that she and Rino were trying to make a man's traveling shoe, and her brother, right afterward, made me swear on my sister Elisa that I would never say a word about it to anyone. They were working in secret from Fernando, Rino had got the skins and the leather from a friend who worked at a tannery at Ponte di Casanova. They would devote five minutes here, ten tomorrow, to making the shoe, because there was no way to persuade their father to help them; in fact when they had brought up the subject Fernando had sent Lila home, shouting that he didn't want to see her in the shop anymore, and meanwhile he had threatened to kill Rino, who at the age of nineteen was lacking in respect and had got it in his head to be better than his father.

I pretended to be interested in their secret undertaking, but in fact I was very sorry about it. Although the two siblings had involved me by choosing me as their confidant, it was still an experience that I could enter only as witness: on that path Lila would do great things by herself, I was excluded. But above all, how, after our intense conversations about love and poetry, could she walk me to the door, as she was doing, far more absorbed in the atmosphere of excitement around a shoe? We had talked with such pleasure about Sarratore and Melina. I couldn't believe that, though she pointed out to me that heap of leathers and skins and tools, she did not still feel, as I did, the anxiety about a woman who was suffering for love. What did I care about shoes. I still had, in my mind's eye, the most secret stages of that affair of violated trust, passion, poetry that became a book, and it was as if she and I had read a novel together, as if we had seen, there in the back of the shop and not in the parish hall on Sunday, a dramatic film. I felt grieved at the waste, because I was compelled to go away, because she preferred the adventure of the shoes to our conversation, because she knew how to be autonomous whereas I needed her, because she had her things that I couldn't be part of, because Pasquale, who was a grown-up, not a boy, certainly would seek other occasions to gaze at her and plead with her and try to persuade her to secretly be his girlfriend, and be kissed, touched, as it was said people did when they became boyfriend and girlfriend—because, in short, she would feel that I was less and less necessary.

Therefore, as if to chase away the feeling of revulsion these thoughts inspired, as if to emphasize my value and my indispensability, I told her in a rush that I was going to the high school. I told her at the doorway of the shop, when I was already in the street. I told her that Maestra Oliviero had insisted to my parents, promising to get me used books, for nothing, herself. I did it because I wanted her to realize that I was special, and that, even if she became rich making shoes with Rino, she couldn't do without me, as I couldn't do without her.

She looked at me perplexed.

"What is high school?" she asked.

"An important school that comes after middle school."

"And what are you going there to do?"

"Study."

"What?"

"Latin."

"That's all?"

"And Greek."

"Greek?"

"Yes."

She had the expression of someone at a loss, finding nothing to say. Finally she murmured, irrelevantly, "Last week I got my period."

And although Rino hadn't called her, she went back inside.

13.

So now she was bleeding, too. The secret movements of the body, which had reached me first, had arrived like the tremor of an earthquake in her as well and would change her, she was already changing. Pasquale—I thought—had realized it before me. He and probably other boys. The fact that I was going to high school quickly lost its aura. For days all I could think of was the unknowability of the changes that would hit Lila. Would she become pretty like Pinuccia Carracci or Gigliola or Carmela? Would she turn ugly like me? I went home and examined myself in the mirror. What was I like, really? What would she, sooner or later, be like?

I began to take more care with myself. One Sunday afternoon, on the occasion of the usual walk from the *stradone* to the gardens, I put on my best dress, which was blue, with a square neckline, and also my mother's silver bracelet. When I met Lila I felt a secret pleasure in seeing her as she was every day, in a worn, faded dress, her black hair untidy. There was nothing to differentiate her from the usual Lila, a restless, skinny girl. Only she seemed taller, she had grown, from a small girl, almost as tall as me, maybe half an inch less. But what was that change? I had a large bosom, a womanly figure.

We reached the gardens, we turned and went back, then walked along the street again to the gardens. It was early, there wasn't yet the Sunday commotion, the sellers of roasted hazelnuts and almonds and *lupini*. Lila was again asking me tentatively about the high school. I told her what I knew, exaggerating as much as possible. I wanted her to be curious, to want at least a little to share my adventure from the outside, to feel she was losing something of me as I always feared losing much of her. I was on the street side, she on the inside. I was talking, she was listening attentively.

The Solaras' 1100 pulled up beside us, Michele was driving, next to him was Marcello, who began to joke with us. With both of us, not just me. He would sing softly, in dialect, phrases like: what lovely young ladies, aren't you tired of going back and forth, look how big Naples is, the most beautiful city in the world, as beautiful as you, get in, half an hour and we'll bring you back here.

I shouldn't have but I did. Instead of going straight ahead as if neither he nor the car nor his brother existed; instead of continuing to talk to Lila and ignoring them, I turned and, out of a need to feel attractive and lucky and on the verge of going to the rich people's school, where I would likely find boys with cars much nicer than the Solaras', said, in Italian:

"Thank you, but we can't."

Marcello reached out a hand. I saw that it was broad and

short, although he was a tall, well-made young man. The five fingers passed through the window and grabbed me by the wrist, while his voice said: "Michè, slow down, you see that nice bracelet the porter's daughter is wearing?"

The car stopped. Marcello's fingers around my wrist made my skin turn cold, and I pulled my arm away in disgust. The bracelet broke, falling between the sidewalk and the car.

"Oh, my God, look what you've made me do," I exclaimed, thinking of my mother.

"Calm down," he said, and, opening the door, got out of the car. "I'll fix it for you."

He was smiling, friendly, he tried again to take my wrist as if to establish a familiarity that would soothe me. It was an instant. Lila, half the size of him, pushed him against the car and whipped the shoemaker's knife under his throat.

She said calmly, in dialect, "Touch her again and I'll show you what happens."

Marcello, incredulous, froze. Michele immediately got out of the car and said in a reassuring tone: "Don't worry, Marcè, this whore doesn't have the guts."

"Come here," Lila said, "come here, and you'll find out if I have the guts."

Michele came around the car, and I began to cry. From where I was I could see that the point of the knife had already cut Marcello's skin, a scratch from which came a tiny thread of blood. The scene is clear in my mind: it was still very hot, there were few passersby, Lila was on Marcello as if she had seen a nasty insect on his face and wanted to chase it away. In my mind there remains the absolute certainty I had then: she wouldn't have hesitated to cut his throat. Michele also realized it.

"O.K., good for you," he said, and with the same composure, as if he were amused, he got back in the car. "Get in, Marcè, apologize to the ladies, and let's go."

Lila slowly removed the point of the blade from Marcello's throat. He gave her a timid smile, his gaze was disoriented.

"Just a minute," he said.

He knelt on the sidewalk, in front of me, as if he wanted to apologize by subjecting himself to the highest form of humiliation. He felt around under the car, recovered the bracelet, examined it, and repaired it by squeezing with his nails the silver link that had come apart. He gave it to me, looking not at me but at Lila. It was to her that he said, "Sorry." Then he got in the car and they drove off.

"I was crying because of the bracelet, not because I was scared," I said.

14.

The boundaries of the neighborhood faded in the course of that summer. One morning my father took me with him. Since I was enrolling in high school, he wanted me to know what public transportation I would have to take and what route when I went in October to the new school.

It was a beautiful, very clear, windy day. I felt loved, coddled, to my affection for him was added a crescendo of admiration. He knew the enormous expanse of the city intimately, he knew where to get the metro or a tram or a bus. Outside he behaved with a sociability, a relaxed courtesy, that at home he almost never had. He was friendly toward everyone, on the metro and the buses, in the offices, and he always managed to let his interlocutor know that he worked for the city and that, if he liked, he could speed up practical matters, open doors.

We spent the entire day together, the only one in our lives, I don't remember any others. He dedicated himself to me, as if he wanted to communicate in a few hours everything useful he had learned in the course of his existence. He showed me

Piazza Garibaldi and the station that was being built: according to him it was so modern that the Japanese were coming from Japan to study it—in particular the columns—and build an identical one in their country. But he confessed that he liked the old station better, he was more attached to it. Ah well. Naples, he said, had always been like that: it's cut down, it's broken up, and then it's rebuilt, and the money flows and creates work.

He took me along Corso Garibaldi, to the building that would be my school. He dealt in the office with extreme good humor, he had the gift of congeniality, a gift that in the neighborhood and at home he kept hidden. He boasted of my extraordinary report card to a janitor whose wedding witness, he discovered on the spot, he knew well. I heard him repeating often: everything in order? Or: everything that can be done is being done. He showed me Piazza Carlo III, the Albergo dei Poveri, the botanical garden, Via Foria, the museum. He took me on Via Costantinopoli, to Port'Alba, to Piazza Dante, to Via Toledo. I was overwhelmed by the names, the noise of the traffic, the voices, the colors, the festive atmosphere, the effort of keeping everything in mind so that I could talk about it later with Lila, the ease with which he chatted with the pizza maker from whom he bought me a pizza melting with ricotta, the fruit seller from whom he bought me a yellow peach. Was it possible that only our neighborhood was filled with conflicts and violence, while the rest of the city was radiant, benevolent?

He took me to see the place where he worked, in Piazza Municipio. There, too, he said, everything had changed, the trees had been cut down, everything was broken up: now see all the space, the only old thing left is the Maschio Angioino, but it's beautiful, little one, there are two real males in Naples, your father and that fellow there. We went to the city hall, he greeted this person and that, everyone knew him. With some he was friendly, and introduced me, repeating yet again that in school I had gotten nine in Italian and nine in Latin; with others he was almost mute, only, indeed, yes, you command and I obey. Finally he said that he would show me Vesuvius from close up, and the sea.

It was an unforgettable moment. We went toward Via Caracciolo, as the wind grew stronger, the sun brighter. Vesuvius was a delicate pastel-colored shape, at whose base the whitish stones of the city were piled up, with the earth-colored slice of the Castel dell'Ovo, and the sea. But what a sea. It was very rough, and loud; the wind took your breath away, pasted your clothes to your body and blew the hair off your forehead. We stayed on the other side of the street in a small crowd, watching the spectacle. The waves rolled in like blue metal tubes carrying an egg white of foam on their peaks, then broke in a thousand glittering splinters and came up to the street with an oh of wonder and fear from those watching. What a pity that Lila wasn't there. I felt dazed by the powerful gusts, by the noise. I had the impression that, although I was absorbing much of that sight, many things, too many, were scattering around me without letting me grasp them.

My father held tight to my hand as if he were afraid that I would slip away. In fact I had the wish to leave him, run, move, cross the street, be struck by the brilliant scales of the sea. At that tremendous moment, full of light and sound, I pretended I was alone in the newness of the city, new myself with all life ahead, exposed to the mutable fury of things but surely triumphant: I, I and Lila, we two with that capacity that together—only together—we had to seize the mass of colors, sounds, things, and people, and express it and give it power.

I returned to the neighborhood as if I had gone to a distant land. Here again the known streets, here again the grocery of Stefano and his sister Pinuccia, Enzo who sold fruit, the Solaras' 1100 parked in front of the bar—now I would have paid any amount for it to be eliminated from the face of the earth. Luckily my mother had never found out about the episode of the bracelet. Luckily no one had reported to Rino what had happened.

I told Lila about the streets, their names, the noise, the extraordinary light. But immediately I felt uncomfortable. If she had been telling the story of that day, I would have joined in with an indispensable counter-melody and, even if I hadn't been present, I would have felt alive and active, I would have asked questions, raised issues, I would have tried to show her that we had to take that same journey together, necessarily, because I would be enriched by it, I would have been a much better companion than her father. She instead listened to me without curiosity, and at first I thought it was malicious, to diminish the force of my enthusiasm. But I had to persuade myself it wasn't so, she simply had her own train of thought that was fed on concrete things, a book, a fountain. With her ears certainly she listened to me, but with her eyes, with her mind, she was solidly anchored to the street, to the few plants in the gardens, to Gigliola, who was walking with Alfonso and Carmela, to Pasquale, who waved at her from the scaffolding of the building site, to Melina, who spoke out loud of Donato Sarratore while Ada tried to drag her into the house, to Stefano, the son of Don Achille, who had just bought a Giardinetta, and had his mother beside him and in the backseat his sister Pinuccia, to Marcello and Michele Solara, who passed in their 1100, with Michele pretending not to see us while Marcello gave us a friendly glance, and, above all, to the secret work, kept hidden from her father, that she applied herself to, advancing the project of the shoes. My story, for her, was at that moment only a collection of useless signals from useless spaces. She would be concerned with those spaces only if she had the opportunity to go there. And in fact, after all my talk, she said only:

"I have to tell Rino that Sunday we should accept Pasquale Peluso's invitation."

There I was, telling her about the center of Naples, and she placed at the center Gigliola's house, in one of the apartment buildings of the neighborhood, where Pasquale wanted to take her dancing. I was sorry. To Peluso's invitations we had always said yes and yet we had never gone, I to avoid arguments with my parents, she because Rino was against it. We often saw him, on holidays, all cleaned up, waiting for his friends, old and young. He was a generous soul, he didn't make distinctions of age, he brought along anyone. He would wait in front of the gas station and, one or two at a time, Enzo and Gigliola, and Carmela who now called herself Carmen, and sometimes Rino himself if he had nothing else to do, and Antonio, who had the weight of his mother, Melina, and, if Melina was calm, also his sister Ada, whom the Solaras had dragged into their car and driven who knows where for an hour. When the day was fine they went to the sea, returning red-faced from the sun. Or, more often, they all met at Gigliola's, whose parents were more tolerant than ours, and there those who knew how to dance danced and those who didn't learned.

Lila began to go to these little parties, and to take me; she had developed, I don't know how, an interest in dancing. Both Pasquale and Rino turned out to be surprisingly good dancers, and we learned from them the tango, the waltz, the polka, and the mazurka. Rino, it should be said, as a teacher got annoyed immediately, especially with his sister, while Pasquale was very patient. At first he would have us dance standing on his feet, so that we learned the steps, then, when we became more skilled, we went whirling through the house.

I discovered that I liked to dance, I would have danced forever. Lila instead wore the expression of someone who wants to understand how it's done, and whose pleasure seems to consist entirely in learning, since often she stayed seated, watching us, studying us, and applauding the couples who were most in synch. Once, at her house, she showed me a book that she had taken from the library: it was all about the dances, and every movement was explained with black-and-white drawings of a man and woman dancing. She was very cheerful in that period, with an exuberance surprising in her. Abruptly she grabbed me around the waist and, playing the man, made me dance the tango as she sang the music. Rino looked in and saw us, and burst into laughter. He wanted to dance, too, first with me, then with his sister, though without music. While we danced he told me that Lila had such a mania for perfection that she was obliged to practice continuously, even if they didn't have a gramophone. But as soon as he said the word—gramophone, gramophone, gramophone—Lila shouted at me from a corner of the room, narrowing her eyes.

"You know what kind of word it is?"

"No."

"Greek."

I looked at her uncertainly. Rino meanwhile let me go and went to dance with his sister, who gave a soft cry, handed me the dance manual, and flew around the room with him. I placed the manual among her books. What had she said? Gramophone was Italian, not Greek. But meanwhile I saw that under *War and Peace*, and bearing the label of Maestro Ferraro's library, a tattered volume was sticking out, entitled *Greek Grammar*. Grammar. Greek. I heard her promising me, out of breath:

"Afterward I'll write gramophone for you in Greek letters."

I said I had things to do and left.

15.

She had begun to study Greek even before I went to high school? She had done it on her own, while I hadn't even thought about it, and during the summer, the vacation? Would she always do the things I was supposed to do, before and better than me? She eluded me when I followed her and meanwhile stayed close on my heels in order to pass me by?

I tried not to see her for a while, I was angry. I went to the library to get a Greek grammar, but there was only one, and the whole Cerullo family had borrowed it in turn. Maybe I should erase Lila from myself like a drawing from the blackboard, I thought, for, I think, the first time. I felt fragile, exposed, I couldn't spend my time following her or discovering that she was following me, either way feeling diminished. I immediately went to find her. I let her teach me how to do the quadrille. I let her show me how many Italian words she could write in the Greek alphabet. She wanted me to learn the alphabet before I went to school, and she forced me to write and read it. I got even more pimples. I went to the dances at Gigliola's with a permanent sense of inadequacy and shame.

I hoped that it would pass, but inadequacy and shame intensified. Once Lila danced a waltz with her brother. They danced so well together that we left them the whole space. I was spellbound. They were beautiful, they were perfect together. As I watched, I understood conclusively that soon she would lose completely her air of a child-old woman, the way a well-known musical theme is lost when it's adapted too fancifully. She had become shapely. Her high forehead, her large eyes that could suddenly narrow, her small nose, her cheekbones, her lips, her ears were looking for a new orchestration and seemed close to finding it. When she combed her hair in a ponytail, her long neck was revealed with a touching clarity. Her chest had small graceful breasts that were more and more visible. Her back made a deep curve before landing at the increasingly taut arc of her behind. Her ankles were still too thin, the ankles of a child; but how long before they adapted to her now feminine figure? I realized that the males, watching as she danced with Rino, were seeing more than I was. Pasquale above all, but also Antonio, also Enzo. They kept their eyes on her as if we others had disappeared. And yet I had bigger breasts. And yet Gigliola was a dazzling blonde, with regular features and nice legs. And yet Carmela had beautiful eyes and, especially, provocative movements. But there was nothing to be done: something had begun to emanate from Lila's mobile body that the males sensed, an energy that dazed them, like the swelling sound of beauty arriving. The music had to stop before they returned to themselves, with uncertain smiles and extravagant applause.

16.

Lila was malicious: this, in some secret place in myself, I still thought. She had shown me not only that she knew how to wound with words but that she would kill without hesitation, and yet those capacities now seemed to me of little importance. I said to myself: she will release something more vicious, and I resorted to the word "evil", an exaggerated word that came to me from childhood tales. But if it was a childish self that unleashed these thoughts in me, they had a foundation of truth. And in fact, it slowly became clear not only to me, who had been observing her since elementary school, but to everyone, that an essence not only seductive but dangerous emanated from Lila.

Toward the end of the summer there was increasing pressure on Rino to take his sister on the group excursions outside the neighborhood for a pizza, for a walk. Rino, however, wanted his own space. He, too, seemed to me to be changing, Lila had kindled his imagination and his hopes. But, to see him, to hear him—the effect hadn't been the best. He had become more of a braggart, he never missed a chance to allude to how good he was at his work and how rich he was going to be, and he often repeated a remark he was fond of: It won't take much, just a little luck, and I'll piss in the Solaras' face. When he was boasting like this, however, it was crucial that his sister not be present. In her presence he was confused, he made a few allusions, then let it go. He realized that Lila was giving him a distrustful look, as if he were betraying a secret pact of behavior, of detachment, and so he preferred not to have her around; they were working together all day anyway in the shoemaker's shop. He escaped and swaggered like a peacock with his friends. But sometimes he had to give in.

One Sunday, after many discussions with our parents, we went out (Rino had generously come to my house and, before my parents, assumed responsibility for my person), in the evening no less. We saw the city lighted up by signs, the crowded streets, we smelled the stench of fish gone bad in the heat but also the fragrance of restaurants, of the fried food stalls, of bar-pastry shops much more lavish than the Solaras'. I don't remember if Lila had already had a chance to go to the center, with her brother or others. Certainly if she had she hadn't told me about it. I remember instead that that night she was absolutely mute. We crossed Piazza Garibaldi, but she stayed behind, lingering to watch a shoeshine, a large painted woman, the dark men, the boys. She stared at people attentively, she looked them right in the face, so that some laughed and others made a gesture meaning "What do you want?" Every so often I gave her a tug, dragging her with me out of fear that we would lose Rino, Pasquale, Antonio, Carmela, Ada.

That night we went to a pizzeria on the Rettifilo. We ate happily. To me it seemed that Antonio wooed me a little, making an effort to overcome his timidity, and I was pleased because at least Pasquale's attentions to Lila were counterbalanced. But at some point the pizza maker, a man in his thirties, began to spin the dough in the air, while he was working it, with extreme virtuosity, and he exchanged smiles with Lila, who looked at him in admiration.

"Stop it," Rino said to her.

"I'm not doing anything," she said and tried to look in another direction.

But things got worse. Pasquale, smiling, said that the man, the pizza maker—who to us girls seemed old, he was wearing a wedding ring, was surely the father of children—had secretly blown a kiss to Lila on the tips of his fingers. We turned suddenly to look at him: he was doing his job, that was all. But Pasquale, still smiling, asked Lila, "Is it true or am I wrong?"

Lila, with a nervous laugh in contrast to Pasquale's broad smile, said, "I didn't see anything."

"Forget it, Pascà," said Rino, giving his sister a cutting look.

But Peluso got up, went to the counter in front of the oven, walked around it, and, a candid smile on his lips, slapped the pizza maker in the face, so that he fell against the mouth of the oven.

The owner of the place, a small, pale man in his sixties, hurried over, and Pasquale explained to him calmly not to worry, he had just made clear to his employee a thing that wasn't clear to him, there would be no more problems. We ended up eating the pizza in silence, eyes lowered, in slow bites, as if it were poisoned. And when we left Rino gave Lila a good lecture that ended with a threat: Go on like that and I'm not taking you anywhere.

What had happened? On the street the men looked at all of us, pretty, less pretty, ugly, and not so much the youths as the grown men. It was like that in the neighborhood and outside of it, and Ada, Carmela, I myself—especially after the incident with the Solaras—had learned instinctively to lower our eyes, pretend not to hear the obscenities they directed at us, and keep going. Lila no. To go out with her on Sunday became a permanent point of tension. If someone looked at her she returned the look. If someone said something to her, she stopped, bewildered, as if she couldn't believe he was talking to her, and sometimes she responded, curious. Especially since—something very unusual—men almost never addressed to her the obscenities that they almost always had for us.

One afternoon at the end of August we went as far as the Villa Comunale park, and sat down in a café there, because Pasquale, acting the grandee, wanted to buy everyone a spumone. At a table across from us was a family eating ice cream, like us: father, mother, and three boys between twelve and seven. They seemed respectable people: the father, a large man, in his fifties, had a professorial look. And I can swear that Lila wasn't showing off in any way: she wasn't wearing lipstick, she had on the usual shabby dress that her mother had made— the rest of us were showing off more, Carmela especially. But that man—this time we all realized it—couldn't take his eyes off her, and Lila, although she tried to control herself, responded to his gaze as if she couldn't get over being so admired. Finally, while at our table the discomfort of Rino, of Pasquale, of Antonio increased, the man, evidently unaware of the risk he ran, rose, stood in front of Lila, and, addressing the boys politely, said:

"You are fortunate: you have here a girl who will become more beautiful than a Botticelli Venus. I beg your pardon, but I said it to my wife and sons, and I felt the need to tell you as well."

Lila burst out laughing because of the strain. The man smiled in turn, and, with a small bow, was about to return to his table when Rino grabbed him by the collar, forced him to retrace his steps quickly, sat him down hard, and, in front of his wife and children, unloaded a series of insults of the sort we said in the neighborhood. Then the man got angry, the wife, yelling, intervened, Antonio pulled Rino away. Another Sunday ruined.

But the worst was a time when Rino wasn't there. What struck me was not the fact in itself but the consolidation around Lila of hostilities from different places. Gigliola's mother gave a party for her name day (her name was Rosa, if I remember right), and invited people of all ages. Since her husband was the baker at the Solara pastry shop, things were done on a grand scale: there was an abundance of cream puffs, pastries with cassata filling, *sfogliatelle*, almond pastries, liqueurs, soft drinks, and dance records, from the most ordinary to the latest fashion. People came who would never come to our kids' parties. For example the pharmacist and his wife and their oldest son, Gino, who was going to high school, like me. For example Maestro Ferraro and his whole large family. For example Maria, the widow of Don Achille, and her son Alfonso and daughter Pinuccia, in a bright-colored dress, and even Stefano.

That family at first caused some unease: Pasquale and Carmela Peluso, the children of the murderer of Don Achille, were also at the party. But then everything arranged itself for the best. Alfonso was a nice boy (he, too, was going to high school, the same one as me), and he even exchanged a few words with Carmela; Pinuccia was just pleased to be at a party, working, as she did, in the store every day; Stefano, having precociously understood that good business is based on the absence of exclusiveness, considered all the residents of the neighborhood potential clients who would spend their money in his store; he produced his lovely, gentle smile for everyone, and so was able to avoid, even for an instant, meeting Pasquale's gaze; and, finally, Maria, who usually turned the other way if she saw Signora Peluso, completely ignored the two children and talked for a long time to Gigliola's mother. And then, as some people started dancing, and the din increased, there was a release of tension, and no one paid attention to anything.

First came the traditional dances, and then we moved on to a new kind of dance, rock and roll, which everyone, old and young, was curious about. I was hot and had retreated to a corner. I knew how to dance rock and roll, of course, I had often done it at home with my brother Peppe, and at Lila's, on Sundays, with her, but I felt too awkward for those jerky, agile moves, and, I decided, though reluctantly, just to watch. Nor did Lila seem particularly good at it: her movements looked silly, and I had even said that to her, and she had taken the criticism as a challenge and persisted in practicing on her own, since even Rino refused to try. But, perfectionist as she was in all things, that night she, too, decided, to my satisfaction, to stand aside with me and watch how well Pasquale and Carmela Peluso danced.

At some point, however, Enzo approached. The child who had thrown stones at us, who had surprisingly competed with Lila in arithmetic, who had once given her a wreath of sorb apples, over the years had been as if sucked up into a short but powerful organism, used to hard work. He looked older even than Rino, who among us was the oldest. You could see in every feature that he rose before dawn, that he had to deal with the Camorra at the fruit-and-vegetable market, that he went in all seasons, in cold, in the rain, to sell fruit and vegetables from his cart, up and down the streets of the neighborhood. Yet in his fair-skinned face, with its blond eyebrows and lashes, in the blue eyes, there was still something of the rebellious child we had known. Enzo spoke rarely but confidently, always in dialect, and it would not have occurred to either of us to joke with him, or even to make conversation. It was he who took the initiative. He asked Lila why she wasn't dancing. She answered: because I don't really know how to do this dance. He was silent for a while, then he said, I don't, either. But when another rock-and-roll song was put on he took her by the arm in a natural way and pushed her into the middle of the room. Lila, who if one simply grazed her without her permission leaped up as if she had been stung by a wasp, didn't react, so great, evidently, was her desire to dance. Rather, she looked at him gratefully and abandoned herself to the music.

It was immediately clear that Enzo didn't know much about it. He moved very little, in a serious, composed way, but he was very attentive to Lila, he obviously wished to do her a favor, let her show off. And although she wasn't as good as Carmen, she managed as usual to win everyone's attention. Even Enzo likes her, I said to myself in desolation. And—I realized right away—Stefano, the grocer: he gazed at her the whole time the way one gazes at a movie star.

But while Lila was dancing the Solara brothers arrived.

The mere sight of them agitated me. They greeted the pastry maker and his wife, they gave Stefano a pat of sympathy, and then they, too, started watching the dancers. First, like masters of the neighborhood, as they felt they were, they looked in a vulgar fashion at Ada, who avoided their gaze; then they spoke to each other and, indicating Antonio, gave him an exaggerated nod of greeting, which he pretended not to see; finally they noticed Lila, stared at her for a long time, then whispered to each other, Michele giving an obvious sign of assent.

I didn't let them out of my sight, and I quickly realized that in particular Marcello—Marcello, whom all the girls liked—didn't seem in the least angered by the knife business. On the contrary. In a few seconds he was completely captivated by Lila's lithe and elegant body, by her face, which was unusual in the neighborhood and perhaps in the whole city of Naples. He gazed without ever taking his eyes off her, as if he had lost the little brain he had. He gazed at her even when the music stopped.

It was an instant. Enzo made as if to push Lila into the corner where I was, Stefano and Marcello moved together to ask her to dance; but Pasquale preceded them. Lila made a gracious skip of consent, clapped her hands happily. At the same moment, four males, of various ages, each convinced in a different way of his own absolute power, reached out toward the figure of a fourteen-year-old girl. The needle scratched on the record, the music started. Stefano, Marcello, Enzo retreated uncertainly. Pasquale began to dance with Lila, and, given his virtuosity, she immediately let go.

At that point Michele Solara, perhaps out of love for his brother, perhaps out of a pure taste for making trouble, decided to complicate the situation in his own way. He nudged Stefano with his elbow and said aloud, "Are you some kind of a sissy? That's the son of the man who killed your father, he's a lousy Communist, and you stand there watching him dance with the girl you wanted to dance with?"

Pasquale certainly didn't hear him, because the music was loud and he was busy performing acrobatics with Lila. But I heard, and Enzo next to me heard, and naturally Stefano heard. We waited for something to happen but nothing happened. Stefano was someone who knew his own business. The grocery was thriving, he was planning to buy a neighboring space to expand it, he felt, in short, fortunate, and in fact he was very sure that life would give him everything he wanted. He said to Michele with his enchanting smile, "Let him dance, he's a good dancer." And he continued to watch Lila as if the only thing that mattered to him at that moment were her. Michele made a grimace of disgust and went to look for the pastry maker and his wife.

What did he want to do now? I saw him talking with the hosts in an agitated manner, he pointed to Maria in one corner, he pointed to Stefano and Alfonso and Pinuccia, he pointed to Pasquale, who was dancing, he pointed to Carmela, who was showing off with Antonio. As soon as the music stopped Gigliola's mother took Pasquale under the arm in a friendly way, led him into a corner, said something in his ear.

"Go ahead," Michele said to his brother, "the way's clear." And Marcello Solara tried again with Lila.

I was sure she would say no, I knew how she detested him. But that wasn't what happened. The music started, and she, with the desire to dance in every muscle, first looked for Pasquale, then, not seeing him, grasped Marcello's hand as if it were merely a hand, as if beyond it there were not an arm, his whole body, and, all sweaty, began again to do what at that moment counted most for her: dance.

I looked at Stefano, I looked at Enzo. Everything was charged with tension. My heart was pounding as Pasquale, scowling, went over to Carmela and spoke sharply to her. Carmela protested in a low voice, in a low voice he silenced her. Antonio approached them, spoke to Pasquale. Together they glared at Michele Solara, who was again talking to Stefano, at Marcello, who was dancing with Lila, pulling her, lifting her, lowering her down. Then Antonio went to drag Ada out of the dancing. The music stopped, Lila returned to my side. I said to her, "Something's happening, we have to go."

She laughed, exclaimed, "Even if there's an earthquake coming I'm going to have another dance," and she looked at Enzo, who was leaning against a wall. But meanwhile Marcello asked and she let him draw her again into a dance.

Pasquale came over and said somberly that we had to go.

"Let's wait till Lila finishes her dance."

"No, right now," he said in a tone that would not admit a response, hard, rude. Then he went straight toward Michele Solara and bumped him hard with one shoulder. Michele laughed, said something obscene out of the corner of his mouth. Pasquale continued toward the door, followed by Carmela, reluctantly, and by Antonio, who had Ada with him.

I turned to see what Enzo was doing, but he was still leaning against the wall, watching Lila dance. The music ended. Lila moved toward me, followed by Marcello, whose eyes were shining with happiness.

"We have to go," I nearly shrieked.

I must have put such anguish into my voice that she finally looked around as if she had woken up. "All right, let's go," she said, puzzled.

I headed toward the door, without waiting any longer, the music started again. Marcello Solara grabbed Lila by the arm, said to her between a laugh and an entreaty: "Stay, I'll take you home."

Lila, as if only then recognizing him, looked at him incredulously: suddenly it seemed to her impossible that he was touching her with such assurance. She tried to free her arm but Marcello held it in a strong grip, saying, "Just one more dance."

Enzo left the wall, grabbed Marcello's wrist without saying a word. I see him before my eyes: he was calm; although younger in years and smaller in size, he seemed to be making no effort. The strength of his grip could be seen only on the face of Marcello Solara, who let go of Lila with a grimace of pain and seized his wrist with his other hand. As we left I heard Lila saying indignantly to Enzo, in the thickest dialect, "He touched me, did you see: me, that shit. Luckily Rino wasn't there. If he does it again, he's dead."

Was it possible she didn't realize that she had danced with Marcello twice? Yes, possible, she was like that.

Outside we found Pasquale, Antonio, Carmela, and Ada. Pasquale was beside himself, we had never seen him like that. He was shouting insults, shouting at the top of his lungs, his eyes like a madman's, and there was no way to calm him. He was angry with Michele, of course, but above all with Marcello and Stefano. He said things that we weren't capable of understanding. He said that the Bar Solara had always been a place for loan sharks from the Camorra, that it was the base for smuggling and for collecting votes for the monarchists. He said that Don Achille had been a spy for the Nazi Fascists, he said that the money Stefano was using to expand the grocery store his father had made on the black market. He yelled, "Papa was right to kill him." He yelled, "The Solaras, father and sons—I'll cut their throats, and then I'll eliminate Stefano and his whole family from the face of the earth." Finally, turning to Lila, he yelled, as if it were the most serious thing, "And you, you were even dancing with that piece of shit."

At that point, as if Pasquale's rage had pumped breath into his chest, Antonio, too, began shouting, and it was almost as if he were angry at Pasquale because he wished to deprive him of a joy: the joy of killing the Solaras for what they had done to Ada. And Ada immediately began to cry and Carmela couldn't restrain herself and she, too, burst into tears. And Enzo tried to persuade all of us to get off the street. "Let's go home," he said. But Pasquale and Antonio silenced him, they wanted to stay and confront the Solaras. Fiercely, but with pretended calm, they kept repeating to Enzo, "Go, go, we'll see you tomorrow." Enzo said softly, "If you stay, I'm going to stay, too." At that point I, too, burst into tears and a moment afterward—the thing that moved me most—Lila, whom I had never seen cry, ever, began weeping.

We were four girls in tears, desperate tears. But Pasquale yielded only when he saw Lila crying. He said in a tone of resignation, "All right, not tonight, I'll settle things with the Solaras some other time, let's go." Immediately, between sobs, Lila and I took him under the arm, dragged him away. For a moment we consoled him by saying mean things about the Solaras, but also insisting that the best thing was to act as if they didn't exist. Then Lila, drying her tears with the back of her hand, asked "Who are the Nazi Fascists, Pascà? Who are the monarchists? What's the black market?"

17.

It's hard to say what Pasquale's answers did to Lila. I'm in danger of getting it wrong, partly because on me, at the time, they had no concrete effect. But she, in her usual way, was moved and altered by them, so that for the entire summer she tormented me with a single concept that I found quite unbearable. I'll try to summarize it, using the language of today, like this: there are no gestures, words, or sighs that do not contain the sum of all the crimes that human beings have committed and commit.

Naturally she said it in another way. But what matters is that she was gripped by a frenzy of absolute disclosure. She pointed to people, things, streets, and said, "That man fought in the war and killed, that one bludgeoned and administered castor oil, that one turned in a lot of people, that one starved his own mother, in that house they tortured and killed, on these stones they marched and gave the Fascist salute, on this corner they inflicted beatings, these people's money comes from the hunger of others, this car was bought by selling bread adulterated with marble dust and rotten meat on the black market, that butcher shop had its origins in stolen copper and vandalized freight trains, behind that bar is the Camorra, smuggling, loan-sharking."

Soon she became dissatisfied with Pasquale. It was as if he had set in motion a mechanism in her head and now her job was to put order into a chaotic mass of impressions. Increasingly intent, increasingly obsessed, probably overcome herself by an urgent need to find a solid vision, without cracks, she complicated his meager information with some book she got from the library. So she gave concrete motives, ordinary faces to the air of abstract apprehension that as children we had breathed in the neighborhood. Fascism, Nazism, the war, the Allies, the monarchy, the republic—she turned them into streets, houses, faces, Don Achille and the black market, Alfredo Peluso the Communist, the Camorrist grandfather of the Solaras, the father, Silvio, a worse Fascist than Marcello and Michele, and her father, Fernando the shoemaker, and my father, all—all—in her eyes stained to the marrow by shadowy crimes, all hardened criminals or acquiescent accomplices, all bought for practically nothing. She and Pasquale enclosed me in a terrible world that left no escape.

Then Pasquale himself began to be silent, defeated by Lila's capacity to link one thing to another in a chain that tightened around you on all sides. I often looked at them walking together and, if at first it had been she who hung on his words, now it was he who hung on hers. He's in love, I thought. I also thought: Lila will fall in love, too, they'll be engaged, they'll marry, they'll always be talking about these political things, they'll have children who will talk about the same things. When school started again, on the one hand I suffered because I knew I wouldn't have time for Lila anymore, on the other I hoped to detach myself from that sum of the misdeeds and compliances and cowardly acts of the people we knew, whom we loved, whom we carried—she, Pasquale, Rino, I, all of us—in our blood.

18.

The first two years of high school were much more difficult than middle school. I was in a class of forty-two students, one of the very rare mixed classes in that school. There were few girls, and I didn't know any of them. Gigliola, after much boasting ("Yes, I'm going to high school, too, definitely, we'll sit at the same desk"), ended up going to help her father in the Solaras' pastry shop. Of the boys, instead, I knew Alfonso and Gino, who, however, sat together in one of the front desks, elbow to elbow, with frightened looks, and nearly pretended not to know me. The room stank, an acid odor of sweat, dirty feet, fear.

For the first months I lived my new scholastic life in silence, constantly picking at my acne-studded forehead and cheeks. Sitting in one of the rows at the back, from which I could barely see the teachers or what they wrote on the blackboard, I was unknown to my deskmate as she was unknown to me. Thanks to Maestra Oliviero I soon had the books I needed; they were grimy and well worn. I imposed on myself a discipline learned in middle school: I studied all afternoon until eleven and then from five in the morning until seven, when it was time to go. Leaving the house, weighed down with books, I often met Lila, who was hurrying to the shoe shop to open up, sweep, wash, get things in order before her father and brother arrived. She questioned me about the subjects I had for the day, what I had studied, and wanted precise answers. If I didn't give them she besieged me with questions that made me fear I hadn't studied enough, that I wouldn't be able to answer the teachers as I wasn't able to answer her. On some cold mornings, when I rose at dawn and in the kitchen went over the lessons, I had the impression that, as usual, I was sacrificing the warm deep sleep of the morning to make a good impression on the daughter of the shoemaker rather than on the teachers in the school for rich people. Breakfast was hurried, too, for her sake. I gulped down milk and coffee and ran out to the street so as not to miss even a step of the way we would go together.

I waited at the entrance. I saw her arriving from her building and noticed that she was continuing to change. She was now taller than I was. She walked not like the bony child she had been until a few months before but as if, as her body rounded, her pace had also become softer. Hi, hi, we immediately started talking. When we stopped at the intersection and said goodbye, she going to the shop, I to the metro station, I kept turning to give her a last glance. Once or twice I saw Pasquale arrive out of breath and walk beside her, keeping her company.

The metro was crowded with boys and girls stained with sleep, with the smoke of the first cigarettes. I didn't smoke, I didn't talk to anyone. During the few minutes of the journey I went over my lessons again, in panic, frantically pasting strange languages into my head, tones different from those used in the neighborhood. I was terrified of failing in school, of the crooked shadow of my displeased mother, of the glares of Maestra Oliviero. And yet I had now a single true thought: to find a boyfriend, immediately, before Lila announced to me that she was going with Pasquale.

Every day I felt more strongly the anguish of not being in time. I was afraid, coming home from school, of meeting her and learning from her melodious voice that now she was making love with Peluso. Or if it wasn't him, it was Enzo. Or if it wasn't Enzo, it was Antonio. Or, what do I know, Stefano Carracci, the grocer, or even Marcello Solara: Lila was unpredictable. The males who buzzed around her were almost men, full of demands. As a result, between the plan for the shoes, reading about the terrible world we had been born into, and boyfriends, she would no longer have time for me. Sometimes, on the way home from school, I made a wide circle in order not to pass the shoemaker's shop. If instead I saw her in person, from a distance, in distress I would change my route. But then I couldn't resist and went to meet her as if it were fated.

Entering and leaving the school, an enormous gloomy, rundown gray building, I looked at the boys. I looked at them insistently, so that they would feel my gaze on them and look at me. I looked at my classmates, some still in short pants, others in knickers or long pants. I looked at the older boys, in the upper classes, who mostly wore jacket and tie, though never an overcoat, they had to prove, especially to themselves, that they didn't suffer from the cold: hair in crew cuts, their necks white because of the high tapering. I preferred them, but I would have been content even with one from the class above mine, the main thing was that he should wear long pants.

One day I was struck by a student with a shambling gait, who was very thin, with disheveled brown hair and a face that seemed to me handsome and somehow familiar. How old could he be: sixteen? Seventeen? I observed him carefully, looked again, and my heart stopped: it was Nino Sarratore, the son of Donato Sarratore, the railroad worker poet. He returned my look, but distractedly, he didn't recognize me. His jacket was shapeless at the elbows, tight at the shoulders, his pants were threadbare, his shoes lumpy. He showed no sign of prosperity, such as Stefano and, especially, the Solaras displayed. Evidently his father, although he had written a book of poems, was not yet wealthy.

I was disturbed by that unexpected apparition. As I left I had a violent impulse to tell Lila right away, but then I changed my mind. If I told her, surely she would ask to go to school with me to see him. And I knew already what would happen. As Nino hadn't noticed me, as he hadn't recognized the slender blond child of elementary school in the fat and pimply fourteen-year-old I had become, so he would immediately recognize Lila and be vanquished. I decided to cultivate the image of Nino Sarratore in silence, as he left school with his head bent and his rocking gait and went off along Corso Garibaldi. Now I went to school as if to see him, even just a glimpse, were the only real reason to go.

The autumn flew by. One morning I was questioned on the Aeneid: it was the first time I had been called to the front of the room. The teacher, an indolent man in his sixties named Gerace, who was always yawning noisily, burst out laughing when I said "or-A-cle" instead of "OR-a-cle." It didn't occur to him that, although I knew the meaning of the word, I lived in a world where no one had ever had any reason to use it. The others laughed, too, especially Gino, sitting at the front desk with Alfonso. I felt humiliated. Days passed, and we had our first homework in Latin. When Gerace brought back the corrected homework he said, "Who is Greco?"

I raised my hand.

"Come here."

He asked me a series of questions on declensions, verbs, syntax. I answered fearfully, especially because he looked at me with an interest that until that moment he hadn't shown in any of us. Then he gave me the paper without any comment. I had got a nine.

It was the start of a crescendo. He gave me eight in the Italian homework, in history I didn't miss a date, in geography I knew perfectly land areas, populations, mineral wealth, agriculture. But in Greek in particular I amazed him. Thanks to what I had learned with Lila, I displayed a knowledge of the alphabet, a skill in reading, a confidence in pronouncing the sounds that finally wrung public praise from the teacher. My cleverness reached the other teachers like a dogma. Even the religion teacher took me aside one morning and asked if I wanted to enroll in a free correspondence course in theology. I said yes. By Christmas people were calling me Greco, some Elena. Gino began to linger on the way out, to wait for me so we could go back to the neighborhood together. One day suddenly he asked me again if I would be his girlfriend, and I, although he was an idiot, drew a sigh of relief: better than nothing. I agreed.

All that exhilarating intensity had a break during the Christmas vacation. I was reabsorbed by the neighborhood, I had more time, I saw Lila more often. She had discovered that I was learning English and naturally she had got a grammar book. Now she knew a lot of words, which she pronounced very approximately, and of course my pronunciation was just as bad. But she pestered me, she said: when you go back to school ask the teacher how to pronounce this, how to pronounce that.

One day she brought me into the shop, showed me a metal box full of pieces of paper: on one side of each she had written an Italian word, on the other the English equivalent: *matita*/pencil, *capire*/to understand, *scarpa*/shoe. It was Maestro Ferraro who had advised her to do this, as an useful way of learning vocabulary. She read me the Italian, she wanted me to say the corresponding word in English. But I knew little or nothing. She seemed ahead of me in everything, as if she were going to a secret school. I noticed also a tension in her, the desire to prove that she was equal to whatever I was studying. I would have preferred to talk about other things, instead she questioned me about the Greek declensions, and deduced that I had stopped at the first while she had already studied the third. She also asked me about the Aeneid, she was crazy about it. She had read it all in a few days, while I, in school, was in the middle of the second book. She talked in great detail about Dido, a figure I knew nothing about, I heard that name for the first time not at school but from her. And one afternoon she made an observation that impressed me deeply. She said, "When there is no love, not only the life of the people becomes sterile but the life of cities." I don't remember exactly how she expressed it, but that was the idea, and I associated it with our dirty streets, the dusty gardens, the country-side disfigured by new buildings, the violence in every house, every family. I was afraid that she would start talking again about Fascism, Nazism, Communism. And I couldn't help it, I wanted her to understand that good things were happening to me, first that I was the girlfriend of Gino, and second that Nino Sarratore came to my school, more handsome than he had been in elementary school.

She narrowed her eyes, I was afraid she was about to tell me: I also have a boyfriend. Instead, she began to tease me. "You go out with the son of the pharmacist," she said. "Good for you, you've given in, you're in love like Aeneas' lover."

Then she jumped abruptly from Dido to Melina and talked about her for a long time, since I knew little or nothing of what was happening in the buildings—I went to school in the morning and studied until late at night. She talked about her relative as if she never let her out of her sight. Poverty was consuming her and her children and so she continued to wash the stairs of the buildings, together with Ada (the money Antonio brought home wasn't enough). But one never heard her singing anymore, the euphoria had passed, now she slaved away mechanically. Lila described Melina in minute detail: bent double, she started from the top floor and, with the wet rag in her hands, wiped step after step, flight after flight, with an energy and an agitation that would have exhausted a more robust person. If someone went down or up, she began shouting insults, she hurled the rag at him. Ada had said that once she had seen her mother, in the midst of a crisis because someone had spoiled her work by walking on it, drink the dirty water from the bucket, and had had to tear it away from her. Did I understand? Step by step, starting with Gino she had ended in Dido, in Aeneas who abandoned her, in the mad widow. And only at that point did she bring in Nino Sarratore, proof that she had listened to me carefully. "Tell him about Melina," she urged me, "tell him he should tell his father." Then she added, maliciously, "Because it's all too easy to write poems." And finally she started laughing and promised with a certain solemnity, "I'm never going to fall in love with anyone and I will never ever ever write a poem."

"I don't believe it."

"It's true."

"But people will fall in love with you."

"Worse for them."

"They'll suffer like that Dido."

"No, they'll go and find someone else, just like Aeneas, who eventually settled down with the daughter of a king."

I wasn't convinced. I went away and came back, I liked those conversations about boyfriends, now that I had one. Once I asked her, cautiously, "What's Marcello Solara up to, is he still after you?"

"Yes."

"And you?"

She made a half smile of contempt that meant: Marcello Solara makes me sick.

"And Enzo?"

"We're friends."

"And Stefano?"

"According to you they're all thinking about me?"

"Yes."

"Stefano serves me first if there's a crowd."

"You see?"

"There's nothing to see."

"And Pasquale, has he said anything to you?"

"Are you mad?"

"I've seen him walking you to the shop in the morning."

"Because he's explaining the things that happened before us."

Thus she returned to the theme of "before," but in a different way than she had at first. She said that we didn't know anything, either as children or now, that we were therefore not in a position to understand anything, that everything in the neighborhood, every stone or piece of wood, everything, anything you could name, was already there before us, but we had grown up without realizing it, without ever even thinking about it. Not just us. Her father pretended that there had been nothing before. Her mother did the same, my mother, my father, even Rino. And yet Stefano's grocery store *before* had been the carpenter shop of Alfredo Peluso, Pasquale's father. And yet Don Achille's money had been made *before*. And the Solaras' money as well. She had tested this out on her father and mother. They didn't know anything, they wouldn't talk about anything. Not Fascism, not the king. No injustice, no oppression, no exploitation. They hated Don Achille and were afraid of the Solaras. But they overlooked it and went to spend their money both at Don Achille's son's and at the Solaras', and sent us, too. And they voted for the Fascists, for the monarchists, as the Solaras wanted them to. And they thought that what had happened before was past and, in order to live quietly, they placed a stone on top of it, and so, without knowing it, they continued it, they were immersed in the things of before, and we kept them inside us, too. That conversation about "before" made a stronger impression than the vague conversations she had drawn me into during the summer. The Christmas vacation passed in deep conversation—in the shoemaker's shop, on the street, in the courtyard. We told each other everything, even the little things, and were happy.

19.

During that period I felt strong. At school I acquitted myself perfectly, I told Maestra Oliviero about my successes and she praised me. I saw Gino, and every day we walked to the Bar Solara: he bought a pastry, we shared it, we went home. Sometimes I even had the impression that it was Lila who depended on me and not I on her. I had crossed the boundaries of the neighborhood, I went to the high school, I was with boys and girls who were studying Latin and Greek, and not, like her, with construction workers, mechanics, cobblers, fruit and vegetable sellers, grocers, shoemakers. When she talked to me about Dido or her method for learning English words or the third declension or what she pondered when she talked to Pasquale, I saw with increasing clarity that it made her somewhat uneasy, as if it were ultimately she who felt the need to continuously prove that she could talk to me as an equal. Even when, one afternoon, with some uncertainty, she decided to show me how far she and Rino were with the secret shoe they were making, I no longer felt that she inhabited a marvelous land without me. It seemed instead that both she and her brother hesitated to talk to me about things of such small value.

Or maybe it was only that I was beginning to feel superior. When they dug around in a storeroom and took out the box, I encouraged them artificially. But the pair of men's shoes they showed me seemed truly unusual; they were size 43, the size of Rino and Fernando, brown, and just as I remembered them in one of Lila's drawings: they seemed both light and strong. I had never seen anything like them on the feet of anyone. While Lila and Rino let me touch them and demonstrated their qualities, I praised them enthusiastically. "Touch here," Rino said, excited by my praise, "and tell me if you feel the stitches." "No," I said, "you can't feel them." Then he took the shoes out of my hands, bent them, widened them, showed me their durability. I approved, I said bravo the way Maestra Oliviero did when she wanted to encourage us. But Lila didn't seem satisfied. The more good qualities her brother listed, the more defects she showed me and said to Rino, "How long would it take Papa to see these mistakes?" At one point she said, seriously, "Let's test with water again." Her brother seemed opposed. She filled a basin anyway, put her hand in one of the shoes as if it were a foot, and walked it in the water a little. "She has to play," Rino said, like a big brother who is annoyed by the childish acts of his little sister.

But as soon as he saw Lila take out the shoe he became preoccupied and asked, "So?"

Lila took out her hand, rubbed her fingers, held it out to him. "Touch."

Rino put his hand in, said, "It's dry."

"It's wet."

"Only you feel the wetness. Touch it, Lenù."

I touched it.

"It's a little damp," I said.

Lila was displeased.

"See? You hold it in the water for a minute and it's already wet, it's no good. We have to unglue it and unstitch it all again."

"What the fuck if there's a little dampness?"

Rino got angry. Not only that: right before my eyes, he went through a kind of transformation. He became red in the face, he swelled up around the eyes and cheekbones, he couldn't contain himself and exploded in a series of curses and expletives against his sister. He complained that if they went on like that they would never finish. He reproached Lila because she first encouraged him and then discouraged him. He shouted that he wouldn't stay forever in that wretched place to be his father's servant and watch others get rich. He grabbed the iron foot, pretended to throw it at her, and if he really had he would have killed her.

I left, on the one hand confused by that rage in a youth who was usually kind and on the other proud of how authoritative, how definitive my opinion had been.

In the following days I found that my acne was drying up.

"You're really doing well, it's the satisfaction you get from school, it's love," Lila said to me, and I felt that she was a little sad.

20.

As the New Year's Eve celebration approached, Rino was seized by the desire to set off more fireworks than anyone else, especially the Solaras. Lila made fun of him, but sometimes she became harsh with him. She told me that her brother, who at first had been skeptical about the possibility of making money with the shoes, had now begun to count on it too heavily, already he saw himself as the owner of the Cerullo shoe factory and didn't want to go back to repairing shoes. This worried her, it was a side of Rino she didn't know. He had always seemed to her only generously impetuous, sometimes aggressive, but not a braggart. Now, though, he posed as what he was not. He felt he was close to wealth. A boss. Someone who could give the neighborhood the first sign of the good fortune the new year would bring by setting off a lot of fireworks, more than the Solara brothers, who had become in his eyes the model of the young man to emulate and indeed to surpass, people whom he envied and considered enemies to be beaten, so that he could assume their role.

Lila never said, as she had with Carmela and the other girls in the courtyard: maybe I planted a fantasy in his head that he doesn't know how to control. She herself believed in the fantasy, felt it could be realized, and her brother was an important element of that realization. And then she loved him, he was six years older, she didn't want to reduce him to a child who can't handle his dreams. But she often said that Rino lacked concreteness, he didn't know how to confront difficulties with his feet on the ground, he tended to get carried away. Like that competition with the Solaras, for example.

"Maybe he's jealous of Marcello," I said once.

"What?"

She smiled, pretending not to understand, but she had told me herself. Marcello Solara passed by and hung around in front of the shoemaker's shop every day, both on foot and in the 1100, and Rino must have been aware of it, since he had said many times to his sister, "Don't you dare get too familiar with that shit." Maybe, who knows, since he wasn't able to beat up the Solaras for chasing after his sister, he wished to demonstrate his strength by means of fireworks.

"If that's true, you'll agree that I'm right?"

"Right about what?"

"That he's acting like a big shot: where's he going to get the money for the fireworks?"

It was true. The last night of the year was a night of battle, in the neighborhood and throughout Naples. Dazzling lights, explosions. The dense smoke from the gunpowder made everything hazy, it entered the houses, burned your eyes, made you cough. But the pop of the poppers, the hiss of the rockets, the cannonades of the missiles had a cost and as usual those who set off the most were those with the most money. We Grecos had no money, at my house the contribution to the end-of-the-year fireworks was small. My father bought a box of sparklers, one of wheels, and one of slender rockets. At midnight he put in my hand, since I was the oldest, the stem of a sparkler or of a Catherine wheel, and lighted it, and I stood motionless, excited and terrified, staring at the whirling sparks, the brief swirls of fire a short distance from my fingers. He then stuck the shafts of the rockets in glass bottles on the marble windowsill, burned the fuses with the tip of his cigarette, and, excitedly, launched the luminous whistles into the sky. Then he threw the bottles, too, into the street.

Similarly at Lila's house they set off just a few or none, and Rino rebelled. From the age of twelve he had gotten into the habit of going out to celebrate midnight with people more daring than his father, and his exploits in recovering unexploded bottles were famous—as soon as the chaos of the celebration was over he would go in search of them. He would assemble them all near the ponds, light them, and delight in the high flare, *trac trac trac*, the final explosion. He still had a dark scar on one hand, a broad stain, from a time when he hadn't pulled back fast enough.

Among the many reasons, open and secret, for that challenge at the end of 1958, it should therefore be added that maybe Rino wanted to make up for his impoverished childhood. So he got busy collecting money here and there to buy fireworks. But we knew—he knew himself, despite the frenzy for grandeur that had seized him—that there was no way to compete with the Solaras. As they did every year, the two brothers went back and forth for days in their 1100, the trunk loaded with explosives that on New Year's Eve would kill birds, frighten dogs, cats, mice, make the buildings quake from the cellars up to the roofs. Rino observed them from the shop with resentment and meanwhile was dealing with Pasquale, with Antonio, and above all with Enzo, who had a little more money, to procure an arsenal that would at least make for a good show.

Things took a small, unexpected turn when Lila and I were sent to Stefano Carracci's grocery by our mothers to do the shopping for the dinner. The shop was full of people. Behind the counter, besides Stefano and Pinuccia, Alfonso was serving customers, and he gave us an embarrassed smile. We settled ourselves for a long wait. But Stefano addressed to me, unequivocally to me, a nod of greeting, and said something in his brother's ear. My classmate came out from behind the counter and asked if we had a list. We gave him our lists and he slipped away. In five minutes our groceries were ready.

We put everything in our bags, paid Signora Maria, and went out. But we hadn't gone far when not Alfonso but Stefano, Stefano himself, called to me with his lovely man's voice, "Lenù."

He joined us. He had a confident expression, a friendly smile. Only his white grease-stained apron spoiled him slightly. He spoke to both of us, in dialect, but looking at me: "Would you like to come and celebrate the new year at my house? Alfonso would really be pleased."

The wife and children of Don Achille, even after the murder of the father, led a very retiring life: church, grocery, home, at most some small celebration they couldn't skip. That invitation was something new. I answered, nodding at Lila: "We're already busy, we'll be with her brother and some friends."

"Tell Rino, too, tell your parents: the house is big and we'll go out on the terrace for the fireworks."

Lila interjected in a dismissive tone: "Pasquale and Carmen Peluso and their mother are coming to celebrate with us."

It was supposed to be a phrase that eliminated any further talk: Alfredo Peluso was at Poggioreale because he had murdered Don Achille, and the son of Don Achille could not invite the children of Alfredo to toast the new year at his house. Instead, Stefano looked at her, very intensely, as if until that moment he hadn't seen her, and said, in the tone one uses when something is obvious: "All right, all of you come: we'll drink spumante, dance—new year, new life."

The words moved me. I looked at Lila, she, too, was confused. She murmured, "We have to talk to my brother."

"Let me know."

"And the fireworks?"

"What do you mean?"

"We'll bring ours, and you?"

Stefano smiled. "How many fireworks do you want?"

"Lots."

The young man again addressed me: "Come to my house and I promise you that we'll still be setting them off at dawn."

21.

The whole way home we laughed till our sides ached, saying things like:

"He's doing it for you."

"No, for you."

"He's in love and to have you at his house he'll invite even the Communists, even the murderers of his father."

"What are you talking about? He didn't even look at me."

Rino listened to Stefano's proposal and immediately said no. But the wish to vanquish the Solaras kept him uncertain and he talked about it with Pasquale, who got very angry. Enzo on the other hand mumbled, "All right, I'll come if I can." As for our parents, they were very pleased with that invitation because for them Don Achille no longer existed and his children and his wife were good, well-to-do people whom it was an honor to have as friends.

Lila at first seemed in a daze, as if she had forgotten where she was, the streets, the neighborhood, the shoemaker's shop. Then she appeared at my house late one afternoon with a look as if she had understood everything and said to me: "We were wrong: Stefano doesn't want me or you."

We discussed it in our usual fashion, mixing facts with fantasies. If he didn't want us, what did he want? We thought that Stefano, too, intended to teach the Solaras a lesson. We recalled when Michele had expelled Pasquale from Gigliola's mother's party, thus interfering in the affairs of the Carraccis and giving Stefano the appearance of a man unable to defend the memory of his father. On that occasion, if you thought about it, the brothers had insulted not only Pasquale but also him. And so now he was raising the stakes, as if to spite them: he was making a conclusive peace with the Pelusos, even inviting them to his house for New Year's Eve.

"And who benefits?" I asked Lila.

"I don't know. He wants to make a gesture that no one would make here in the neighborhood."

"Forgive?"

Lila shook her head skeptically. She was trying to understand, we were both trying to understand, and understanding was something that we loved to do. Stefano didn't seem the type capable of forgiveness. According to Lila he had something else in mind. And slowly, proceeding from one of the

ideas she hadn't been able to get out of her head since the
moment she started talking to Pasquale, she seemed to find a
solution.

"You remember when I said to Carmela that she could be
Alfonso's girlfriend?"

"Yes."

"Stefano has in mind something like that."

"Marry Carmela?"

"More."

Stefano, according to Lila, wanted to clear away everything.
He wanted to try to get out of the *before*. He didn't want to
pretend it was nothing, as our parents did, but rather to set in
motion a phrase like: I know, my father was what he was, but
now I'm here, we are us, and so, enough. In other words, he
wanted to make the whole neighborhood understand that he
was not Don Achille and that the Pelusos were not the former
carpenter who had killed him. That hypothesis pleased us, it
immediately became a certainty, and we had an impulse of
great fondness for the young Carracci. We decided to take his
part.

We went to explain to Rino, to Pasquale, to Antonio that
Stefano's invitation was more than an invitation, that behind it
were important meanings, that it was as if he were saying:
before us some ugly things happened; our fathers, some in one
way, some in another, didn't behave well; from this moment,
we take note of that and show that we children are better than
they were.

"Better?" Rino asked, with interest.

"Better," I said. "The complete opposite of the Solaras,
who are worse than their grandfather and their father."

I spoke with great excitement, in Italian, as if I were in
school. Lila herself glanced at me in amazement, and Rino,
Pasquale, and Antonio muttered, embarrassed. Pasquale even
tried to answer in Italian but he gave up. He said somberly:

"His father made money on the black market, and now Stefano is using it to make more money. His shop is in the place where my father's carpenter shop was."

Lila narrowed her eyes, so you almost couldn't see them.

"It's true. But do you prefer to be on the side of someone who wants to change or on the side of the Solaras?"

Pasquale said proudly, partly out of conviction, partly because he was visibly jealous of Stefano's unexpected central role in Lila's words, "I'm on my own side and that's it."

But he was an honest soul, he thought it over again and again. He talked to his mother, he discussed it with the whole family. Giuseppina, who had been a tireless, good-natured worker, relaxed and exuberant, had become after her husband's imprisonment a slovenly woman, depressed by her bad luck, and she turned to the priest. The priest went to Stefano's shop, talked for a long time with Maria, then went back to talk to Giuseppina Peluso. In the end everyone was persuaded that life was already very difficult, and that if it was possible, on the occasion of the new year, to reduce its tensions, it would be better for everyone. So at 11:30 P.M. on December 31st, after the New Year's Eve dinner, various families—the family of the former carpenter, the family of the porter, that of the shoemaker, that of the fruit and vegetable seller, the family of Melina, who that night had made an effort with her appearance—climbed up to the fifth floor, to the old, hated home of Don Achille, to celebrate the new year together.

22.

Stefano welcomed us with great cordiality. I remember that he had dressed with care, his face was slightly flushed because of his agitation, he was wearing a white shirt and a tie, and a blue sleeveless vest. I found him very handsome, with the manners of a prince. I calculated that he was seven years older than me and Lila, and I thought then that to have Gino as a boyfriend, a boy of my own age, was a small thing: when I asked him to come to the Carraccis' with me, he had said that he couldn't, because his parents wouldn't let him go out after midnight, it was dangerous. I wanted an older boyfriend, one like those young men, Stefano, Pasquale, Rino, Antonio, Enzo. I looked at them, I hovered about them all evening. I nervously touched my earrings, my mother's silver bracelet. I had begun to feel pretty again and I wanted to read the proof in their eyes. But they all seemed taken up by the fireworks that would start at midnight. They were waiting for their war of men and didn't pay attention even to Lila.

Stefano was kind especially to Signora Peluso and to Melina, who didn't say a word, she had wild eyes and a long nose, but she had combed her hair, and, with her earrings, and her old black widow's dress, she looked like a lady. At midnight the master of the house filled first his mother's glass with spumante and right afterward that of Pasquale's mother. We toasted all the marvelous things that would happen in the new year, then we began to swarm toward the terrace, the old people and children in coats and scarves, because it was very cold. I realized that the only one who lingered indifferently downstairs was Alfonso. I called him, out of politeness, but he didn't hear me, or pretended not to. I ran up. Above me was a tremendous cold sky, full of stars and shadows.

The boys wore sweaters, except Pasquale and Enzo, who were in shirtsleeves. Lila and Ada and Carmela and I had on the thin dresses we wore for dancing parties and were trembling with cold and excitement. Already we could hear the first whizz of the rockets as they furrowed the sky and exploded in bright-colored flowers. Already the thud of old things flying out the windows could be heard, with shouts and laughter. The whole neighborhood was in an uproar, setting off firecrackers.

I lighted sparklers and pinwheels for the children, I liked to see in their eyes the fearful wonder that I had felt as a child. Lila persuaded Melina to light the fuse of a Bengal light with her: the jet of flame sprayed with a colorful crackle. They shouted with joy and hugged each other.

Rino, Stefano, Pasquale, Enzo, Antonio transported cases and boxes and cartons of explosives, proud of all those supplies they had managed to accumulate. Alfonso also helped, but he did it wearily, reacting to his brother's pressure with gestures of annoyance. He seemed intimidated by Rino, who was truly frenzied, pushing him rudely, grabbing things away from him, treating him like a child. So finally, rather than get angry, Alfonso withdrew, mingling less and less with the others. Meanwhile the matches flared as the adults lighted cigarettes for each other with cupped hands, speaking seriously and cordially. If there should be a civil war, I thought, like the one between Romulus and Remus, between Marius and Silla, between Caesar and Pompey, they will have these same faces, these same looks, these same poses.

Except for Alfonso, all the boys filled their shirts with firecrackers and missiles and arranged rows of rockets in ranks of empty bottles. Rino, increasingly agitated, shouting louder and louder, assigned to me, Lila, Ada, and Carmela the job of supplying everyone with ammunition. Then the very young, the young, the not so young—my brothers Peppe and Gianni, but also my father, also the shoemaker, who was the oldest of all—began moving around in the dark and the cold lighting fuses and throwing fireworks over the parapet or into the sky, in a celebratory atmosphere of growing excitement, of shouts like did you see those colors, wow what a bang, come on, come on—all scarcely disturbed by Melina's faint yet terrified wails, by Rino as he snatched the fireworks from my brothers and used them himself, yelling that it was a waste because the boys threw them without waiting for the fuse to really catch fire.

The glittering fury of the city slowly faded, died out, letting the sound of the cars, the horns emerge. Broad zones of dark sky reappeared. The Solaras' balcony became, even through the smoke, amid the flashes, more visible.

They weren't far, we could see them. The father, the sons, the relatives, the friends were, like us, in the grip of a desire for chaos. The whole neighborhood knew that what had happened so far was minor, the real show would begin when the penurious had finished with their little parties and petty explosions and fine rains of silver and gold, when only the masters of the revels remained.

And so it was. From the balcony the fire intensified abruptly, the sky and the street began to explode again. At every burst, especially if the firecracker made a sound of destruction, enthusiastic obscenities came from the balcony. But, unexpectedly, here were Stefano, Pasquale, Antonio, Rino ready to respond with more bursts and equivalent obscenities. At a rocket from the Solaras they launched a rocket, a string of firecrackers was answered by a string of firecrackers, and in the sky miraculous fountains erupted, and the street below flared, trembled. At one point Rino climbed up onto the parapet shouting insults and throwing powerful firecrackers while his mother shrieked with terror, yelling, "Get down or you'll fall."

At that point panic overwhelmed Melina, who began to wail. Ada was furious, it was up to her to get her home, but Alfonso indicated that he would take care of her, and he disappeared down the stairs with her. My mother immediately followed, limping, and the other women began to drag the children away. The Solaras' explosions were becoming more and more violent, one of their rockets instead of heading into the sky burst against the parapet of our terrace with a loud red flash and suffocating smoke.

"They did it on purpose," Rino yelled at Stefano, beside himself.

Stefano, a dark profile in the cold, motioned him to calm down. He hurried to a corner where he himself had placed a box that we girls had received orders not to touch, and he dipped into it, inviting the others to help themselves.

"Enzo," he cried, with not even a trace now of the polite shopkeeper's tones, "Pascà, Rino, Antò, here, come on, here, we'll show them what we've got."

They all ran laughing. They repeated: yeah, we'll let them have it, fuck those shits, fuck, take this, and they made obscene gestures in the direction of the Solaras' balcony. Shivering with cold, we looked at their frenetic black forms. We were alone, with no role. Even my father had gone downstairs, with the shoemaker. Lila, I don't know, she was silent, absorbed by the spectacle as if by a puzzle.

The thing was happening to her that I mentioned and that she later called dissolving margins. It was—she told me—as if, on the night of a full moon over the sea, the intense black mass of a storm advanced across the sky, swallowing every light, eroding the circumference of the moon's circle, and disfiguring the shining disk, reducing it to its true nature of rough insensate material. Lila imagined, she saw, she felt—as if it were true—her brother break. Rino, before her eyes, lost the features he had had as long as she could remember, the features of the generous, candid boy, the pleasing features of the reliable young man, the beloved outline of one who, as far back as she had memory, had amused, helped, protected her. There, amid the violent explosions, in the cold, in the smoke that burned the nostrils and the strong odor of sulfur, something violated the organic structure of her brother, exercising over him a pressure so strong that it broke down his outlines, and the matter expanded like a magma, showing her what he was truly made of. Every second of that night of celebration horrified her, she had the impression that, as Rino moved, as he expanded around himself, every margin collapsed and her own margins, too, became softer and more yielding. She struggled to maintain control, and succeeded: on the outside her anguish hardly showed. It's true that in the tumult of explosions and colors I didn't pay much attention to her. I was struck, I think, by her expression, which seemed increasingly fearful. I also realized that she was staring at the shadow of her brother—the most active, the most arrogant, shouting the loudest, bloodiest insults in the direction of the Solaras' terrace—with repulsion. It seemed that she, she who in general feared nothing, was afraid. But they were impressions I recalled only later. At the moment I didn't notice, I felt closer to Carmela, to Ada, than to her. She seemed as usual to have no need of male attention. We, instead, out in the cold, in the midst of that chaos, without that attention couldn't give ourselves meaning. We would have preferred that Stefano or Enzo or Rino stop the war, put an arm around our shoulders, press us to them, side to side, and speak soft words. Instead, we were holding on to each other to get warm, while they rushed to grab cylinders with fat fuses, astonished by Stefano's infinite reserves, admiring of his generosity, disturbed by how much money could be transformed into fiery trails, sparks, explosions, smoke for the pure satisfaction of winning.

They competed with the Solaras for I don't know how long, explosions from one side and the other as if terrace and balcony were trenches, and the whole neighborhood shook, vibrated. You couldn't understand anything—roars, shattered glass, splintered sky. Even when Enzo shouted, "They're finished, they've got nothing left," ours continued, Rino especially kept going, until there remained not a fuse to light. Then they raised a victorious chorus, jumping and embracing. Finally they calmed down, silence fell.

But it didn't last; it was broken by the rising cry of a child in the distance, shouts and insults, cars advancing through the streets littered with debris. And then we saw flashes on the Solaras' balcony, sharp sounds reached us, *pah, pah*. Rino shouted in disappointment, "They're starting again." But Enzo, who immediately understood what was happening, pushed us inside, and after him Pasquale, Stefano. Only Rino went on yelling vulgar insults, leaning over the parapet, so that Lila dodged Pasquale and ran to pull her brother inside, yelling insults at him in turn. We girls cried out as we went downstairs. The Solaras, in order to win, were shooting at us.

23.

As I said, many things about that night escaped me. But above all, overwhelmed by the atmosphere of celebration and danger, by the swirl of males whose bodies gave off a heat hotter than the fires in the sky, I neglected Lila. And yet it was then that her first inner change took place.

I didn't realize, as I said, what had happened to her, the action was difficult to perceive. But I was aware of the consequences almost immediately. She became lazier. Two days later, I got up early, even though I didn't have school, to go with her to open the shop and help her do the cleaning, but she didn't appear. She arrived late, sullen, and we walked through the neighborhood avoiding the shoemaker's shop.

"You're not going to work?"

"No."

"Why?"

"I don't like it anymore."

"And the new shoes?"

"They're nowhere."

"And so?"

It seemed to me that even she didn't know what she wanted. The only definite thing was that she seemed very worried about her brother, much more than I had seen recently. And it was precisely as a result of that worry that she began to modify her speeches about wealth. There was always the pressure to become wealthy, there was no question about it, but the goal was no longer the same as in childhood: no treasure chests, no sparkle of coins and precious stones. Now it seemed that money, in her mind, had become a cement: it consolidated, reinforced, fixed this and that. Above all, it fixed Rino's head. The pair of shoes that they had made together he now considered ready, and wanted to show them to Fernando. But Lila knew well (and according to her so did Rino) that the work was full of flaws, that their father would examine the shoes and throw them away. So she told him that they had to try and try again, that the route to the shoe factory was a difficult one; but he was unwilling to wait longer, he felt an urgent need to become like the Solaras, like Stefano, and Lila couldn't make him see reason. Suddenly it seemed to me that wealth in itself no longer interested her. She no longer spoke of money with any excitement, it was just a means of keeping her brother out of trouble. But since it wasn't around the corner, she wondered, with cruel eyes, what she had to come up with to soothe him.

Rino was in a frenzy. Fernando, for example, never reproached Lila for having stopped coming to the shop, in fact he let her understand that he was happy for her to stay home and help her mother. Her brother instead got furious and in early January I witnessed another ugly quarrel. Rino approached us with his head down, he blocked our path, he said to her, "Come to work right now." Lila answered that she wouldn't think of it. He then dragged her by the arm, she defied him with a nasty insult, Rino slapped her, shouted at her, "Then go home, go and help Mamma." She obeyed, without even saying goodbye to me.

The climax came on the day of the Befana.[1] She, it seems, woke up and found next to her bed a sock full of coal. She knew

---

[1] In Italian folklore, the Befana is an old woman who delivers gifts to children, mostly in southern Italy, on the eve of the Epiphany (the night of January 5th), like St. Nicholas or Santa Claus.

it was from Rino and at breakfast she set the table for everyone but him. Her mother appeared: Rino had left a sock full of candies and chocolate hanging on a chair, which had moved her, she doted on that boy. So, when she realized that Rino's place wasn't set, she tried to set it but Lila prevented her. While mother and daughter argued, Rino appeared and Lila immediately threw a piece of coal at him. Rino laughed, thinking it was a game, that she had appreciated the joke, but when he realized that his sister was serious he tried to hit her. Then Fernando arrived, in underpants and undershirt, a cardboard box in his hand.

"Look what the Befana brought me," he said, and it was clear that he was furious.

He pulled out of the box the new shoes that his children had made in secret. Lila was openmouthed with surprise. She didn't know anything about it. Rino had decided on his own to show his father their work, as if it were a gift from the Befana.

When she saw on her brother's face a small smile that was amused and at the same time tormented, when she caught his worried gaze on his father's face, it seemed to her she had the confirmation of what had frightened her on the terrace, amid the smoke and fireworks: Rino had lost his usual outline, she now had a brother without boundaries, from whom something irreparable might emerge. In that smile, in that gaze she saw something unbearably wretched, the more unbearable the more she loved her brother, and felt the need to stay beside him to help him and be helped.

"How beautiful they are," said Nunzia, who was ignorant of the whole business.

Fernando, without saying a word, and now looking like an angry Randolph Scott, sat down and put on first the right shoe, then the left.

"The Befana," he said, "made them precisely for my feet."

He got up, tried them, walked back and forth in the kitchen as his family watched.

"Very comfortable," he commented.

"They're gentleman's shoes," his wife said, giving her son admiring looks.

Fernando sat down again. He took them off, he examined them above, below, inside and outside.

"Whoever made these shoes is a master," he said, but his face didn't brighten at all. "Brava, Befana."

In every word you heard how much he suffered and how that suffering was charging him with a desire to smash everything. But Rino didn't seem to realize it. At every sarcastic word of his father's he became prouder, he smiled, blushing, formulated half-phrases: I did like this, Papa, I added this, I thought that. Lila wanted to get out of the kitchen, out of the way of her father's imminent rage, but she couldn't make up her mind, she didn't want to leave her brother alone.

"They're light but also strong," Fernando continued, "there's no cutting corners. And I've never seen anything like them on anyone's feet, with this wide tip they're very original."

He sat down, he put them on again, he laced them. He said to his son: "Turn around Rinù, I have to thank the Befana."

Rino thought it was a joke that would conclusively end the whole long controversy and he appeared happy and embarrassed. But as soon as he started to turn his back his father kicked him violently in the rear, called him animal, idiot, and threw at him whatever came to hand, finally even the shoes.

Lila got involved only when she saw that her brother, at first intent only on protecting himself from punching and kicking, began shouting, too, overturning chairs, breaking plates, crying, swearing that he would kill himself rather than continue to work for his father for nothing, terrorizing his mother, the other children, and the neighbors. But in vain. Father and son first had to explode until they wore themselves out. Then they went back to working together, mute, shut up in the shop with their desperations.

There was no mention of the shoes for a while. Lila decided that her role was to help her mother, do the marketing, cook, wash the clothes and hang them in the sun, and she never went to the shoemaker's shop. Rino, saddened, sulky, felt the thing as an incomprehensible injustice and began to insist that he find socks and underpants and shirts in order in his drawer, that his sister serve him and show him respect when he came home from work. If something wasn't to his liking he protested, he said unpleasant things like you can't even iron a shirt, you shit. She shrugged, she didn't resist, she continued to carry out her duties with attention and care.

He himself, naturally, wasn't happy with the way he was behaving, he was tormented, he tried to calm down, he made not a few efforts to return to being what he had been. On good days, Sunday mornings for example, he wandered around joking, taking on a gentle tone of voice. "Are you mad at me because I took all the credit for the shoes? I did it," he said, lying, "to keep Papa from getting angry at you." And then he asked her, "Help me, what should we do now? We can't stop here, I have to get out of this situation." Lila was silent: she cooked, she ironed, at times she kissed him on the cheek to let him know that she wasn't mad anymore. But in the meantime he would get angry again, he always ended up smashing something. He shouted that she had betrayed him, and would betray him yet again, when, sooner or later, she would marry some imbecile and go away, leaving him to live in this wretchedness forever.

Sometimes, when no one was home, Lila went into the little room where she had hidden the shoes and touched them, looked at them, marveled to herself that for good or ill there they were and had come into being as the result of a design on a sheet of graph paper. How much wasted work.

24.

I returned to school, I was dragged inside the torturous rhythms that the teachers imposed on us. Many of my companions began to give up, the class thinned out. Gino got low marks and asked me to help him. I tried to but really all he wanted was for me to let him copy my homework. I did, but reluctantly: even when he copied he didn't pay attention, he didn't try to understand. Even Alfonso, although he was very disciplined, had difficulties. One day he burst into tears during the Greek interrogation, something that for a boy was considered very humiliating. It was clear that he would have preferred to die rather than shed a single tear in front of the class, but he couldn't control it. We were all silent, extremely disturbed, except Gino, who, perhaps for the satisfaction of seeing that even for his deskmate things could go badly, burst out laughing. As we left school I told him that because of that laughter he was no longer my boyfriend. He responded by asking me, worried, "You like Alfonso?" I explained that I simply didn't like him anymore. He stammered that we had scarcely started, it wasn't fair. Not much had happened between us as boyfriend and girlfriend: we'd kissed but without tongues, he had tried to touch my breasts and I had got angry and pushed him away. He begged me to continue just for a little, I was firm in my decision. I knew that it would cost me nothing to lose his company on the way to school and the way home.

A few days had passed since the break with Gino when Lila confided that she had had two declarations almost at the same time, the first in her life. Pasquale, one morning, had come up to her while she was doing the shopping. He was marked by fatigue, and extremely agitated. He had said that he was worried because he hadn't seen her in the shoemaker's shop and thought she was sick. Now that he found her in good health, he was happy. But there was no happiness in his face at all as he spoke. He broke off as if he were choking and, to free his voice, had almost shouted that he loved her. He loved her so much that, if she agreed, he would come and speak to her brother, her parents, whoever, immediately, so that they could be engaged. She was dumbstruck, for a few minutes she thought he was joking. I had said a thousand times that Pasquale had his eyes on her, but she had never believed me. Now there he was, on a beautiful spring day, almost with tears in his eyes, and was begging her, telling her his life was worth nothing if she said no. How difficult the sentiments of love were to untangle. Lila, very cautiously, but without ever saying no, had found words to refuse him. She had said that she loved him, but not as one should love a fiancé. She had also said that she would always be grateful to him for all the things he had explained to her: Fascism, the Resistance, the monarchy, the republic, the black market, Comandante Lauro, the neo-fascists, Christian Democracy, Communism. But to be his girlfriend, no, she would never be anyone's girlfriend. And she had concluded: "I love all of you, Antonio, you, Enzo, the way I love Rino." Pasquale had then murmured, "I, however, don't love you the way I do Carmela." He had escaped and gone back to work.

"And the other declaration?" I asked her, curious but also a little anxious.

"You'd never imagine."

The other declaration had come from Marcello Solara.

In hearing that name I felt a pang. If Pasquale's love was a sign of how much someone could like Lila, the love of Marcello—a young man who was handsome and wealthy, with a car, who was harsh and violent, a Camorrist, used, that is, to taking the women he wanted—was, in my eyes, in the eyes of all my contemporaries, and in spite of his bad reputation, in fact perhaps even because of it, a promotion, the transition from skinny little girl to woman capable of making anyone bend to her will.

"How did it happen?"

Marcello was driving the 1100, by himself, without his brother, and had seen her as she was going home along the *stradone*. He hadn't driven up alongside her, he hadn't called to her from the window. He had left the car in the middle of the street, with the door open, and approached her. Lila had kept walking, and he followed. He had pleaded with her to forgive him for his behavior in the past, he admitted she would have been absolutely right to kill him with the shoemaker's knife. He had reminded her, with emotion, how they had danced rock and roll so well together at Gigliola's mother's party, a sign of how well matched they might be. Finally he had started to pay her compliments: "How you've grown up, what lovely eyes you have, how beautiful you are." And then he told her a dream he had had that night: he asked her to become engaged, she said yes, he gave her an engagement ring like his grandmother's, which had three diamonds in the band of the setting. At last Lila, continuing to walk, had spoken. She had asked, "In that dream I said yes?" Marcello confirmed it and she replied, "Then it really was a dream, because you're an animal, you and your family, your grandfather, your brother, and I would never be engaged to you even if you tell me you'll kill me."

"You told him that?"

"I said more."

"What?"

When Marcello, insulted, had replied that his feelings were delicate, that he thought of her only with love, night and day, that therefore he wasn't an animal but one who loved her, she had responded that if a person behaved as he had behaved with Ada, if that same person on New Year's Eve started shooting people with a gun, to call him an animal was to insult animals. Marcello had finally understood that she wasn't joking, that she really considered him less than a frog, a salamander, and he was suddenly depressed. He had murmured weakly, "It was my brother who was shooting." But even as he spoke he had realized that that excuse would only increase her contempt. Very true. Lila had started walking faster and when he tried to follow had yelled, "Go away," and started running. Marcello then had stopped as if he didn't remember where he was and what he was supposed to be doing, and so he had gone back to the 1100.

"You did that to Marcello Solara?"

"Yes."

"You're crazy: don't tell anyone you treated him like that."

At the moment it seemed to me superfluous advice, I said it just to demonstrate that I was concerned. Lila by nature liked talking and fantasizing about facts, but she never gossiped, unlike the rest us, who were continuously talking about people. And in fact she spoke only to me of Pasquale's love, I never discovered that she had told anyone else. But she told everyone about Marcello Solara. So that when I saw Carmela she said, "Did you know that your friend said no to Marcello Solara?" I met Ada, who said to me, "Your friend said no to Marcello Solara, no less." Pinuccia Carracci, in the shop, whispered in my ear, "Is it true that your friend said no to Marcello Solara?" Even Alfonso said to me one day at school, astonished, "Your friend said no to Marcello Solara?"

When I saw Lila I said to her, "You shouldn't have told everyone, Marcello will get angry."

She shrugged. She had work to do, her siblings, the housework, her mother, her father, and she didn't stop to talk much. Now, as she had been since New Year's Eve, she was occupied only with domestic things.

25.

So it was. For the rest of the term Lila was totally uninterested in what I did in school. And when I asked her what books she was taking out of the library, what she was reading, she answered, spitefully, "I don't take them out anymore, books give me a headache."

Whereas I studied, reading now was like a pleasant habit. But I soon had to observe that, since Lila had stopped pushing me, anticipating me in my studies and my reading, school, and even Maestro Ferraro's library, had stopped being a kind of adventure and had become only a thing that I knew how to do well and was much praised for.

I realized this clearly on two occasions.

Once I went to get some books out of the library. My card was dense with borrowings and returns, and the teacher first congratulated me on my diligence, then asked me about Lila, showing regret that she and her whole family had stopped taking out books. It's hard to explain why, but that regret made me suffer. It seemed to be the sign of a true interest in Lila, something much stronger than the compliments for my discipline as a constant reader. It occurred to me that if Lila had taken out just a single book a year, on that book she would have left her imprint and the teacher would have felt it the moment she returned it, while I left no mark, I embodied only the persistence with which I added volume to volume in no particular order.

The other circumstance had to do with school exercises. The literature teacher, Gerace, gave back, corrected, our Italian papers (I still remember the subject: "The Various Phases of the Tragedy of Dido"), and while he generally confined himself to saying a word or two to justify the eight or nine I usually got, this time he praised me eloquently in front of the class and revealed only at the end that he had given me a ten. At the end of the class he called me into the corridor, truly impressed by how I had treated the subject, and when the religion teacher came by he stopped him and summarized my paper enthusiastically. A few days passed and I realized that Gerace had not limited himself to the priest but had circulated that paper of mine among the other teachers, and not only in my section. Some teachers in the upper grades now smiled at me in the corridors, or even made comments. For example, Professor Galiani, a woman who was highly regarded and yet avoided, because she was said to be a Communist, and because with one or two comments she could dismantle any argument that did not have a solid foundation, stopped me in the hall and spoke with particular admiration about the idea, central to my paper, that if love is exiled from cities, their good nature becomes an evil nature. She asked me:

"What does 'a city without love' mean to you?"

"A people deprived of happiness."

"Give me an example."

I thought of the discussions I'd had with Lila and Pasquale in September and I suddenly felt that they were a true school, truer than the one I went to every day.

"Italy under Fascism, Germany under Nazism, all of us human beings in the world today."

She scrutinized me with increased interest. She said that I wrote very well, she recommended some reading, she offered to lend me books. Finally, she asked me what my father did, I answered, "He's a porter at the city hall." She went off with her head down.

The interest shown by Professor Galiani naturally filled me with pride, but it had no great consequence; the school routine returned to normal. As a result, even the fact that, in my first year, I was a student with a small reputation for being clever soon seemed to me unimportant. In the end what did it prove? It proved how fruitful it had been to study with Lila and talk to her, to have her as a goad and support as I ventured into the world outside the neighborhood, among the things and persons and landscapes and ideas of books. Of course, I said to myself, the essay on Dido is mine, the capacity to formulate beautiful sentences comes from me; of course, what I wrote about Dido belongs to me; but didn't I work it out with her, didn't we excite each other in turn, didn't my passion grow in the warmth of hers? And that idea of the city without love, which the teachers had liked so much, hadn't it come to me from Lila, even if I had developed it, with my own ability? What should I deduce from this?

I began to expect new praise that would prove my autonomous virtuosity. But Gerace, when he gave another assignment on the Queen of Carthage ("Aeneas and Dido: An Encounter Between Two Refugees"), was not enthusiastic, he gave me only an eight. Still, from Professor Galiani I got cordial nods of greeting and the pleasant discovery that she was the Latin and Greek teacher of Nino Sarratore. I urgently needed some reinforcements of attention and admiration, and hoped that maybe they would come from him. I hoped that, if his professor of literature had praised me in public, let's say in his class, he would remember me and finally would speak to me. But nothing happened, I continued to glimpse him on the way out, on the way in, always with that absorbed expression, never a glance. Once I even followed him along Corso Garibaldi and Via Casanova, hoping he would notice me and say: Hello, I see we're taking the same route, I've heard a lot about you. But he walked quickly, eyes down, and never turned. I got tired, I despised myself. Depressed, I turned onto Corso Novara and went home.

I kept on day after day, committed to asserting, with increasing thoroughness, to the teachers, to my classmates, to myself my application and diligence. But inside I felt a growing sense of solitude, I felt I was learning without energy. I tried to report to Lila Maestro Ferraro's regret, I told her to go back to the library. I also mentioned to her how well the assignment on Dido had been received, without telling her what I had written but letting her know that it was also her success. She listened to me without interest, maybe she no longer even remembered what we had said about that character, she had other problems. As soon as I left her an opening she told me that Marcello Solara had not resigned himself like Pasquale but continued to pursue her. If she went out to do the shopping he followed her, without bothering her, to Stefano's store, to Enzo's cart, just to look at her. If she went to the window she found him at the corner, waiting for her to appear. This constancy made her anxious. She was afraid that her father might notice, and, especially, that Rino might notice. She was frightened by the possibility that one of those stories of men would begin, in which they end up fighting all the time—there were plenty of those in the neighborhood. "What do I have?" she said. She saw herself as scrawny, ugly: why had Marcello become obsessed with her? "Is there something wrong with me?" she said. "I make people do the wrong thing."

Now she often repeated that idea. The conviction of having done more harm than good for her brother had solidified. "All you have to do is look at him," she said. Even with the disappearance of the Cerullo shoe factory project, Rino was gripped by the mania of getting rich like the Solaras, like Stefano, and even more, and he couldn't resign himself to the dailiness of the work in the shop. He said, trying to rekindle her old enthusiasm, "We're intelligent, Lina, together no one can stop us, tell me what we should do." He also wanted to buy a car, a television, and he detested Fernando, who didn't understand the importance of these things. But when Lila showed that she wouldn't support him anymore, he treated her worse than a servant. Maybe he didn't even know that he had changed for the worse, but she, who saw him every day, was alarmed. She said to me once, "Have you seen that when people wake up they're ugly, all disfigured, can't see?"

Rino in her view had become like that.

26.

One Sunday, in the middle of April, I remember, five of us went out: Lila, Carmela, Pasquale, Rino, and I. We girls were dressed up as well as we could and as soon as we were out of the house we put on lipstick and a little eye makeup. We took the metro, which was very crowded, and Rino and Pasquale stood next to us, on the lookout, the whole way. They were afraid that someone might touch us, but no one did, the faces of our escorts were too dangerous.

We walked down Toledo. Lila insisted on going to Via Chiaia, Via Filangieri, and then Via dei Mille, to Piazza Amedeo, an area where she knew there would be wealthy, elegant people. Rino and Pasquale were opposed, but they couldn't or wouldn't explain, and responded only by muttering in dialect and insulting indeterminate people they called "dandies." We three ganged up and insisted. Just then we heard honking. We turned and saw the Solaras' 1100. We didn't even notice the two brothers, we were so struck by the girls who were waving from the windows: Gigliola and Ada. They looked pretty, with pretty dresses, pretty hairdos, sparkling earrings, they waved and shouted happy greetings to us. Rino and Pasquale turned their faces away, Carmela and I were too surprised to respond. Lila was the only one to shout enthusiastically and wave, with broad motions of her arms, as the car disappeared in the direction of Piazza Plebiscito.

For a while we were silent, then Rino said to Pasquale he had always known that Gigliola was a whore, and Pasquale gravely agreed. Neither of the two mentioned Ada, Antonio was their friend and they didn't want to offend him. Carmela, however, said a lot of mean things about Ada. More than anything, I felt bitterness. That image of power had passed in a flash, four young people in a car—that was the right way to leave the neighborhood and have fun. Ours was the wrong way: on foot, in shabby old clothes, penniless. I felt like going home. Lila reacted as if that encounter had never taken place, insisting again that she wanted to go for a walk where the fancy people were. She clung to Pasquale's arm, she yelled, she laughed, she performed what she thought of as a parody of the respectable person, with waggling hips, a broad smile, and simpering gestures. We hesitated a moment and then went along with her, resentful at the idea that Gigliola and Ada were having fun in the 1100 with the handsome Solaras while we were on foot, in the company of Rino who resoled shoes and Pasquale who was a construction worker.

This dissatisfaction of ours, naturally unspoken, must somehow have reached the two boys, who looked at each other, sighed, and gave in. All right, they said, and we turned onto Via Chiaia.

It was like crossing a border. I remember a dense crowd and a sort of humiliating difference. I looked not at the boys but at the girls, the women: they were absolutely different from us. They seemed to have breathed another air, to have eaten other food, to have dressed on some other planet, to have learned to walk on wisps of wind. I was astonished. All the more so that, while I would have paused to examine at leisure dresses, shoes, the style of glasses if they wore glasses, they passed by without seeming to see me. They didn't see any of the five of us. We were not perceptible. Or not interesting. And in fact if at times their gaze fell on us, they immediately turned in another direction, as if irritated. They looked only at each other.

Of this we were all aware. No one mentioned it, but we understood that Rino and Pasquale, who were older, found on those streets only confirmation of things they already knew, and this put them in a bad mood, made them sullen, resentful at the certainty of being out of place, while we girls discovered it only at that moment and with ambiguous sentiments. We felt uneasy and yet fascinated, ugly but also impelled to imagine what we would become if we had some way to re-educate ourselves and dress and put on makeup and adorn ourselves properly. Meanwhile, in order not to ruin the evening, we became mocking, sarcastic.

"Would you ever wear that dress?"

"Not if you paid me."

"I would."

"Good for you, you'd look like a cream puff, like that lady there."

"And did you see the shoes?"

"What, those are shoes?"

We went as far as Palazzo Cellammare laughing and joking. Pasquale, who did his best to avoid being next to Lila and when she took his arm immediately, politely, freed himself (he spoke to her often, of course, he felt an evident pleasure in hearing her voice, in looking at her, but it was clear that the slightest contact overwhelmed him, might even make him cry), staying close to me, asked derisively:

"At school do your classmates look like that?"

"No."

"That means it's not a good school."

"It's a classical high school," I said, offended.

"It's not a good one," he insisted, "you can be sure that if there are no people like that it's no good: right, Lila, it's no good?"

"Good?" Lila said, and pointed to a blond girl who was coming toward us with a tall, dark young man, in a white V-neck sweater. "If there's no one like that, your school stinks." And she burst out laughing.

The girl was all in green: green shoes, green skirt, green jacket, and on her head—this was above all what made Lila laugh—she wore a bowler, like Charlie Chaplin, also green.

The hilarity passed from her to the rest of us. When the couple went by Rino made a vulgar comment on what the young woman in green should do, with the bowler hat, and Pasquale stopped, he was laughing so hard, and leaned against the wall with one arm. The girl and her companion took a few steps, then stopped. The boy in the white pullover turned, was immediately restrained by the girl, who grabbed his arm. He wriggled free, came back, addressed directly to Rino a series of insulting phrases. It was an instant. Rino punched him in the face and knocked him down, shouting:

"What did you call me? I didn't get it, repeat, what did you call me? Did you hear, Pascà, what he called me?"

Our laughter abruptly turned to fear. Lila first of all hurled herself at her brother before he started kicking the young man on the ground and dragged him off, with an expression of disbelief, as if a thousand fragments of our life, from childhood to this, our fourteenth year, were composing an image that was finally clear, yet which at that moment seemed to her incredible.

We pushed Rino and Pasquale away, while the girl in the bowler helped her boyfriend get up. Lila's incredulity meanwhile was changing into fury. As she tried to get her brother off she assailed him with the coarsest insults, pulled him by the arm, threatened him. Rino kept her away with one hand, a nervous laugh on his face, and meanwhile he turned to Pasquale:

"My sister thinks this is a game, Pascà," he said in dialect, his eyes wild, "my sister thinks that even if I say it's better for us not to go somewhere, she can do it, because she always knows everything, she always understands everything, as usual, and she can go there like it or not." A short pause to regain his breath, then he added, "Did you hear that shit called me 'hick'? Me a hick? A hick?" And still, breathless, "My sister brought me here and now she sees if I'm called a hick, now she sees what I do if they call me a hick."

"Calm down, Rino," Pasquale said, looking behind him every so often, in alarm.

Rino remained agitated, but subdued. Lila, however, had calmed down. We stopped at Piazza dei Martiri. Pasquale said, almost coldly, addressing Carmela: "You girls go home now."

"Alone?"

"Yes."

"No."

"Carmè, I don't want to discuss it: go."

"We don't know how to get there."

"Don't lie."

"Go," Rino said to Lila, trying to contain himself. "Take some money, buy an ice cream on the way."

"We left together and we're going back together."

Rino lost patience again, gave her a shove: "Will you stop it? I'm older and you do what I tell you. Move, go, in a second I'll bash your face in."

I saw that he was ready to do it seriously, I dragged Lila by the arm. She also understood the risk: "I'll tell Papa."

"Who gives a fuck. Walk, come on, go, you don't even deserve the ice cream."

Hesitantly we went up past Santa Caterina. But after a while Lila had second thoughts, stopped, said that she was going back to her brother. We tried to persuade her to stay with us, but she wouldn't listen. Just then we saw a group of boys, five, maybe six, they looked like the rowers we had sometimes admired on Sunday walks near Castel dell'Ovo. They were all tall, sturdy, well dressed. Some had sticks, some didn't. They quickly passed by the church and headed toward the piazza. Among them was the young man whom Rino had struck in the face; his V-necked sweater was stained with blood.

Lila freed herself from my grip and ran off, Carmela and I behind her. We arrived in time to see Rino and Pasquale backing up toward the monument at the center of the piazza, side by side, while those well-dressed youths chased them, hitting them with their sticks. We called for help, we began to cry, to stop people passing, but the sticks were frightening, no one helped. Lila grabbed the arm of one of the attackers but was thrown to the ground. I saw Pasquale on his knees, being kicked, I saw Rino protecting himself from the blows with his arm. Then a car stopped and it was the Solaras' 1100.

Marcello got out immediately. First he helped Lila up and then, incited by her, as she shrieked with rage and shouted at her brother, threw himself into the fight, hitting and getting hit. Only at that point Michele got out of the car, opened the trunk in a leisurely way, took out something that looked like a shiny iron bar, and joined in, hitting with a cold ferocity that I hope never to see again in my life. Rino and Pasquale got up furiously, hitting, choking, tearing—they seemed like strangers, they were so transformed by hatred. The well-dressed young men were routed. Michele went up to Pasquale, whose nose was bleeding, but Pasquale rudely pushed him away and wiped his face with the sleeve of his white shirt, then saw that it was soaked red. Marcello picked up a bunch of keys and handed it to Rino, who thanked him uneasily. The people who had kept their distance before now came over, curious. I was paralyzed with fear.

"Take the girls away," Rino said to the two Solaras, in the grateful tone of someone who makes a request that he knows is unavoidable.

Marcello made us get in the car, first Lila, who resisted. We were all jammed in the back seat, sitting on each other's knees. I turned to look at Pasquale and Rino, who were heading toward the Riviera, Pasquale limping. I felt as if our neighborhood had expanded, swallowing all Naples, even the streets where respectable people lived. In the car there were immediate tensions. Gigliola and Ada were annoyed, protesting that the ride was uncomfortable. "It's impossible," they said. "Then get out and walk," Lila shouted and they were about to start hitting each other. Marcello braked, amused. Gigliola got out and went to sit in front, on Michele's knees. We made the journey like that, with Gigliola and Michele kissing each other in front of us. I looked at her and she, though kissing passionately, looked at me. I turned away.

Lila said nothing until we reached the neighborhood. Marcello said a few words, his eyes looking for her in the rearview mirror, but she never responded. They let us out far from our houses, so that we wouldn't be seen in the Solaras' car. The rest of the way we walked, the five of us. Apart from Lila, who seemed consumed by anger and worry, we all admired the behavior of the two brothers. Good for them, we said, they behaved well. Gigliola kept repeating, "Of course," "What did you think," "Naturally," with the air of one who, working in the pastry shop, knew very well what first-rate people the Solaras were. At one point she asked me, but in a teasing tone:

"How's school?"

"Great."

"But you don't have fun the way I do."

"It's a different type of fun."

When she, Carmela, and Ada left us at the entrance of their building, I said to Lila:

"The rich people certainly are worse than we are."

She didn't answer. I added, cautiously, "The Solaras may be shit, but it's lucky they were there: those people on Via dei Mille might have killed Rino and Pasquale."

She shook her head energetically. She was paler than usual

and under her eyes were deep purple hollows. She didn't agree but she didn't tell me why.

27.

I was promoted with nines in all my subjects, I would even receive something called a scholarship. Of the forty we had been, thirty-two remained. Gino failed, Alfonso had to retake the exams in three subjects in September. Urged by my father, I went to see Maestra Oliviero—my mother was against it, she didn't like the teacher to interfere in her family and claim the right to make decisions about her children in her place—with the usual two packets, one of sugar and one of coffee, bought at the Bar Solara, to thank her for her interest in me.

She wasn't feeling well, she had something in her throat that hurt her, but she was full of praise, congratulated me on how hard I had worked, said that I looked a little too pale and that she intended to telephone a cousin who lived on Ischia to see if she would let me stay with her for a little while. I thanked her, but said nothing to my mother of that possibility. I already knew that she wouldn't let me go. Me on Ischia? Me alone on the ferry traveling over the sea? Not to mention me on the beach, swimming, in a bathing suit?

I didn't even mention it to Lila. Her life in a few months had lost even the adventurous aura associated with the shoe factory, and I didn't want to boast about the promotion, the scholarship, a possible vacation in Ischia. In appearance things had improved: Marcello Solara had stopped following her. But after the violence in Piazza dei Martiri something completely unexpected happened that puzzled her. He came to the shop to ask about Rino's condition, and the honor conferred by that visit perturbed Fernando. But Rino, who had been careful not to tell his father what had happened (to explain the bruises on his face and his body he made up a story that he had fallen off a friend's Lambretta), and worried that Marcello might say one word too many, had immediately steered him out into the street. They had taken a short walk. Rino had reluctantly thanked Solara both for his intervention and for the kindness of coming to see how he was. Two minutes and they had said goodbye. When he returned to the shop his father had said:

"Finally you're doing something good."

"What?"

"A friendship with Marcello Solara."

"There's no friendship, Papa."

"Then it means you were a fool and a fool you remain."

Fernando wanted to say that something was changing and that his son, whatever he wanted to call that thing with the Solaras, would do well to encourage it. He was right. Marcello returned a couple of days later with his grandfather's shoes to resole; then he invited Rino to go for a drive. Then he urged him to apply for a license, assuming the responsibility for getting him to practice in the 1100. Maybe it wasn't friendship, but the Solaras certainly had taken a liking to Rino.

When Lila, ignorant of these visits, which took place entirely at the shoemaker's shop, where she never went, heard about them, she, unlike her father, felt an increasing worry. First she remembered the battle of the fireworks and thought: Rino hates the Solaras too much, it can't be that he'll let himself be taken in. Then she had had to observe that Marcello's attentions were seducing her older brother even more than her parents. She now knew Rino's fragility, but still she was angry at the way the Solaras were getting into his head, making him a kind of happy little monkey.

"What's wrong with it?" I objected once.

"They're dangerous."

"Here everything is dangerous."

"Did you see what Michele took out of the car, in Piazza dei Martiri?"

"No."

"An iron bar."

"The others had sticks."

"You don't see it, Lenù, but the bar was sharpened into a point: if he wanted he could have thrust it into the chest, or the stomach, of one of those guys."

"Well, you threatened Marcello with the shoemaker's knife."

At that point she grew irritated and said I didn't understand. And probably it was true. It was her brother, not mine; I liked to be logical, while she had different needs, she wanted to get Rino away from that relationship. But as soon as she made some critical remark Rino shut her up, threatened her, sometimes beat her. And so things, willy-nilly, proceeded to the point where, one evening in late June—I was at Lila's house, I was helping her fold sheets, or something, I don't remember—the door opened and Rino entered, followed by Marcello.

He had invited Solara to dinner, and Fernando, who had just returned from the shop, very tired, at first was irritated, and then felt honored, and behaved cordially. Not to mention Nunzia: she became agitated, thanked Marcello for the three bottles of good wine that he had brought, pulled the other children into the kitchen so they wouldn't be disruptive.

I myself was involved with Lila in the preparations for dinner.

"I'll put roach poison in it," Lila said, furious, at the stove, and we laughed, while Nunzia shut us up.

"He's come to marry you," I said to provoke her, "he's going to ask your father."

"He is deceiving himself."

"Why," Nunzia asked anxiously, "if he likes you do you say no?"

"Ma, I already told him no."

"Really?"

"Yes."

"What are you saying?"

"It's true," I said in confirmation.

"Your father must never know, otherwise he'll kill you."

At dinner only Marcello spoke. It was clear that he had invited himself, and Rino, who didn't know how to say no to him, sat at the table nearly silent, or laughed for no reason. Solara addressed himself mainly to Fernando, but never neglected to pour water or wine for Nunzia, for Lila, for me. He said to him how much he was respected in the neighborhood because he was such a good cobbler. He said that his father had always spoken well of his skill. He said that Rino had an unlimited admiration for his abilities as a shoemaker.

Fernando, partly because of the wine, was moved. He muttered something in praise of Silvio Solara, and even went so far as to say that Rino was a good worker and was becoming a good shoemaker. Then Marcello started to praise the need for progress. He said that his grandfather had started with a cellar, then his father had enlarged it, and today the bar-pastry shop Solara was what it was, everybody knew it, people came from all over Naples to have coffee, eat a pastry.

"What an exaggeration," Lila exclaimed, and her father gave her a silencing look.

But Marcello smiled at her humbly and admitted, "Yes, maybe I'm exaggerating a little, but just to say that money has to circulate. You begin with a cellar and from generation to generation you can go far."

At this point, with Rino showing evident signs of uneasiness, he began to praise the idea of making new shoes. And from that moment he began to look at Lila as if in praising the energy of the generations he were praising her in particular. He said: if someone feels capable, if he's clever, if he can invent

good things, which are pleasing, why not try? He spoke in a
nice, charming dialect and as he spoke he never stopped staring at my friend. I felt, I saw that he was in love as in the songs,
that he would have liked to kiss her, that he wanted to breathe
her breath, that she would be able to make of him all she
wanted, that in his eyes she embodied all possible feminine
qualities.

"I know," Marcello concluded, "that your children made a
very nice pair of shoes, size 43, just my size."

A long silence fell. Rino stared at his plate and didn't dare
look up at his father. Only the sound of the goldfinch at the
window could be heard. Fernando said slowly, "Yes, they're
size 43."

"I would very much like to see them, if you don't mind?"

Fernando stammered, "I don't know where they are.
Nunzia, do you know?"

"She has them," Rino said, indicating his sister.

"I did have them, yes, I had put them in the storeroom. But
then Mamma told me to clean it out the other day and I threw
them away. Since no one liked them."

Rino said angrily, "You're a liar, go and get the shoes right
now."

Fernando said nervously, "Go get the shoes, go on."

Lila burst out, addressing her father, "How is it that now you
want them? I threw them away because you said you didn't like
them."

Fernando pounded the table with his open hand, the wine
trembled in the glasses.

"Get up and go get the shoes, right now."

Lila pushed away her chair, stood up.

"I threw them away," she repeated weakly and left the
room.

She didn't come back.

The time passed in silence. The first to become alarmed was

Marcello. He said, with real concern, "Maybe I was wrong, I didn't know that there were problems."

"There's no problem," Fernando said, and whispered to his wife, "Go see what your daughter is doing."

Nunzia left the room. When she came back she was embarrassed, she couldn't find Lila. We looked for her all over the house, she wasn't there. We called her from the window: nothing. Marcello, desolate, took his leave. As soon as he had gone Fernando shouted at his wife, "God's truth, this time I'm going to kill your daughter."

Rino joined his father in the threat, Nunzia began to cry. I left almost on tiptoe, frightened. But as soon as I closed the door and came out on the landing Lila called me. She was on the top floor, I went up on tiptoe. She was huddled next to the door to the terrace, in the shadows. She had the shoes in her lap, for the first time I saw them finished. They shone in the feeble light of a bulb hanging on an electrical cable. "What would it cost you to let him see them?" I asked, confused.

She shook her head energetically. "I don't even want him to touch them."

But she was as if overwhelmed by her own extreme reaction. Her lower lip trembled, something that never happened.

Gradually I persuaded her to go home, she couldn't stay hiding there forever. I went with her, counting on the fact that my presence would protect her. But there were shouts, insults, some blows just the same. Fernando screamed that on a whim she had made him look foolish in the eyes of an important guest. Rino tore the shoes out of her hand, saying that they were his, the work had been done by him. She began to cry, murmuring, "I worked on them, too, but it would have been better if I'd never done it, you've become a mad beast." It was Nunzia who put an end to that torture. She turned pale and in a voice that was not her usual voice she ordered her children, and even her husband—she who was always so submissive—to stop it immediately, to give the shoes to her, not to venture a single word if they didn't want her to jump out the window. Rino gave her the shoes and for the moment things ended there. I slipped away.

28.

But Rino wouldn't give in, and in the following days he continued to attack his sister with words and fists. Every time Lila and I met I saw a new bruise. After a while I felt that she was resigned. One morning he insisted that they go out together, that she come with him to the shoemaker's shop. On the way they both sought, with wavy moves, to end the war. Rino said that he loved her but that she didn't love anyone, neither her parents nor her siblings. Lila murmured, "What do you mean by love, what does love mean for our family? Let's hear." Step by step, he revealed to her what he had in mind.

"If Marcello likes the shoes, Papa will change his mind."

"I don't think so."

"Yes, he will. And if Marcello buys them, Papa will understand that your designs are good, that they're profitable, and he'll have us start work."

"The three of us?"

"He and I and maybe you, too. Papa is capable of making a pair of shoes, completely finished, in four days, at most five. And I, if I work hard, I'll show you that I can do the same. We make them, we sell them, and we finance ourselves."

"Who do we sell them to, always Marcello Solara?"

"The Solaras market them; they know people who count. They'll do the publicity for us."

"They'll do it free?"

"If they want a small percentage we'll give it to them."

"And why should they be content with a small percentage?"

"They've taken a liking to me."

"The Solaras?"

"Yes."

Lila sighed. "Just one thing: I'll tell Papa and see what he thinks."

"Don't you dare."

"This way or not at all."

Rino was silent, very nervous.

"All right. Anyway, you speak, you can speak better."

That evening, at dinner, in front of her brother, whose face was fiery red, Lila said to Fernando that Marcello not only had shown great curiosity about the shoe enterprise but might even be interested in buying the shoes for himself, and that in fact, if he was enthusiastic about the matter from a commercial point of view, he would advertise the product in the circles he frequented, in exchange, naturally, for a small percentage of the sales.

"This I said," Rino explained with lowered eyes, "not Marcello."

Fernando looked at his wife: Lila understood that they had talked about it and had already, secretly, reached a conclusion.

"Tomorrow," he said, "I'll put your shoes in the shop window. If someone wants to see them, wants to try them, wants to buy them, whatever fucking thing, he has to talk to me, I am the one who decides."

A few days later I passed by the shop. Rino was working, Fernando was working, both heads bent over the work. I saw in the window, among boxes of shoe polish and laces, the beautiful, elegant shoes made by the Cerullos. A sign pasted to the window, certainly written by Rino, said, pompously: "Shoes handmade by the Cerullos here." Father and son waited for good luck to arrive.

But Lila was skeptical, sulky. She had no faith in the ingenuous hypothesis of her brother and was afraid of the indecipherable agreement between her father and mother. In other words she expected bad things. A week passed, and no one showed the least interest in the shoes in the window, not even Marcello. Only because he was cornered by Rino, in fact almost dragged to the shop, did Solara glance at them, but as if he had other things on his mind. He tried them, of course, but said they were a little tight, took them off immediately, and disappeared without even a word of compliment, as if he had a stomachache and had to hurry home. Disappointment of father and son. But two minutes later Marcello reappeared. Rino jumped up, beaming, and took his hand as if some agreement, by that pure and simple reappearance, had already been made. But Marcello ignored him and turned directly to Fernando. He said, all in one breath:

"I have very serious intentions, Don Fernà. I would like the hand of your daughter Lina."

29.

Rino reacted to that turn with a violent fever that kept him away from work for days. When, abruptly, the fever went down, he had disturbing symptoms: he got out of bed in the middle of the night, and, while still sleeping, silent, and extremely agitated, he went to the door and struggled to open it, with his eyes wide open. Nunzia and Lila, frightened, dragged him back to bed.

Fernando, however, who with his wife had immediately guessed Marcello's true intentions, spoke with his daughter calmly. He explained to her that Marcello Solara's proposal was important not only for her future but for that of the whole family. He told her that she was still a child and didn't have to say yes immediately, but added that he, as her father, advised her to consent. A long engagement at home would slowly get her used to the marriage.

Lila answered with equal tranquility that rather than be engaged to Marcello Solara and marry him she would go and drown herself in the pond. A great quarrel arose, but she didn't change her mind.

I was stunned by the news. I knew that Marcello wanted to be Lila's boyfriend at all costs, but it would never have entered my mind that at our age one could receive a proposal of marriage. And yet Lila had received one, and she wasn't yet fifteen, she hadn't yet had a secret boyfriend, had never kissed anyone. I sided with her immediately. Get married? To Marcello Solara? Maybe even have children? No, absolutely no. I encouraged her to fight that new war against her father and swore I would support her, even if he had already lost his composure and now was threatening her, saying that for her own good he would break every bone in her body if she didn't accept a proposal of that importance.

But I couldn't stay with her. In the middle of July something happened that I should have thought of but that instead caught me unawares and overwhelmed me. One late afternoon, after the usual walk through the neighborhood with Lila, discussing what was happening to her and how to get out of it, I came home and my sister Elisa opened the door. She said in a state of excitement that in the dining room was her teacher, that is, Maestra Oliviero. She was talking to our mother.

I looked timidly into the room, my mother stammered, in annoyance, "Maestra Oliviero says you need to rest, you're worn out."

I looked at the teacher without understanding. She seemed the one in need of rest, she was pale and her face was puffy. She said to me, "My cousin responded just yesterday: you can go to her in Ischia, and stay there until the end of August. She'll be happy to have you, you just have to help a little in the house."

She spoke to me as if she were my mother and as if my

mother, the real one, with the injured leg and the wandering eye, were only a disposable living being, and as such not to be taken into consideration. Nor did she go away after that communication, but stayed another hour showing me one by one the books that she had brought to lend to me. She explained to me which I should read first and which after, she made me swear that before reading them I would make covers for them, she ordered me to give them all back at the end of the summer without a single dog-ear. My mother endured all this patiently. She sat attentively, even though her wandering eye gave her a dazed expression. She exploded only when the teacher, finally, took her leave, with a disdainful farewell and not even a caress for my sister, who had counted on it and would have been proud. She turned to me, overwhelmed by bitterness for the humiliation that it seemed to her she had suffered on my account. She said, "The signorina must go and rest on Ischia, the signorina is too exhausted. Go and make dinner, go on, or I'll hit you."

Two days later, however, after taking my measurements and rapidly making me a bathing suit—I don't know where she copied it from—she herself took me to the ferry. Along the street to the port, while she bought me the ticket, and then while she waited for me to get on, she besieged me with warnings. What frightened her most was the crossing. "Let's hope the sea isn't rough," she said almost to herself, and swore that when I was a child she had taken me to Coroglio every day, so my catarrh would dry out, and that the sea was beautiful and I had learned to swim. But I didn't remember Coroglio or the sea or learning to swim, and I told her. And her tone became resentful, as if to say that if I drowned it would not be her fault—that what she was supposed to do to avoid it she had done—but because of my own forgetfulness. Then she ordered me not to go far from the shore even when the sea was calm, and to stay home if it was rough or there was a red flag. "Especially," she said, "if you have a full stomach or your period, you mustn't even get your feet wet." Before she left she asked an old sailor to keep an eye on me. When the ferry left the wharf I was terrified and at the same time happy. For the first time I was leaving home, I was going on a journey, a journey by sea. The large body of my mother—along with the neighborhood, and Lila's troubles—grew distant, and vanished.

30.

I blossomed. The teacher's cousin was called Nella Incardo and she lived in Barano. I arrived in the town by bus, and found the house easily. Nella was a big, kind woman, very lively, talkative, unmarried. She rented rooms to vacationers, keeping for herself one small room and the kitchen. I would sleep in the kitchen. I had to make up my bed in the evening and take it all apart (boards, legs, mattress) in the morning. I discovered that I had some mandatory obligations: to get up at six-thirty, make breakfast for her and her guests—when I arrived there was an English couple with two children—tidy up and wash cups and bowls, set the table for dinner, and wash the dishes before going to sleep. Otherwise I was free. I could sit on the terrace and read with the sea in front of me, or walk along a steep white road toward a long, wide, dark beach that was called Spiaggia dei Maronti.

In the beginning, after all the fears that my mother had inoculated me with and all the troubles I had with my body, I spent the time on the terrace, dressed, writing a letter to Lila every day, each one filled with questions, clever remarks, lively descriptions of the island. But one morning Nella made fun of me, saying, "What are you doing like this? Put on your bathing suit." When I put it on she burst out laughing, she thought it was old-fashioned. She sewed me one that she said was more modern, very low over the bosom, more fitted around the bottom, of a beautiful blue. I tried it on and she was enthusiastic, she said it was time I went to the sea, enough of the terrace.

The next day, amid a thousand fears and a thousand curiosities, I set out with a towel and a book toward the Maronti. The trip seemed very long, I met no one coming up or going down. The beach was endless and deserted, with a granular sand that rustled at every step. The sea gave off an intense odor and a sharp, monotonous sound.

I stood looking for a long time at that great mass of water. Then I sat on the towel, uncertain what to do. Finally I got up and stuck my feet in. How had it happened that I lived in a city like Naples and never thought, not once, of swimming in the sea? And yet it was so. I advanced cautiously, letting the water rise from my feet to my ankles, to my thighs. Then I missed a step and sank. Terrified, I gasped for air, swallowed water, returned to the surface, to the air. I realized that it came naturally to move my feet and arms in a certain way to keep myself afloat. So I knew how to swim. My mother really had taken me to the sea as a child and there, while she took the sand treatments, I had learned to swim. I saw her in a flash, younger, less ravaged, sitting on the black sand in the midday sun, in a flowered white dress, her good leg covered to the knee by her dress, the injured one completely buried in the burning sand.

The seawater and the sun rapidly erased the inflammation of the acne from my face. I burned, I darkened. I waited for letters from Lila, we had promised when we said goodbye, but none came. I practiced speaking English a little with the family at Nella's. They understood that I wanted to learn and spoke to me with increasing kindness, and I improved quite a lot. Nella, who was always cheerful, encouraged me, and I began to interpret for her. Meanwhile she didn't miss any opportunity to compliment me. She made me enormous meals, and she was a really good cook. She said that I had been a stick when I arrived and now, thanks to her treatment, I was beautiful.

In other words, the last ten days of July gave me a sense of well-being that I had never known before. I felt a sensation that later in my life was often repeated: the joy of the new. I liked everything: getting up early, making breakfast, tidying up, walking in Barano, taking the road to the Maronti, uphill and down, lying in the sun and reading, going for a swim, returning to my book. I did not feel homesick for my father, my brothers and sister, my mother, the streets of the neighborhood, the public gardens. I missed only Lila, Lila who didn't answer my letters. I was afraid of what was happening to her, good or bad, in my absence. It was an old fear, a fear that has never left me: the fear that, in losing pieces of her life, mine lost intensity and importance. And the fact that she didn't answer emphasized that preoccupation. However hard I tried in my letters to communicate the privilege of the days in Ischia, my river of words and her silence seemed to demonstrate that my life was splendid but uneventful, which left me time to write to her every day, while hers was dark but full.

At the end of July Nella told me that on the first of August, in place of the English, a Neapolitan family was to arrive. It was the second year they had come. Very respectable people, very polite, refined: especially the husband, a true gentleman who always said wonderful things to her. And then the older son, really a fine boy: tall, thin but strong, this year he was seventeen. "You won't be alone anymore," she said to me, and I was embarrassed, immediately filled with anxiety about this young man who was arriving, fearful that we wouldn't be able to speak two words to each other, that he wouldn't like me.

As soon as the English departed—they left me a couple of novels to practice my reading, and their address, so that if I ever decided to go to England I should go and see them—Nella had me help her clean the rooms, do the laundry, remake the beds. I was glad to do it, and as I was washing the floor she called to me from the kitchen: "How clever you are, you can even read in English. Are the books you brought not enough?"

And she went on praising me from a distance, in a loud voice, for how disciplined I was, how sensible, for how I read all day and also at night. When I joined her in the kitchen I found her with a book in her hand. She said that the man who was arriving the next day had written it himself. Nella kept it on her night table, every evening she read a poem, first to herself and then aloud. Now she knew them all by heart.

"Look what he wrote to me," she said, and handed me the book.

It was *Attempts at Serenity*, by Donato Sarratore. The dedication read: "*To darling Nella, and to her jams.*"

31.

I immediately wrote to Lila: pages and pages of apprehension, joy, the wish to flee, intense foreshadowing of the moment when I would see Nino Sarratore, I would walk to the Maronti with him, we would swim, we would look at the moon and the stars, we would sleep under the same roof. All I could think of was that intense moment when, holding his brother by the hand, a century ago—ah, how much time had passed—he had declared his love. We were children then: now I felt grown-up, almost old.

The next day I went to the bus stop to help the guests carry their bags. I was very agitated, I hadn't slept all night. The bus arrived, stopped, the travelers got out. I recognized Donato Sarratore, I recognized Lidia, his wife, I recognized Marisa, although she was very changed, I recognized Clelia, who was always by herself, I recognized little Pino, who was now a solemn kid, and I imagined that the capricious child who was annoying his mother must be the one who, the last time I had seen the entire Sarratore family, was still in a carriage, under the projectiles hurled by Melina. But I didn't see Nino.

Marisa threw her arms around my neck with an enthusiasm I would never have expected: in all those years I had never, absolutely never, thought of her, while she said she had often thought of me with great nostalgia. When she alluded to the days in the neighborhood and told her parents that I was the daughter of Greco, the porter, Lidia, her mother, made a grimace of distaste and hurried to grab her little child to scold him for something or other, while Donato Sarratore saw to the luggage without even a remark like: How is your father.

I felt depressed. The Sarratores settled in their rooms, and I went to the sea with Marisa, who knew the Maronti and all Ischia well, and was already impatient, she wanted to go to the Port, where there was more activity, and to Forio, and to Casamicciola, anywhere but Barano, which according to her was a morgue. She told me that she was studying to be a secretary and had a boyfriend whom I would meet soon because he was coming to see her, but secretly. Finally she told me something that tugged at my heart. She knew all about me, she knew that I went to the high school, that I was very clever, and that Gino, the pharmacist's son, was my boyfriend.

"Who told you?"

"My brother."

So Nino had recognized me, so he knew who I was, so it was not inattention but perhaps timidity, perhaps uneasiness, perhaps shame for the declaration he had made to me as a child.

"I stopped going with Gino ages ago," I said. "Your brother isn't very well informed."

"All he thinks about is studying, it's already a lot that he told me about you, usually he's got his head in the clouds."

"He's not coming?"

"He'll come when Papa leaves."

She spoke to me very critically about Nino. He had no feelings. He was never excited about anything, he didn't get angry but he wasn't nice, either. He was closed up in himself, all he cared about was studying. He didn't like anything, he was cold-blooded. The only person who managed to get to him a little was his father. Not that they quarreled, he was a respectful and obedient son. But Marisa knew very well that Nino couldn't stand his father. Whereas she adored him. He was the best and most intelligent man in the world.

"Is your father staying long? When is he leaving?" I asked her with perhaps excessive interest.

"Just three days. He has to work."

"And Nino arrives in three days?"

"Yes. He pretended that he had to help the family of a friend of his move."

"And it's not true?"

"He doesn't have any friends. And anyway he wouldn't carry that stone from here to there even for my mamma, the only person he loves even a little, imagine if he's going to help a friend."

We went swimming, we dried off walking along the shore. Laughing, she pointed out to me something I had never noticed. At the end of the black beach were some motionless white forms. She dragged me, still laughing, over the burning sand and at a certain point it became clear that they were people. Living people, covered with mud. It was some sort of treatment, we didn't know for what. We lay on the sand, rolling over, shoving each other, pretending to be mummies like the people down the beach. We had fun playing, then went swimming again.

In the evening the Sarratore family had dinner in the kitchen and invited Nella and me to join them. It was a wonderful evening. Lidia never mentioned the neighborhood, but, once her first impulse of hostility had passed, she asked about me. When Marisa told her that I was very studious and went to the same school as Nino she became particularly nice. The most congenial of all, however, was Donato Sarratore. He loaded Nella with compliments, praised my scholastic record, was extremely considerate toward Lidia, played with Ciro, the baby, wanted to clean up himself, kept me from washing the dishes.

I studied him carefully and he seemed different from the way I remembered him. He was thinner, certainly, and had grown a mustache, but apart from his looks there was something more that I couldn't understand and that had to do with his behavior. Maybe he seemed to me more paternal than my father and uncommonly courteous.

This sensation intensified in the next two days. Sarratore, when we went to the beach, wouldn't allow Lidia or us two girls to carry anything. He loaded himself up with the umbrella, the bags with towels and food for lunch, on the way and, equally, on the way back, when the road was all uphill. He gave the bundles to us only when Ciro whined and insisted on being carried. He had a lean body, without much hair. He wore a bathing suit of an indefinable color, not of fabric, it seemed a light wool. He swam a lot but didn't go far out, he wanted to show me and Marisa how to swim freestyle. His daughter swam like him, with the same very careful, slow arm strokes, and I immediately began to imitate them. He expressed himself more in Italian than in dialect and tended somewhat insistently, especially with me, to come out with convoluted sentences and unusual phrasings. He summoned us cheerfully, me, Lidia, Marisa, to run back and forth on the beach with him to tone our muscles, and meanwhile he made us laugh with funny faces, little cries, comical walks. When he swam with his wife they stayed together, floating, they talked in low voices, and often laughed. The day he left, I was sorry as Marisa was sorry, as Lidia was sorry, as Nella was sorry. The house, though it echoed with our voices, seemed silent, a tomb. The only consolation was that finally Nino would arrive.

32.

I tried to suggest to Marisa that we should go and wait for him at the Port, but she refused, she said her brother didn't deserve that attention. Nino arrived in the evening. Tall, thin, in a blue shirt, dark pants, and sandals, with a bag over his shoulder, he showed not the least emotion at finding me in Ischia, in that house, so I thought that in Naples they must have a telephone, that Marisa had found a way of warning him. At dinner he spoke in monosyllables, and he didn't appear at breakfast. He woke up late, we went late to the beach, and he carried little or nothing. He dove in immediately, decisively, and swam out to sea effortlessly, without the ostentatious virtuosity of his father. He disappeared: I was afraid he had drowned, but neither Marisa nor Lidia was worried. He reappeared almost two hours later and began reading, smoking one cigarette after another. He read for the entire day, without saying a word to us, arranging the cigarette butts in the sand in a row, two by two. I also started reading, refusing the invitation of Marisa to walk along the shore. At dinner he ate in a hurry and went out. I cleared, I washed the dishes thinking of him. I made my bed in the kitchen and started reading again, waiting for him to come back. I read until one, then fell asleep with the light on and the book open on my chest. In the morning I woke up with the light off and the book closed. I thought it must have been him and felt a flare of love in my veins that I had never experienced before.

In a few days things improved. I realized that every so often he would look at me and then turn away. I asked him what he was reading, I told him what I was reading. We talked about our reading, annoying Marisa. At first he seemed to listen attentively, then, just like Lila, he started talking and went on, increasingly under the spell of his own arguments. Since I wanted him to be aware of my intelligence I endeavored to interrupt him, to say what I thought, but it was difficult, he seemed content with my presence only if I was silently listening, which I quickly resigned myself to doing. Besides, he said things that I could never have thought, or at least said, with the same assurance, and he said them in a strong, engaging Italian.

Marisa sometimes threw balls of sand at us, and sometimes burst in, shouting "Stop it, who cares about this Dostoyevsky, who gives a damn about the Karamazovs." Then Nino abruptly broke off and walked along the shore, head lowered, until he became a tiny speck. I spent some time with Marisa talking about her boyfriend, who couldn't come to see her, which made her cry. Meanwhile I felt better and better, I couldn't believe that life could be like this. Maybe, I thought, the girls of Via dei Mille—the one dressed all in green, for example—had a life like this.

Every three or four days Donato Sarratore returned, but stayed at most for twenty-four hours, then left. He said that all he could think of was the thirteenth of August, when he would settle in Barano for two full weeks. As soon as his father appeared, Nino became a shadow. He ate, disappeared, reappeared late at night, and didn't say a single word. He listened to him with a compliant sort of half smile, and whatever his father uttered he gave no sign of agreement but neither did he oppose it. The only time he said something definite and explicit was when Donato mentioned the longed-for thirteenth of August. Then, a moment later, he reminded his mother—his mother, not Donato—that right after the mid-August holiday he had to return to Naples because he had arranged with some school friends to meet—they planned to get together in a country house in the Avellinese—and begin their summer homework. "It's a lie," Marisa whispered to me, "he has no homework." But his mother praised him, and even his father. In fact, Donato started off right away on one of his favorite topics: Nino was fortunate to be able to study; he himself had barely finished the second year of vocational school when he had had to go to work, but if he had been able to study as his son was doing, who knows where he might have gone. And he concluded, "Study, Ninù, go on, make Papa proud, and do what I was unable to do."

That tone bothered Nino more than anything else. Sometimes, just to get away, he went so far as to invite Marisa and me to go out with him. He would say gloomily to his parents, as if we had been tormenting him, "They want to get an ice cream, they want to go for a little walk, I'll take them."

Marisa hurried eagerly to get ready and I regretted that I always had the same shabby old dress. But it seemed to me that he didn't much care if I was pretty or ugly. As soon as we left the house he started talking, which made Marisa uncomfortable, she said it would have been better for her to stay home. I, however, hung on Nino's every word. It greatly astonished me that, in the tumult of the Port, among the young and not so young men who looked at Marisa and me purposefully, he showed not a trace of that disposition to violence that Pasquale, Rino, Antonio, Enzo showed when they went out with us and someone gave us one glance too many. As an intimidating guardian of our bodies he had little value. Maybe because he was engrossed in the things that were going on in his head, by an eagerness to talk to me about them, he would let anything happen to us.

That was how Marisa made friends with some boys from Forio, they came to see her at Barano, and she brought them with us to the beach at the Maronti. And so the three of us began to go out every evening. We all went to the Port, but once we arrived she went off with her new friends (when in the world would Pasquale have been so free with Carmela, Antonio with Ada?) and we walked along the sea. Then we met her around ten and returned home.

One evening, as soon as we were alone, Nino said suddenly that as a boy he had greatly envied the relationship between Lila and me. He saw us from a distance, always together, always talking, and he would have liked to be friends with us, but never had the courage. Then he smiled and said, "You remember the declaration I made to you?"

"Yes."

"I liked you a lot."

I blushed, I whispered stupidly, "Thank you."

"I thought we would become engaged and we would all three be together forever, you, me, and your friend."

"Together?"

He smiled at himself as a child.

"I didn't understand anything about engagements."

Then he asked me about Lila.

"Did she go on studying?"

"No."

"What does she do?"

"She helps her parents."

"She was so smart, you couldn't keep up with her, she made my head a blur."

He said it just that way—*she made my head a blur*—and if at first I had been a little disappointed because he had said that his declaration of love had been only an attempt to introduce himself into my and Lila's relationship, this time I suffered in an obvious way, I felt a real pain in my chest.

"She's not like that anymore," I said. "She's changed."

And I felt an urge to add, "Have you heard how the teachers at school talk about me?" Luckily I managed to restrain myself. But, after that conversation, I stopped writing to Lila:

I had trouble telling her what was happening to me, and anyway she wouldn't answer. I devoted myself instead to taking care of Nino. I knew that he woke up late and I invented excuses of every sort not to have breakfast with the others. I waited for him, I went to the beach with him, I got his things ready, I carried them, we went swimming together. But when he went out to sea I didn't feel able to follow, I returned to the shoreline to watch apprehensively the wake he left, the dark speck of his head. I became anxious if I lost him, I was happy when I saw him return. In other words I loved him and knew it and was content to love him.

But meanwhile the mid-August holiday approached. One evening I told him that I didn't want to go to the Port, I would rather walk to the Maronti, there was a full moon. I hoped that he would come with me, rather than take his sister, who was eager to go to the Port, where by now she had a sort of boyfriend with whom, she told me, she exchanged kisses and embraces, betraying the boyfriend in Naples. Instead he went with Marisa. As a matter of principle, I set out on the rocky road that led to the beach. The sand was cold, gray-black in the moonlight, the sea scarcely breathed. There was not a living soul and I began to weep with loneliness. What was I, who was I? I felt pretty again, my pimples were gone, the sun and the sea had made me slimmer, and yet the person I liked and whom I wished to be liked by showed no interest in me. What signs did I carry, what fate? I thought of the neighborhood as of a whirlpool from which any attempt at escape was an illusion. Then I heard the rustle of sand, I turned, I saw the shadow of Nino. He sat down beside me. He had to go back and get his sister in an hour. I felt he was nervous, he was hitting the sand with the heel of his left foot. He didn't talk about books, he began suddenly speaking of his father.

"I will devote my life," he said, as if he were speaking of a mission, "to trying not to resemble him."

"He's a nice man."

"Everyone says that."

"And so?"

He had a sarcastic expression that for a few seconds made him ugly.

"How is Melina?"

I looked at him in astonishment. I had been very careful never to mention Melina in those days of intense conversation, and here he was talking about her.

"All right."

"He was her lover. He knew perfectly well that she was a fragile woman, but he took her just the same, out of pure vanity. Out of vanity he would hurt anyone and never feel responsible. Since he is convinced that he makes everyone happy, he thinks that everything is forgiven him. He goes to Mass every Sunday. He treats us children with respect. He is always considerate of my mother. But he betrays her continually. He's a hypocrite, he makes me sick."

I didn't know what to say. In the neighborhood terrible things could happen, fathers and sons often came to blows, like Rino and Fernando, for example. But the violence of those few carefully constructed sentences hurt me. Nino hated his father with all his strength, that was why he talked so much about the Karamazovs. But that wasn't the point. What disturbed me profoundly was that Donato Sarratore, as far as I had seen with my own eyes, heard with my own ears, was not repellent, he was the father that every girl, every boy should want, and Marisa in fact adored him. Besides, if his sin was the capacity to love, I didn't see anything particularly evil, even of my father my mother would say angrily, Who knows what he had been up to. As a result those lashing phrases, that cutting tone seemed to me terrible. I murmured, "He and Melina were overcome by passion, like Dido and Aeneas. These are things that are hurtful, but also very moving."

"He swore faithfulness to my mother before God," he exclaimed suddenly. "He doesn't respect her or God." And he jumped up in agitation, his eyes were beautiful, shining. "Not even you understand me," he said, walking off with long strides.

I caught up to him, my heart pounding.

"I understand you," I murmured, and cautiously took his arm.

We had scarcely touched, the contact burned my fingers, I immediately let go. He bent over and kissed me on the lips, a very light kiss.

"I'm leaving tomorrow," he said.

"But the thirteenth is the day after tomorrow."

He didn't answer. We went back to Barano speaking of books, then we went to get Marisa at the Port. I felt his mouth on mine.

33.

I cried all night, in the silent kitchen. I fell asleep at dawn. Nella came to wake me and reproached me, she said that Nino had wanted to have breakfast on the terrace in order not to disturb me. He had left.

I dressed in a hurry, and she saw that I was suffering. "Go on," she yielded, finally, "maybe you'll be in time." I ran to the Port hoping to get there before the ferry left, but the boat was already out at sea.

Some difficult days passed. Cleaning the rooms I found a blue paper bookmark that belonged to Nino and I hid it among my things. At night, in my bed in the kitchen, I sniffed it, kissed it, licked it with the tip of my tongue and cried. My own desperate passion moved me and my weeping fed on itself.

Then Donato Sarratore arrived for his two-week holiday. He was sorry that his son had left, but pleased that he had joined his schoolmates in the Avellinese to study. "He's a truly serious boy," he said to me, "like you. I'm proud of him, as I imagine your father must be proud of you."

The presence of that reassuring man calmed me. He wanted to meet Marisa's new friends, he invited them one evening to have a big bonfire on the beach. He himself gathered all the wood he could find and piled it up, and he stayed with us until late. The boy with whom Marisa was carrying on a half-steady relationship strummed a guitar and Donato sang, he had a beautiful voice. Then, late at night, he himself began to play and he played well, he improvised dance tunes. Some began to dance, Marisa first.

I looked at that man and thought: he and his son have not even a feature in common. Nino is tall, he has a delicate face, the forehead buried under black hair, the mouth always half-closed, with inviting lips; Donato instead is of average height, his features are pronounced, he has a receding hairline, his mouth is compact, almost without lips. Nino has brooding eyes that see beyond things and persons and seem to be frightened; Donato has a gaze that is always receptive, that adores the appearance of every thing or person and is always smiling on them. Nino has something that's eating him inside, like Lila, and it's a gift and a suffering; they aren't content, they never give in, they fear what is happening around them; this man, no, he appears to love every manifestation of life, as if every lived second had an absolute clarity.

From that evening on, Nino's father seemed to me a solid remedy not only against the darkness into which his son had driven me, departing after an almost imperceptible kiss, but also—I realized with amazement—against the darkness into which Lila had driven me by never responding to my letters. She and Nino scarcely know each other, I thought, they have never been friends, and yet now they seem to me very similar: they have no need of anything or anyone, and they always know what's right and what isn't. But if they're wrong? What is especially terrible about Marcello Solara, what is especially terrible about Donato Sarratore? I didn't understand. I loved both Lila and Nino, and now in a different way I missed them, but I was grateful to that hated father, who made me, and all us children, important, who gave us joy and peace that night at the Maronti. Suddenly I was glad that neither of the two was present on the island.

I began reading again, I wrote a last letter to Lila, in which I said that, since she hadn't ever answered me, I wouldn't write anymore. I bound myself instead to the Sarratore family, I felt I was the sister of Marisa, Pinuccio, and little Ciro, who now loved me tremendously and with me, only with me, wasn't naughty but played happily; we went looking for shells together. Lidia, whose hostility had conclusively turned into sympathy and fondness, often praised me for the precision that I put into everything: setting the table, cleaning the rooms, washing the dishes, entertaining the baby, reading and studying. One morning she made me try on a sundress that was too tight for her, and, since Nella and even Sarratore, called urgently to give an opinion, thought it very becoming, she gave it to me. At certain moments she even seemed to prefer me to Marisa. She said, "She's lazy and vain, I brought her up badly, she doesn't study; whereas you are so sensible about everything." "Just like Nino," she added once, "except that you're sunny and he is always irritable." But Donato, hearing those criticisms, responded sharply, and began to praise his oldest son. "He's as good as gold," he said, and with a look asked me for confirmation and I nodded yes with great conviction.

After his long swims Donato lay beside me to dry in the sun and read his newspaper, *Roma*, the only thing he read. I was struck by the fact that someone who wrote poems, who had even collected them in a volume, never opened a book. He hadn't brought any with him and was never curious about mine. At times he read aloud to me some passage from an article, words and sentiments that would have made Pasquale extremely angry and certainly Professor Galiani, too. But I was silent, I didn't feel like arguing with such a kind and courteous person, and spoiling the great esteem he had for me. Once he read me an entire article, from beginning to end, and every two lines he turned to Lidia smiling, and Lidia responded with a complicit smile. At the end he asked me, "Did you like it?"

It was an article on the speed of train travel as opposed to the speed of travel in the past, by horse carriage or on foot, along country lanes. It was written in high-flown sentences that he read with great feeling.

"Yes, very much," I said.

"See who wrote it: what do you read here?"

He held it out toward me, put the paper under my eyes. With emotion, I read: "Donato Sarratore."

Lidia burst out laughing and so did he. They left me on the beach to keep an eye on Ciro while they swam in their usual way, staying close to each other and whispering. I looked at them, I thought, Poor Melina, but without bitterness toward Sarratore. Assuming that Nino was right and that there really had been something between the two of them; assuming, in other words, that Sarratore really had betrayed Lidia, now, even more than before—now that I knew him somewhat—I couldn't feel that he was guilty, especially since it seemed to me that not even his wife felt he was guilty, although at the time she had compelled him to leave the neighborhood. As for Melina, I understood her, too. She had felt the joy of love for that so far from ordinary man—a conductor on the railroad but also a poet, a journalist—and her fragile mind had been unable to readjust to the rough normality of life without him. I was satisfied with these thoughts. I was pleased with everything, in those days, with my love for Nino, with my sadness, with the affection that I felt surrounded by, with my own capacity to read, think, reflect in solitude.

34.

Then, at the end of August, when that extraordinary period was about to come to an end, two important things happened, suddenly, on the same day. It was the twenty-fifth, I remember with precision because my birthday fell on that day. I got up, I prepared breakfast for everyone, at the table I said, "Today I'm fifteen," and as I said it I remembered that Lila had turned fifteen on the eleventh, but, in the grip of so many emotions, I hadn't remembered. Although customarily it was the saint's day that was celebrated—birthdays were considered irrelevant at the time—the Sarratores and Nella insisted on having a party, in the evening. I was pleased. They went to get ready for the beach, I began to clear the table, when the postman arrived.

I stuck my head out the window, the postman said there was a letter for Greco. I ran down with my heart pounding. I ruled out the possibility that my parents had written to me. Was it a letter from Lila, from Nino? It was from Lila. I tore open the envelope. There were five closely written pages, and I devoured them, but I understood almost nothing of what I read. It may seem strange today, and yet it really was so: even before I was overwhelmed by the contents, what struck me was that the writing contained Lila's voice. Not only that. From the first lines I thought of *The Blue Fairy*, the only text of hers that I had read, apart from our elementary-school homework, and I understood what, at the time, I had liked so much. There was, in *The Blue Fairy*, the same quality that struck me now: Lila was able to speak through writing; unlike me when I wrote, unlike Sarratore in his articles and poems, unlike even many writers I had read and was reading, she expressed herself in sentences that were well constructed, and without error, even though she had stopped going to school, but—further— she left no trace of effort, you weren't aware of the artifice of the written word. I read and I saw her, I heard her. The voice set in the writing overwhelmed me, enthralled me even more than when we talked face to face: it was completely cleansed of the dross of speech, of the confusion of the oral; it had the vivid orderliness that I imagined would belong to conversation if one were so fortunate as to be born from the head of Zeus and not from the Grecos, the Cerullos. I was ashamed of the childish pages I had written to her, the overwrought tone, the frivolity, the false cheer, the false grief. Who knows what Lila had thought of me. I felt contempt and bitterness toward Professor Gerace, who had deluded me by giving me a nine in Italian. The first effect of that letter was to make me feel, at the age of fifteen, on the day of my birthday, a fraud. School, with me, had made a mistake and proof was there, in Lila's letter.

Then, slowly, the contents reached me as well. Lila sent me good wishes for my birthday. She hadn't written because she was pleased that I was having fun in the sun, that I was comfortable with the Sarratores, that I loved Nino, that I liked Ischia so much, the beach of the Maronti, and she didn't want to spoil my vacation with her terrible stories. But now she had felt an urge to break the silence. Immediately after my departure Marcello Solara, with the consent of Fernando, had begun to appear at dinner every night. He came at eight-thirty and left exactly at ten-thirty. He always brought something: pastries, chocolates, sugar, coffee. She didn't touch anything, she kept him at a distance, he looked at her in silence. After the first week of that torture, since Lila acted as if he weren't there, he had decided to surprise her. He showed up in the morning with a big fellow, all sweaty, who deposited in the dining room an enormous cardboard box. Out of the box emerged an object that we all knew about but that very few in the neighborhood had in their house: a television, an apparatus, that is, with a screen on which one saw images, just as at the cinema, but the images came not from a projector but rather from the air, and inside the apparatus was a mysterious tube that was called a cathode. Because of that tube, mentioned continuously by the large sweaty man, the machine hadn't worked for days. Then, after various attempts, it had started, and now half the neighborhood, including my mother, my father, and my sister and brothers, came to the Cerullo house to see the miracle. Not Rino. He was better, the fever had definitely gone, but he no longer spoke to Marcello. When Marcello showed up, he began to disparage the television and after a while he either went to bed without eating or went out and wandered around with Pasquale and Antonio until late at night. Lila said that she herself loved the television. She especially liked to watch it with Melina, who came every night and sat silently for a long time, completely absorbed. It was the only moment of peace. Otherwise, everyone's anger was unloaded on her: her brother's anger because she had abandoned him to his fate as the slave of their father while she set off on a marriage that would make her a lady; the anger of Fernando and Nunzia because she was not nice to Solara but, rather, treated him like dirt; finally the anger of Marcello, who, although she hadn't accepted him, felt increasingly that he was her fiancé, in fact her master, and tended to pass from silent devotion to attempts to kiss her, to suspicious questions about where she went during the day, whom she saw, if she had had other boyfriends, if she had even just touched anyone. Since she wouldn't answer, or, worse still, teased him by telling him of kisses and embraces with nonexistent boyfriends, he one evening had whispered to her seriously, "You tease me, but remember when you threatened me with the knife? Well, if I find out that you like someone else, remember, I won't merely threaten you, I'll kill you." So she didn't know how to get out of this situation and she still carried her weapon, just in case. But she was terrified. She wrote, in the last pages, of feeling all the evil of the neighborhood around her. Rather, she wrote obscurely, good and evil are mixed together and reinforce each other in turn. Marcello, if you thought about it, was really a good arrangement, but the good tasted of the bad and the bad tasted of the good, it was a mixture that took your breath away. A few evenings earlier, something had happened that had really scared her. Marcello had left, the television was off, the house was empty, Rino was out, her parents were going to bed. She was alone in the kitchen washing the dishes and was tired, really without energy, when there was an explosion. She had turned suddenly and realized that the big copper pot had exploded. Like that, by itself. It was hanging on the nail where it normally hung, but in the middle there was a large hole and the rim was lifted and twisted and the pot itself was all deformed, as if it could no longer maintain its appearance as a pot. Her mother had hurried in in her nightgown and had blamed her for dropping it and ruining it. But a copper pot, even if you drop it, doesn't break and doesn't become mis-shapen like that. "It's this sort of thing," Lila concluded, "that frightens me. More than Marcello, more than anyone. And I feel that I have to find a solution, otherwise, everything, one thing after another, will break, everything, everything." She sent me many more good wishes, and, even if she wished the opposite, even if she couldn't wait to see me, even if she urgently needed my help, she hoped I would stay in Ischia with kind Signora Nella and never return to the neighborhood again.

35.

This letter disturbed me greatly. Lila's world, as usual, rapidly superimposed itself on mine. Everything that I had written in July and August seemed to me trivial, I was seized by a frenzy to redeem myself. I didn't go to the beach, I tried immediately to answer her with a serious letter, one that had the essential, pure yet colloquial tone of hers. But if the other letters had come easily to me—I dashed off pages and pages in a few minutes, without ever correcting—this I wrote, rewrote, rewrote again, and yet Nino's hatred of his father, the role that the affair of Melina had had in the origin of that ugly sentiment, my entire relationship with the Sarratore family, even my anxiety about what was happening to her, came out badly. Donato, who in reality was a remarkable man, on the page became a banal family man; and, as far as Marcello was concerned, I was capable only of superficial advice. In the end all that seemed true was my disappointment that she had a television at home and I didn't.

In other words I couldn't answer her, even though I deprived myself of the sea, the sun, the pleasure of being with Ciro, with Pino, with Clelia, with Lidia, with Marisa, with Sarratore. Thankfully Nella, at some point, came to keep me company on the terrace, bringing me an *orzata*. And when the Sarratores came back from the beach, they were sorry that I had stayed home and began celebrating me again. Lidia herself wanted to make a cake filled with pastry cream, Nella opened a bottle of vermouth, Donato Sarratore began singing Neapolitan songs, Marisa gave me an oakum seahorse she had bought at the Port the night before.

I grew calmer, yet I couldn't get out of my mind Lila in trouble while I was so well, so celebrated. I said, in a slightly dramatic way, that I had received a letter from a friend, that my friend needed me, and so I was thinking of leaving before the appointed time. "The day after tomorrow at the latest," I announced, but without really believing it. In fact I said it only to hear Nella say how sorry she was, Lidia how Ciro would suffer, Marisa how desperate she would be, and Sarratore exclaim sadly, "How will we manage without you?" All this moved me, making my birthday even happier.

Then Pino and Ciro began to nod and Lidia and Donato took them to bed. Marisa helped me wash the dishes, Nella said that if I wanted to sleep a little later in the morning she would get up to make breakfast. I protested, that was my job. One by one, they withdrew, and I was alone. I made my bed in the usual corner, I looked around to see if there were cockroaches, if there were mosquitoes. My gaze fell on the copper pots.

How evocative Lila's writing was; I looked at the pots with increasing distress. I remembered that she had always liked their brilliance, when she washed them she took great care in polishing them. On them, not coincidentally, four years earlier, she had placed the blood that spurted from the neck of Don Achille when he was stabbed. On them now she had deposited that sensation of threat, the anguish over the difficult choice she had, making one of them explode like a sign, as if its shape had decided abruptly to cede. Would I know how to imagine those things without her? Would I know how to give life to every object, let it bend in unison with mine? I turned off the light. I got undressed and got in bed with Lila's letter and Nino's blue bookmark, which seemed to me at that moment the most precious things that I possessed.

From the window the white light of the moon rained down. I kissed the bookmark as I did every night, I tried to reread my friend's letter in the weak glow. The pots shone, the table creaked, the ceiling weighed oppressively, the night air and the sea pressed on the walls. Again I felt humbled by Lila's ability to write, by what she was able to give form to and I was not, my eyes misted. I was happy, yes, that she was so good even without school, without books from the library, but that happiness made me guiltily unhappy.

Then I heard footsteps. I saw the shadow of Sarratore enter the kitchen, barefoot, in blue pajamas. I pulled up the sheet. He went to the tap, he took a glass of water, drank. He remained standing for a few seconds in front of the sink, put down the glass, moved toward my bed. He squatted beside me, his elbows resting on the edge of the sheet.

"I know you're awake," he said.

"Yes."

"Don't think of your friend, stay."

"She's in trouble, she needs me."

"It's I who need you," he said, and he leaned over, kissed me on the mouth without the lightness of his son, half opening my lips with his tongue.

I was immobilized.

He pushed the sheet aside, continuing to kiss me with care, with passion, and he sought my breast with his hand, he caressed me under the nightgown. Then he let go, descended between my legs, pressed two fingers hard over my underpants. I said, did nothing, I was terrified by that behavior, by the horror it created, by the pleasure that I nevertheless felt. His mustache pricked my upper lip, his tongue was rough. Slowly he left my mouth, took away his hand.

"Tomorrow night we'll take a nice walk, you and I, on the beach," he said, a little hoarsely. "I love you and I know that you love me very much. Isn't it true?"

I said nothing. He brushed my lips again with his, murmured good night, got up and left the kitchen. I didn't move, I don't know for how long. However I tried to distance the sensation of his tongue, his caresses, the pressure of his hand, I couldn't. Nino had wanted to warn me, did he know what would happen? I felt an uncontainable hatred for Donato Sarratore and disgust for myself, for the pleasure that lingered in my body. However unlikely it may seem today, as long as I could remember until that night I had never given myself pleasure, I didn't know about it, to feel it surprised me. I remained in the same position for many hours. Then, at first light, I shook myself, collected all my things, took apart the bed, wrote two lines of thanks to Nella, and left.

The island was almost noiseless, the sea still, only the smells were intense. Using the money that my mother had left me more than a month before, I took the first departing ferry. As soon as the boat moved and the island, with its tender early-morning colors, was distant enough, I thought that I finally had a story to tell that Lila could not match. But I knew immediately that the disgust I felt for Sarratore and the revulsion that I had toward myself would keep me from saying anything. In fact this is the first time I've sought words for that unexpected end to my vacation.

36.

I found Naples submerged in a stinking, devastating heat. My mother, without saying a word about how I had changed—the acne gone, my skin sun-darkened—reproached me because I had returned before the appointed time.

"What have you done," she said, "you've behaved rudely, did the teacher's friend throw you out?"

It was different with my father, whose eyes shone and who showered me with compliments, the most conspicuous of which, repeated a hundred times, was: "Christ, what a pretty daughter I have." As for my siblings, they said with a certain contempt, "You look like a negro."

I looked at myself in the mirror and I also marveled: the sun had made me a shining blonde, but my face, my arms, my legs were as if painted with dark gold. As long as I had been immersed in the colors of Ischia, amid sunburned faces, my transformation had seemed suitable; now, restored to the context of the neighborhood, where every face, every street had a sick pallor, it seemed to me excessive, anomalous. The people, the buildings, the dusty, busy *stradone* had the appearance of a poorly printed photograph, like the ones in the newspapers.

As soon as I could I hurried to find Lila. I called her from the courtyard, she looked out, emerged from the doorway. She hugged me, kissed me, gave me compliments, so that I was overwhelmed by all that explicit affection. She was the same and yet, in little more than a month, she had changed further. She seemed no longer a girl but a woman, a woman of at least eighteen, an age that then seemed to me advanced. Her old clothes were short and tight, as if she had grown inside them in the space of a few minutes, and they hugged her body more than they should. She was even taller, more developed, her back was straight. And the pale face above her slender neck seemed to me to have a delicate, unusual beauty.

She seemed nervous, she kept looking around on the street, behind her, but she didn't explain. She said only, "Come with me," and wanted me to go with her to Stefano's grocery. She added, taking my arm, "It's something I can only do with you, thank goodness you've come back. I thought I'd have to wait till September."

We had never walked those streets toward the public gardens so close to one another, so together, so happy to see each other. She told me that things were getting worse every day. Just the night before Marcello had arrived with sweets and spumante and had given her a ring studded with diamonds. She had accepted it, had put it on her finger to avoid trouble in the presence of her parents, but just before he left, at the door, she had given it back to him rudely. Marcello had protested, he had threatened her, as he now did more and more often, then had burst into tears. Fernando and Nunzia had immediately realized that something was wrong. Her mother had grown very fond of Marcello, she liked the good things he brought to the house every night, she was proud of being the owner of a television; and Fernando felt as if he had stopped suffering, because, thanks to a close relationship with the Solaras, he could look to the future without anxieties.

Thus, as soon as Marcello left, both had harassed her more than usual to find out what was happening. Result: for the first time in a long, long time, Rino had defended her, had insisted that if his sister didn't want a halfwit like Marcello, it was her sacrosanct right to refuse him and that, if they insisted on giving him to her, he, in person, would burn down everything, the house and the shoemaker's shop and himself and the entire family. Father and son had started fighting, Nunzia had got involved, all the neighbors had woken up. Not only: Rino had thrown himself on the bed in distress, had abruptly fallen asleep, and an hour later had had another episode of sleep-walking. They had found him in the kitchen lighting matches, and passing them in front of the gas valve as if to check for leaks. Nunzia, terrified, had wakened Lila, saying, "Rino really does want to burn us all alive," and Lila had hurried in and reassured her mother: Rino was sleeping, and in sleep, unlike when he was awake, he wanted to make sure that there was no gas escaping. She had taken him back to bed.

"I can't bear it anymore," she concluded, "you don't know what torture this is, I have to get out of this situation."

She clung to me as if I could give her the energy.

"You're well," she said, "everything's going well for you: you have to help me."

I answered that she could count on me for everything and she seemed relieved, she squeezed my arm, whispered, "Look."

I saw in the distance a sort of red spot that radiated light.

"What is it?"

"Don't you see?"

I couldn't see clearly.

"It's Stefano's new car."

We walked to where the car was parked, in front of the grocery store, which had been enlarged, had two entrances now, and was extremely crowded. The customers, waiting to be served, threw admiring glances at that symbol of well-being and prestige: a car like that had never been seen in the neighborhood, all glass and metal, with a roof that opened. A car for wealthy people, nothing like the Solaras' 1100.

I wandered around it while Lila stood in the shadows and surveyed the street as if she expected violence to erupt at any moment. Stefano looked out from the doorway of the grocery, in his greasy apron, his large head and his high forehead giving a not unpleasant sense of disproportion. He crossed the street, greeted me cordially, said, "How well you look, like an actress."

He, too, looked well: he had been in the sun as I had, maybe we were the only ones in the whole neighborhood who appeared so healthy. I said to him:

"You're very dark."

"I took a week's vacation."

"Where?"

"In Ischia."

"I was in Ischia, too."

"I know, Lina told me: I looked for you but didn't see you."

I pointed to the car. "It's beautiful."

Stefano's face wore an expression of moderate agreement. He said, indicating Lila, with laughing eyes: "I bought it for your friend, but she won't believe it." I looked at Lila, who was standing in the shadows, her expression serious, tense. Stefano said to her, vaguely ironic, "Now Lenuccia's back, what are you doing?"

Lila said, as if the thing annoyed her, "Let's go. But remember, you invited her, not me: I only came along with the two of you."

He smiled and went back into the shop.

"What's happening?" I asked her, confused.

"I don't know," she said, and meant that she didn't know exactly what she was getting into. She looked the way she did when she had to do a difficult calculation in her head, but without her usual impudent expression; she was visibly preoccupied, as if she were attempting an experiment with an uncertain result. "It all began," she said, "with the arrival of that car." Stefano, first as if joking, then with increasing seriousness, had sworn to her that he had bought the car for her, for the pleasure of opening the door and having her get in at least once. "It was made just for you," he had said. And since it had been delivered, at the end of July, he had been asking her constantly, not in an aggressive way, but politely, first to take a drive with him and Alfonso, then with him and Pinuccia, then even with him and his mother. But she had always said no. Finally she had promised him, "I'll go when Lenuccia comes back from Ischia." And now we were there, and what was to happen would happen.

"But he knows about Marcello?"

"Of course he knows."

"And so?"

"So he insists."

"I'm scared, Lila."

"Do you remember how many things we've done that scared you? I waited for you on purpose."

Stefano returned without his apron, dark eyes, dark face, shining black eyes, white shirt and dark pants. He opened the car door, sat behind the wheel, put the top down. I was about to get into the narrow back space but Lila stopped me, she settled herself in the back. I sat uneasily next to Stefano, he started off immediately, heading toward the new buildings.

The heat dissipated in the wind. I felt good, intoxicated by the speed and by the tranquil certainties released by Carracci's body. It seemed to me that Lila had explained everything without explaining anything. There was, yes, this brand-new sports car that had been bought solely to take her for a ride that had just begun. There was, yes, that young man who, though he knew about Marcello Solara, was violating men's rules of masculinity without any visible anxiety. There was me, yes, dragged furiously into that business to hide by my presence secret words between them, maybe even a friendship. But what type of friendship? Certainly, with that drive, something significant was happening, and yet Lila had been unable or unwilling to provide me with the elements necessary for understanding. What did she have in mind? She had to know that she was setting in motion an earthquake worse than when she threw the ink-soaked bits of paper. And yet it might be that she wasn't aiming at anything precise. She was like that, she threw things off balance just to see if she could put them back in some other way. So here we were racing along, hair blowing in the wind, Stefano driving with satisfied skill, I sitting beside him as if I were his girlfriend. I thought of how he had looked at me, when he said I looked like an actress. I thought of the possibility of him liking me more than he now liked my friend. I thought with horror of the idea that Marcello Solara might shoot him. His beautiful person with its confident gestures would lose substance like the copper of the pot that Lila had written about.

We were driving among the new buildings in order to avoid passing the Bar Solara.

"I don't care if Marcello sees us," Stefano said without emphasis, "but if it matters to you it's fine like this."'

We went through the tunnel, we turned toward the Marina. It was the road that Lila and I had taken many years earlier, when we had gotten caught in the rain. I mentioned that episode, she smiled, Stefano wanted us to tell him about it. We told him everything, it was fun, and meanwhile we arrived at the Granili.

"What do you think, fast, isn't it?"

"Incredibly fast," I said, enthusiastically.

Lila made no comment. She looked around, at times she

touched my shoulder to point out the houses, the ragged poverty along the street, as if she saw a confirmation of something and I was supposed to understand it right away. Then she asked Stefano, seriously, without preamble, "Are you really different?"

He looked at her in the rearview mirror. "From whom?"

"You know."

He didn't answer immediately. Then he said in dialect, "Do you want me to tell you the truth?"

"Yes."

"The intention is there, but I don't know how it will end up."

At that point I was sure that Lila must not have told me quite a few things. That allusive tone was evidence that they were close, that they had talked other times and not in jest but seriously. What had I missed in the period of Ischia? I turned to look at her, she delayed replying, I thought that Stefano's answer had made her nervous because of its vagueness. I saw her flooded by sunlight, eyes half closed, her shirt swelled by her breast and by the wind.

"The poverty here is worse than among us," she said. And then, without connection, laughing, "Don't think I've forgotten about when you wanted to prick my tongue."

Stefano nodded.

"That was another era," he said.

"Once a coward, always a coward—you were twice as big as me."

He gave a small, embarrassed smile and, without answering, accelerated in the direction of the port. The drive lasted less than half an hour, we went back on the Rettifilo and Piazza Garibaldi.

"Your brother isn't well," Stefano said when we had returned to the outskirts of the neighborhood. He looked at her again in the mirror and asked, "Are those shoes displayed in the window the ones you made?"

"What do you know about the shoes?"

"It's all Rino talks about."

"And so?"

"They're very beautiful."

She narrowed her eyes, squeezed them almost until they were closed.

"Buy them," she said in her provocative tone.

"How much will you sell them for?"

"Talk to my father."

Stefano made a decisive U turn that threw me against the door, we turned onto the street where the shoe repair shop was.

"What are you doing?" Lila asked, alarmed now.

"You said to buy them and I'm going to buy them."

37.

He stopped the car in front of the shoemaker's shop, came around and opened the door for me, gave me his hand to help me out. He didn't concern himself with Lila, who got out herself and stayed behind. He and I stopped in front of the window, under the eyes of Fernando and Rino, who looked at us from inside the shop with sullen curiosity.

When Lila joined us Stefano opened the door of the shop, let me go first, went in without making way for her. He was very courteous with father and son, and asked if he could see the shoes. Rino rushed to get them, and Stefano examined them, praised them: "They're light and yet strong, they really have a nice line." He asked me, "What do you think, Lenù?"

I said, with great embarrassment, "They're very handsome."

He turned to Fernando: "Your daughter said that all three of you worked on them and that you have a plan to make others, for women as well."

"Yes," said Rino, looking in wonder at his sister.

"Yes," said Fernando, puzzled, "but not right away."

Rino said to his sister, a little worked up, because he was afraid she would refuse, "Show him the designs."

Lila, continuing to surprise him, didn't resist. She went to the back of the shop and returned, handing the sheets of paper to her brother, who gave them to Stefano. They were the models that she had designed almost two years earlier.

Stefano showed me a drawing of a pair of women's shoes with a very high heel.

"Would you buy them?"

"Yes."

He went back to examining the designs. Then he sat down on a stool, took off his right shoe.

"What size is it?"

"43, but it could be a 44," Rino lied.

Lila, surprising us again, knelt in front of Stefano and using the shoehorn helped him slip his foot into the new shoe. Then she took off the other shoe and did the same.

Stefano, who until that moment had been playing the part of the practical, businesslike man, was obviously disturbed. He waited for Lila to get up, and remained seated for some seconds as if to catch his breath. Then he stood, took a few steps.

"They're tight," he said.

Rino turned gray, disappointed.

"We can put them on the machine and widen them," Fernando interrupted, but uncertainly.

Stefano turned to me and asked, "How do they look?"

"Nice," I said.

"Then I'll take them."

Fernando remained impassive, Rino brightened.

"You know, Ste', these are an exclusive Cerullo design, they'll be expensive."

Stefano smiled, took an affectionate tone: "And if they

weren't an exclusive Cerullo design, do you think I would buy them? When will they be ready?"

Rino looked at his father, radiant.

"We'll keep them in the machine for at least three days," Fernando said, but it was clear that he could have said ten days, twenty, a month, he was so eager to take his time in the face of this unexpected novelty.

"Good: you think of a friendly price and I'll come in three days to pick them up."

He folded the pieces of paper with the designs and put them in his pocket before our puzzled eyes. Then he shook hands with Fernando, with Rino, and headed toward the door.

"The drawings," Lila said coldly.

"Can I bring them back in three days?" Stefano asked in a cordial tone, and without waiting for an answer opened the door. He made way for me to pass and went out after me.

I was already settled in the car next to him when Lila joined us. She was angry.

"You think my father is a fool, that my brother is a fool?"

"What do you mean?"

"If you think you'll make fools of my family and me, you are mistaken."

"You are insulting me: I'm not Marcello Solara."

"And who are you?"

"A businessman: the shoes you've designed are unusual. And I don't mean just the ones I bought, I mean all of them."

"So?"

"So let me think and we'll see each other in three days."

Lila stared at him as if she wanted to read his mind, she didn't move away from the car. Finally she said something that I would never have had the courage to utter:

"Look, Marcello tried in every possible way to buy me but no one is going to buy me."

Stefano looked her straight in the eyes for a long moment.

"I don't spend a lira if I don't think it can produce a hundred."

He started the engine and we left. Now I was sure: the drive had been a sort of agreement reached at the end of many encounters, much talk. I said weakly, in Italian, "Please, Stefano, leave me at the corner? If my mother sees me in a car with you she'll bash my face in."

38.

Lila's life changed decisively during that month of September. It wasn't easy, but it changed. As for me, I had returned from Ischia in love with Nino, branded by the lips and hands of his father, sure that I would weep night and day because of the mixture of happiness and horror I felt inside. Instead I made no attempt to find a form for my emotions, in a few hours everything was reduced. I put aside Nino's voice, the irritation of his father's mustache. The island faded, lost itself in some secret corner of my head. I made room for what was happening to Lila.

In the three days that followed the astonishing ride in the convertible, she, with the excuse of doing the shopping, went often to Stefano's grocery, but always asked me to go with her. I did it with my heart pounding, frightened by the possible appearance of Marcello, but also pleased with my role as confidante generous with advice, as accomplice in weaving plots, as apparent object of Stefano's attentions. We were girls, even if we imagined ourselves wickedly daring. We embroidered on the facts—Marcello, Stefano, the shoes—with our usual eagerness and it seemed to us that we always knew how to make things come out right. "I'll say this to him," she hypothesized, and I would suggest a small variation: "No, say this." Then she and Stefano would be deep in conversation in a corner behind the counter, while Alfonso exchanged a few words with me, Pinuccia, annoyed, waited on the customers, and Maria, at the cash register, observed her older son apprehensively, because he had been neglecting the job lately, and was feeding the gossip of the neighbors.

Naturally we were improvising. In the course of that back and forth I tried to understand what was really going through Lila's head, so as to be in tune with her goals. At first I had the impression that she intended simply to enable her father and brother to earn some money by selling Stefano, for a good price, the only pair of shoes produced by the Cerullos, but soon it seemed to me that her principal aim was to get rid of Marcello by making use of the young grocer. In this sense, she was decisive when I asked her:

"Which of the two do you like more?"

She shrugged.

"I've never liked Marcello, he makes me sick."

"You would become engaged to Stefano just to get Marcello out of your house?"

She thought for a moment and said yes.

From then on the ultimate goal of all our plotting seemed to us that—to fight by every means possible Marcello's intrusion in her life. The rest came crowding around almost by chance and we merely gave it a rhythm and, at times, a true orchestration. Or so at least we believed. In fact, the person who was acting was only and was always Stefano.

Punctually, three days later, he went to the store and bought the shoes, even though they were tight. The two Cerullos with much hesitation asked for twenty-five thousand lire, but were ready to go down to ten thousand. He didn't bat an eye and put down another twenty thousand in exchange for Lila's drawings, which—he said—he liked, he wanted to frame them.

"Frame?" Rino asked.

"Yes."

"Like a picture by a painter?"

"Yes."

"And you told my sister that you're buying her drawings?"

"Yes."

Stefano didn't stop there. In the following days he again poked his head in at the shop and announced to father and son that he had rented the space adjacent to theirs. "For now it's there," he said, "but if you one day decide to expand, remember that I am at your disposal."

At the Cerullos' they discussed for a long time what that statement meant. "Expand?" Finally Lila, since they couldn't get there on their own, said:

"He's proposing to transform the shoe shop into a workshop for making Cerullo shoes."

"And the money?" Rino asked cautiously.

"He'll invest it."

"He told you?" Fernando, incredulous, was alarmed, immediately followed by Nunzia.

"He told the two of you," Lila said, indicating her father and brother.

"But he knows that handmade shoes are expensive?"

"You showed him."

"And if they don't sell?"

"You've wasted the work and he's wasted the money."

"And that's it?"

"That's it."

The entire family was upset for days. Marcello moved to the background. He arrived at night at eight-thirty and dinner wasn't ready. Often he found himself alone in front of the television with Melina and Ada, while the Cerullos talked in another room.

Naturally the most enthusiastic was Rino, who regained energy, color, good humor, and, as he had been the close friend of the Solaras, so he began to be Stefano's close friend, Alfonso's,

Pinuccia's, even Signora Maria's. When, finally, Fernando's last reservation dissolved, Stefano went to the shop and, after a small discussion, came to a verbal agreement on the basis of which he would put up the expenses and the two Cerullos would start production of the model that Lila and Rino had already made and all the other models, it being understood that they would split the possible profits half and half. He took the documents out of a pocket and showed them to them one after another.

"You'll do this, this, this," he said, "but let's hope that it won't take two years, as I know happened with the other."

"My daughter is a girl," Fernando explained, embarrassed, "and Rino hasn't yet learned the job well."

Stefano shook his head in a friendly way.

"Leave Lina out of it. You'll have to take on some workers."

"And who will pay them?" Fernando asked.

"Me again. You choose two or three, freely, according to your judgment."

Fernando, at the idea of having, no less, employees, turned red and his tongue was loosened, to the evident annoyance of his son. He spoke of how he had learned the trade from his late father. He told of how hard the work was on the machines, in Casoria. He said that his mistake had been to marry Nunzia, who had weak hands and no wish to work, but if he had married Ines, a flame of his youth who had been a great worker, he would in time have had a business all his own, better than Campanile, with a line to display perhaps at the regional trade show. He told us, finally, that he had in his head beautiful shoes, perfect, that if Stefano weren't set on those silly things of Lina's, they could start production now and you know how many they would sell. Stefano listened patiently, but repeated that he, for now, was interested only in having Lila's exact designs made. Rino then took his sister's sheets of paper, examined them carefully, and asked him in a lightly teasing tone:

"When you get them framed where will you hang them?"

"In here."

Rino looked at his father, but he had turned sullen again and said nothing.

"My sister agrees about everything?" he asked.

Stefano smiled: "Who can do anything if your sister doesn't agree?"

He got up, shook Fernando's hand vigorously, and headed toward the door. Rino went with him and, with sudden concern, called to him from the doorway, as Stefano was going to the red convertible:

"The brand of the shoes is Cerullo."

Stefano waved to him, without turning: "A Cerullo invented them and Cerullo they will be called."

39.

That same night Rino, before he went out with Pasquale and Antonio, said, "Marcè, have you seen that car Stefano's got?"

Marcello, stupefied by the television and by sadness, didn't even answer.

Then Rino drew his comb out of his pocket, pulled it through his hair, and said cheerfully: "You know that he bought our shoes for twenty-five thousand lire?"

"You see he's got money to throw away," Marcello answered, and Melina burst out laughing, it wasn't clear if she was reacting to that remark or to what was showing on the television.

From that moment Rino found a way, night after night, to annoy Marcello, and the atmosphere became increasingly tense. Besides, as soon as Solara, who was always greeted kindly by Nunzia, arrived, Lila disappeared, saying she was tired, and went to bed. One night Marcello, very depressed, talked to Nunzia.

"If your daughter goes to bed as soon as I arrive, what am I coming here for?"

Evidently he hoped that she would comfort him, saying something that would encourage him to persevere. But Nunzia didn't know what to say and so he stammered, "Does she like someone else?"

"But no."

"I know she goes to do the shopping at Stefano's."

"And where should she go, my boy, to do the shopping?"

Marcello was silent, eyes lowered.

"She was seen in the car with the grocer."

"Lenuccia was there, too: Stefano is interested in the porter's daughter."

"Lenuccia doesn't seem to me a good companion for your daughter. Tell her not to see her anymore."

I was not a good companion? Lila was not supposed to see me anymore? When my friend reported that request of Marcello's I went over conclusively to Stefano's side and began to praise his tactful ways, his calm determination. "He's rich," I said to her finally. But even as I said that I realized how the idea of the riches girls dreamed of was changing further. The treasure chests full of gold pieces that a procession of servants in livery would deposit in our castle when we published a book like *Little Women*—riches and fame—had truly faded. Perhaps the idea of money as a cement to solidify our existence and prevent it from dissolving, together with the people who were dear to us, endured. But the fundamental feature that now prevailed was concreteness, the daily gesture, the negotiation. This wealth of adolescence proceeded from a fantastic, still childish illumination—the designs for extraordinary shoes—but it was embodied in the petulant dissatisfaction of Rino, who wanted to spend like a big shot, in the television, in the meals, and in the ring with which Marcello wanted to buy a feeling, and, finally, from step to step, in that courteous youth

Stefano, who sold groceries, had a red convertible, spent forty-five thousand lire like nothing, framed drawings, wished to do business in shoes as well as in cheese, invested in leather and a workforce, and seemed convinced that he could inaugurate a new era of peace and well-being for the neighborhood: it was, in short, wealth that existed in the facts of every day, and so was without splendor and without glory.

"He's rich," I heard Lila repeat, and we started laughing. But then she added, "Also nice, also good," and I agreed, these last were qualities that Marcello didn't have, a further reason for being on Stefano's side. Yet those two adjectives confused me, I felt that they gave the final blow to the shine of childish fantasies. No castle, no treasure chest—I seemed to understand—would concern Lila and me alone, intent on writing our *Little Women*. Wealth, incarnated in Stefano, was taking the form of a young man in a greasy apron, was gaining features, smell, voice, was expressing kindness and goodness, was a male we had known forever, the oldest son of Don Achille.

I was disturbed.

"But he wanted to prick your tongue," I said.

"He was a child," she answered, with emotion, sweet as I had never heard her before, so that only at that moment did I realize that she was much farther along than what she had said to me in words.

In the following days everything became clearer. I saw how she talked to Stefano and how he seemed shaped by her voice. I adapted to the pact they were making, I didn't want to be cut out. And we plotted for hours—the two of us, the three of us—to act in a way that would quickly silence people, feelings, the arrangement of things. A worker arrived in the space next to the shoe shop and took down the dividing wall. The shoemaker's shop was reorganized. Three nearly silent apprentices appeared, country boys, from Melito. In one corner they continued to do resoling, in the rest of the space Fernando arranged benches, shelves, his tools, his wooden forms according to the various sizes, and began, with sudden energy, unsuspected in a man so thin, consumed by a bitter discontent, to talk about a course of action.

Just that day, when the new work was about to begin, Stefano showed up. He carried a package done up in brown paper. They all jumped to their feet, even Fernando, as if he had come for an inspection. He opened the package, and inside were a number of small pictures, all the same size, in narrow brown frames. They were Lila's notebook pages, under glass, like precious relics. He asked permission from Fernando to hang them on the walls, Fernando grumbled something, and Stefano had Rino and the apprentices help him put in the nails. When the pictures were hung, Stefano asked the three helpers to go get a coffee and handed them some lire. As soon as he was alone with the shoemaker and his son, he announced quietly that he wanted to marry Lila.

An unbearable silence fell. Rino confined himself to a knowing little smile and Fernando said finally, weakly, "Stefano, Lina is engaged to Marcello Solara."

"Your daughter doesn't know it."

"What do you mean?"

Rino interrupted, cheerfully: "He's telling the truth: you and Mamma let that shit come to our house, but Lina never wanted him and doesn't want him."

Fernando gave his son a stern look. The grocer said gently, looking around: "We've started out on a job now, let's not get worked up. I ask of you a single thing, Don Fernà: let your daughter decide. If she wants Marcello Solara, I will resign myself. I love her so much that if she's happy with someone else I will withdraw and between us everything will remain as it is now. But if she wants me—if she wants me—there's no help for it, you must give her to me."

"You're threatening me," Fernando said, but halfheartedly, in a tone of resigned observation.

"No, I'm asking you to do what's best for your daughter."

"I know what's best for her."

"Yes, but she knows better than you."

And here Stefano got up, opened the door, called me, I was waiting outside with Lila.

"Lenù."

We went in. How we liked feeling that we were at the center of those events, the two of us together, directing them toward their outcome. I remember the extreme tension of that moment. Stefano said to Lila, "I'm saying to you in front of your father: I love you, more than my life. Will you marry me?"

Lila answered seriously, "Yes."

Fernando gasped slightly, then murmured, with the same subservience that in times gone by he had manifested toward Don Achille: "We're offending not only Marcello but all the Solaras. Who's going to tell that poor boy?"

Lila said, "I will."

40.

In fact two nights later, in front of the whole family except Rino, who was out, before they sat down at the table, before the television was turned on, Lila asked Marcello, "Will you take me to get some ice cream?"

Marcello couldn't believe his ears.

"Ice cream? Without eating first? You and me?" And he suddenly asked Nunzia, "Signora, would you come, too?"

Nunzia turned on the television and said, "No, thank you, Marcè. But don't be too long. Ten minutes, you'll go and be back."

"Yes," he promised, happily, "thank you."

He repeated thank you at least four times. It seemed to him that the longed-for moment had arrived, Lila was about to say yes.

But as soon as they were outside the building she confronted him and said, with the cold cruelty that had come easily to her since her first years of life, "I never told you that I loved you."

"I know. But now you do?"

"No."

Marcello, who was heavily built, a healthy, ruddy youth of twenty-three, leaned against a lamppost, brokenhearted.

"Really no?"

"No. I love someone else."

"Who is it?"

"Stefano."

"I knew it, but I couldn't believe it."

"You have to believe it, it's true."

"I'll kill you both."

"With me you can try right now."

Marcello left the lamppost in a rush, but, with a kind of death rattle, he bit his clenched right fist until it bled.

"I love you too much, I can't do it."

"Then get your brother, your father to do it, some friend, maybe they're capable. But make it clear to all of them that you had better kill me first. Because if you touch anyone else while I'm alive, I will kill you, and you know I will, starting with you."

Marcello continued to bite his finger stubbornly. Then he repressed a sort of sob that shook his breast, turned, and went off.

She shouted after him: "Send someone to get the television, we don't need it."

41.

Everything happened in little more than a month and Lila

in the end seemed to me happy. She had found an outlet for the shoe project, she had given an opportunity to her brother and the whole family, she had gotten rid of Marcello Solara and had become the fiancée of the most respectable wealthy young man in the neighborhood. What more could she want? Nothing. She had everything. When school began again I felt the dreariness of it more than usual. I was reabsorbed by the work and, so that the teachers would not find me unprepared, I went back to studying until eleven and setting my alarm for five-thirty. I saw Lila less and less.

On the other hand, my relationship with Stefano's brother, Alfonso, solidified. Although he had worked in the grocery all summer, he had passed the makeup exams successfully, with seven in each of the subjects: Latin, Greek, and English. Gino, who had hoped that he would fail so that they could repeat the first year of high school together, was disappointed. When he realized that the two of us, now in our second year, went to school and came home together every day, he grew even more bitter and became mean. He no longer spoke to me, his former girlfriend, or to Alfonso, his former deskmate, even though he was in the classroom next to ours and we often met in the hallways, as well as in the streets of the neighborhood. But he did worse: soon I heard that he was telling nasty stories about us. He said that I was in love with Alfonso and touched him during class even though Alfonso didn't respond, because, as he knew very well, he who had sat next to him for a year, he didn't like girls, he preferred boys. I reported this to Alfonso, expecting him to beat up Gino, as was the rule in such cases, but he confined himself to saying, contemptuously, in dialect, "Everyone knows that he's the fag."

Alfonso was a pleasant, fortunate discovery. He gave an impression of cleanliness and good manners. Although his features were very similar to Stefano's, the same eyes, same nose, same mouth; although his body, as he grew, was taking the same form, the large head, legs slightly short in relation to the torso; although in his gaze and in his gestures he manifested the same mildness, I felt in him a total absence of the determination that was concealed in every cell of Stefano's body, and that in the end, I thought, reduced his courtesy to a sort of hiding place from which to jump out unexpectedly. Alfonso was soothing, that type of human being, rare in the neighborhood, from whom you know you needn't expect any cruelty. We didn't talk a lot, but we didn't feel uncomfortable. He always had what I needed and if he didn't he hurried to get it. He loved me without any tension and I felt quietly affectionate toward him. The first day of school we ended up sitting at the same desk, a thing that was audacious at the time, and even if the other boys made fun of him because he was always near me and the girls asked me continuously if he was my boyfriend, neither of us decided to change places. He was a trusted person. If he saw that I needed my own time, he either waited for me at a distance or said goodbye and went off. If he realized that I wanted him to stay with me, he stayed even if he had other things to do.

I used him to escape Nino Sarratore. When, for the first time after Ischia, we saw each other from a distance, Nino came toward me in a friendly way, but I dismissed him with a few cold remarks. And yet I liked him so much, if his tall slender figure merely appeared I blushed and my heart beat madly. And yet now that Lila was really engaged, officially engaged— and to such a fiancé, a man of twenty-two, not a boy: kind, decisive, courageous—it was more urgent than ever that I, too, should have an enviable fiancé and so rebalance our relationship. It would be lovely to go out as four, Lila with her betrothed, I with mine. Of course, Nino didn't have a red convertible. Of course, he was a student in the fourth year of high school, and thus didn't have a lira. But he was a lot taller than I, while Stefano was an inch or so shorter than Lila. And he spoke a literary Italian, when he wanted to. And he read and discussed everything and was aware of the great questions of the human condition, while Stefano lived shut off in his grocery, spoke almost exclusively in dialect, had not gone past the vocational school, at the cash register had his mamma, who did the accounts better than he, and, though he had a good character, was sensitive above all to the profitable turnover of money. Yet, although passion consumed me, although I saw clearly the prestige I would acquire in Lila's eyes if I were bound to him, for the second time since seeing him and falling in love I felt incapable of establishing a relationship. The motive seemed to me much stronger than that of childhood. Seeing him brought immediately to mind Donato Sarratore, even if they didn't resemble each other at all. And the disgust, the rage aroused by the memory of what his father had done without my being able to repulse him extended to Nino. Of course, I loved him. I longed to talk to him, walk with him, and at times I thought, racking my brains: Why do you behave like that, the father isn't the son, the son isn't the father, behave as Stefano did with the Pelusos. But I couldn't. As soon as I imagined kissing him, I felt the mouth of Donato, and a wave of pleasure and revulsion mixed father and son into a single person.

An alarming episode occurred, which made the situation more complicated. Alfonso and I had got into the habit of walking home. We went to Piazza Nazionale and then reached Corso Meridionale. It was a long walk, but we talked about homework, teachers, classmates, and it was pleasant. Then one day, just beyond the ponds, at the start of the *stradone*, I turned and seemed to see on the railway embankment, in his conductor's uniform, Donato Sarratore. I started with rage and horror, and immediately turned away. When I looked again, he was gone.

Whether that apparition was true or false, the sound my heart made in my chest, like a gunshot, stayed with me, and, I don't know why, I thought of the passage in Lila's letter about the sound that the copper pot had made when it burst. That same sound returned the next day, at the mere sight of Nino. Then, frightened, I took cover in affection for Alfonso, and at both the start and the end of school I kept near him. As soon as the lanky figure of the boy I loved appeared, I turned to the younger son of Don Achille as if I had the most urgent things to tell him, and we walked away chattering.

It was, in other words, a confusing time, I would have liked to be attached to Nino and yet I was careful to stay glued to Alfonso. In fact, out of fear that he would get bored and leave me for other company, I behaved more and more kindly toward him, sometimes I even spoke sweetly. But as soon as I realized that I risked encouraging his liking me I changed my tone. What if he misunderstands and says he loves me? I worried. It would have been embarrassing, I would have had to reject him: Lila, my contemporary, was engaged to a man, Stefano, and it would be humiliating to be with a boy, the little brother of her fiancé. Yet my mind swirled without restraint, I daydreamed. Once, as I walked home along Corso Meridionale, with Alfonso beside me like a squire escorting me through the thousand dangers of the city, it seemed to me right that the duty had fallen to two Carraccis, Stefano and him, to protect, if in different forms, Lila and me from the blackest evil in the world, from that very evil that we had experienced for the first time going up the stairs that led to their house, when we went to retrieve the dolls that their father had stolen.

42.

I liked to discover connections like that, especially if they concerned Lila. I traced lines between moments and events distant from one another, I established convergences and divergences. In that period it became a daily exercise: the better off I had been in Ischia, the worse off Lila had been in the desolation of the neighborhood; the more I had suffered upon leaving the island, the happier she had become. It was as if, because of an evil spell, the joy or sorrow of one required the sorrow or joy of the other; even our physical aspect, it seemed to me, shared in that swing. In Ischia I had felt beautiful, and the impression had lingered on my return to Naples—during the constant plotting with Lila to help her get rid of Marcello, there had even been moments when I thought again that I was prettier, and in some of Stefano's glances I had caught the possibility of his liking me. But Lila now had retaken the upper hand, satisfaction had magnified her beauty, while I, overwhelmed by schoolwork, exhausted by my frustrated love for Nino, was growing ugly again. My healthy color faded, the acne returned. And suddenly one morning the specter of glasses appeared.

Professor Gerace questioned me about something he had written on the blackboard, and realized that I could see almost nothing. He told me that I must go immediately to an oculist, he would write it down in my notebook, he expected the signature of one of my parents the next day. I went home and showed them the notebook, full of guilt for the expense that glasses would involve. My father darkened, my mother shouted, "You're always with your books, and now you've ruined your eyesight." I was extremely hurt. Had I been punished for pride in wishing to study? What about Lila? Hadn't she read much more than I had? So then why did she have perfect vision while mine deteriorated? Why should I have to wear glasses my whole life and she not?

The need for glasses intensified my mania for finding a pattern that, in good as in evil, would bind my fate and hers: I was blind, she a falcon; I had an opaque pupil, she narrowed her eyes, with darting glances that saw more; I clung to her arm, among the shadows, she guided me with a stern gaze. In the end my father, thanks to his dealings at the city hall, found the money. The fantasies diminished. I went to the oculist, he diagnosed a severe myopia, the glasses materialized. When I looked at myself in the mirror, the clear image was a hard blow: blemished skin, broad face, wide mouth, big nose, eyes imprisoned in frames that seemed to have been drawn insistently by an angry designer under eyebrows already too thick. I felt disfigured, and decided to wear the glasses only at home or, at most, if I had to copy something from the blackboard. But one day, leaving school, I forgot them on the desk. I hurried back to the classroom, the worst had happened. In the haste that seized us all at the sound of the last bell, they had ended up on the floor: one sidepiece was broken, a lens cracked. I began to cry.

I didn't have the courage to go home, I took refuge with Lila. I told her what had happened, and gave her the glasses. She examined them and said to leave them with her. She spoke with a different sort of determination, calmer, as if it were no longer necessary to fight to the death for every little thing. I imagined some miraculous intervention by Rino with his shoemaker's tools and I went home hoping that my parents wouldn't notice that I was without my glasses.

A few days afterward, in the late afternoon, I heard someone calling from the courtyard. Below was Lila, she had my glasses on her nose and at first I was struck not by the fact that they were as if new but by how well they suited her. I ran down thinking, why is it that they look nice on her when she doesn't need them and they make me, who can't do without them, look ugly? As soon as I appeared she took off the glasses with amusement and put them on my nose herself, exclaiming, "How nice you look, you should wear them all the time." She had given the glasses to Stefano, who had had them fixed by an optician in the city. I murmured in embarrassment that I could never repay her, she replied ironically, perhaps with a trace of malice:

"Repay in what sense?"

"Give you money."

She smiled, then said proudly, "There's no need, I do what I like now with money."

43.

Money gave even more force to the impression that what I lacked she had, and vice versa, in a continuous game of exchanges and reversals that, now happily, now painfully, made us indispensable to each other.

She has Stefano, I said to myself after the episode of the glasses. She snaps her fingers and immediately has my glasses repaired. What do I have?

I answered that I had school, a privilege she had lost forever. That is my wealth, I tried to convince myself. And in fact that year all the teachers began to praise me again. My report cards were increasingly brilliant, and even the correspondence course in theology went well, I got a Bible with a black cover as a prize.

I displayed my successes as if they were my mother's silver bracelet, and yet I didn't know what to do with that virtuosity. In my class there was no one to talk to about what I read, the ideas that came into my mind. Alfonso was a diligent student; after the failure of the preceding year he had got back on track and was doing well in all the subjects. But when I tried to talk to him about *The Betrothed*, or the marvelous books I still borrowed from Maestro Ferraro's library, or about the Holy Spirit, he merely listened, and, out of timidity or ignorance, never said anything that would inspire me to further thoughts. Besides, while in school he used a good Italian; when it was just the two of us he never abandoned dialect, and in dialect it was hard to discuss the corruption of earthly justice, as it could be seen during the lunch at the house of Don Rodrigo, or the relations between God, the Holy Spirit, and Jesus, who, although they were a single person, when they were divided in three, I thought, necessarily had to have a hierarchy, and then who came first, who last?

I remembered what Pasquale had once said: that my high school, even if it was a classical high school, was surely not one of the best. I concluded that he was right. Rarely did I see my schoolmates dressed as well as the girls of Via dei Mille. And, when school was out, you never saw elegantly dressed young men, in cars more luxurious than those of Marcello and Stefano, waiting to pick them up. Intellectually, too, they were deficient. The only student who had a reputation like mine was Nino, but now, because of the coldness with which I had treated him, he went off with his head down, he didn't even look at me. What to do, then?

I needed to express myself, my head was bursting. I turned to Lila, especially when school was on vacation. We met, we talked. I told her in detail about the classes, the teachers. She listened intently, and I hoped that she would become curious and go back to the phase when in secret or openly she would eagerly get the books that would allow her to keep up with me. But it never happened, it was as if one part of her kept a tight rein on the other part. Instead she developed a tendency to interrupt right away, in general in an ironic manner. Once, just to give an example, I told her about my theology course and said, to impress her with the questions that tormented me, that I didn't know what to think about the Holy Spirit, its function wasn't clear to me. "Is it," I argued aloud, "a subordinate entity, in the service of both God and Jesus, like a messenger? Or an emanation of the first two, their miraculous essence? But in the first case how can an entity who acts as a messenger possibly be one with God and his son? Wouldn't it be like saying that my father who is a porter at the city hall is the same as the mayor, as Comandante Lauro? And, if you look at the second case, well, essence, sweat, voice are part of the person from whom they emanate: how can it make sense, then, to consider the Holy Spirit separate from God and Jesus? Or is the Holy Spirit the most important person and the other two his mode of being, or I don't understand what his function is." Lila, I remember, was preparing to go out with Stefano: they were going to a cinema in the center with Pinuccia, Rino, and Alfonso. I watched while she put on a new skirt, a new jacket, and she was truly another person now, even her ankles were no longer like sticks. Yet I saw that her eyes narrowed, as when she tried to grasp something fleeting. She said, in dialect, "You still waste time with those things, Lenù? We are flying over a ball of fire. The part that has cooled floats on the lava. On that part we construct the buildings, the bridges, and the streets, and every so often the lava comes out of Vesuvius or causes an earthquake that destroys everything. There are microbes everywhere that make us sick and die. There are wars. There is a poverty that makes us all cruel. Every second something might happen that will cause you such suffering that you'll never have enough tears. And what are you doing? A theology course in which you struggle to understand what the Holy Spirit is? Forget it, it was the Devil who invented the world, not the Father, the Son, and the Holy Spirit. Do you want to see the string of pearls that Stefano gave me?" That was how she talked, more or less, confusing me. And not only in a situation like that but more and more often, until that tone became established, became her way of standing up to me. If I said something about the Very Holy Trinity, she with a few hurried but good-humored remarks cut off any possible conversation and went on to show me Stefano's presents, the engagement ring, the necklace, a new dress, a hat, while the things that I loved, that made me shine in front of the teachers, so that they considered me clever, slumped in a corner, deprived of their meaning. I let go of ideas, books. I went on to admire all those gifts that contrasted with the humble house of Fernando the shoemaker; I tried on the dresses and the jewelry; I almost immediately noticed that they would never suit me as they did her; and I was depressed.

44.

In the role of fiancée, Lila was much envied and caused quite a lot of resentment. After all, her behavior had been irritating when she was a skinny little child, imagine now that she was a very fortunate young girl. She herself told me of an increasing hostility on the part of Stefano's mother and, especially, Pinuccia. Their spiteful thoughts were stamped clearly on their faces. Who did the shoemaker's daughter think she was? What evil potion had she made Stefano drink? How was it that as soon as she opened her mouth he opened his wallet? She wants to come and be mistress in our house?

If Maria confined herself to a surly silence, Pinuccia couldn't contain herself, she exploded, speaking to her brother like this: "Why do you buy all those things for her, while for me you've never bought anything, and as soon as I buy something nice you criticize me, you say I'm wasting money?"

Stefano displayed his tranquil half smile and didn't answer. But soon, in accord with his habit of accommodation, he began to give his sister presents, too. Thus a contest began between the two girls, they went to the hairdresser together, they bought the same dresses. This, however, only embittered Pinuccia the more. She wasn't ugly, she was a few years older than us, maybe her figure was more developed, but there was no comparison between the effect made by any dress or object when Lila had it on and when Pinuccia wore it. It was her mother who realized this first. Maria, when she saw Lila and

Pinuccia ready to go out, with the same hairstyle, in similar dresses, always found a way to digress and, by devious means, end up criticizing her future daughter-in-law, with false good humor, for something she had done days earlier—leaving the light on in the kitchen or the tap open after getting a glass of water. Then she turned the other way, as if she had a lot to do, and muttered, "Be home soon."

We girls of the neighborhood soon had similar problems. On holidays Carmela, who still wanted to be called Carmen, and Ada and Gigliola started dressing up, without admitting it, without admitting it to themselves, in competition with Lila. Gigliola in particular, who worked in the pastry shop, and who, although she wasn't officially with Michele Solara, bought and had him buy pretty things, just to show off on walks or in the car. But there was no contest, Lila seemed inaccessible, a dazzling figurine against the light.

At first we tried to keep her, to impose on her the old habits. We drew Stefano into our group, embraced him, coddled him, and he seemed pleased, and so one Saturday, perhaps impelled by his sympathy for Antonio and Ada, he said to Lila, "See if Lenuccia and Melina's children will come and eat with us tomorrow evening." By "us" he meant the two of them plus Pinuccia and Rino, who now liked to spend his free time with his future brother-in-law. We accepted, but it was a difficult evening. Ada, afraid of making a bad impression, borrowed a dress from Gigliola. Stefano and Rino chose not a pizzeria but a restaurant in Santa Lucia. Neither I nor Antonio nor Ada had ever been in a restaurant, it was something for rich people, and we were overcome by anxiety: how should we dress, what would it cost? While the four of them went in the Giardinetta, we took the bus to Piazza Plebiscito and walked the rest of the way. At the restaurant, they casually ordered many dishes, and we almost nothing, out of fear that the bill would be more than we could afford. We were almost silent the whole time, because

Rino and Stefano talked, mainly about money, and never thought of involving even Antonio in their conversations. Ada, not resigned to marginality, tried all evening to attract Stefano's attention by flirting outrageously, which upset her brother. Then, when it was time to pay, we discovered that Stefano had already taken care of the bill, and, while it didn't bother Rino at all, Antonio went home in a rage, because although he was the same age as Stefano and Lila's brother, although he worked as they did, he felt he had been treated like a pauper. But the most significant thing was that Ada and I, with different feelings, realized that in a public place, outside of our intimate, neighborhood relationship, we didn't know what to say to Lila, how to treat her. She was so well dressed, so carefully made up, that she seemed right for the Giardinetta, the convertible, the restaurant in Santa Lucia, but physically unsuited now to go on the metro with us, to travel on the bus, to walk around the neighborhood, to get a pizza in Corso Garibaldi, to go to the parish cinema, to dance at Gigliola's house.

That evening it became evident that Lila was changing her circumstances. In the days, the months, she became a young woman who imitated the models in the fashion magazines, the girls on television, the ladies she had seen walking on Via Chiaia. When you saw her, she gave off a glow that seemed a violent slap in the face of the poverty of the neighborhood. The girl's body, of which there were still traces when we had woven the plot that led to her engagement to Stefano, was soon banished to dark lands. In the light of the sun she was instead a young woman who, when on Sundays she went out on the arm of her fiancé, seemed to apply the terms of their agreement as a couple, and Stefano, with his gifts, seemed to wish to demonstrate to the neighborhood that, if Lila was beautiful, she could always be more so; and she seemed to have discovered the joy of dipping into the inexhaustible well of her beauty, and to feel and show that no shape, however beautifully drawn, could contain her conclusively, since a new hairstyle, a new dress, a new way of making up her eyes or her mouth were only more expansive outlines that dissolved the preceding ones. Stefano seemed to seek in her the most palpable symbol of the future of wealth and power that he intended; and she seemed to use the seal that he was placing on her to make herself, her brother, her parents, her other relatives safe from all that she had confusedly confronted and challenged since she was a child.

I still didn't know anything about what she secretly called, in herself, after the bad experience of New Year's, dissolving margins. But I knew the story of the exploded pot, it was always lying in ambush in some corner of my mind; I thought about it over and over again. And I remember that, one night at home, I reread the letter she had sent me on Ischia. How seductive was her way of talking about herself and how distant it seemed now. I had to acknowledge that the Lila who had written those words had disappeared. In the letter there was still the girl who had written *The Blue Fairy*, who had learned Latin and Greek on her own, who had consumed half of Maestro Ferraro's library, even the girl who had drawn the shoes framed and hanging in the shoe store. But in the life of every day I no longer saw her, no longer heard her. The tense, aggressive Cerullo was as if immolated. Although we both continued to live in the same neighborhood, although we had had the same childhood, although we were both living our fifteenth year, we had suddenly ended up in two different worlds. I was becoming, as the months ran by, a sloppy, disheveled, spectacled girl bent over tattered books that gave off a moldy odor, volumes bought at great sacrifice at the secondhand store or obtained from Maestra Oliviero. She went around on Stefano's arm in the clothes of an actress or a princess, her hair styled like a diva's.

I looked at her from the window, and felt that her earlier shape had broken, and I thought again of that wonderful passage of the letter, of the cracked and crumpled copper. It was an image that I used all the time, whenever I noticed a fracture in her or in me. I knew—perhaps I hoped—that no form could ever contain Lila, and that sooner or later she would break everything again.

45.

After the terrible evening in the restaurant in Santa Lucia there were no more occasions like that, and not because the boyfriends didn't ask us again but because we now got out of it with one excuse or another. Instead, when I wasn't exhausted by my homework, I let myself be drawn out to a dance at someone's house, to have a pizza with the old group. I preferred to go, however, only when I was sure that Antonio would come; for a while he had been courting me, discreetly, attentively. True, his face was shiny and full of blackheads, his teeth here and there were bluish; he had broad hands and strong fingers—he had once effortlessly unscrewed the screws on the punctured tire of an old car that Pasquale had acquired. But he had black wavy hair that made you want to caress it, and although he was very shy the rare times he opened his mouth he said something witty. Besides, he was the only one who noticed me. Enzo seldom appeared; he had a life of which we knew little or nothing, and when he was there he devoted himself, in his detached, slow way, and never excessively, to Carmela. As for Pasquale, he seemed to have lost interest in girls after Lila's rejection. He took very little notice even of Ada, who flirted with him tirelessly, even if she kept saying that she couldn't stand always seeing our mean faces.

Naturally on those evenings we sooner or later ended up talking about Lila, even if it seemed that no one wanted to name her: the boys were all a little disappointed, each one would have liked to be in Stefano's place. But the most unhappy was Pasquale: if his hatred for the Solaras hadn't been of such long standing, he would probably have sided publicly with Marcello against the Cerullo family. His sufferings in love had dug deep inside him and a mere glimpse of Lila and Stefano together dimmed his joy in life. Yet he was by nature honest and good-hearted, so he was careful to keep his reactions under control and to take sides according to what was just. When he found out that Marcello and Michele had confronted Rino one evening, and though they hadn't laid a finger on him had grossly insulted him, Pasquale had entirely taken Rino's part. When he found out that Silvio Solara, the father of Michele and Marcello, had gone in person to Fernando's renovated shoe store and calmly reproached him for not having brought up his daughter properly, and then, looking around, had observed that the shoemaker could make all the shoes he wanted, but then where would he sell them, he would never find a store that would take them, not to mention that with all that glue around, with all that thread and pitch and wooden forms and soles and heels, it wouldn't take much to start a fire, Pasquale had promised that, if there was a fire at the Cerullo shoe shop, he would go with a few trusted companions and burn down the Solara bar and pastry shop. But he was critical of Lila. He said that she should have run away from home rather than allow Marcello to go there and court her all those evenings. He said she should have smashed the television with a hammer and not watched it with anyone who knew that he had bought it only to have her. He said, finally, that she was a girl too intelligent to be truly in love with a hypocritical idiot like Stefano Carracci.

On those occasions I was the only one who did not remain silent but explicitly disagreed with Pasquale's criticisms. I refuted him, saying things like: It's not easy to leave home; it's not easy to go against the wishes of the people you love; nothing is easy, especially when you criticize her rather than being angry at your friend Rino—he's the one who got her in that trouble with Marcello, and if Lila hadn't found a way of getting out of it, she would have had to marry Marcello. I concluded by praising Stefano, who of all the boys who had known Lila since she was a child and loved her was the only one with the courage to support her and help her. A terrible silence fell and I was very proud of having countered every criticism of my friend in a tone and language that, among other things, had subdued him.

But one night we ended up quarreling unpleasantly. We were all, including Enzo, having a pizza on the Rettifilo, in a place where a margherita and a beer cost fifty lire. This time it was the girls who started: Ada, I think, said she thought Lila was ridiculous going around always fresh from the hairdresser and in clothes like Princess Soraya, even though she was sprinkling roach poison in front of the house door. We all, some more, some less, laughed. Then, one thing leading to another, Carmela ended up saying outright that Lila had gone with Stefano for the money, to settle her brother and the rest of the family. I was starting my usual official defense when Pasquale interrupted me and said, "That's not the point. The point is that Lina knows where that money comes from."

"Now you want to drag in Don Achille and the black market and the trafficking and loan sharking and all the nonsense of before and after the war?" I said.

"Yes, and if your friend were here now she would say I was right."

"Stefano is just a shopkeeper who's a good salesman."

"And the money he put into the Cerullos' shoe store he got from the grocery?"

"Why, what do you think?"

"It comes from the gold objects taken from mothers and

hidden by Don Achille in the mattress. Lina acts the lady with the blood of all the poor people of this neighborhood. And she is kept, she and her whole family, even before she's married."

I was about to answer when Enzo interrupted with his usual detachment: "Excuse me, Pascà, what do you mean by 'is kept'?"

As soon as I heard that question I knew that things would turn ugly. Pasquale turned red, embarrassed. "Keep means keep. Who pays, please, when Lina goes to the hairdresser, when she buys dresses and purses? Who put money into the shoe shop so that the shoe-repair man can play at making shoes?"

"Are you saying that Lina isn't in love, isn't engaged, won't soon marry Stefano, but has sold herself?"

We were all quiet. Antonio murmured, "No, Enzo, Pasquale doesn't mean that; you know that he loves Lina as we all of us love her."

Enzo nodded at him to be quiet.

"Be quiet, Anto', let Pasquale answer."

Pasquale said grimly, "Yes, she sold herself. And she doesn't give a damn about the stink of the money she spends every day."

I tried again to have my say, at that point, but Enzo touched my arm.

"Excuse me, Lenù, I want to know what Pasquale calls a girl who sells herself."

Here Pasquale had an outburst of violence that we all read in his eyes and he said what for months he had wanted to say, to shout out to the whole neighborhood: "Whore, I call her a whore. Lina has behaved and is behaving like a whore."

Enzo got up and said, almost in a whisper: "Come outside."

Antonio jumped up, restrained Pasquale, who was getting up, and said, "Now, let's not overdo it, Enzo. Pasquale is only saying something that's not an accusation, it's a criticism that we'd all like to make."

Enzo answered, this time aloud, "Not me." And he headed

toward the door, announcing, "I'll wait outside for both of you."

We kept Pasquale and Antonio from following him, and nothing happened. They didn't speak for several days, then everything was as before.

46.

I've recounted that quarrel to say how that year passed and what the atmosphere was around Lila's choices, especially among the young men who had secretly or explicitly loved her, desired her, and in all probability loved and desired her still. As for me, it's hard to say in what tangle of feelings I found myself. I always defended Lila, and I liked doing so, I liked to hear myself speak with the authority of one who is studying difficult subjects. But I also knew that I could have just as well recounted, and willingly, if with some exaggeration, how Lila had really been behind each of Stefano's moves, and I with her, linking step to step as if it were a mathematics problem, to achieve that result: to settle herself, settle her brother, attempt to realize the plan of the shoe factory, and even get money to repair my glasses if they broke.

I passed Fernando's old workshop and felt a vicarious sense of triumph. Lila, clearly, had made it. The shoemaker's shop, which had never had a sign, now displayed over the door a kind of plaque that said "Cerullo." Fernando, Rino, the three apprentices worked at joining, stitching, hammering, polishing, bent over their benches from morning till late at night. It was known that father and son often quarreled. It was known that Fernando maintained that the shoes, especially the women's, couldn't be made as Lila had invented them, that they were only a child's fantasy. It was known that Rino maintained the opposite and that he went to Lila to ask her to intervene. It was known that Lila said she didn't want to know about it, and so Rino went to Stefano and dragged him to the shop to give his father specific orders. It was known that Stefano went in and looked for a long time at Lila's designs framed on the walls, smiled to himself and said tranquilly that he wanted the shoes to be exactly as they were in those pictures, he had hung them there for that purpose. It was known, in short, that things were proceeding slowly, that the workers first received instructions from Fernando and then Rino changed them and everything stopped and started over, and Fernando noticed the changes and changed them back, and Stefano arrived and so back to square one: they ended up yelling, breaking things.

I glanced in and immediately fled. But the pictures hanging on the walls made an impression. Those drawings, for Lila, were fantasies, I thought. Money has nothing to do with it, selling has nothing to do with it. All that activity is the result of a whim of hers, celebrated by Stefano merely out of love. She's lucky to be so loved, to love. Lucky to be adored for what she is and for what she invents. Now that she's given her brother what he wanted, now that she's taken him out of danger, surely she'll invent something else. So I don't want to lose sight of her. Something will happen.

But nothing happened. Lila established herself in the role of Stefano's fiancée. And even in our conversations, when she had time to talk, she seemed satisfied with what she had become, as if she no longer saw anything beyond it, didn't *want* to see anything beyond it, except marriage, a house, children.

I was disappointed. She seemed sweeter, without the hardness she had always had. I realized this later, when through Gigliola Spagnuolo I heard disgraceful rumors about her. Gigliola said to me rancorously, in dialect, "Now your friend is acting like a princess. But does Stefano know that when Marcello went to her house she gave him a blow job every night?"

I didn't know what a blow job was. The term had been

familiar to me since I was a child but the sound of it recalled only a kind of disfigurement, something very humiliating.

"It's not true."

"Marcello says so."

"He's a liar."

"Yes? And would he lie even to his brother?"

"Did Michele tell you?"

"Yes."

I hoped that those rumors wouldn't reach Stefano. Every day when I came home from school I said to myself: maybe I should warn Lila, before something bad happens. But I was afraid she would be furious and that, because of how she had grown up, because of how she was made, she would go directly to Marcello Solara with the shoemaker's knife. But in the end I decided: it was better to report to her what I had learned, so she would be prepared to confront the situation. But I discovered that she already knew about it. Not only that: she was better informed than me about what a blow job was. I realized it from the fact that she used a clearer formulation to tell me it was so disgusting to her that she would never do it to any man, let alone Marcello Solara. Then she told me that Stefano had heard the rumor and he had asked her what type of relations she had had with Marcello during the period when he went to the Cerullo house. She had said angrily, "None, are you crazy?" And Stefano had said immediately that he believed her, that he had never had doubts, that he had asked the question only to let her know that Marcello was saying obscene things about her. Yet he seemed distracted, like someone who, even against his will, is following scenes of disaster that are forming in his mind. Lila had realized it and they had discussed it for a long time, she had confessed that she, too, felt a need for revenge. But what was the use? After talk and more talk, they had decided by mutual consent to rise a step above the Solaras, above the logic of the neighborhood.

"A step above?" I asked, marveling.

"Yes, to ignore them: Marcello, his brother, the father, the grandfather, all of them. Act as if they didn't exist."

So Stefano had continued to go to work, without defending the honor of his fiancée, Lila had continued her life as a fiancée without resorting to the knife or anything else, the Solaras had continued to spread obscenities. I was astonished. What was happening? I didn't understand. The Solaras' behavior seemed more comprehensible, it seemed to me consistent with the world that we had known since we were children. What, instead, did she and Stefano have in mind, where did they think they were living? They were behaving in a way that wasn't familiar even in the poems that I studied in school, in the novels I read. I was puzzled. They weren't reacting to the insults, even to that truly intolerable insult that the Solaras were making. They displayed kindness and politeness toward everyone, as if they were John and Jacqueline Kennedy visiting a neighborhood of indigents. When they went out walking together, and he put an arm around her shoulders, it seemed that none of the old rules were valid for them: they laughed, they joked, they embraced, they kissed each other on the lips. I saw them speeding around in the convertible, alone even in the evening, always dressed like movie stars, and I thought, They go wherever they want, without a chaperone, and not secretly but with the consent of their parents, with the consent of Rino, and do whatever they like, without caring what people say. Was it Lila who had persuaded Stefano to behave in a way that was making them the most admired and most talked about couple in the neighborhood? Was this her latest invention? Did she want to leave the neighborhood by staying in the neighborhood? Did she want to drag us out of ourselves, tear off the old skin and put on a new one, suitable for what she was inventing?

47.

Everything returned abruptly to the usual track when the rumors about Lila reached Pasquale. It happened one Sunday, when Carmela, Enzo, Pasquale, Antonio, and I were walking along the *stradone*. Antonio said, "I hear that Marcello Solara is telling everyone that Lina was with him."

Enzo didn't blink. Pasquale immediately flared up: "Was how?"

Antonio was embarrassed by my and Carmela's presence and said, "You understand."

They moved away, to talk among themselves. I saw and heard that Pasquale was increasingly enraged, that Enzo was becoming physically more compact, as if he no longer had arms, legs, neck, as if he were a block of hard material. Why is it, I wondered, that they are so angry? Lila isn't a sister of theirs or even a cousin. And yet they feel it's their duty to be indignant, all three of them, more than Stefano, much more than Stefano, as if they were the true fiancés. Pasquale especially seemed ridiculous. He who only a short time before had said what he had said shouted, at one point, and we heard him clearly, with our own ears: "I'll smash the face of that shit, calling her a whore. Even if Stefano allows it, I'm not going to allow it." Then silence, they rejoined us, and we wandered aimlessly, I talking to Antonio, Carmela between her brother and Enzo. After a while they took us home. I saw them going off, Enzo, who was the shortest, in the middle, flanked by Antonio and Pasquale.

The next day and on those which followed there was a big uproar about the Solaras' 1100. It had been demolished. Not only that: the two brothers had been savagely beaten, but they couldn't say by whom. They swore they had been attacked on a dark street by at least ten people, men from outside the neighborhood. But Carmela and I knew very well that there were only three attackers, and we were worried. We waited for the inevitable reprisal, one day, two, three. But evidently things had been done right. Pasquale continued as a construction worker, Antonio as a mechanic, Enzo made his rounds with the cart. The Solaras, instead, for some time went around only on foot, battered, a little dazed, always with four or five of their friends. I admit that seeing them in that condition pleased me. I was proud of my friends. Along with Carmen and Ada I criticized Stefano and also Rino because they had acted as if nothing had happened. Then time passed, Marcello and Michele bought a green Giulietta and began to act like masters of the neighborhood again. Alive and well, bigger bullies than before. A sign that perhaps Lila was right: with people like that, you had to fight them by living a superior life, such as they couldn't even imagine. While I was taking my exams in the second year of high school, she told me that in the spring, when she was barely sixteen and a half, she would be married.

48.

This news upset me. When Lila told me about her wedding it was June, just before my oral exams. It was predictable, of course, but now that a date had been fixed, March 12th, it was as if I had been strolling absentmindedly and banged into a door. I had petty thoughts. I counted the months: nine. Maybe nine months was long enough so that Pinuccia's treacherous resentment, Maria's hostility, Marcello Solara's gossip—which continued to fly from mouth to mouth throughout the neighborhood, like Fama in the Aeneid—would wear Stefano down, leading him to break the engagement. I was ashamed of myself, but I was no longer able to trace a coherent design in the division of our fates. The concreteness of that date made concrete the crossroads that would separate our lives. And, what was worse, I took it for granted that her fate would be better than mine. I felt more strongly than ever the meaninglessness of school, I knew clearly that I had embarked on that path years earlier only to seem enviable to Lila. And now instead books had no importance for her. I stopped preparing for my exams, I didn't sleep that night. I thought of my meager experience of love: I had kissed Gino once, I had scarcely grazed Nino's lips, I had endured the fleeting and ugly contact of his father: that was it. Whereas Lila, starting in March, at sixteen, would have a husband and within a year, at seventeen, a child, and then another, and another, and another. I felt I was a shadow, I wept in despair.

The next day I went unwillingly to take the exams. But something happened that made me feel better. Professor Gerace and Professor Galiani, who were part of the committee, praised my Italian paper to the skies. Gerace in particular said that my exposition was further improved. He wanted to read a passage to the rest of the committee. And only as I listened did I realize what I had tried to do in those months whenever I had to write: to free myself from my artificial tones, from sentences that were too rigid; to try for a fluid and engaging style like Lila's in the Ischia letter. When I heard my words in the teacher's voice, with Professor Galiani listening and silently nodding agreement, I realized that I had succeeded. Naturally it wasn't Lila's way of writing, it was mine. And it seemed to my teachers something truly out of the ordinary.

I was promoted to the third year with all tens, but at home no one was surprised or celebrated me. I saw that they were satisfied, yes, and I was pleased, but they gave the event no weight. My mother, in fact, found my scholastic success completely natural, my father told me to go right away to Maestra Oliviero to ask her to get ahead of time the books for next year. As I went out my mother cried, "And if she wants to send you to Ischia again, tell her that I'm not well and you have to help me in the house."

The teacher praised me, but carelessly, partly because by now she took my ability for granted, partly because she wasn't well, the illness she had in her mouth was very troublesome. She never mentioned my need to rest, her cousin Nella, Ischia. Instead, surprisingly, she began to talk about Lila. She had seen her on the street, from a distance. She was with her fiancé, she said, the grocer. Then she added a sentence that I will always remember: "The beauty of mind that Cerullo had from childhood didn't find an outlet, Greco, and it has all ended up in her face, in her breasts, in her thighs, in her ass, places where it soon fades and it will be as if she had never had it."

I had never heard her say a rude word since I had known her. That day she said "ass," and then muttered, "Excuse me." But that wasn't what struck me. It was the regret, as if the teacher were realizing that something of Lila had been ruined because she, as a teacher, hadn't protected and nurtured it well. I felt that I was her most successful student and went away relieved.

The only one who congratulated me without reserve was Alfonso, who had also been promoted, with all sevens. I felt that his admiration was genuine, and this gave me pleasure. In front of the posted grades, in the presence of our schoolmates and their parents, he, in his excitement, did something inappropriate, as if he had forgotten that I was a girl and he wasn't supposed to touch me: he hugged me tight, and kissed me on the cheek, a noisy kiss. Then he became confused, apologized, and yet he couldn't contain himself, he cried, "All tens, impossible, all tens." On the way home we talked a lot about the wedding of his brother, of Lila. Since I felt especially at ease, I asked him for the first time what he thought of his future sister-in-law. He took some time before he answered. Then he said:

"You remember the competitions they made us do at school?"

"Who could forget them?"

"I was sure I would win, you were all afraid of my father."

"Lina, too: in fact for a while she tried not to beat you."

"Yes, but then she decided to win and she humiliated me. I went home crying."

"It's not nice to lose."

"Not because of that: it seemed to me intolerable that everyone was terrified of my father, me first of all, and that girl wasn't."

"Were you in love with her?"

"Are you kidding? She always made me uncomfortable."

"In what sense?"

"In the sense that my brother really shows some courage in marrying her."

"What do you mean?"

"I mean that you are better, and that if it were me choosing I would marry you."

This, too, pleased me. We burst out laughing, we said good-bye, still laughing. He was condemned to spend the summer in the grocery store, I, thanks to a decision of my mother more than my father, had to find a job for the summer. We promised to meet, to go at least once to the beach together. We didn't.

In the following days I reluctantly made the rounds of the neighborhood. I asked Don Paolo, the pharmacist on the *stradone*, if he needed a clerk. No. I asked the newspaper seller: I wasn't useful to him, either. I went by the stationer's, she started laughing: she needed someone, yes, but not now. I should come back in the fall when school began. I was about to go and she called me back. She said, "You're a serious girl, Lenù, I trust you: would you be able to take my girls swimming?"

I was really happy when I left the shop. The stationer would pay me—and pay well—if I took her three little girls to the beach for the month of July and the first ten days of August.

Sea, sun, and money. I was to go every day to a place between Mergellina and Posillipo that I knew nothing about, it had a foreign name: Sea Garden. I went home in great excitement, as if my life had taken a decisive turn. I would earn money for my parents, I would go swimming, I would become smooth and golden in the sun as I had during the summer in Ischia. How sweet everything is, I thought, when the day is fine and every good thing seems to be waiting for you alone.

I had gone a short distance when that impression of privileged hours was solidified. Antonio joined me, in his grease-stained overalls. I was pleased, whoever I had met at that moment of happiness would have been greeted warmly. He had seen me passing and had run after me. I told him about the stationer, he must have read in my face that it was a happy moment. For months I had been grinding away, feeling alone, ugly. Although I was sure I loved Nino Sarratore, I had always avoided him and hadn't even gone to see if he had been promoted, and with what grades. Lila was about to complete a definitive leap beyond my life, I would no longer be able to follow her. But now I felt good and I wanted to feel even better. When Antonio, guessing that I was in the right mood, asked if I wanted to be his girlfriend, I said yes right away, even though I loved someone else, even if I felt for him nothing but some friendliness. To have him as a boyfriend, he who was an adult, the same age as Stefano, a worker, seemed to me a thing not different from being promoted with all tens, from the job of taking, with pay, the daughters of the stationer to the Sea Garden.

49.

My job began, and life with a boyfriend. The stationer gave me a sort of bus pass, and every morning I crossed the city with the three little girls, on the crowded buses, and took them to that bright-colored place of beach umbrellas, blue sea, concrete platforms, students, well-off women with a lot of free time, showy women, with greedy faces. I was polite to the attendants who tried to start conversations. I looked after the children, taking them for long swims, and showing off the bathing suit that Nella had made for me the year before. I fed them, played with them, let them drink endlessly at the jet of a stone fountain, taking care that they didn't slip and break their teeth on the basin.

We got back to the neighborhood in the late afternoon. I returned the children to the stationer, and hurried to my secret date with Antonio, burned by the sun, salty from the sea water. We went to the ponds by back streets, I was afraid of being seen by my mother and, perhaps still more, by Maestra Oliviero. With him I exchanged my first real kisses. I soon let him touch my breasts and between my legs. One evening I touched his penis, straining, large, inside his pants, and when he took it out I held it willingly in one hand while we kissed. I accepted those practices with two very clear questions in my mind. The first was: does Lila do these things with Stefano? The second was: is the pleasure I feel with Antonio the same that I felt the night Donato Sarratore touched me? In both cases Antonio was ultimately only a useful phantom to evoke on the one hand the love between Lila and Stefano, on the other the strong emotion, difficult to categorize, that Nino's father had inspired in me. But I never felt guilty. Antonio was so grateful to me, he showed such an absolute dependence on me for those few moments of contact at the ponds, that I soon convinced myself that it was he who was indebted to me, that the pleasure I gave him was by far superior to that which he gave me.

Sometimes, on Sunday, he went with me and the children to the Sea Garden. He spent money with pretended casualness, though he earned very little, and he also hated getting sunburned. But he did it for me, just to be near me, without any immediate reward, since there was no way to kiss or touch each other. And he entertained the children, with clowning and athletic diving. While he played with them I lay in the sun reading, dissolving into the pages like a jellyfish.

One of those times I looked up for a second and saw a tall, slender, graceful girl in a stunning red bikini. It was Lila. By now she was used to having men's gaze on her, she moved as if there were no one in that crowded place, not even the young attendant who went ahead of her, leading her to her umbrella. She didn't see me and I didn't know whether to call her. She was wearing sunglasses, she carried a purse of bright-colored fabric. I hadn't yet told her about my job or even about Antonio: probably I was afraid of her judgment of both. Let's wait for her to notice me, I thought, and turned back to my book, but I was unable to read. Soon I looked in her direction again. The attendant had opened the chaise, she was sitting in the sun. Meanwhile Stefano was arriving, very white, in a blue bathing suit, in his hand his wallet, lighter, cigarettes. He kissed Lila on the lips the way princes kiss sleeping beauties, and also sat down on a chaise.

Again I tried to read. I had long been used to self-discipline and this time for a few minutes I really did manage to grasp the meaning of the words, I remember that the novel was *Oblomov*. When I looked up again Stefano was still sitting, staring at the sea, Lila had disappeared. I searched for her and saw that she was talking to Antonio, and Antonio was pointing to me. I gave her a warm wave to which she responded as warmly, and she turned to call Stefano.

We went swimming, the three of us, while Antonio watched the stationer's daughters. It was a day of seeming cheerfulness. At one point Stefano took us to the bar, ordered all kinds of things: sandwiches, drinks, ice cream, and the children immediately abandoned Antonio and turned their attention to him.

When the two young men began to talk about some problems with the convertible, a conversation in which Antonio had a lot to say, I took the little girls away so that they wouldn't bother them. Lila joined me.

"How much does the stationer pay you?" she asked.

I told her.

"Not much."

"My mother thinks she pays me too much."

"You should assert yourself, Lenù."

"I'll assert myself when I take your children to the beach."

"I'll give you treasure chests full of gold pieces, I know the value of spending time with you."

I looked at her to see if she was joking. She wasn't joking, but she joked right afterward when she mentioned Antonio:

"Does he know your value?"

"We've been together for three weeks."

"Do you love him?"

"No."

"So?"

I challenged her with a look.

"Do you love Stefano?"

She said seriously, "Very much."

"More than your parents, more than Rino?"

"More than everyone, but not more than you."

"You're making fun of me."

But meanwhile I thought: even if she's kidding, it's nice to talk like this, in the sun, sitting on the warm concrete, with our feet in the water; never mind if she didn't ask what book I'm reading; never mind if she didn't find out how the exams went. Maybe it's not all over: even after she's married, something between us will endure. I said to her:

"I come here every day. Why don't you come, too?"

She was enthusiastic about the idea, she spoke to Stefano about it and he agreed. It was a beautiful day on which all of us, miraculously, felt at our ease. Then the sun began to go down, it was time to take the children home. Stefano went to pay and discovered that Antonio had taken care of everything. He was really sorry, he thanked him wholeheartedly. On the street, as soon as Stefano and Lila went off in the convertible, I reproached him. Melina and Ada washed the stairs of the buildings, he earned practically nothing in the garage.

"Why did you pay?" I almost yelled at him, in dialect, angrily.

"Because you and I are better-looking and more refined," he answered.

50.

I grew fond of Antonio almost without realizing it. Our sexual games became a little bolder, a little more pleasurable. I thought that if Lila came again to the Sea Garden I would ask her what happened between her and Stefano when they went off in the car alone. Did they do the same things that Antonio and I did or more, for example the things that the rumors started by the two Solaras said she did? I had no one to compare myself with except her. But there was no chance to ask her those questions, she didn't come back to the Sea Garden.

In mid-August my job was over and, with it, the joy of sun and sea. The stationer was extremely satisfied with the way I had taken care of the children and although they, in spite of my instructions, had told their mother that sometimes a young man who was my friend came to the beach, with whom they did some lovely dives, instead of reproaching me embraced me, saying, "Thank goodness, let go a little, please, you're too sensible for your age. And she added maliciously, "Think of Lina Cerullo, all she gets up to."

At the ponds that evening I said to Antonio, "It's always

been like that, since we were little: everyone thinks she's bad and I'm good."

He kissed me, murmuring ironically, "Why, isn't that true?"

That response touched me and kept me from telling him that we had to part. It was a decision that seemed to me urgent, the affection wasn't love, I loved Nino, I knew I would love him forever. I had a gentle speech prepared for Antonio, I wanted to say to him: It's been wonderful, you helped me a lot at a time when I was sad, but now school is starting and this year is going to be difficult, I have new subjects, I'll have to study a lot; I'm sorry but we have to stop. I felt it was necessary and every afternoon I went to our meeting at the ponds with my little speech ready. But he was so affectionate, so passionate, that my courage failed and I put it off. In the middle of August. By the end of the month. I said: you can't kiss, touch a person and be touched, and be only a little fond of him; Lila loves Stefano very much, I did not love Antonio.

The time passed and I could never find the right moment to speak to him. He was worried. In the heat Melina generally got worse, but in the second half of August the deterioration became very noticeable. Sarratore returned to her mind, whom she called Donato. She said she had seen him, she said he had come to get her; her children didn't know how to soothe her. I became anxious that Sarratore really had appeared on the streets of the neighborhood and that he was looking not for Melina but for me. At night I woke with a start, under the impression that he had come in through the window and was in the room. Then I calmed down, I thought: he must be on vacation in Barano, at the Maronti, not here, in this heat, with the flies, the dust.

But one morning when I was going to do the shopping I heard my name called. I turned and at first I didn't recognize him. Then I brought into focus the black mustache, the pleasing features gilded by the sun, the thin-lipped mouth. I kept going, he followed me. He said that he had been pained not to find me at Nella's house, in Barano, that summer. He said that he thought only of me, that he couldn't live without me. He said that to give a form to our love he had written many poems and would like to read them to me. He said that he wanted to see me, talk to me at leisure, that if I refused he would kill himself. Then I stopped and whispered that he had to leave me alone, I had a boyfriend, I never wanted to see him again. He despaired. He murmured that he would wait for me forever, that every day at noon he would be at the entrance to the tunnel on the *stradone*. I shook my head forcefully: I would never go there. He leaned forward to kiss me, I jumped back with a gesture of disgust, he gave a disappointed smile. He murmured, "You're clever, you're sensitive, I'll bring you the poems I like best," and he went off.

I was very frightened, I didn't know what to do. I decided to turn to Antonio. That evening, at the ponds, I told him that his mother was right, Donato Sarratore was wandering around the neighborhood. He had stopped me in the street. He had asked me to tell Melina that he would wait for her always, every day, at the entrance to the tunnel, at midday. Antonio turned somber, he said, "What should I do?" I told him that I would go with him to the appointment and that together we would give Sarratore a candid speech about the state of his mother's health.

I was too worried to sleep that night. The next day we went to the tunnel. Antonio was silent, he seemed in no hurry, I felt he had a weight on him that was slowing him down. One part of him was furious and the other subdued. I thought angrily, He was capable of confronting the Solaras for his sister Ada, for Lila, but now he's intimidated, in his eyes Donato Sarratore is an important person, of a certain standing. To feel him like that made me more determined, I would have liked to shake

286 · ELENA FERRANTE

him, shout at him: You haven't written a book but you are much better than that man. I merely took his arm.

When Sarratore saw us from a distance he tried to disappear quickly into the darkness of the tunnel. I called him: "Signor Sarratore."

He turned reluctantly.

Using the formal *lei*, something that at the time was unusual in our world, I said, "I don't know if you remember Antonio, he is the oldest son of Signora Melina."

Sarratore pulled out a bright, very affectionate voice: "Of course I remember him, hello, Antonio."

"He and I are together."

"Ah, good."

"And we've talked a lot—now he'll explain to you."

Antonio understood that his moment had arrived and, extremely pale and tense, he said, struggling to speak in Italian, "I am very pleased to see you, Signor Sarratore, I haven't forgotten. I will always be grateful for what you did for us after the death of my father. I thank you in particular for having found me a job in Signor Gorresio's shop. I owe it to you if I have learned a trade."

"Tell him about your mother," I pressed him, nervously.

He was annoyed, and gestured at me to be quiet. He continued, "However, you no longer live in the neighborhood and you don't understand the situation. My mother, if she merely hears your name, loses her head. And if she sees you, if she sees you even one single time, she'll end up in the insane asylum."

Sarratore gasped. "Antonio, my boy, I never had any intention of doing harm to your mother. You justly recall how much I did for you. And in fact I have always and only wanted to help her and all of you."

"Then if you wish to continue to help her don't look for her, don't send her books, don't show up in the neighborhood."

"This you cannot ask of me, you cannot keep me from seeing again the places that are dear to me," Sarratore said, in a warm, falsely emotional voice.

That tone made me indignant. I knew it, he had used it often at Barano, on the beach at the Maronti. It was rich, caressing, the tone that he imagined a man of depth who wrote poems and articles in *Roma* should have. I was on the point of intervening, but Antonio, to my surprise, was ahead of me. He curved his shoulders, drew in his head, and extended one hand toward the chest of Donato Sarratore, pressing it with his powerful fingers. He said in dialect, "I won't hinder you. But I promise you that if you take away from my mother the little reason that she still has, you will lose forever the desire to see these shitty places again."

Sarratore turned very pale.

"Yes," he said quickly. "I understand, thank you."

He turned on his heels and hurried off toward the station.

I slipped in under Antonio's arm, proud of that burst of anger, but I realized that he was trembling. I thought, perhaps for the first time, of what the death of his father must have been for him, as a boy, and then the job, the responsibility that had fallen on him, the collapse of his mother. I drew him away, full of affection, and gave myself another deadline: I'll leave him after Lila's wedding.

51.

The neighborhood remembered that wedding for a long time. Its preparations were tangled up with the slow, elaborate, rancorous birth of Cerullo shoes: two undertakings that, for one reason or another, it seemed, would never come to fruition.

The wedding put a strain on the shoemaker's shop. Fernando and Rino labored not only on the new shoes, which for the moment brought in nothing, but also on the thousand other little jobs that provided immediate income, which they needed urgently. They had to put together enough money to provide Lila with a small dowry and to meet the expenses of the refreshments, which they intended to take on, no matter what, in order not to seem like poor relations. As a result, the Cerullo household was extremely tense for months: Nunzia embroidered sheets night and day, and Fernando made constant scenes, pining for the happy days when, in the tiny shop where he was king, he glued, sewed, and hammered in peace, with the tacks between his lips.

The only ones who seemed unruffled were the engaged couple. There were just two small moments of friction between them. The first had to do with their future home. Stefano wanted to buy a small apartment in the new neighborhood, Lila would have preferred to live in the old buildings. They argued. The apartment in the old neighborhood was larger but dark and had no view, like all the apartments there. The apartment in the new neighborhood was smaller but had an enormous bathtub, like the ones in the Palmolive ad, a bidet, and a view of Vesuvius. It was useless to point out that, while Vesuvius was a shifting and distant outline that faded into the cloudy sky, less than two hundred yards away ran the gleaming tracks of the railroad. Stefano was seduced by the new, by the shiny floors, by the white walls, and Lila soon gave in. What counted more than anything else was that, not yet seventeen, she would be the mistress of a house of her own, with hot water that came from the taps, and a house not rented but owned.

The second cause of friction was the honeymoon. Stefano proposed Venice, and Lila, revealing a tendency that would mark her whole life, insisted on not going far from Naples. She suggested a stay on Ischia, Capri, and maybe the Amalfi coast, all places she had never been. Her future husband almost immediately agreed.

Otherwise, there were small tensions, more than anything echoes of problems within their families. For example, if

Stefano went into the Cerullo shoe shop, he always let slip a few rude words about Fernando and Rino when he saw Lila later, and she was upset, she leaped to their defense. He shook his head, unpersuaded, he was beginning to see in the business of the shoes an excessive investment, and at the end of the summer, when the strain between him and the two Cerullos increased, he imposed a precise limit on the making and unmaking by father, son, helpers. He said that by November he wanted the first results: at least the winter styles, men's and women's, ready to be displayed in the window for Christmas. Then, rather nervously, he admitted to Lila that Rino was quicker to ask for money than to work. She defended her brother, he replied, she bristled, he immediately retreated. He went to get the pair of shoes that had given birth to the whole project, shoes bought and never worn, kept as a valuable witness to their story, and he fingered them, smelled them, became emotional talking of how he felt about them, saw them, had always seen in them her small, almost childish hands working alongside her brother's large ones. They were on the terrace of the old house, the one where we had set off the fireworks in competition with the Solaras. He took her fingers and kissed them, one by one, saying that he would never again allow them to be spoiled.

Lila herself told me, happily, about that act of love. She told me the day she took me to see the new house. What splendor: floors of polished majolica tile, the tub in which you could have a bubble bath, the inlaid furniture in the dining room and the bedroom, a refrigerator and even a telephone. I wrote down the number, with great excitement. We had been born and lived in small houses, without our own rooms, without a place to study. I still lived like that, soon she would not. We went out on the balcony that overlooked the railroad and Vesuvius, and I asked her warily:

"Do you and Stefano come here by yourselves?"

"Yes, sometimes."

"And what happens?"

She looked at me as if she didn't understand.

"In what sense?"

I was embarrassed.

"Do you kiss?"

"Sometimes."

"And then?"

"That's all, we're not married yet."

I was confused. Was it possible? So much freedom and nothing? So much gossip in the neighborhood, the Solaras' obscenities, and there had been only a few kisses?

"But he doesn't ask you?"

"Why, does Antonio ask you?"

"Yes."

"No, he doesn't. He agrees that we should be married first."

But she seemed struck by my questions, much as I was struck by her answers. So she yielded nothing to Stefano, even if they went out in the car by themselves, even if they were about to get married, even if they already had a furnished house, a bed with a mattress, still in its packing. And I, who certainly would not get married, had long ago gone beyond kissing. When she asked me, genuinely curious, if I gave Antonio the things he asked for, I was ashamed to tell her the truth. I said no and she seemed content.

52.

I made the dates at the ponds less frequent, partly because school was about to start again. I was sure that Lila, because of my classes, my homework, would keep me out of the wedding preparations, she had got used to my disappearance during the school year. But it wasn't to be. The conflicts with Pinuccia had intensified over the summer. It was no longer a matter of dresses or hats or scarves or jewelry. One day Pinuccia said to her brother, in Lila's presence and unambiguously, that either his betrothed came to work in the grocery, if not immediately then at least after the honeymoon—to work as the whole family always had, as even Alfonso did whenever school allowed him to—or she would stop working. And this time her mother supported her outright.

Lila didn't blink, she said she would start immediately, even tomorrow, in whatever role the Carracci family wanted. That answer, as Lila's answers always were, always had been, though intended to be conciliatory, had something arrogant, scornful, about it, which made Pinuccia even angrier. It became clear that the two women saw the shoemaker's daughter as a witch who had come to be the mistress, to throw money out the window without lifting a finger to earn it, to subdue the master by her arts, making him act unjustly against his own flesh and blood, that is to say against his sister and even his mother.

Stefano, as usual, did not respond immediately. He waited until his sister's outburst was over, then, as if the problem of Lila and her placement in the small family business had never been raised, said calmly that it would be better if Pinuccia, rather than work in the grocery, would help his fiancée with the preparations for the wedding.

"You don't need me anymore?" she snapped.

"No: starting tomorrow I have Ada, Melina's daughter, coming to replace you."

"Did she suggest it?" cried his sister, pointing to Lila.

"It's none of your business."

"Did you hear that, Ma? Did you hear what he said? He thinks he's the absolute boss in here."

There was an unbearable silence, then Maria got up from the seat behind the cash register and said to her son, "Find someone for this place, too, because I'm tired and I don't want to work anymore."

Stefano at that point yielded a little. "Calm down, I'm not the boss of anything, the business of the grocery doesn't have to do with me alone but all of us. We have to make a decision. Pinù, do you need to work? No. Mammà, do you need to sit back there all day? No. Then let's give work to those who need it. I'll put Ada behind the counter and I'll think about the cash register. Otherwise, who will take care of the wedding?"

I don't know for sure if Lila was behind the expulsion of Pinuccia and her mother from the daily running of the grocery, behind the hiring of Ada (certainly Ada was convinced of it and so, especially, was Antonio, who began referring to our friend as a good fairy). Of course, she wasn't pleased that her sister-in-law and mother-in-law had a lot of free time to devote to her wedding. The two women complicated life, there were conflicts about every little thing: the guests, the decoration of the church, the photographer, the cake, the wedding favors, the rings, even the honeymoon, since Pinuccia and Maria considered it a poor thing to go to Sorrento, Positano, Ischia, and Capri. So all of a sudden I was drawn in, apparently to give Lila an opinion on this or that, in reality to support her in a difficult battle.

I was starting my third year of high school, I had a lot of new, hard subjects. My usual stubborn diligence was already killing me, I studied relentlessly. But once, coming home from school, I ran into Lila and she said to me; point-blank, "Please, Lenù, tomorrow will you come and give me some advice?"

I didn't even know what she meant. I had been tested in chemistry and hadn't done well, and was suffering.

"Advice about what?"

"Advice about my wedding dress. Please, don't say no, because if you don't come I'll murder my sister-in-law and mother-in-law."

I went. I joined her, Pinuccia, and Maria uneasily. The shop was on the Rettifilo and I remember I had stuck some books in a bag, hoping to find some way of studying. It was impossible. From four in the afternoon to seven in the evening we looked at styles, we fingered fabrics, Lila tried on the wedding dresses displayed on the shop mannequins. Whatever she put on, her beauty enhanced the dress, the dress enhanced her beauty. Stiff organza, soft satin, airy tulle became her. A lace bodice, puff sleeves became her. A full skirt and a narrow skirt became her, a long train and a short one, a flowing veil and a short one, a crown of rhinestones, of pearls, of orange blossoms. And she, obediently, examined styles or tried on the models that were flattering on the mannequins. But occasionally, when she could no longer bear the fussiness of her future relatives, the old Lila rose up and, looking me straight in the eye, said, alarming mother-in-law, sister-in-law, "What if we chose a beautiful green satin, or a red organza, or a nice black tulle, or, better still, yellow?" It took my laughter to indicate that the bride was joking, to return to serious, rancorous consideration of fabrics and styles. The dressmaker merely kept repeating enthusiastically, "Please, whatever you choose, bring me the wedding pictures so that I can display them in the shop window, and say: I dressed that girl."

The problem, however, was choosing. Every time Lila preferred a style, a fabric, Pinuccia and Maria lined up in favor of another style, another fabric. I said nothing, stunned by all those discussions and by the smell of new fabric. Finally Lila asked me in vexation:

"What do you think, Lenù?"

There was silence. I suddenly perceived, with a certain astonishment, that the two women had been expecting that moment and feared it. I set in motion a technique I had learned at school, which consisted of this: whenever I didn't know how to answer a question, I was lavish in setting out premises in the confident voice of someone who knows clearly where he wishes to end up. I said first—in Italian—that I liked very much the styles favored by Pinuccia and her mother. I launched not into praise but into arguments that demonstrated how suitable they were to Lila's figure. At the moment when, as in class with the teachers, I felt I had the admiration, the sympathy of mother and daughter, I chose one of the styles at random, truly at random, careful not to pick one of those that Lila favored, and went on to demonstrate that it incorporated the qualities of the styles favored by the two women, and the qualities of the ones favored by my friend. The dressmaker, Pinuccia, the mother were immediately in agreement with me. Lila merely looked at me with narrowed eyes. Then her gaze returned to normal and she said that she agreed, too.

On the way out both Pinuccia and Maria were in a very good mood. They addressed Lila almost with affection and, commenting on the purchase, kept dragging me in with phrases like: as Lenuccia said, or, Lenuccia rightly said. Lila maneuvered so that we were a little behind them, in the evening crowd of the Rettifilo. She asked me:

"You learn this in school?"

"What?"

"To use words to con people."

I felt wounded. I murmured, "You don't like the style we chose?"

"I like it immensely."

"So?"

"So do me the favor of coming with us whenever I ask you."

I was angry. I said, "You want to use me to con them?"

She understood that she had offended me, she squeezed my hand hard. "I didn't intend to say something unkind. I meant only that you are good at making yourself liked. The difference between you and me, always, has been that people are afraid of me and not of you."

"Maybe because you're mean," I said, even angrier.

"Maybe," she said, and I saw that I had hurt her as she had hurt me. Then, repenting, I added immediately, to make up: "Antonio would get himself killed for you: he said to thank you for giving his sister a job."

"It's Stefano who gave the job to Ada," she replied. "I'm mean."

53.

From then on, I was constantly called on to take part in the most disputed decisions, and sometimes—I discovered—not at Lila's request but Pinuccia and her mother's. I chose the favors. I chose the restaurant, in Via Orazio. I chose the photographer, persuading them to include a film in super 8. In every circumstance I realized that, while I was deeply interested in everything, as if each of those questions were practice for when my turn came to get married, Lila, at the stations of her wedding, paid little attention. I was surprised, but that was certainly the case. What truly engaged her was to make sure, once and for all, that in her future life as wife and mother, in her house, her sister-in-law and her mother-in-law would have no say. But it wasn't the ordinary conflict between mother-in-law, daughter-in-law, sister-in-law. I had the impression, from the way she used me, from the way she handled Stefano, that she was struggling to find, from inside the cage in which she was enclosed, a way of being, all her own, that was still obscure to her.

Naturally I wasted entire afternoons settling their affairs, I didn't study much, and a couple of times ended up not even going to school. The result was that my report card for the first trimester was not especially brilliant. My new teacher of Latin and Greek, the greatly respected Galiani, had a high opinion of me, but in philosophy, chemistry, and mathematics I barely passed. Then one morning I got into serious trouble. Since the religion teacher was constantly delivering tirades against the Communists, against their atheism, I felt impelled to react, I don't really know if by my affection for Pasquale, who had always said he was a Communist, or simply because I felt that all the bad things the priest said about Communists concerned me directly as the pet of the most prominent Communist, Professor Galiani. The fact remains that I, who had successfully completed a theological correspondence course, raised my hand and said that the human condition was so obviously exposed to the blind fury of chance that to trust in a God, a Jesus, the Holy Spirit—this last a completely superfluous entity, it was there only to make up a trinity, notoriously nobler than the mere binomial father-son—was the same thing as collecting trading cards while the city burns in the fires of hell. Alfonso had immediately realized that I was overdoing it and timidly tugged on my smock, but I paid no attention and went all the way, to that concluding comparison. For the first time I was sent out of the classroom and had a demerit on my class record.

Once I was in the hall, I was disoriented at first—what had happened, why had I behaved so recklessly, where had I gotten the absolute conviction that the things I was saying were right and should be said?—and then I remembered that I had had those conversations with Lila, and saw that I had landed myself in trouble because, in spite of everything, I continued to assign her an authority that made me bold enough to challenge the religion teacher. Lila no longer opened a book, no longer went to school, was about to become the wife of a grocer, would probably end up at the cash register in place of Stefano's mother, and I? I had drawn from her the energy to invent an image that defined religion as the collecting of trading cards while the city burns in the fires of hell? Was it not true, then, that school was my personal wealth, now far from her influence? I wept silently outside the classroom door.

But things changed unexpectedly. Nino Sarratore appeared at the end of the hall. After the new encounter with his father, I had all the more reason to behave as if he didn't exist, but seeing him in that situation revived me, I quickly dried my tears. He must have realized that something was wrong, and he came toward me. He was more grown-up: he had a prominent Adam's apple, features hollowed out by a bluish beard, a firmer gaze. It was impossible to avoid him. I couldn't go back into the class, I couldn't go to the bathroom, either of which would have made my situation more complicated if the religion teacher looked out. So when he joined me and asked why I was outside, what had happened, I told him. He frowned and said, "I'll be right back." He disappeared and reappeared a few minutes later with Professor Galiani.

Galiani was full of praise. "But now," she said, as if she were giving me and Nino a lesson, "after the full attack, it's time to mediate." She knocked on the door of the classroom, closed it behind her, and five minutes later looked out happily. I could go back provided I apologized to the professor for the aggressive tone I had used. I apologized, wavering between anxiety about probable reprisals and pride in the support I had received from Nino and from Professor Galiani.

I was careful not to say anything to my parents, but I told Antonio everything, and he proudly reported the incident to Pasquale, who ran into Lila one morning and, so overcome by his love for her that he could barely speak, seized on my adventure like a life vest, and told her about it. Thus I became, in the blink of an eye, the heroine both of my old friends and of the small but seasoned group of teachers and students who challenged the lectures of the teacher of religion. Meanwhile, aware that my apologies to the priest were not enough, I made an effort to regain credit with him and with his like-minded colleagues. I easily separated my words from myself: toward all the teachers who had become hostile to me I was respectful, helpful, cooperative, so that they went back to thinking of me as a person who came out with odd, but forgivable, assertions. I thus discovered that I was able to behave like Professor Galiani: present my opinions firmly and, at the same time, soften them, and regain respect, through my irreproachable behavior. Within a few days it seemed to me that I had returned, along with Nino Sarratore, who was in his fifth year and would graduate, to the top of the list of the most promising students in our shabby high school.

It didn't end there. A few weeks later, unexpectedly, Nino, with his shadowy look, asked me if I could quickly write half a page recounting the conflict with the priest.

"To do what with?"

He told me that he wrote for a little journal called *Naples, Home of the Poor*. He had described the incident to the editors and they had said that if I could write an account in time they would try to put it in the next issue. He showed me the journal. It was a pamphlet of fifty pages, of a dirty gray. In the contents he appeared, first name and last name, with an article entitled "The Numbers of Poverty." I thought of his father, and the satisfaction, the vanity with which he had read to me at the Maronti the article he'd published in *Roma*.

"Do you also write poetry?" I asked.

He denied it with such disgusted energy that I immediately promised: "All right, I'll try."

I went home in great agitation. My head was already churning with the sentences I would write, and on the way I talked about it in great detail to Alfonso. He became anxious for me, he begged me not to write anything.

"Will they sign it with your name?"

"Yes."

"Lenù, the priest will get angry again and fail you: he'll get chemistry and mathematics on his side."

He transmitted his anxiety to me and I lost confidence. But, as soon as we separated, the idea of being able to show the journal, with my little article, my name in print, to Lila, to my parents, to Maestra Oliviero, to Maestro Ferraro, got the upper hand. I would mend things later. It had been very energizing to win praise from those who seemed to me better (Professor Galiani, Nino) taking sides against those who seemed to me worse (the priest, the chemistry teacher, the mathematics teacher), and yet to behave toward the adversaries in such a way as not to lose their friendship and respect. I would make an effort to repeat this when the article was published.

I spent the afternoon writing and rewriting. I found concise, dense sentences. I tried to give my position the maximum theoretical weight by finding difficult words. I wrote, "If God is present everywhere, what need does he have to disseminate himself by way of the Holy Spirit?" But the half page was soon used up, merely in the premise. And the rest? I started again. And since I had been trained since elementary school to try and stubbornly keep trying, in the end I got a creditable result and turned to my lessons for the next day.

But half an hour later my doubts returned, I felt the need for confirmation. Who could I ask to read my text and give an opinion? My mother? My brothers? Antonio? Naturally not, the only one was Lila. But to turn to her meant to continue to recognize in her an authority, when in fact I, by now, knew more than she did. So I resisted. I was afraid that she would dismiss my half page with a disparaging remark. I was even more afraid that that remark would nevertheless work in my mind, pushing me to extreme thoughts that I would end up transcribing onto my half page, throwing off its equilibrium. And yet finally I gave in and went to look for her. She was at her parents' house. I told her about Nino's proposal and gave her the notebook.

She looked at the page unwillingly, as if the writing

wounded her eyes. Exactly like Alfonso, she asked, "Will they put your name on it?"

I nodded yes.

"Elena Greco?"

"Yes."

She held out the notebook: "I'm not capable of telling you if it's good or not."

"Please."

"No, I'm not capable."

I had to insist. I said, though I knew it wasn't true, that if she didn't like it, if in fact she refused to read it, I wouldn't give it to Nino to print.

In the end she read it. It seemed to me that she shrank, as if I had unloaded a weight on her. And I had the impression that she was making a painful effort to free from some corner of herself the old Lila, the one who read, wrote, drew, made plans spontaneously—the naturalness of an instinctive reaction. When she succeeded, everything seemed pleasantly light.

"Can I erase?"

"Yes."

She erased quite a few words and an entire sentence.

"Can I move something?"

"Yes."

She circled a sentence and moved it with a wavy line to the top of the page.

"Can I recopy it for you onto another page?"

"I'll do it."

"No, let me do it."

It took a while to recopy. When she gave me back the notebook, she said, "You're very clever, of course they always give you ten."

I felt that there was no irony, it was a real compliment. Then she added with sudden harshness:

"I don't want to read anything else that you write."

"Why?"

She thought about it.

"Because it hurts me," and she struck her forehead with her hand and burst out laughing.

54.

I went home happy. I shut myself in the toilet so that I wouldn't disturb the rest of the family and studied until three in the morning, when finally I went to sleep. I dragged myself up at six-thirty to recopy the text. But first I read it over in Lila's beautiful round handwriting, a handwriting that had remained the same as in elementary school, very different now from mine, which had become smaller and plainer. On the page was exactly what I had written, but it was clearer, more immediate. The erasures, the transpositions, the small additions, and, in some way, her handwriting itself gave me the impression that I had escaped from myself and now was running a hundred paces ahead with an energy and also a harmony that the person left behind didn't know she had.

I decided to leave the text in Lila's handwriting. I brought it to Nino like that in order to keep the visible trace of her presence in my words. He read it, blinking his long eyelashes. At the end he said, with sudden, unexpected sadness, "Professor Galiani is right."

"About what?"

"You write better than I do."

And although I protested, embarrassed, he repeated that phrase again, then turned his back and went off without saying goodbye. He didn't even say when the journal would come out or how I could get a copy, nor did I have the courage to ask him. That behavior bothered me. And even more because, as he walked away, I recognized for a few moments his father's gait.

This was how our new encounter ended. We got everything wrong again. For days Nino continued to behave as if writing better than him was a sin that had to be expiated. I became irritated. When suddenly he reassigned me body, life, presence, and asked me to walk a little way with him, I answered coldly that I was busy, my boyfriend was supposed to pick me up.

For a while he must have thought that the boyfriend was Alfonso, but any doubt was resolved when, one day, after school, his sister Marisa appeared, to tell him something or other. We hadn't seen each other since the days on Ischia. She ran over to me, she greeted me warmly, she said how sorry she was that I hadn't returned to Barano that summer. Since I was with Alfonso I introduced him. She insisted, as her brother had already left, on going part of the way with us. First she told us all her sufferings in love. Then, when she realized that Alfonso and I were not boyfriend and girlfriend, she stopped talking to me and began to chat with him in her charming way. She must have told her brother that between Alfonso and me there was nothing, because right away, the next day, he began hovering around me again. But now the mere sight of him made me nervous. Was he vain like his father, even if he detested him? Did he think that others couldn't help liking him, loving him? Was he so full of himself that he couldn't tolerate good qualities other than his own?

I asked Antonio to come and pick me up at school. He obeyed immediately, confused and at the same time pleased by that request. What surely surprised him most was that there in public, in front of everyone, I took his hand and entwined my fingers with his. I had always refused to walk like that, either in the neighborhood or outside it, because it made me feel that I was still a child, going for a walk with my father. That day I did it. I knew that Nino was watching us and I wanted him to understand who I was. I wrote better than he did, I would publish in the magazine where he published, I was as good at school and better than he was, I had a man, look at him: and so I would not run after him like a faithful beast.

55.

I also asked Antonio to go with me to Lila's wedding, not to leave me alone, and maybe always to dance with me. I dreaded that day, I felt it as a definitive break, and I wanted someone there who would support me.

This request was to complicate life further. Lila had sent invitations to everyone. In the houses of the neighborhood the mothers, the grandmothers had been working for months to make dresses, to get hats and purses, to shop for a wedding present, I don't know, a set of glasses, of plates, of silverware. It wasn't so much for Lila that they made that effort; it was for Stefano, who was very decent, and allowed you to pay at the end of the month. But a wedding was, above all, an occasion where no one should make a bad showing, especially girls without fiancés, who there would have a chance of finding one and getting settled, marrying, in their turn, within a few years.

It was really for that last reason that I wanted Antonio to go with me. I had no intention of making the thing official—we were careful to keep our relationship absolutely hidden—but I wished to keep under control my anxiety about being attractive. I wanted, that day, to feel calm, tranquil, despite my glasses, the modest dress made by my mother, my old shoes, and at the same time think: I have everything a sixteen-year-old girl should have, I don't need anything or anyone.

But Antonio didn't take it like that. He loved me, he considered me the luckiest thing that had ever happened to him. He often asked aloud, with a hint of anguish straining under an appearance of amusement, how in the world I had chosen him, who was stupid and couldn't put two words together. In fact, he couldn't wait to appear at my parents' house and make our relationship official. And so at that request of mine he must have thought that I had finally decided to let him come out of hiding, and he went into debt to buy a suit, in addition to what he was spending for the wedding gift, clothes for Ada and the other children, a presentable appearance for Melina.

I didn't notice anything. I struggled on, between school, the urgent consultations whenever things got tangled up between Lila and her sister-in-law and mother-in-law, the pleasant nervousness about the article that I might see published at any time. I was secretly convinced that I would truly exist only at the moment when my signature, Elena Greco, appeared in print, and as I waited for that day I didn't pay much attention to Antonio, who had got the idea of completing his wedding outfit with a pair of Cerullo shoes. Every so often he asked me, "Do you know what point they've reached?" I answered, "Ask Rino, Lila doesn't know anything."

It was true. In November the Cerullos summoned Stefano without bothering to show the shoes to Lila first, even though she was still living at home with them. Instead, Stefano showed up for the occasion with his fiancée and Pinuccia, all three looking as if they had emerged from the television screen. Lila told me that, on seeing the shoes she had designed years earlier made real, she had felt a very violent emotion, as if a fairy had appeared and fulfilled a wish. The shoes really were as she had imagined them at the time. Even Pinuccia was amazed. She wanted to try on a pair she liked and she complimented Rino effusively, letting him understand that she considered him the true craftsman of those masterpieces of sturdy lightness, of dissonant harmony. The only one who seemed displeased was Stefano. He interrupted the warm greetings Lila was giving her father and brother and the workers, silenced the sugary voice of Pinuccia, who was congratulating Rino, raising an ankle to show him her extraordinarily shod foot, and, style after style, he criticized the modifications made to the original designs. He was especially persistent in the comparison between the man's shoe as it had been made by Rino and Lila in secret from Fernando, and the same shoe as the father and son had refined it. "What's this fringe, what are these stitches, what is this gilded pin?" he asked in annoyance. And no matter how Fernando explained all the modifications, for reasons of durability or to disguise some defect in the idea, Stefano was adamant. He said he had invested too much money to obtain ordinary shoes and not—precisely identical—Lila's shoes.

The tension was extreme. Lila gently defended her father, she told her fiancé to let it go: her designs were the fantasies of a child, and surely the modifications were necessary, and, besides, were not so great. But Rino supported Stefano and the discussion went on for a long time. It broke off only when Fernando, utterly worn out, sat down in a corner and, looking at the pictures on the wall, said, "If you want the shoes for Christmas take them like that. If you want them exactly the way my daughter designed them, have someone else make them."

Stefano gave in, Rino, too, gave in.

At Christmas the shoes appeared in the window, a window with the comet star made of cotton wool. I went by to see them: they were elegant objects, carefully finished: just to look at them gave an impression of wealth that did not accord with the humble shop window, with the desolate landscape outside, with the shop's interior, all pieces of hide and leather and benches and awls and wooden forms and boxes of shoes piled up to the ceiling, waiting for customers. Even with Fernando's modifications, they were the shoes of our childish dreams, not invented for the reality of the neighborhood.

In fact at Christmas not a single pair sold. Only Antonio appeared, asked Rino for a 44, tried it. Later he told me the pleasure he had had in feeling so well shod, imagining himself with me at the wedding, in his new suit, with those shoes on his feet. But when he asked the price and Rino told him, he was dumbstruck: "Are you crazy?" and when Rino said, "I'll sell them to you on a monthly installment," he responded, laughing, "Then I'll buy a Lambretta."

56.

At the moment Lila, taken up by the wedding, didn't realize that her brother, until then cheerful, playful, even though he was exhausted by work, was becoming depressed again, sleeping badly, flying into a rage for no reason. "He's like a child," she said to Pinuccia, as if to apologize for some of his outbursts, "his mood changes according to whether his whims are satisfied immediately or not, he doesn't know how to wait." She, like Fernando, did not feel in the least that the failure of the shoes to sell at Christmas was a fiasco. After all, the production of the shoes had not followed any plan: they had originated in Stefano's wish to see Lila's purest caprice made concrete, there were heavy ones, light ones, spanning most of the seasons. And this was an advantage. In the white boxes piled up in the Cerullos' shop was a considerable assortment. They had only to wait, and in winter, in spring, in autumn the shoes would sell.

But Rino was increasingly agitated. After Christmas, on his own initiative, he went to the owner of the dusty shoe store at the end of the *stradone* and, although he knew the man was bound hand and foot to the Solaras, proposed that he display some of the Cerullo shoes, without obligation, just to see how they went. The man said no politely, that product was not suitable for his customers. Rino took offense and an exchange of vulgarities followed, which became known in the whole neighborhood. Fernando was furious with his son, Rino insulted him, and Lila again experienced her brother as an element of disorder, a manifestation of the destructive forces that had frightened her. When the four of them went out, she noticed with apprehension that her brother maneuvered to let her and Pinuccia go on ahead while he stayed behind to talk to Stefano. In general the grocer listened to him without showing signs of irritation. Only once Lila heard him say:

"Excuse me, Rino, do you think I put so much money in the shoe store like that, without any security, just for love of your sister? We have the shoes, they're beautiful, we have to sell them. The problem is to find the right place."

That "just for love of your sister" didn't please her. But she let it go, because the words had a good effect on Rino, who calmed down and began to talk, in particular to Pinuccia, about strategies for selling the shoes. He said they had to think on a grand scale. Why did so many good initiatives fail? Why had the Gorresio auto repair shop given up motorbikes? Why had the dressmaker in the dry goods store lasted only six months? Because they were undertakings that lacked breadth. The Cerullo shoes, instead, would as soon as possible leave the local market and become popular in the wealthier neighborhoods.

Meanwhile the date of the wedding approached. Lila hurried to fittings for her wedding dress, gave the final touches to her future home, fought with Pinuccia and Maria, who, among many things, were intolerant of Nunzia's intrusions. The situation was increasingly tense. But the damaging attacks came from elsewhere. There were two events in particular, one after the other, that wounded Lila deeply.

One cold afternoon in February she asked me out of the blue if I could come with her to see Maestra Oliviero. She had never displayed any interest in her, no affection, no gratitude. Now, though, she felt the need to bring her the invitation in person. Since in the past I had never reported to her the hostile tones that the teacher had often used about her, it didn't seem to me right to tell her then, especially since the teacher had recently seemed less aggressive, more melancholy: maybe she would welcome her kindly.

Lila dressed with extreme care. We walked to the building where the teacher lived, near the parish church. As we climbed the stairs, I realized that she was nervous. I was used to that journey, to those stairs; she wasn't, and didn't say a word. I rang the bell, I heard the teacher's dragging steps.

"Who is it?"

"Greco."

She opened the door. Over her shoulders she wore a purple shawl and half her face was wrapped in a scarf. Lila smiled and said, "Maestra, do you remember me?"

The teacher stared at her as she used to do in school when Lila was annoying, then she turned to me, speaking with difficulty, as if she had something in her mouth.

"Who is it? I don't know her."

Lila was confused and said quickly, in Italian, "I'm Cerullo. I've brought you an invitation, I'm getting married. And I would be so happy if you would come to my wedding."

The teacher turned to me, said: "I know Cerullo, I don't know who this girl is."

She closed the door in our faces.

We stood without moving on the landing for some moments, then I touched her hand to comfort her. She withdrew it, stuck the invitation under the door, and started down the stairs. On the street she began talking about all the bureaucratic problems at the city hall and the parish, and how helpful my father had been.

The other sorrow, perhaps more profound, came, surprisingly, from Stefano and the business of the shoes. He had long since decided that the role of speech master would be entrusted to a relative of Maria's who had emigrated to Florence after the war and had set up a small trade in old things of varied provenance, especially metal objects. This relative had married a Florentine woman and had taken on the local accent. Because of his cadences he enjoyed in the family a certain prestige, and also for that reason had been Stefano's confirmation sponsor. But, abruptly, the bridegroom changed his mind.

At first, Lila spoke as if it were a sign of last-minute nervousness. For her, it was completely indifferent who the speech master was, the important thing was to decide. But for several days Stefano gave her only vague, confused answers, and she couldn't understand who was to replace the Florentine couple. Then, less than a week before the wedding, the truth came out. Stefano told her, as a thing done, without any explanation, that the speech master would be Silvio Solara, the father of Marcello and Michele.

Lila, who until that moment hadn't considered the possibility that even a distant relative of Marcello Solara might be present at *her* wedding, became again the girl I knew very well. She insulted Stefano grossly, she said she didn't want to ever see him again. She shut herself up in her parents' house, stopped concerning herself with anything, didn't go to the last fitting of the dress, did absolutely nothing that had to do with the imminent wedding.

The procession of relatives began. First came her mother, Nunzia, who spoke to her desperately about the good of the family. Then Fernando arrived, gruff, and told her not to be a child: for anyone who wanted to have a future in the neighborhood, to have Silvio Solara as speech master was obligatory. Finally Rino came, and, in an aggressive tone of voice, and with the air of a businessman who is interested only in profit, explained to her how things stood: Solara the father was like a bank and, above all, was the channel by which the Cerullo shoe styles could be placed in shops. "What are you doing?" he shouted at her with puffy, bloodshot eyes. "You want to ruin me and the whole family and all the work we've done up to now?" Right afterward even

Pinuccia appeared, and said to her, in a somewhat artificial tone of voice, how pleased she, too, would have been to have the metal merchant from Florence as the speech master, but you had to be reasonable, you couldn't cancel a wedding and eradicate a love for a matter of such little importance.

A day and a night passed. Nunzia sat mutely in a corner without moving, without caring for the house, without sleeping. Then she slipped out in secret from her daughter and came to summon me, to speak to Lila, to put in a word. I was flattered, I thought for a long time which side to take. There was at stake a wedding, a practical, highly complex thing, crammed with affections and interests. I was frightened. I knew that, although I could argue publicly with the Holy Spirit, challenging the authority of the professor of religion, if I were in Lila's place I would never have the courage to throw it all away. But she, yes, she would be capable of it, even though the wedding was about to be celebrated. What to do? I felt that it would take very little for me to urge her along that path, and that to work for that conclusion would give me great pleasure. Inside, it was what I truly wanted: to bring her back to pale, ponytailed Lila, with the narrowed eyes of a bird of prey, in her tattered dress. No more of those airs, that acting like the Jacqueline Kennedy of the neighborhood.

But, unfortunately for her and for me, it seemed a small-minded act. Thinking it would be for her good, I would not restore her to the bleakness of the Cerullo house, and so a single idea became fixed in my mind and all I could do was tell her over and over again, with gentle persuasion: Silvio Solara, Lila, isn't Marcello, or even Michele; it's wrong to confuse them, you know better than I do, you've said it yourself on other occasions. He's not the one who pulled Ada into the car, he's not the one who shot at us the night of New Year's, he's not the one who forced his way into your house, he's not the one who said vulgar things about you; Silvio will be the speech master and will help Rino and Stefano sell the shoes, that's all—he'll have no importance in your future life. I reshuffled the cards that by now we knew well enough. I spoke of the before and the after, of the old generation and of ours, of how we were different, of how she and Stefano were different. And this last argument made a breach, seduced her, I returned to it passionately. She listened to me in silence, evidently she wanted to be helped to compose herself, and slowly she did. But I read in her eyes that that move of Stefano's had shown her something about him that she still couldn't see clearly and that just for that reason frightened her even more than the ravings of Rino. She said to me:

"Maybe it's not true that he loves me."

"What do you mean he doesn't love you? He does everything you tell him to."

"Only when I don't put real money at risk," she said in a tone of contempt that I had never heard her use for Stefano Carracci.

In any case she returned to the world. She didn't appear in the grocery, she didn't go to the new house, in other words she was not the one who would seek to reconcile. She waited for Stefano to say to her: "Thank you, I love you dearly, you know there are things one is obliged to do." Only then did she let him come up behind her and kiss her on the neck. But then she turned suddenly and looking him straight in the eyes said to him, "Marcello Solara must absolutely not set foot in my wedding."

"How can I prevent it?"

"I don't know, but you must swear to me."

He snorted and said smiling, "All right, Lina, I swear."

57.

March 12th arrived, a mild day that was almost like spring.

Lila wanted me to come early to her old house, so that I could help her wash, do her hair, dress. She sent her mother away, we were alone. She sat on the edge of the bed in underpants and bra. Next to her was the wedding dress, which looked like the body of a dead woman; in front of us, on the hexagonal-tiled floor, was the copper tub full of boiling water. She asked me abruptly: "Do you think I'm making a mistake?"

"How?"

"By getting married."

"Are you still thinking about the speech master?"

"No, I'm thinking of the teacher. Why didn't she want me to come in?"

"Because she's a mean old lady."

She was silent for a while, staring at the water that sparkled in the tub, then she said, "Whatever happens, you'll go on studying."

"Two more years: then I'll get my diploma and I'm done."

"No, don't ever stop: I'll give you the money, you should keep studying."

I gave a nervous laugh, then said, "Thanks, but at a certain point school is over."

"Not for you: you're my brilliant friend, you have to be the best of all, boys and girls."

She got up, took off her underpants and bra, said, "Come on, help me, otherwise I'll be late."

I had never seen her naked, I was embarrassed. Today I can say that it was the embarrassment of gazing with pleasure at her body, of being the not impartial witness of her sixteen-year-old's beauty a few hours before Stefano touched her, penetrated her, disfigured her, perhaps, by making her pregnant. At the time it was just a tumultuous sensation of necessary awkwardness, a state in which you cannot avert the gaze or take away the hand without recognizing your own turmoil, without, by that retreat, declaring it, hence without coming into conflict with the undisturbed innocence of the one who is the cause of the turmoil, without expressing by that rejection the violent emotion that overwhelms you, so that it forces you to stay, to rest your gaze on the childish shoulders, on the breasts and stiffly cold nipples, on the narrow hips and the tense buttocks, on the black sex, on the long legs, on the tender knees, on the curved ankles, on the elegant feet; and to act as if it's nothing, when instead everything is there, present, in the poor dim room, amid the worn furniture, on the uneven, water-stained floor, and your heart is agitated, your veins inflamed.

I washed her with slow, careful gestures, first letting her squat in the tub, then asking her to stand up: I still have in my ears the sound of the dripping water, and the impression that the copper of the tub had a consistency not different from Lila's flesh, which was smooth, solid, calm. I had a confusion of feelings and thoughts: embrace her, weep with her, kiss her, pull her hair, laugh, pretend to sexual experience and instruct her in a learned voice, distancing her with words just at the moment of greatest closeness. But in the end there was only the hostile thought that I was washing her, from her hair to the soles of her feet, early in the morning, just so that Stefano could sully her in the course of the night. I imagined her naked as she was at that moment, entwined with her husband, in the bed in the new house, while the train clattered under their windows and his violent flesh entered her with a sharp blow, like the cork pushed by the palm into the neck of a wine bottle. And it suddenly seemed to me that the only remedy against the pain I was feeling, that I would feel, was to find a corner secluded enough so that Antonio could do to me, at the same time, the exact same thing.

I helped her dry off, dress, put on the wedding dress that I—I, I thought with a mixture of pride and suffering—had chosen for her. The fabric became living, over its whiteness ran Lila's heat, the red of her mouth, her hard black eyes. Finally she put on the shoes that she herself had designed. Pressed by Rino, who if she hadn't worn them would have felt a kind of betrayal, she had chosen a pair with low heels, to avoid seeming too much taller than Stefano. She looked at herself in the mirror, lifting the dress slightly.

"They're ugly," she said.

"It's not true."

She laughed nervously.

"But yes, look: the mind's dreams have ended up under the feet."

She turned with a sudden expression of fear.

"What's going to happen to me, Lenù?"

58.

In the kitchen, waiting impatiently for us, were Fernando and Nunzia. I had never seen them so well dressed and groomed. At that time Lila's parents, mine—all parents—seemed to me old. I didn't make much of a distinction between them and my grandparents, maternal and paternal, creatures who in my eyes all led a sort of cold life, an existence that had nothing in common with mine, with Lila's, Stefano's, Antonio's, Pasquale's. It was we who were truly consumed by the heat of feelings, by the outburst of thoughts. Only now, as I write, do I realize that Fernando at that time couldn't have been more than forty-five, Nunzia was certainly a few years younger, and together, that morning, he, in a white shirt and dark suit, with his Randolph Scott face, and she, all in blue, with a blue hat and blue veil, made an impressive sight. The same goes for my parents, about whose age I can be more precise, my father was thirty-nine, my mother thirty-five. I looked at them for a long time in the church. I felt with vexation that, that day, my success in school consoled them not at all, that in fact they felt, especially my mother, that it was pointless, a waste of time. When Lila, splendid in the dazzling white cloud of her dress and the gauzy veil, processed through the Church of the Holy Family on the arm of the shoemaker and joined Stefano, who looked extremely handsome, at the flower-decked altar—lucky the florist who had provided such abundance—my mother, even if her wandering eye seemed to gaze elsewhere, looked at me to make me regret that I was there, in my glasses, far from the center of the scene, while my bad friend had acquired a wealthy husband, economic security for her family, a house of her own, not rented but bought, with a bathtub, a refrigerator, a television, and a telephone.

The ceremony was long, the priest drew it out for an eternity. Coming into the church the relatives and friends of the bridegroom had all sat together on one side, the relatives and friends of the bride on the other. Throughout the ceremony the photographer kept shooting—flash, spotlights—while his young assistant filmed the important moments.

Antonio sat devotedly next to me, in his new tailor-made suit, leaving to Ada—who was really annoyed because, as the clerk in the bridegroom's grocery store, she might have aspired to a better place—the job of sitting at the back next to Melina and keeping an eye on her, along with the younger children. Once or twice he whispered something in my ear, but I didn't answer. He was supposed simply to sit next to me, without showing a particular intimacy, to avoid gossip. I let my eyes wander through the crowded church, people were bored and, like me, kept looking around. There was an intense fragrance of flowers, a smell of new clothes. Gigliola looked pretty, and so did Carmela Peluso. And the boys were their equal. Enzo and especially Pasquale seemed to want to demonstrate that there, at the altar, next to Lila, they would have made a better showing than Stefano. As for Rino, while the construction worker and the fruit and vegetable seller stood at the back of the church, like sentinels for the success of the ceremony, he, the brother of the bride, breaking the order of family ranks, had gone to sit next to Pinuccia, on the side of the bridegroom's relatives, and he, too, was perfect in his new suit, Cerullo shoes on his feet, as shiny as his brilliantined hair. What a display! It was clear that no one who had received an invitation wanted to miss it, and they came dressed like grand ladies and gentlemen, something that, as far as I knew, as far as everyone knew, meant that not a few—perhaps first of all Antonio, who was sitting next to me—had had to borrow money. Then I looked at Silvio Solara, a large man in a dark suit, standing next to the bridegroom, with a lot of gold glittering on his wrists. I looked at his wife, Manuela, dressed in pink, and loaded down with jewels, who stood beside the bride. The money for the display came from them. With Don Achille dead, it was that man with his purple complexion and blue eyes, bald at the temples, and that lean woman, with a long nose and thin lips, who lent money to the whole neighborhood (or, to be precise, Manuela managed the practical side: famous and feared was the ledger book with the red cover in which she put down figures, due dates). Lila's wedding was an affair not only for the florist, not only for the photographer, but, above all, for that couple, who had also provided the cake, and the favors.

Lila, I realized, never looked at them. She didn't even turn toward Stefano, she stared only at the priest. I thought that, seen like that, from behind, they were not a handsome couple. Lila was taller, he shorter. Lila gave off an energy that couldn't be ignored, he seemed a faded little man. Lila seemed extremely absorbed, as if she were obliged to understand fully what that ritual truly signified, he instead turned every so often toward his mother or exchanged a smile with Silvio Solara or scratched his head. At one point I was seized by anxiety. I thought: and if Stefano really isn't what he seems? But I didn't follow that thought to the end for two reasons. First of all, the bride and groom said yes clearly, decisively, amid the general commotion: they exchanged rings, they kissed, I had to understand that Lila was really married. And then suddenly I stopped paying attention to the bride and groom. I realized that I had seen everyone except Alfonso, I looked for him among the relatives of the bridegroom, among those of the bride, and found him at the back of the church, almost hidden by a pillar. But behind him appeared in full splendor Marisa Sarratore. And right behind her, lanky, disheveled, hands in his pockets, in the rumpled jacket and pants he wore to school, was Nino.

59.

There was a confused crowding around the newlyweds, who came out of the church accompanied by the vibrant sounds of the organ, the flashes of the photographer. Lila and Stefano stood in the church square amid kisses, embraces, the chaos of the cars and the nervousness of the relatives who were left waiting, while others, not even blood relations—but perhaps more important, more loved, more richly dressed, ladies with especially elegant hats?—were loaded immediately into cars and driven to Via Orazio, to the restaurant.

Alfonso was all dressed up. I had never seen him in a dark suit, white shirt, tie. Outside of his modest school clothes, outside of the grocery apron, he seemed to me not only older than his sixteen years but suddenly—I thought—physically different from his brother Stefano. He was taller now, slender, and was handsome, like a Spanish dancer I had seen on television, with large eyes, full lips, still no trace of a beard. Marisa had evidently stuck with him, their relationship had developed, they must have been seeing each other without my realizing it.

Had Alfonso, however devoted to me, been won over by Marisa's curls and her unstoppable chatter, which exempted him, who was so shy, from filling the gaps in conversation? Were they together officially? I doubted it, he would have told me. But things were clearly going well, since he had invited her to his brother's wedding. And she, surely in order to get her parents' permission, had dragged Nino along.

So there he was, in the church square, the young Sarratore, completely out of place in his shabby old clothes, too tall, too thin, hair too long and uncombed, hands sunk too deep in the pockets of his trousers, wearing the expression of one who doesn't know what to do with himself, his eyes on the newly-weds like everyone else's, but without interest, only to rest them somewhere. That unexpected presence added greatly to the emotional disorder of the day. We greeted each other in the church, a whisper and that was it, hello, hello. Nino had fol-lowed his sister and Alfonso, I had been grabbed firmly by the arm by Antonio and, although I immediately freed myself, had still ended up in the company of Ada, Melina, Pasquale, Carmela, Enzo. Now, in the uproar, while the newlyweds got into a big white car with the photographer and his assistant, to go and have pictures taken at the Parco della Rimembranza, I became anxious that Antonio's mother would recognize Nino, that she would read in his face some feature of Donato's. It was a needless worry. Lila's mother, Nunzia, led that addled woman, along with Ada and the smaller children, to a car and they drove away.

In fact no one recognized Nino, not even Gigliola, not even Carmela, not even Enzo. Nor did they notice Marisa, although her features still resembled those of the girl she had been. The two Sarratores, for the moment, passed completely unob-served. And meanwhile Antonio was pushing me toward Pasquale's old car, and Carmela and Enzo got in with us, and we were about to leave, and all I could say was, "Where are my parents? I hope someone is taking care of them." Enzo said that he had seen them in some car, and so there was nothing to do, we left, and I barely had time to glance at Nino, standing in the church square, in a daze, while Alfonso and Marisa were talking to each other. Then I lost him.

I became nervous. Antonio, sensitive to my every change of mood, whispered, "What is it?"

"Nothing."

"Did something upset you?"

"No."

Carmela laughed. "She's annoyed that Lina is married and she'd like to get married, too."

"Why, wouldn't you like to?" Enzo asked.

"If it were up to me, I'd get married tomorrow."

"Who to?"

"I know who."

"Shut up," Pasquale said, "no one would have you."

We went down toward the Marina, Pasquale was a ferocious driver. Antonio had fixed up the car for him so that it drove like a race car. He sped along, making a racket and ignoring the jolts caused by the bumpy streets. He would speed toward the cars ahead of him as if he wanted to go through them, stop a few inches before hitting them, turn the wheel abruptly, pass. We girls cried out in terror or uttered indignant instructions that made him laugh and inspired him to do still worse. Antonio and Enzo didn't blink, at most they made vulgar comments about the slow drivers, lowered the windows, and, as Pasquale sped past, shouted insults.

It was during that journey to Via Orazio that I began to be made unhappy by my own alienness. I had grown up with those boys, I considered their behavior normal, their violent language was mine. But for six years now I had also been following daily a path that they were completely ignorant of and in the end I had confronted it brilliantly. With them I couldn't use any of what I learned every day, I had to suppress myself, in some way diminish myself. What I was in school I was there obliged to put aside or use treacherously, to intimidate them. I asked myself what I was doing in that car. They were my friends, of course, my boyfriend was there, we were going to Lila's wedding celebration. But that very celebration confirmed that Lila, the only person I still felt was essential even though our lives had diverged, no longer belonged to us and, without her, every intermediary between me and those youths, that car racing through the streets, was gone. Why then wasn't I with Alfonso, with whom I shared both origin and flight? Why, above all, hadn't I stopped to say to Nino, Stay, come to the reception, tell me when the magazine with my article's coming out, let's talk, let's dig ourselves a cave that can protect us from Pasquale's driving, from his vulgarity, from the violent tones of Carmela and Enzo, and also—yes, also—of Antonio?

60.

We were the first young people to enter the reception room. My bad mood got worse. Silvio and Manuela Solara were already at their table, along with the metal merchant, his Florentine wife, Stefano's mother. Lila's parents were also at a long table with other relatives, my parents, Melina, Ada, who was furious and greeted Antonio angrily. The band was taking its place, the musicians tuning their instruments, the singer at the microphone. We wandered around embarrassed. We didn't know where to sit, none of us dared ask the waiters, Antonio clung to me, trying to divert me.

My mother called me, I pretended not to hear. She called me again and I didn't answer. Then she got up, came over to me with her limping gait. She wanted me to sit next to her. I refused. She whispered, "Why is Melina's son always around you?"

"No one is around me, Ma."

"Do you think I'm an idiot?"

"No."

"Come and sit next to me."

"No."

"I told you come. We're not sending you to school to let you ruin yourself with an auto mechanic who has a crazy mother."

I did what she said; she was furious. Other young people began arriving, all friends of Stefano. Among them I saw Gigliola, who nodded to me to join them. My mother restrained me. Pasquale, Carmela, Enzo, Antonio finally sat down with Gigliola's group. Ada, who had succeeded in getting rid of her mother by entrusting her to Nunzia, stopped to whisper in my ear, saying, "Come." I tried to get up but my mother grabbed my arm angrily. Ada made a face and went to sit next to her brother, who every so often looked at me, while I signaled to him, raising my eyes to the ceiling, that I was a prisoner.

The band began to play. The singer, who was around forty, and nearly bald, with very delicate features, hummed something as a test. Other guests arrived, the room grew crowded. None of the guests disguised their hunger, but naturally we had to wait for the newlyweds. I tried again to get up and my mother whispered, "You are going to stay near me."

Near her. I thought how contradictory she was, without realizing it, with her rages, with those imperious gestures. She hadn't wanted me to go to school, but now that I was going to school she considered me better than the boys I had grown up with, and she understood, as I myself now did, that my place was not among them. Yet here she was insisting that I stay with her, to keep me from who knows what stormy sea, from who knows what abyss or precipice, all dangers that at that moment were represented in her eyes by Antonio. But staying near her meant staying in her world, becoming completely like her. And if I became like her, who would be right for me if not Antonio?

Meanwhile the newlyweds entered, to enthusiastic applause. The band started immediately, with the marriage processional. I was indissolubly welded to my mother, to her body, the alienness that was expanding inside me. Here was Lila celebrated by the neighborhood, she seemed happy. She smiled, elegant, courteous, her hand in her husband's. She was very beautiful. As a child I had looked to her, to her progress, to learn how to escape my mother. I had been mistaken. Lila had remained there, chained in a glaring way to that world, from which she imagined she had taken the best. And the best was that young man, that marriage, that celebration, the game of shoes for Rino and her father. Nothing that had to do with my path as a student. I felt completely alone.

The newlyweds were obliged to dance amid the flashes of the photographer. They spun through the room, precise in their movements. I should take note, I thought: not even Lila, in spite of everything, has managed to escape from my mother's world. I have to, I can't be acquiescent any longer. I have to eliminate her, as Maestra Oliviero had been able to do when she arrived at our house to impose on her what was good for me. She was restraining me by one arm but I had to ignore her, remember that I was the best in Italian, Latin, and Greek, remember that I had confronted the religion teacher, remember that an article would appear with my signature in the same journal in which a handsome, clever boy in his last year of high school wrote.

At that moment Nino Sarratore entered. I saw him before I saw Alfonso and Marisa, I saw him and jumped up. My mother tried to hold me by the hem of my dress and I pulled the dress away. Antonio, who hadn't let me out of his sight, brightened, threw me a glance of invitation. But I, moving away from Lila and Stefano, who were now going to take their place in the middle of the table, between the Solaras and the couple from Florence, headed straight toward the entrance, toward Alfonso, Marisa, Nino.

61.

We found a seat. I made general conversation with Alfonso and Marisa, and I hoped that Nino would say something to me. Meanwhile Antonio came up behind me, leaned over, and whispered in my ear.

"I've kept a place for you."

I whispered, "Go away, my mother has understood everything."

He looked around uncertainly, very intimidated. He returned to his table.

There was a noise of discontent in the room. The more rancorous guests had immediately begun to notice the things that weren't right. The wine wasn't the same quality for all the tables. Some were already on the first course when others still hadn't been served their antipasto. Some were saying aloud that the service was better where the relatives and friends of the bridegroom were sitting than where the relatives and friends of the bride were. I hated those conflicts, their mounting clamor. Boldly I drew Nino into the conversation, asking him to tell me about his article on poverty in Naples, thinking I would ask him afterward, naturally, for news of the next issue of the journal and my half page. He started off with really interesting and informed talk on the state of the city. His assurance struck me. In Ischia he had still had the features of the tormented boy, now he seemed to me almost too grown-up. How was it possible that a boy of eighteen could speak not generically, in sorrowful accents, about poverty, the way Pasquale did, but concretely, impersonally, citing precise facts.

"Where did you learn those things?"

"You just have to read."

"What?"

"Newspapers, journals, the books that deal with these problems."

I had never even leafed through a newspaper or a magazine, I read only novels. Lila herself, in the time when she read, had never read anything but the dog-eared old novels of the circulating library. I was behind in everything, Nino could help me make up ground.

I began to ask more and more questions, he answered. He answered, yes, but he didn't give instant answers, the way Lila did, he didn't have her capacity to make everything fascinating. He constructed speeches with the attitude of a scholar, full of concrete examples, and every one of my questions was a small push that set off a landslide: he spoke without stopping, without embellishment, without any irony, harsh, cutting. Alfonso and Marisa soon felt isolated. Marisa said, "Goodness, what a bore my brother is." And they began to talk to each other. Nino and I also were isolated. We no longer heard what was happening around us: we didn't know what was served on the plates, what we ate or drank. I struggled to find questions, I listened closely to his endless answers. I quickly grasped, however, that a single fixed idea constituted the thread of his conversation and animated every sentence: the rejection of vague words, the necessity of distinguishing problems clearly, hypothesizing practical solutions, intervention. I kept nodding yes, I declared myself in agreement on everything. I assumed a puzzled expression only when he spoke ill of literature. "If they want to be windbags," he repeated two or three times, very angry at his enemies, that is to say anyone who was a windbag, "let them write novels, I'll read them willingly; but if you really want to change things, then it's a different matter." In reality—I seemed to understand—he used the word "literature" to be critical of anyone who ruined people's minds by means of what he called idle chatter. When I protested weakly, for example, he answered like this: "Too many bad gallant novels, Lenù, make a Don Quixote; but here in Naples we, with all due respect to Don Quixote, have no need to tilt against windmills, it's only wasted courage: we need people who know how the mills work and will make them work."

In a short while I wished I could talk every day to a boy on that level: how many mistakes I had made with him; what foolishness it had been to want him, love him, and yet always avoid him. His father's fault. But also my fault: I—I who was so upset by my mother—I had let the father throw his ugly shadow over the son? I repented, I reveled in my repentance, in the novel I felt myself immersed in. Meanwhile I often raised my voice to be heard over the clamor of the room, the music, and so did he. From time to time I looked at Lila's table: she laughed, she ate, she talked, she didn't realize where I was, the person I was talking to. Rarely, however, did I look toward Antonio's table, I was afraid he would make me a sign to join him. But I felt that he kept his eyes on me, that he was nervous, getting angry. Never mind, I thought, I've already decided, I'll break up tomorrow: I can't go on with him, we're too different. Of course, he adored me, he was entirely devoted to me, but like a dog. I was dazzled instead by the way Nino talked to me: without any subservience. He set out his future, the ideas on the basis of which he would build it. To listen to him lighted up my mind almost the way Lila once had. His devotion to me made me grow. He, yes, he would take me away from my mother, he who wanted only to leave his father.

I felt someone touch my shoulder, it was Antonio again. He said, "Let's dance."

"My mother doesn't want me to," I whispered.

He replied, tensely, "Everyone's dancing, what's the problem?"

I half-smiled at Nino, embarrassed, he knew that Antonio was my boyfriend. He looked at me seriously, he turned to Alfonso. I left.

"Don't hold me close."

"I'm not holding you close."

There was a loud din, a drunken gaiety. Young people, adults, children were dancing. But I could feel the reality behind the appearance of festivity. The distorted faces of the bride's relatives signaled a quarrelsome discontent. Especially the women. They had spent their last cent for the gift, for what they were wearing, had gone into debt, and now they were treated like poor relations, with bad wine, intolerable delays in service? Why didn't Lila intervene, why didn't she protest to Stefano? I knew them. They would restrain their rage for love of Lila but at the end of the reception, when she went to change, when she came back, dressed in her beautiful traveling clothes, when she handed out the wedding favors, when she had left, with her husband, then a huge fight would erupt, and it would be the start of hatreds lasting months, years, and offenses and insults that would involve husbands, sons, all with an obligation to prove to mothers and sisters and grandmothers that they knew how to be men. I knew all the women, the men. I saw the gazes of the young men turned fiercely to the singer, to the musicians who looked insultingly at their girlfriends or made allusive remarks to one another. I saw how Enzo and Carmela talked while they danced, I saw also Pasquale and Ada sitting at the table: it was clear that before the end of the party they would be together and then they would be engaged and in all probability in a year, in ten, they would marry. I saw Rino and Pinuccia. In their case everything would happen more quickly: if the Cerullo shoe factory seriously got going, in a year at most they would have a wedding celebration no less ostentatious than this. They danced, they looked into each other's eyes, they held each other closely.

Love and interest. Grocery plus shoes. Old houses plus new houses. Was I like them? Was I still?

"Who's that?" Antonio asked.

"Who do you think? You don't recognize him?"

"No."

"It's Nino, Sarratore's oldest son. And that's Marisa, you remember her?"

He didn't care at all about Marisa, about Nino he did. He said nervously, "So first you bring me to Sarratore to threaten him, and then you sit talking to his son for hours? I have a new suit made so I can sit watching you amuse yourself with that kid, who doesn't even get a haircut, doesn't even wear a tie?"

He left me in the middle of the room and headed quickly toward the glass door that opened onto the terrace.

For a few seconds I was uncertain what to do. Join Antonio. Return to Nino. I had on me my mother's gaze, even if her wandering eye seemed to be looking elsewhere. I had on me my father's gaze, and it was an ugly gaze. I thought: if I go back to Nino, if I don't join Antonio on the terrace, it will be he who leaves me and for me it will be better like that. I crossed the room while the band kept playing, couples continued to dance. I sat down.

Nino seemed not to have taken the least notice of what had happened. Now he was speaking in his torrential way about Professor Galiani. He was defending her to Alfonso, who I knew detested her. He was saying that he, too, often ended up disagreeing with her—too rigid—but as a teacher she was extraordinary, she had always encouraged him, had transmitted the capacity to study. I tried to enter the conversation. I felt an urgent need to be caught up again by Nino, I didn't want him to start talking to my classmate exactly the way, until a moment earlier, he had been talking to me. I needed—in order not to rush to make up with Antonio, to tell him, in tears: yes, you're right, I don't know what I am and what I really want, I use you and then I throw you away, but it's not my fault, I feel half and half, forgive me—Nino to draw me exclusively into the things he knew, into his powers, to recognize me as like him. So I almost cut him off and, while he tried to resume the interrupted conversation, I enumerated the books that the teacher had lent me since the beginning of the year, the advice she had given me. He nodded yes, somewhat sulkily, he remembered that the teacher, some time earlier, had lent one of those texts to him and he began to talk about it. But I had an increasing urgency for gratifications that would distract me from Antonio, and I asked him, without any connection:

"When will the magazine come out?"

He stared at me uncertainly, slightly apprehensive.

"It came out a couple of weeks ago."

I had a start of joy, I asked, "Where can I find it?"

"They sell it at the Guida bookstore. Anyway I can get it for you."

"Thank you."

He hesitated, then he said, "But they didn't put your piece in, it turned out there wasn't room."

Alfonso suddenly smiled with relief and murmured, "Thank goodness."

62.

We were sixteen. I was sitting with Nino Sarratore, Alfonso, Marisa, and I made an effort to smile, I said with pretended indifference, "All right, another time." Lila was at the other end of the room—she was the bride, the queen of the celebration—and Stefano was whispering in her ear and she was smiling.

The long, exhausting wedding lunch was ending. The band was playing, the singer was singing. Antonio, with his back to me, was suppressing in his chest the pain I had caused him, and looking at the sea. Enzo was perhaps murmuring to Carmela that he loved her. Rino certainly had already done so with Pinuccia, who, as she talked, was staring into his eyes. Pasquale in all likelihood was wandering around frightened, but Ada would manage so that, before the party was over, she would tear out of his mouth the necessary words. For a while toasts with obscene allusions had been tumbling out; the metal merchant shone in that art. The floor was splattered with sauces from a plate dropped by a child, wine spilled by Stefano's grandfather. I swallowed my tears. I thought: maybe they'll publish my piece in the next issue, maybe Nino didn't insist enough, maybe I should have taken care of it myself. But I said nothing, I kept smiling, I even found the energy to say, "Anyway, I already argued once with the priest, to argue a second time would have been pointless."

"Right," said Alfonso.

But nothing diminished the disappointment. I struggled to detach myself from a sort of fog in my mind, a painful drop of tension, and I couldn't. I discovered that I had considered the publication of those few lines, my name in print, as a sign that I really had a destiny, that the hard work of school would surely lead upward, somewhere, that Maestra Oliviero had been right to push me forward and to abandon Lila. "Do you know what the plebs are?" "Yes, Maestra." At that moment I knew what the plebs were, much more clearly than when, years earlier, she had asked me. The plebs were us. The plebs were that fight for food and wine, that quarrel over who should be served first and better, that dirty floor on which the waiters clattered back and forth, those increasingly vulgar toasts. The plebs were my mother, who had drunk wine and now was leaning against my father's shoulder, while he, serious, laughed, his mouth gaping, at the sexual allusions of the metal dealer. They were all laughing, even Lila, with the expression of one who has a role and will play it to the utmost.

Probably disgusted by the spectacle in progress, Nino got up, said he was going. He made an arrangement with Marisa for returning home together, and Alfonso promised to take her at the agreed-on time to the agreed-on place. She seemed very proud of having such a dutiful knight. I said uncertainly to Nino:

"Don't you want to greet the bride?"

He gestured broadly, he muttered something about his outfit, and, without even a handshake, or a nod to me or Alfonso, he headed toward the door with his usual swinging gait. He could enter and leave the neighborhood as he wished, without being contaminated by it. He could do it, he was capable of doing it, maybe he had learned years before, at the time of the stormy move that had almost cost him his life.

I doubted that I could make it. Studying was useless: I could get the highest possible marks on my work, but that was only school: instead, those who worked at the journal had sniffed my report, my and Lila's report, and hadn't printed it. Nino could do anything: he had the face, the gestures, the gait of one who would always do better. When he left it seemed that the only person in the whole room who had the energy to take me away had vanished.

Later I had the impression that a gust of wind had shut the door of the restaurant. In reality there was no wind or even a banging of doors. There happened only what could have been predicted to happen. Just in time for the cake, for the favors, the very handsome, very well-dressed Solara brothers appeared. They moved through the room greeting this one and that in their lordly way. Gigliola threw her arms around Michele's neck and drew him down next to her. Lila, with a sudden flush on her throat and around her eyes, pulled her husband energetically by the arm and said something in his ear. Silvio nodded slightly to his children, Manuela looked at them with a mother's pride. The singer started *Lazzarella*, modestly imitating Aurelio Fierro. Rino with a friendly smile invited Marcello to sit down. Marcello sat down, loosened his tie, crossed his legs.

The unpredictable revealed itself only at that point. I saw Lila lose her color, become as pale as when she was a child, whiter than her wedding dress, and her eyes had that sudden contraction that turned them into cracks. She had in front of her a bottle of wine and I was afraid that her gaze would go through it with a violence that would shatter it, with the wine spraying everywhere. But she wasn't looking at the bottle. She was looking farther away, she was looking at the shoes of Marcello Solara.

They were Cerullo shoes for men. Not the model for sale, not the ones with the gilded pin. Marcello had on his feet the shoes bought earlier by Stefano, her husband. It was the pair she had made with Rino, making and unmaking them for months, ruining her hands.

About the Author

Elena Ferrante is the author of *The Days of Abandonment* (Europa, 2005), *Troubling Love* (Europa, 2006), *The Lost Daughter* (Europa, 2008) and the four volumes of the Neapolitan Quartet (*My Brilliant Friend*, *The Story of a New Name*, *Those Who Leave and Those Who Stay*, and *The Story of the Lost Child*), published by Europa Editions between 2012 and 2015. She is also the author of a children's picture book illustrated by Mara Cerri, *The Beach at Night*, and a work of non-fiction, *Frantumaglia: A Writer's Journey*.

THE NEAPOLITAN QUARTET
By Elena Ferrante

BOOK 1

"Ferrante's novels are intensely, violently personal, and because of this they seem to dangle bristling key chains of confession before the unsuspecting reader."
—James Wood, *The New Yorker*

978-1-60945-078-6 • September 2012

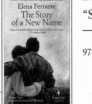

BOOK 2

"Stunning . . . cinematic in the density of its detail."
—The *Times Literary Supplement*

978-1-60945-134-9 • September 2013

BOOK 3

"Everyone should read anything with Ferrante's name on it."—Eugenia Williamson, *The Boston Globe*

978-1-60945-233-9 • September 2014

BOOK 4

"One of modern fiction's richest portraits of a friendship."—John Powers, *NPR's Fresh Air*

978-1-60945-286-5 • September 2015

"Imagine if Jane Austen got angry and you'll have some idea how explosive these works are."
—John Freeman, critic and author of *How to Read a Novelist*